THE RED STAR OF DEATH

1200   400

MARC LIEBMAN

ROTOR
HEAD
MEDIA, LLC

Publisher:

Rotorhead Media, LLC
Savannah, TX

ISBN Paperback —979-8-9883127-6-5

Cover images from Vecteezy.
Proofreader: Diane Blythe
Book interior design by – Deena Rae; E-BookBuilders, adaptation for ebook

BISAC Subject Headings:
    FIC – 014030 – Historical/Thrillers
    FIC – 031050 – Thrillers/Military
    FIC – 06000 – Thrillers/Espionage
    FIC – 031090 – Thrillers/Terrorism

File version: 202304025-04.022

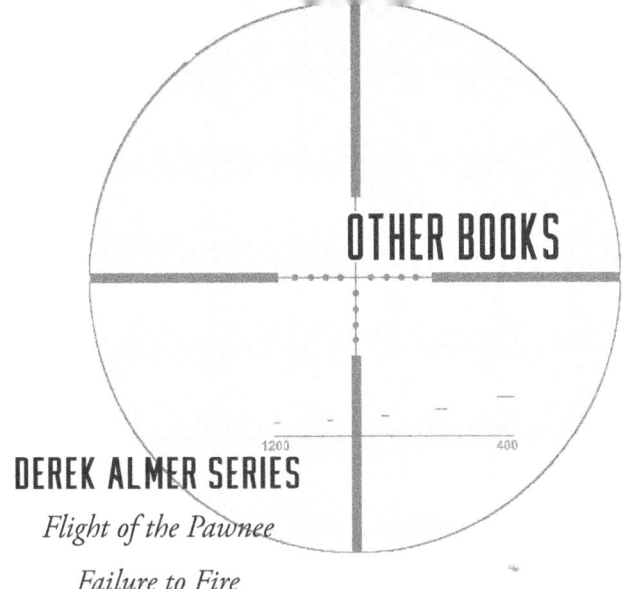

OTHER BOOKS

DEREK ALMER SERIES
Flight of the Pawnee

Failure to Fire

Insidious Dragon

JOSH HAMAN SERIES
Cherubs 2

Big Mother 40

Render Harmless

Forgotten

Inner Look

Moscow Airlift

The Simushir Island Incident

AGE OF SAIL SERIES
Raider of the Scottish Coast

Carronade

Death of A Lady

CONTENTS

Other Books iii
Discover Rotorhead Media vii
Authors Note ix
Dedication xi
Chapter 1 — Old History 1
Chapter 2 — Hezbollah Strikes 11
Chapter 3 — The Searchers 33
Chapter 4 — It Is Better To Be Lucky Than Good 57
Chapter 5 — Weak Leads 73
Chapter 6 — Dinner Break 91
Chapter 7 — The Reluctant Recruit 105
Chapter 8 — Enemies May Become Bedfellows 121
Chapter 9 — Revelatons 137
Chapter 10 — The Deal 141
Chapter 11 — First Joint Ops 157
Chapter 12 — First Failures 177
Chapter 13 — Death Near The Tulips 193
Chapter 14 — Solo Mission 201
Chapter 15 — Into The Wolf's Lair 223
Chapter 16 — Ugly News 239
Chapter 17 — Conundrums 247
Chapter 18 — More Questions Than Answers 255
Chapter 19 — Prejudices And The World's Oldest Profession 271
Chapter 20 — Bunker Watch 283
Chapter 21 — Tidbits 297
Chapter 22 — High Seas Taketown 313
Chapter 23 — To Catch A Cuban 327
Chapter 24 — Taking Care Of Our Own 337
Chapter 25 — But This Is Texas 351
Chapter 26 — Not The Final Solution 357
Chapter 27 — The Fight Goes On 371
Meet The Author 377

DISCOVER ROTORHEAD MEDIA

Visit Marc Liebman's website – *https://marcliebman.com* – for information about Marc, his books, blog, and podcasts.

Check out Marc's blog on the period of approximately 1770 to 1816 which is the end of the War of 1812. Through his blog, you'll learn about events in American history that do not appear in American history textbooks.

You can also subscribe to Marc's newsletter by clicking on Contact Marc on the link *https://marcliebman.com/contact/*. His monthly newsletter contains information on what books he is working on, speaking events, podcasts, and other information.

You can also find Marc on Facebook at *https://www.facebook.com/marcliebmanauthor/* and you can watch his history and aviation podcasts on his YouTube channel at *https://www.youtube.com/channel/UC_sDoFQM5wupNaCeGIvKL1g*.

Marc hopes you enjoy this book. If you spot any problems, please contact him via the Contact Marc tab on his website and describe what you found.

If you have a moment, the author would appreciate you taking the time to leave a review for this book at the retailer's site where you purchased it.

Thank you for your support

AUTHORS NOTE

T *he Red Star of Death* is on one hand, a stand-alone novel about terrorism. On the other, it is the continuation of the fourth novel of the Josh Haman Series called *Forgotten* in that one of its main characters – Janet Pulaski – is brought back to life as the main character in the story. In *Forgotten,* Janet is dubbed *The Red Star of Death* by the man she knew as The Broker who was the cut out between the customer wanting someone assassinated and Janet.

At its core, *Red Star of Death* is a novel about the on-going fight against global terrorism perpetrated on the world by organizations such as Hamas and Hezbollah which are nurtured, funded, supported, and equipped by Iran.

Considering events that occurred in Gaza beginning on October 7th, 2023, the fight will never end until those who foment terrorists are eradicated from the face of the earth.

DEDICATION

This novel is dedicated to all the victims of the vicious Hamas attack on October 7th and their families.

THE RED
STAR OF
DEATH

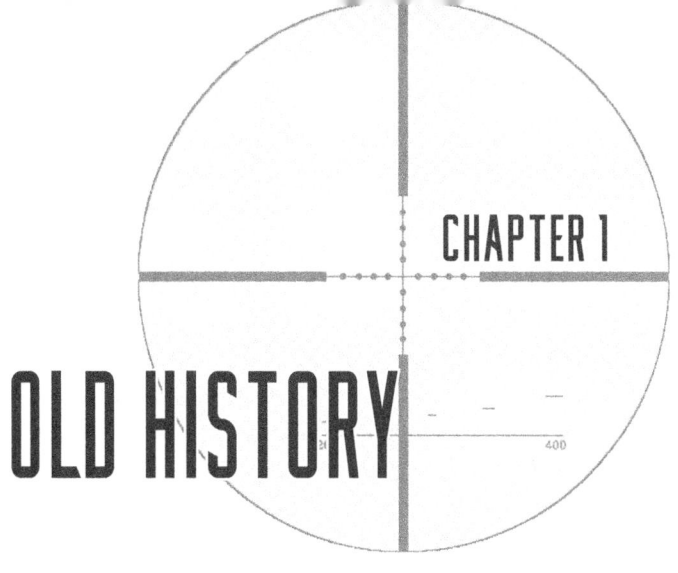

CHAPTER 1

OLD HISTORY

THURSDAY, FEBRUARY 12TH, 1976, 6:17 P.M. LOCAL TIME, BARILOCHE, ARGENTINA

The longer Janet Pulaski stayed in Bariloche, the more uncomfortable she became. Two years into the reign of Isabella Peron, rumors of a coup by the military to take power abounded. Janet overheard conversations in coffee shops and Argentine pundits speculated that Juan Peron's third wife who took over the presidency when he died would be deposed and arrested. She didn't know what to believe.

Escape after executing her contract was foremost on Janet's mind. As an assassin, escape was equally important as the actual hit.

There were six flights each day from the resort city of Bariloche to Buenos Aires if the two-hour-long flights flew as scheduled. Argentina's capital was 1,600 kilometers (976 miles) to the northeast and was 23 hours away by train or a two-day trek by car.

If a coup occurred and the airports and ports closed, departing Argentina would be difficult, if not impossible even as a foreigner. Janet could stay after the contract was executed and hide in plain sight which was an option albeit not an attractive one.

1

Her plan was to check out of the lakeside hotel in the morning, take the first flight to Buenos Aires and board an American Airlines flight to Miami that left around 2 p.m. If all went according to her plan, she would be in the air when Freiburg's body was found.

Janet pushed her worries to the back of her mind as she left the Hotel Heumel and focused on the job that would bring her another million-dollar payday. The temperature had already dropped from the daytime high of 19°C (66°F) to 10°C (50°F), making her dark gray insulated jacket necessary.

Surveillance over the past week suggested her target, *SS-Gruppenführer und General Leutnant der Waffen-SS Reinhard Freiburg*, returned to his house from his job as Managing Director of Andes Ski and Hiking Tours around six every evening. His predictable routine made him vulnerable 32 years after he left Nazi Germany, traveled to Spain, and then Argentina.

Freiburg was wanted for a long list of war crimes, including the murder of 200 Moroccan soldiers captured in 1940 during the Battle of France. As a commander of an *Einsatzgruppe* in the Soviet Union, he ordered his men to murder thousands of Soviet Jews.

A newsreel clip captured by the Allies after the war showed him laughing as he walked down a row of Soviet Jews, shooting them in the head one by one. At the end of the line, he stood in front of a man who was holding an infant and pressed the muzzle of his P-38 pistol against the child's chest. Freiburg pulled the trigger, confident that the bullet would go through the baby and into the father. The mortally wounded man dropped to the ground holding his dead child and Freiburg bent over and said, according to the subtitles, "We will kill all you Jews."

A month later in 1941, a bullet from a Soviet sniper ripped his left bicep apart. What remained of his arm was removed at the shoulder. After leaving the hospital, Freiburg was sent to Lithuania and Latvia to lead the men who sent thousands of Lithuanian and Latvian Jews to death camps.

In early March 1944, Heinrich Himmler, the head of the SS, summoned Freiburg to his office in Berlin to tell him he was going to Argentina. Freiburg's mission: help escaping SS officers build new identities so they could live in the South American country. For the task, 10 million Reichmarks ($4,000,000 in U.S. dollars at the 1944 exchange rate of 1RM = $.40) were deposited into a Swiss bank with offices in Buenos Aires. All this was in his SS personnel file that also noted his promotion to *SS-Gruppenführer und General Leutnant der Waffen SS* in February 1945.

Before Janet accepted the contract, she was sent copies of the U.S., British, French, Israeli, and Soviet arrest warrants charging Freiburg with crimes against humanity. These came with the Argentine government's repeated denials of Allied extradition requests. Why? Argentina's policy was not to allow it to arrest or extradite criminals where a guilty verdict could result in the death penalty. Since Freiburg would not be tried in a court of law, Janet would be his judge, jury, and executioner.

Soon after he arrived in Argentina, Reinhard Freiburg earned a real-estate license and sold houses in Buenos Aires to make money. Right after World War II ended, he brought his 16-year-old daughter Gertrude to Argentina. At the time, she was enrolled at a Swiss boarding school.

Freiburg's next move was to buy a travel agency. By 1950, his businesses had helped 22 other wanted SS officers settle in Argentina. By 1955, the number was 29.

The war crimes trials in West Germany ended when West Germany became a member of NATO in the spring of 1955. None of the NATO nations wanted the trials to be reminders of Germany's past now that it was a member of the alliance.

Nazi hunting was now passé for the Allies and Freiburg, and many of his fellow SS officers felt the danger of arrest was over. What was in the past, was in the past. In 1956, Freiburg moved to San Carlos de Bariloche where he saw the area's potential as a ski resort as well as a summer retreat.

Freiburg was not hard for Janet to find or to learn his routine. She suspected he'd become complacent, confident that he was not about to be arrested for his wartime activities.

Janet didn't need much convincing to believe Freiburg should have been tried and executed or spend the rest of his life in a jail cell. Even though the assignment came through the man she knew as The Broker, Janet suspected she was hired by the Israeli government or a group that wanted Nazi war criminals executed. Her role was not to investigate who or why. What mattered most to Janet was that her fee was paid.

She made a phone call from a pay phone in the Bariloche post office once she had the details worked out on how she would carry out the hit. Two days later, a Browning Hi-Power, suppressor, four 13-round magazines, and ammunition arrived in a duffel bag she took from a locker at the train station. It was time to execute the contract.

Standing at the pedestrian crossing at Avenida Exquiel de Bustillo, Janet searched for signs she was under surveillance. After several cars passed, she crossed the road along the bank of Lago Nahuel Huapi before walking through a stand of trees toward a house 200 yards up an unnamed lane. At the back door of the three-story house, trees shielded her from being seen from neighboring buildings. Janet pulled on latex gloves noting on her cheap Timex watch that the time was 4:01 p.m.

Inside the stairwell from the garage into the house to the second floor, Janet pressed her back against the wall, listening for sounds of human activity. Hearing none, Janet pulled the ski mask down over her head so only her eyes were visible.

She lifted the 9mm Browning Hi-Power from the shoulder holster and pulled the suppressor from the back pocket of her jeans. When she inspected the semi-automatic pistol, the markings said it was made under license by Fabricaciones Militares for the Argentine military. The tinny, metallic sound of the suppressor being screwed onto the barrel was the only noise in the vacant house with a red-tiled roof.

Armed and ready, Janet searched each room taking care not to disturb anything. Confident no one was home Janet closed the drapes to the living room and went back upstairs with a glass taken from a kitchen cabinet. She was not a safecracker by trade, but with the glass pressed against the door of the safe mounted in the wall, she could hear tumblers turn.

The lock gave up its security in less than two minutes. Inside, Janet stuffed the documents and the $5,200 in U.S. $50 and $100 bills she found into her backpack. The cash she would keep, the documents would go to The Broker who would pass them on to his customer.

In the living room, Janet selected a chair where she could watch the stairs through which she entered and the front door. With the Hi-Power in her lap, she closed her eyes and forced herself to be calm while she waited for *SS-Gruppenführer und General Leutnant der Waffen SS* Reinhard Freiburg.

When The Broker contacted her about another assignment in Argentina, Janet said yes if The Broker's client paid her $1 million fee plus $25,000 for expenses.

In all her hits, Janet forced herself not to be judgmental. She was being paid by someone to kill someone and always kept her distance, so as not to become emotionally involved.

This one, like the others in Argentina, was different. Freiburg was a monster and should have been tried and executed for what he did during World War 2. Knowing that Reinhard Freiburg was about to pay for his war crimes gave Janet a sense of purpose.

The waiting gave Janet time to review how she got to this moment. Her reminiscing was spurred on by an article she read in *American Way* on the way down called "12 Sentences That Define your Life." In it, a psychologist posited how difficult it was to write 12 short declarative sentences that describe the most significant events in one's life.

In her mind, Janet began writing her own list:

1. March 27th, 1967 – As a member of the Students for a Democratic Society's Action Wing, I fire-bombed an Armed Forces Recruiting Center and killed my accomplice so there were no witnesses.

2. June 1st, 1968 – My parents disowned me for my radical political views on the day I graduated from the University of Wisconsin, Madison campus and I moved to Fresno, CA.

3. June 13th, 1968 – I legally changed my name from Julia Amy Lucas to Janet Anne Williams, the first of my many aliases.

4. April 18th, 1969 – I, Julia Amy Lucas, met and married Lieutenant Junior Grade Randy Pulaski, a Naval Aviator and A-7 pilot in VA-146.

5. October 22nd, 1970 – Randy was shot down and declared MIA.

6. December 12th, 1979 –Helen Starkey, the wife of another POW and I start a torrid affair through which I become a confirmed lesbian.

7. May 17th, 1971 – SDS orders me to Cuba to learn how to be an assassin, a task at which I now excel.
8. December 17th, 1971 – I execute my first contract for the Cubans in Miami.
9. April 13th, 1972 – With Randy probably going to be declared KIA, I sell our house in Lemoore and buy a ranch in Stallion Springs, CA.
10. June 30th, 1972 – A card sent to one of my P.O. boxes leads to an introduction to The Broker who now provides my contracts.
11. January 23rd, 1973– Randy is declared MIA, presumed KIA so now I am a widow.

The crunching of tires on gravel ended Janet's reminiscing and thinking about what she now called The List. She made a mental note to complete it sometime in the future and then decided to not to because it was incriminating.

Moments later, she heard voices at the door through which she had come and moved to where she could not be seen unless Freiburg crossed the living room and turned around.

Freiburg's empty sleeve was pinned to his jacket and made him easy to identify and the young woman matched the pictures she had of his daughter. Janet spoke in a soft, authoritative voice in German. "*SS-Gruppenführer und General Leutnant der Waffen SS* Reinhard Freiburg."

Freiburg turned to the sound of the voice 15 feet behind him. Belligerently, he spoke in Spanish. "Yes. Who the hell are you?"

Gertrude stood frozen next to her father with a fearful, horrified look as she stared at the Hi-Power and the suppressor. She said nothing.

Even though his brain said he was in mortal danger, Freiburg spoke as a general to a junior officer, "Who sent you, the Jews?"

Janet said nothing. *It's a contract, pure and simple. Some people deserve to be killed for what they have done and you, Herr Freiburg, are one of them. Your daughter is in the wrong place at the wrong time and as a witness, she is also going to die.*

"Then you are a professional. I'll pay you double or triple what you are being paid to leave us alone."

"Sorry, I took a contract. To do anything else would be unethical to say unprofessional."

Freiburg gave a knowing smile. "Then, it must be the Jews who paid you since they don't have the guts to do their own dirty work. We should have exterminated all of them. Had we won the war, there wouldn't be a *Gottverdammt* Jew left in the world."

Janet squeezed the trigger thinking enough is enough. The 115-grain hollow point bullet entered Freiburg's head just to the left of his nose and it disintegrated as it shredded his brain, sending him to the dark brown tile floor, dead.

Gertrud dropped to her knees by her father whose head was leaking blood and looked at Janet. "You've killed him. Why?"

"Your father was a war criminal wanted in at least four countries. And you, Gertrude, helped him." The Browning Hi-Power spat again. Gertrude, now a corpse, fell on top of her father, her blood mixing with his. Janet dropped Freiburg's SS insignia, his SS identification card, and a copy of his SS personnel file from her backpack on his body.

MONDAY, JANUARY 21ST, 1980, 10:31 A.M. LOCAL TIME, BUENOS AIRES

Four years after killing Freiburg in Bariloche, Janet stood in line for those going through immigration at Ministro Pistarini International Airport south-southwest of Buenos Aires. With only four booths open, the lines to the immigration officers were long. She waited patiently, her Jamie Symonds passport, ticket, boarding pass, and immigration form in hand.

Off to one side, the senior officer on duty, *Segundo Commandante* (the equivalent of a U.S. Army major) Benjamin DeMedina of the *Gendarmería Nacional Argentina,* looked over the departing passengers in each line. Having just left a briefing that described a woman of medium build with light brown hair suspected of assassinating *SS-Obersturmbahnführer* Hans Straussner, a naturalized Argentine citizen, two days before on January 19th. The description was vague and bordering on useless.

Gendarmería officers at all Argentine airports and ports and the *Policía Federal* Argentina had been alerted to detain and question anyone fitting the attacker's description. DeMedina had broad discretion on what, if any, action, he might take.

In the briefing, DeMedina learned an attacker killed Straussner, his bodyguard and two guards from a private security company with a Browning Hi-Power pistol equipped with a suppressor. The shoot-out was recorded on a black-and-white security camera and lasted less than 30 seconds. The assailant was seen taking off the ski mask and shaking out her hair. Based on the shade of gray, the woman's hair was thought to be light brown. One could not see her face, but the assumption was that the killer was a woman. So far, neither the pistol nor the ski mask had been found.

The bulletin circulated to all *Gendarmería Nacional Argentina* posts included a fuzzy, still photo taken from the back. A footnote stated Straussner was wanted for war crimes by the United States and the Soviet Union. De Medina believed that in cases that involved heinous crimes, Argentina should allow extradition.

This was not the first time a former SS officer was assassinated in Argentina. In the *Gendarmerie's* archives, Benjamin DeMedina found reports on the assassinations of six more wanted Nazis living in Argentina with the blessing of the country's dictator, Juan Peron. They were being killed at the rate of about one per year. Each time the man was shot, investigators found no witnesses or traces of the killer.

This time was different. They had a picture and a woman waiting patiently in line matched the description.

DeMedina politely asked Ms. Symonds to follow him to an interview room. A check of immigration records showed Symonds departed Argentina on two occasions two days after three other SS officers were killed. A search of her luggage found no gray clothing or anything that matched the photo. With nothing more than the photo, DeMedina couldn't hold the American and escorted her to the first-class lounge so she could catch her flight to Miami.

DeMedina wrote in the immigration log for the day that Ms. Symonds was interviewed as part of a routine, random screen. He deliberately did not state that she matched the vague description that could also describe thousands of other women.

During his career in the *Gendarmerie,* DeMedina collected photos from investigations and newspaper articles on Nazis murdered in Argentina. They were all cataloged and went into a folder he kept at home. He believed Nazis wanted for war crimes shouldn't be allowed to live in his country. That policy was not within his power to change or even influence.

The folder stayed in his small safe at home. He figured that one day, it might be helpful.

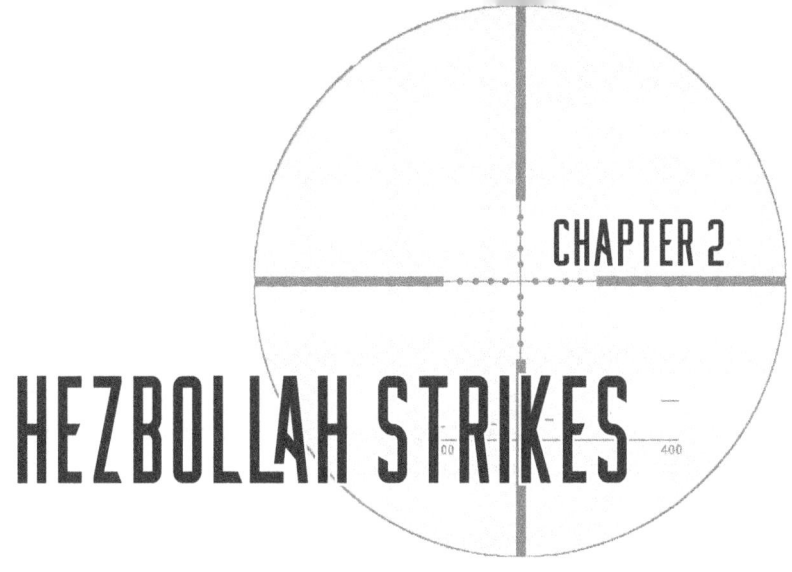

CHAPTER 2

HEZBOLLAH STRIKES

Argentina's papers were still buzzing about Brazil's recent win in the World Cup and their country's shameful loss to Romania in Round of 16. Even with an aging Diego Maradona and rising star Gabriel Batistuta, sports pundits believed Argentina's team had enough talent to reach the tournament's championship game.

None of this passion for soccer interested Hussein Berro as he navigated through the lunch-hour traffic to his target on July 18ᵗʰ. This was the day after Brazil beat Italy in the Rose Bowl in front of 100,000 screaming, passionate fans who vicariously lived and died with every pass.

Once Hussein spotted the building housing the *Asociación Mutual Israelita Argentina,* he mashed the accelerator to the floor and crashed through the gate at 2:42 p.m. Once inside the grounds, he pressed the button that set off 275 kilograms of ammonium nitrate and diesel fuel mixed in barrels and arranged as a shaped charge. The explosion caused the load-bearing external wall to fail and collapse into a pile of rubble.

The blast killed Berro and 84 people, 300 more were injured. Within hours of the bomb exploding, Ansar Allah, a front for

Hezbollah claimed responsibility. The bombing in Buenos Aires was not their first attack outside Europe or the Middle East.

The Israeli response was prompt. As it did after the 1992 attack on the Israeli Embassy in Buenos Aires that killed 30 and wounded 242, the Mossad sent a team to the Argentine capital, one of whom was Aliyah Skylar.

1994 was déjà vu all over again and Aliyah Skylar had been on the ground in Buenos Aires for 48 hours and her body was still on Tel Aviv time. She was already making phone calls to contacts from her work in Argentina which had the sixth-largest Jewish community in the world.

Aliyah was not a sabra or native-born Israeli. She was two years old in 1959 when her parents were one of the few Ukrainian families allowed to immigrate to Israel. They promptly renamed her Aliyah after the Hebrew word denoting the return of Jews to Israel from around the world.

At 18, when Aliyah reported for her required stint in the Israeli Defense Forces, she spoke Ukrainian, Russian, Hebrew, Yiddish, and Arabic. Her flair for languages led to her being recruited by the Mossad. After an immersion course in Spanish in 1978, she was sent to Buenos Aires.

Her job at that time was to gain intelligence on high-ranking Nazis living in Argentina, Chile, and Paraguay. During this assignment, the attractive, dark haired, dark skinned, Aliyah had no trouble passing as a native Argentinian. She built relationships within the *Policia Federal Argentina* – the country's equivalent of the American FBI – and the *Gendarmería Nacional Argentina.*

An old friend – Benjamin DeMedina – was one of her first calls. He'd recently retired from the *Gendarmería* with the rank of *Commandante-mayor,* a rank equivalent to a full colonel in the U.S. military. He suggested a leisurely lunch at a restaurant off the Avendia de 9th of Julio.

DeMedina was already at a table when Aliyah arrived. On it was a package wrapped in gold paper with a blue bow. The man she remembered had aged – there was more gray than black in his hair, but he had the same wonderful smile and perfect white teeth.

Rather than shake hands, Benjamin DeMedina hugged the petite Aliyah before they sat down. They talked about the years since the last time they saw each other. DeMedina was now a grandfather, and the Argentine was surprised Aliyah was still single.

DeMedina waited until there was a break in the conversation while the main course was served and changed the subject. "As I told you on the phone, I now work as a security consultant for Aerolíneas Argentinas. There is not a lot I can do."

"Would you make some calls?"

"I would rather you work through your official contacts. If you get nowhere, I will make some introductions. You know I will always help you, but you must follow the protocols, or all the doors will close."

Aliyah nodded and used her fingers to move her dark hair off her right ear. DeMedina said what she thought he would say.

While they were sipping their coffee and waiting for dessert, DeMedina slid the box to Aliyah. He leaned over and said in a serious tone, "Open that in your office. It is a present that may not be helpful during this visit to my country but may be in others."

The Israeli gave DeMedina a quizzical look and then nodded in agreement.

"Good, now that our business has been concluded, can you come for Shabbat dinner tomorrow night? My lovely Ester would love to see you again."

FRIDAY, SEPTEMBER 22ND, 1995, 10:16 A.M. LOCAL TIME, LOS ANGELES

Despite the numbered prints of famous female athletes on the wall, the OBGYN doctor's examining room still looked sterile. Karin Egger sat on the examining table chair and Janis Rhonda Goodrich, at one time known as Janet Pulaski, cradled her lover's hand in both of hers.

Doctor Ava Rogers, whom they'd both been seeing for years, came into the room with a blue folder and a grim look. "Karin, I do not have good news. The mammogram and X-rays show a mass which I am sure is some type of melanoma. Let me show you."

The doctor clipped the X-ray film onto a lightbox, and both women stepped forward. Dr. Rogers pointed to a small cylinder about an inch long and maybe an eighth of an inch in diameter with the tip of her pen. Janis found it while fondling her lover's breasts three days before.

"I recommend we remove the mass immediately and run some tests. Experience tells me the tumor is stage II and maybe stage III. If the tumor is malignant, the surgeon will suggest a radical mastectomy. Once you recover from the surgery, an oncologist will recommend a treatment that will kill the cancer cells. Your chances of a full recovery are excellent based on what I know about your health and age."

Karin did her best to hold back her tears. Dr. Rogers patiently answered her questions, treading carefully on the line between sugarcoating and being too blunt.

When she finished, Dr. Rogers nodded and left the two women alone. Karin started sobbing, and Janis wrapped her arms around her lover to comfort her. Once the tears ended and Karin composed herself, the couple stopped by the desk to check out and schedule an appointment with the surgeon Dr. Rogers recommended. They were also given the name of an oncologist who was a breast cancer specialist.

SUNDAY, OCTOBER 13TH, 1996, 2:16 A.M. LOCAL TIME, NEAR SOHMOR, LEBANON

The temperature was still in the low seventies and, walking across the airfield ramp, Aliyah could feel a slight chill in the air. Nonetheless, even the fittest commandos lugging 20 kilos of rifle, pistol, ammunition, and grenades generated a sweat.

Sweating from the walk to the helicopter, Aliyah needed a push from behind to clamber aboard the U.S.-made Sikorsky Blackhawk known in the Israeli Air Force as the *Yanshuf* or Owl. From where she sat just behind the two pilots and between the door gunners, Aliyah had to lean forward or backward to see out. The helicopters had just entered the Israeli Air Force inventory. Operation Grapes of Wrath was the first time the *Yanshufs* were used in combat.

Enroute to the landing zone, the door gunners scanned for surface-to-air missiles fired at either of the two low-flying helicopters. Behind Aliyah, 11 Israeli commandos sat stoically while the helicopter bounced and banked 100 feet over the Lebanese countryside.

Operational planning for the raid began when Mossad received two tips about a meeting of five high-level members of Hezbollah. The gathering was at an olive farm west of Sohmor in Lebanon's Bekaa Valley. Abd al Bari Ghulam, who the Mossad believed was a high-level operational planner and in Hezbollah's leadership circle, was supposed to be there. Ghulam was also suspected of masterminding several terrorist attacks in Israel.

The more Aliyah tried to verify the source of the tips, the more inconsistencies she found. Alarmed, Aliyah's strongly recommended the raid be called off. Her persistence led to a meeting with the head of Mossad; the general responsible for planning and executing the raid; and Eitan Kohan whose source provided the tips.

Headquartered in Beirut, Hezbollah was funded, supplied, and often directed by the Iranian Revolutionary Guards Corps. Rarely did more than three Hezbollah leaders meet outside heavily guarded locations in Beirut. Four, much less five, was highly unusual and set off alarm bells in Aliyah's mind.

After listening to her argument, the general said the mission would go as planned, rationalizing that if they kill or capture just one Hezbollah leader, the raid will be a success. He agreed to increase the size of the quick reaction force and have it waiting closer to the target.

Aliyah didn't ask for permission to get on the helicopter; she just told Noah Milgram, the *Segen* (or first lieutenant) and leader of the men who would attack the farmhouse, she was boarding. Aliyah thought it was significant that Kohan stayed in the Israeli Defense Forces command center rather than going in with the assault force.

"Two minutes."

Aliyah raised her hand to acknowledge the alert. Her Galil SAR carbine was ready to fire. It had a round in the chamber and was pointed at the floor with the safety on. Aliyah's web gear carrying eight extra magazines, each with thirty-five 5.56mm rounds and two grenades was tight. She leaned back and closed her eyes hoping she was wrong.

A shout by one of the door gunners was followed by a shriek she heard over the noise of the engines and rotor blades. A red-orange fireball engulfed the tail of the helicopter while machine gun bullets tattooed the *Yanshuf.*

The helicopter dropped like a rock and smashed hard into the ground, ripping off one wheel but the fuselage stayed upright. As she followed the commandos out, Aliyah stepped on a soft mass. She looked down and gagged when she saw her foot in the belly of the door gunner whose body was torn apart by a 12.7mm round.

Aliyah ran to where two commandos knelt behind a meter-high rock wall. She popped her head above the wall, spotted a target squeezed off a three-round burst. *Segen* Noam Milgram pulled her down and pointed to the left of where they crouched. "Welcome to a goat fuck. Find some cover over there and then kill anyone approaching from that direction."

As she low crawled along the wall, Aliyah looked at the helicopter. The tips of the broken rotor blades were touching the ground, and the tail pylon was 10 meters from the fuselage.

Tracers whined over her head, and bullets smacked into the stonewall. Aliyah spotted a figure peering out from behind a tree and waited a second until he further exposed himself before she squeezed the trigger. The AK-47 flew out of the man's hand as he fell.

She was searching for another target when Milgram yelled, "Aliyah, get down." Aliyah heard the distinctive popping sound of a Bell Cobra gunship known in the IDF as a *Tzefa* (Viper) and the whoosh of rockets. Dirt, rocks, chunks of trees and Aliyah suspected parts of human beings flew over where she lay. After the second Cobra flashed overhead, Aliyah peeked over the wall and seeing no one, looked at Milgram who was lying on his side, talking into the radio.

Aliyah was mad as hell. Mad because they walked into a trap just as she thought. And, mad since she could die in Lebanon.

Behind her, the first H-53 touched down and 30 men spread out as they exited the helicopter. Milgram stood up, waved, and vaulted over the stonewall. He took two steps toward the building that was their target and collapsed with a bullet in his head.

Aliyah was the second one to reach the house and when there were four, stacked two on each side, one man kicked down the door.

Aliyah had never done this before, but instincts took over. In seconds, they cleared the building. No one was inside.

Now, the five of them in the building had to make it back to their comrades. When they exited, tracers came from both sides. One commando went down and was picked up by a comrade who supported him with one hand and fired with the other. Aliyah was on automatic pilot. See a target; shoot a target. See a muzzle flash, fire at it. Reload when the Galil clicked empty. Keep moving.

As Aliyah leapt over the wall, a bullet from an AK-47 slammed into her left hip. The force spun her around and she landed heavily on her side. Aliyah tried to stand up and fell over. A commando shoved a battle compress on her hip and said hold it tight against the wound. Two men carried her to where the commandos had set up a perimeter near the downed helicopter. Then, there was a bright flash.

The next thing Aliyah remembered was waking up in a hospital where she was told she was hit by two bullets. One fractured her pelvis which was now wired together. The other broke her femur so the surgeons put plates on the bone so it could heal. She was lucky the bullets didn't sever her femoral artery, or she would have bled to death. The flash was a mortar shell that landed about 10 meters from her and peppered her with fragments.

On the third day in the hospital, a physical therapist taught her to walk using crutches. Instead of resting on the seventh day, rehab started in earnest.

During her stay in the hospital, Aliyah learned six Israelis died that night – Milgram, two crewmembers on her helicopter, and 3 commandos. The unsuccessful raid was, she thought, not a good night for the Israeli Defense Forces.

TUESDAY, DECEMBER 10TH, 1996, 1:59 P.M. LOCAL TIME, DAMASCUS, SYRIA

Abd al Bari Ghulam leaned his head against the headrest on the Iran Air flight from Damascus to Tehran and closed his eyes. He was thinking about playing on the beach in his carefree childhood in

Sidon, Lebanon. Since then, the world, and more importantly, his world, had changed. The Lebanese Civil War was in full swing.

Even though he was a college graduate who spent a year in the U.S., al Bari was out of work. Hezbollah a.k.a., The Party of God, offered a job and a chance to strike back at the Israelis. Abd attributed his promotions to following his motto – "do everything with excellence."

Two weeks ago, Hezbollah's leader, Hassan Nasrallah, told him that he was being sent to Iran to set up a training center. His mission – create a special commando unit called al-Musawi Corps that would conduct attacks in Israel and on Jews around the world. The unit was named after Abbas al-Musawi, the co-founder of Hezbollah who was assassinated by the Israelis. Nasrallah wanted 100 trained fighters plus supporting intelligence and logistics units operational in six months. In a year, Nasrallah wanted 500 commandos. When the camp was ready, Hezbollah would begin sending volunteers.

The al-Musawi Corps would attack at Hezbollah's discretion as either Islamic Jihad or the al-Musawi Corps to show its global reach. Credit for other attacks would be claimed under new names to confuse Western intelligence agencies.

Abd al Bari thought the start of this trip – two days after the holiday of al Isra' wal Mi'raj – was a good omen. The holiday commemorates the date God took Mohammed on a journey from Mecca to Jerusalem and then on to heaven. Some Muslims believe Mohammed left for heaven from where the Dome of the Rock sanctuary now stands in Jerusalem.

SUNDAY, DECEMBER 15ᵀᴴ, 1996, 6:49 P.M. LOCAL TIME, HAIFA

Friday night dinners were family events for the Skylars. Attendance was mandatory unless one was out of the country or on duty with the Israeli Defense Forces. The elder Skylars – Golda and Yuri – wanted their three children – Elon, age 43, Aliyah, age 39, and Ariel, age 35 – and four grandchildren around the table.

During the meal, the grandchildren were expected to participate in the conversation and answer questions from their grandparents. As a reward, they were excused to go play outside so the adults could enjoy coffee and even an after-dinner drink. The gatherings showed Golda had fulfilled one of her purposes in life – create a new generation of Skylars.

Of the three children, only Aliyah was not married. Golda first heard her only daughter was not interested in men when she was 15. Golda wrote it off, thinking Aliyah wasn't ready to date boys.

Just before Aliyah began her mandatory Army service, her mother suggested that the IDF was an excellent place to look for a husband. Aliyah shook her head, saying said she was a lesbian and would look for a lover.

Golda spent her teenage years living in Ukrainian forests and caves to hide from the Nazis. Her three brothers fought with the partisans, and one was killed by the Nazis.

She was horrified when she heard the word lesbian and blamed herself for her daughter's sexual preference. Her dismay turned to anger that simmered just below the surface and affected what had been a healthy mother/daughter relationship.

Offers to invite men to meet Aliyah led to shouting matches. Often Aliyah would storm out of the apartment, only to be brought back by her brothers who wanted peace in the family, not turmoil. What emerged was an agreement not to talk about Aliyah's social life or sexual preference.

SUNDAY, JULY 6TH, 2001, 4:26 P.M. LOCAL TIME, PALMDALE, CA

Before they left in late August for a three-week trip to Denali National Park in Alaska, Karin made her appointment for her annual check. When she made it, she said to Janis that she wasn't feeling well. Both women wrote it off as maybe the early onset of menopause.

In Janis' Socata TBM 850, Karin slept in one of the reclining chairs in the cabin until just before they landed in Juneau for a potty and fuel stop. She again slept until the airplane touched down at Tehachapi Airport, where Janis kept the airplane. Janis wrote off Karin's fatigue to the long hikes they'd taken in the park.

While Janis waited for Dr. Rogers to finish her exam, Janis thought about the life the two women shared for the past 19 years since she retired from being a freelance assassin. After they started living together, Janis began taking flying lessons. When the chief flight instructor suggested she start with the simpler, Cessna 150, Janis said she wanted to start in the Piper Arrow. Why? The plane was equipped with retractable landing gear and a constant-speed prop. In FAA parlance, and for insurance purposes, the Arrow was considered a "complex" airplane.

By flying almost every day, Janis earned her private pilot license in two months and learned to fly on instruments. With 100 hours in her logbook, she passed the check ride for an instrument rating.

The flight school's insurance policy wouldn't let her rent the faster F-Series Bonanza it had in its rental fleet since she didn't have at least 250 hours in a "complex aircraft." Janis offered to pay any additional premium required, but the insurance company refused.

Janis wanted an airplane and bought a six-seat, Piper Turbo Saratoga that had a constant-speed propeller, retractable landing gear, and cruised at 175 knots. In the cabin, the plane carried anything within reason Karin or Janis wanted.

Two years later and with 500 hours in her logbook, Janis traded the Turbo Saratoga for a Piper Malibu. The plane had longer range, flew 35 knots faster, and a pressurized cabin that let her cruise at 20,000 feet.

Janis' love affair with the Malibu led to wanting a faster airplane. After a demo flight in a Socata TBM 850, she bought a used one with 420 hours on the airframe and engine. Her insurance policy required that she fly with an instructor in the TBM for 25 hours after successfully finishing Socata's transition course. She and an instructor flew 2.5-hour hops twice a day and he signed her logbook as safe for solo 10 days after she completed the mandatory course.

The couple flew in the pressurized TBM, which cruised at over 300 knots (~345 mph) all over the U.S., Canada and down the Antilles to Aruba. Before the Alaskan trip, they took a two month-long trip that took them to Cabo de Hormos on the southern tip of Chile.

Janis' reflections were interrupted when the nurse asked her to come to the examining room where Karin sat on the examining table. While Dr. Roger's didn't say it exactly, Janis' takeaway was, "Karin's cancer was back with a vengeance." Dr. Rogers wanted to admit Karin into the hospital today to run a battery of tests to determine treatment.

The drive back to the hospital in Palmdale was as grim a trip in a car Janis had ever taken. Both women suspected but would not say that Karin's cancer was terminal.

Late in the afternoon, Dr. Rogers came entered Karin's hospital room with a radiologist and Dr. Cass, the oncologist who supervised Karin's first treatment for breast cancer. All three were grim.

The radiologist showed where the tumors were in Karin's body. His work done; Dr. Cass departed leaving the four women in the room. Dr. Rogers said, "Karin, you have uterine serous uterine carcinoma that is an undifferentiated sarcoma. Unfortunately, the cancer has metastasized into all but four of your lymph nodes. Surgery is out of the question because we'd have to cut you open in so many places, it is just not practical. Dr. Cass and I recommend that we try chemo first. If we can kill enough of the tumors, we can then take the resistant ones out."

Karin took a deep breath and Janis could see the tears in her eyes. Her lover was just given a death sentence. "With the chemo, how long do I have?"

"If we stop the growth of the tumors and kill them, we have a fighting chance that you'll live to a ripe old age."

"If you don't?"

"Without chemo, it is hard to forecast but I would guess three to four months."

"With chemo, assuming it just slows the growth down."

Dr. Rogers turned to Dr. Cass who said, "A year at most."

Janis held her lover's hand when Karin spoke, her voice cracked. "How soon do I have to let you know?"

"The sooner the better. We can start the chemo within hours of you giving us the go ahead. Please let us know what you want to do."

The two doctors left Karin and Janis alone. Karin had a decision to make.

SUNDAY, NOVEMBER 11TH, 2001, 6:21 A.M. LOCAL TIME, STALLION SPRINGS, CA

Janis woke up with a start and knew instantly the nightmare of the last two months was finally over. After finding no pulse, Janis closed Karin's eyes that were staring at a ceiling she could no longer see. Karin had fulfilled her wish of dying in her own bed.

Janis's first thought was, "You dumb cancer, now that you won, you die."

Then, Janis called 911 and the funeral home in Palmdale where Karin wished to be cremated.

With a timeline fleshing out in her head, Janis made the call to Germany she dreaded to tell Karin's parents their daughter had passed away. Their last conversation with Karin was two days ago and despite the morphine Janis was injecting for the pain, Karin managed a coherent conversation. What made the call more painful for the elder Eggers was that her mother was a 20-year breast cancer survivor.

Janis told the Eggers she would buy three tickets so her brother, Edgar could come as he did in October when they saw Karin alive for the last time. By then, it was clear that the chemotherapy wasn't killing the cancer and Karin had said, "Stop, let me die in peace."

MONDAY, NOVEMBER 19TH, 2001, 12:09 P.M. LOCAL TIME, KAUAI, HI

The trail to the Nepali Coast from the Kalalau Lookout off Highway 550 is difficult to walk. On average, 400 inches of rain falls in Waimea Canyon every year, making it one of the wettest places on earth. The trail to the Nā Pali Coast is narrow, slippery, and steep. Rarely does one see the sun, and most of the hike is made in or just below the clouds. If you can see something other than the damp trail and trees, it is the valleys below.

As they drove along Route 550, the Eggers said little. They were awed by the beauty of the rainforest. Both Janis and Karin came to Kauai once a year, and on each trip, they hiked to the Nepali Coast where they pitched a tent, spent two days on the beach before climbing back to their rental car.

Janis patiently let the 72-year-old Ursula Egger set a slow but deliberate pace. Edgar followed behind with his father Stefan, who was a spritely 75. The walk was taking an emotional and physical toll on the couple who were determined to reach the outcropping where Karin's ashes would be spread.

At the point in the trail where it began to drop down to the ocean, Janis led the Eggers to the rocky outlook. The gray clouds had parted, letting a shaft of sunshine light up the valley, the volcanic black and green cliffs, and the dark blue Pacific Ocean. This was *THE SPOT* where Karin and Janis always stopped to peer into the valley before following the trail down to the beach. It was also where Karin wanted her ashes spread.

Janis opened the urn and gave it to Ursula. She looked down at the light gray ash that was all that remained of her daughter, unsure what to do. Stefan gently took the porcelain urn and put her hands under his.

Ursula gave out a wail of grief and as they tossed the ash into the wind. When it was half empty, the couple gave it to their son, Edgar. Tears streamed down 44-year-old Edgar's face as he offered the urn to his sister's lover. "Janis, Karin loved you more than anyone or anything in the world. You finish."

WEDNESDAY, NOVEMBER 21ST, 2001, 8:12 P.M. LOCAL TIME, LOS ANGELES

After spending another day in Kauai after the hike, Janis and the Eggers flew to Los Angeles. After checking in late in the evening at the Marriott Hotel on West Century Boulevard, just down the street from the terminal, they agreed to meet in the Concierge Lounge for breakfast.

The hotel's shuttle bus dropped them off at the Tom Bradley International Terminal and Janis waited for the Eggers to check-in. Just before the German family approached the security checkpoint to go to the business class lounge for their flight to Frankfurt, Janis yelled. "Edgar!"

The young German turned to see Janis waving at him. The security officer nodded, and he ducked under the plastic lines that formed the lines.

Janis slipped off the six-carat Aascher-cut diamond ring she gave Karin in 1982 when she asked her to live together for the rest of their lives. "Take this. I gave it to Karin as a token of my love for her. Give it to your wife or daughter."

Edgar looked at her and started to cry. "I will. Thank you so much."

As she hugged him, Janis said, "I'll mail you the appraisal, receipt and a letter saying I gave it to you as a gift."

He nodded numbly and headed back to his parents.

Instead of driving back to Stallion Springs, Janis went to her accountant's office. She had been Sandra Santorelli's client since 1973 and Sandra, now 71 was working part-time.

Every quarter, Janis visited with Sandra to ensure her return would not appear on the IRS's radar. She didn't want the IRS digging into the source of her money and was willing to pay more in taxes to keep taxman out of her hair.

On every visit, Sandra also had a complete set of reports on her investments. When she retired in 1982, Janis's portfolio totaled $39.7 million.

With Sandra's help and network of advisors, in the 19 years since, Janis' portfolio grew at an average post-tax rate of 12 percent per year, over what she spent to live. Net-net, Sandra smiled when she slid the summary of her portfolio across the table. The total even surprised Janis who hadn't thought about in the past three months. The bottom line said her portfolio was worth $343.4 million. The number didn't include the value of her 500-acre ranch in Stallion Springs which was, at least for tax purposes, assessed to be worth $4.50 million. On the market, Janis though she could get closer to five million.

As Janis sifted through the charts and tables, Sandra, still pert and attractive with her hair now stylishly whiter than gray stood behind her. Her hands started massaging Janis' shoulders before sliding down to her breasts.

"Can you stay for dinner?"

"Yes." Before Karin, visits to Sandra's office started with business and ended with a pleasure-filled threesome. When Janis became a client and was still active as an assassin, Sandra's current lover was always a woman no older than 25. As Sandra aged, they were now '40 somethings. With Karin, they became foursomes.

"Good. My friend Angie and I will be happy to feed you."

Janis reached up and pulled Sandra's head down so she could kiss her. "Thanks. I need a good fucking." Her comment was driven by the comment that she hadn't had sex for the last two months and was very horny.

"I figured you did. We loved Karin and will miss her. I'm so sorry she had to pass away so young."

Janis nodded numbly. She'd been grieving ever since Karin's diagnosis. The pain of her loss was still there, but she was ready to move on.

"Janis, can you stay the weekend?"

"No, I must go back home. I have a long list of honey-dos that went undone while Karin was sick."

"Angie and I will take good care of you tonight."

Janis put her hands over Sandra's and whispered, "I'm counting on that."

TUESDAY, NOVEMBER 27TH, 2001, 8:19 A.M. LOCAL TIME, STALLION SPRINGS

Weather permitting, Janis started every day with a workout on the large porch in front of her house. It was her own private dojo and couldn't be seen from Banducci Road, half a mile down the driveway. Her nearest neighbor was, as the crow flies, a mile away.

Hanging from a beam was a large, well-used heavy punching bag. Janis screamed as she hammered at it, driven by the anger and fury of losing Karin. When the burst of emotion subsided, she started practicing tae kwon do katas. The yells with each strike or hit came from deep within her soul. The workout helped her vent the anger that formed when she learned she would lose Karin.

Sweating in the dry mountain air, Janis tied her running shoes and made sure the pouch with her cell phone, driver's license, half a dozen or so 20s, and credit cards was around her waist. She took a bottle of water and headed down the gravel driveway for a six-mile run that averaged about 45 minutes. While she was out, she extended it to 10 miles, and now home, her tired legs and thighs ached.

As Janis gulped down more water from another bottle she took from the refrigerator, her body glistened with sweat. She went into the bedroom that felt so empty now that Karin was gone and slowly stripped off her shoes and socks.

The full-length mirror on the back of the bathroom door drew her like a magnet. The socks and soaking wet t-shirt were tossed in the hamper along with the sports bra. Using her thumbs, both her running shorts and panties dropped to the floor. They too were tossed in the laundry basket.

Janis stood in front of the mirror studying her image. At 54, her sandy brown hair was showing some gray and she had small crow's feet at the corner of her eyes.

Her hands were drawn to her breasts. Janis barely filled a 34A bra. Long ago, she had become accustomed to being flat-chested. Janis smiled thinking that as she got older, there wasn't much to sag!

After cupping and caressing her breasts long enough to make the nipples stand at attention, her right hand ran down her toned body. She admired what daily workouts, running and sessions in a dojo created. Janis was, at 5' 8" and at 120 pounds, muscular but not overly so.

As she took stock, Janis didn't think of herself as beautiful yet both Karin and her ex-husband thought she was both beautiful and sexy. Looking at the image in the mirror, Janis believed she was aging gracefully, and that was, in her mind, "very cool."

MONDAY, DECEMBER 10TH, 2001, 8:36 A.M. LOCAL TIME, DALLAS

Janis never told Karin that she had decided to sell the ranch in Stallion Springs after she passed away. Every room, every part of the 500 acres, brought back memories of Karin. With her lover gone, it was time for a change.

So, where would she live? Janis hated the way California was governed and started with a list of eight cities. New York, Chicago, and Boston went into the trashcan due to their climate. She loved visiting winter to ski but did not want to live in it.

Denver was so-so in Janis' mind and was eliminated along with Atlanta leaving Dallas and Miami as two cities that met her criteria – a warm climate and a large gay community. Janis loved the beach, but the drug money flowing through the city and the crime rate made her feel uncomfortable so that left Dallas. In the TBM, she made it from Tehachapi to Dallas Love Field in 3.5 hours.

A back issue of D Magazine with an article on the top 10 realtors in Dallas was sitting on the coffee table in her hotel room in The Mansion at Turtle Creek. Number one was Darla Joyce, an agent from Sotheby's International Realty office in Dallas.

The surprised receptionist asked if Janis had an appointment when she entered. "No, I understand that Mrs. Darla Joyce is the top realtor in Dallas. Or am I mistaken? If she is, I'd like her to help me buy a house in Highland Park."

Flustered, the receptionist asked her to wait a minute. Janis turned away and smiled. She'd deliberately ignored the "by appointment only" note in the ad. While she waited to see if they were "stuck up" and if the rating had gone to the agency's collective head, Janis put her backpack on the floor. It was a combination purse and briefcase and had a copy of her November portfolio statement along with her laptop.

"Hi, I'm Darla Joyce." Janis was looking at an impeccably dressed woman with short blond hair, probably about her age and height, holding out her hand.

"Janis Goodrich." Janis wore a pair of clean, but faded designer jeans, a simple white blouse under a brown leather vest and a pair of worn and comfortable cowboy boots with round toes. In Texas, the boots are called ropers. Janis preferred the 'rancher' look and rarely wore dresses or skirts.

"Let's go into my office where we can talk. Coffee?"

"No thanks, but some water would be wonderful."

Darla pointed with her hand to an open doorway down the hall. Neither said anything until they sat down at the table. A bottle of water appeared by Janis' side, and she heard the door close.

"So, where are you from?" Joyce slid a yellow-lined pad next to her and uncapped a Waterman fountain pen.

Old fashioned. I like that! "Stallion Springs, California. It is a small town in the mountains 125 miles north, northeast of LA." While Darla wrote down the name of the small city where she lived, Janis guessed that Darla had no idea where the Stallion Springs was. *I'll bet Darla's pearl necklace and matching earrings are real. Her engagement ring has a stone that's at least five carats which means both she and her husband have done well.*

"Why are you moving to Dallas?"

"Because I want to."

Darla looked at the woman across the table. *That's a very interesting answer. Blunt and I'll bet it's the truth. She has an aura about her that says don't mess with me. The hairdo is dyke ish.*

"What kind of work do you do?"

"I don't. I'm retired."

"What type of house are you looking for?"

"A one-story house preferably in Highland Park with three bedrooms, two and a half-bathrooms. I need at least a four-car garage, but it doesn't have to be attached to the house."

"Janis, do you want it near middle or high schools?" *I'll see if she has any kids.*

"No. I'm single."

"Do you have a price range in mind?"

"No. If I like the house, I'll buy it."

"Do you have a mortgage commitment yet?"

"I don't need one. I'm paying cash."

I wonder if you know how much homes in Highland Park cost. She looked at Janis thinking she needed ask more qualifying questions to make sure if Janis Goodrich was a real buyer. "How big is your place in California?"

"The house is a little over 3,500 square feet and the ranch is just over 500 acres."

The place must be worth millions, even if it is out in the sticks. "Is it up for sale yet?"

"No, but it will be when I get back. They're staging the house and taking photographs this week."

"I presume you have a realtor and an asking price."

"I do. It'll go on the market at $4,995,000 and want to net around four point seven-five."

"How long do you think it will take to sell?" *I need to find out if we are looking at dragging this on for months.*

"The answer to your real question is that I don't need the cash from the ranch sale to buy a house in Highland Park. The ranch will sell when it sells, I am not going to give it away."

The edge in Janis's voice took Darla by surprise. "How soon do you want to move to Dallas?"

"As soon as practical. Depending on the house, it can either be move-in ready or I'll do what is needed to renovate it. I'm more interested in the house than a move-in date."

"Got it." Darla leaned back and glanced at the clock on her credenza. "I have a few houses in mind. How about if we meet for lunch at 11:30 and by then I'll have some houses picked out to visit. Where are you staying?"

"The Mansion." Janis suspected she didn't need to add the words, At Turtle Creek.

Why am I not surprised? Darla put her hand on Janis' and was not surprised that it wasn't withdrawn. "See you 11:30."

"Cool."

TUESDAY, DECEMBER 11TH, 2001, 5:49 P.M. LOCAL TIME, DALLAS

Even though a cold front came through the night before, the temperature was a delightful 65° Fahrenheit. The house was set back from the street and partially hidden by large oak trees in the front yard. Water from an early afternoon shower darkened the concrete driveway that went up the side of the house to a building behind the pool that was either an apartment for a maid or elderly parents. The rest of the building that stretched across the back of the lot was a five-car garage.

This was Janis' second visit, and the more she saw of the house, the more she liked. Darla said the home was tied up in a probate fight, and the children wanted more money than the house was worth.

From the island in the kitchen, Janis looked over the sunken living room that was two steps down and out to the patio and pool. Above the living room, there was a loft on three sides. The owners had turned the loft into a library with built-in bookshelves running its entire length and added several long tables along with a desk at the end.

The rear of the house was all glass and overlooked the pool full of decaying leaves, suggesting that it hadn't been serviced in months. The ultra-modern cement exterior made it different from the other homes in the area. Each bedroom had a large closet. In the one she planned to convert into an office, the closet would be turned into a gun vault. To Janis, the house was perfect, assuming its structure was still sound.

Darla stood in the corner of the kitchen taking notes while she was on a call with another client. Janis walked around the house again as she decided what to offer.

With a price and deal structure worked out in her mind, her brain wandered back to the weekend. Friday night, she went to Mary's, a club The Mansion's concierge said was Dallas' best lesbian bar. Janis arrived around 8:30 p.m. when it was still not crowded and took a seat at the end of the bar. She was not disappointed since she could see single women of all ages.

Three '20 somethings' gave her the once over. One made a pass, but Janis was looking for someone closer to her age.

The bartender's nametag said her name was Shelli and she smiled when Janis said she was moving from Southern California to Dallas. "You'll like it here. I'm from San Francisco and while the community is not as big, it is much more laid back."

Janis wasn't a big fan of the bar scene, but her sexual needs overruled her hesitation. Standing at the bar, the music wasn't too loud or soft. As she looked out at the crowd, a random thought crossed her mind that made her smile.

Karin, early in their relationship right after she retired, said that she was a 'badass, freelance, nymphomaniac lesbian assassin' and that it would make the basis of a best-selling novel. She was still thinking of Karin's dark sense of humor when Shelli refilled Janis's glass of Glenfiddich. Leaning over the bar, she said. "If you're interested, I can make an introduction to someone you might like. And, if you don't hit it off, she can introduce you to her more mature friends who are always looking for someone new."

That conversation was, as Janis noted on her gold, diamond studded Rolex President, at 9:05 in the evening. The woman, Staci Gilbright, and she hit it off right away. By 10:30, they were on their way to Staci's condominium in Turtle Creek a few blocks from Janis' hotel. On the way out, Janis left a C note on the counter for Shelli.

Staci started French kissing Janis in the elevator. Once the door to Staci's condo closed, their clothes started coming off. By midnight, they were spent and sitting on the bed drinking wine while Staci showed Janis her collection of sex toys.

The distinctive smell of applewood bacon being cooked woke Janis Saturday morning. Just as she was sitting up, Staci stuck her head in the door and asked her how Janis liked her eggs.

Darla's voice brought Janis back to reality. "Do you want to keep looking, or is this the place for you?"

"I want to make an offer on this house and here's how I would like to proceed. You said the owners have two appraisals that are far apart. Why don't I pay for one from a third neither party has used. We'll use the average of the three as the starting point for negotiations. In the meantime, I'd like the name of an engineer who can tell me what is wrong with the house and the pool so I can factor that into the final deal."

"Great. I'll let them know and I don't think they'll object. How much earnest money can you put down?"

"Darla, I want enough to ensure the house is off the market until we see if we can make a deal. This will also give me time to have the engineer and a general contractor prepare formal estimates on the repairs and the changes I want to make. I don't mind forfeiting part of the earnest money if necessary."

"The more you want to put on the table, the better."

"How about twenty-five thousand and if we can't reach a deal, they can keep five grand."

"That's more than fair. We can say the firm offer will be contingent on the average of the appraisals and the result of engineer's report." Darla opened her portfolio. "Here's the name of the engineer I suggest you use. I'll let him know you will be calling."

"Thanks."

"Is this still going to be a cash sale?"

"Yup."

"I'll need proof that you can write that size check."

"No problem." Janis reached into her backpack and placed the bound blue folder on the kitchen counter. Darla stood closer than normal, so their biceps and arms were touching as Janis opened the report to the summary page. "Will this do?"

Darla looked at the summary and gently squeezed Janis's hand. She wasn't sure if Darla was one of those 'touchy feely' women or was genuinely interested in making love to another woman. Until she closed on this or another house, nothing sexual was going to happen.

Darla nodded. "Oh yes, this is just fine. I'll call the owner's agent on the way back to my office."

CHAPTER 3

THE SEARCHERS

Colonel Hector Ordonez sat with his elbows on the edge of his desk and his hands tented beneath his chin. The large ceiling fan rotated just enough to stir the hot, humid air and cause the single piece of paper in the center of his desk to flutter. The document on which he was focused had five numbered items.

Ordonez' specialty in the *Dirección de Inteligencia* – Cuba's equivalent of the CIA – was advising friendly governments on how to stay in power. During his career, he had used legal and illegal means and was considered an expert in what was known as 'wet work,' i.e., assassinations, kidnappings, and bombings. At an earlier meeting with a member of the foreign ministry and the head of the Operations Department, Ordonez was told to find a way to kill Venezuela's President Hugo Chavez's opponents, so the blame does not fall on the Venezuelan dictator's shoulders.

The paunchy 175-centimeter-tall (~5' 9") Ordonez was debating the merits of five courses of action he'd written down.

> Option one – use Cuban assets. Cuban involvement in an assassination of a Chavez opposition leader could be exposed and would lead to an unacceptable outcome.

Option two – hire the Chinese. The Chinese may want more money and favors than the Cuban government would pay.

Option three – ask the Russian FSB for help. No one lies working with the FSB or its predecessor, the KGB.

Option four – hire Iranians –An Iranian officer in their embassy offered to help if the action stuck a sharp stick in the eye of the Great Satan. What would they want in return?

Option five – use a freelance assassin. But who? One could be hired through a series of cut-outs which would give us deniability. Cost???

In what Ordonez thought was a moment of absolute brilliance, he remembered that in the 1970s, the *Dirección de Inteligencia* trained fellow revolutionaries as assassins. As a junior officer, he visited the camp in the Escambray Mountains, 50 kilometers north of Trinidad. If one of the graduates were still active, he or she would be perfect.

He called Lieutenant Colonel Hector Ruiz, the head of the *Dirección de Inteligencia's* archive section to bring him the records on the assassins Cuba trained. From them, he hoped to determine if the agency still maintained contact with the graduates. Ruiz knew exactly what camp he was talking about because when he joined the *Dirección de Inteligencia,* his first assignment was maintaining the camp's training records.

THURSDAY, MARCH 14ᵀᴴ, 2002, 4:28 P.M. LOCAL TIME, EVANSTON, IL

Janis could feel the rented Chevy Malibu rock from the gusty wind as she studied the house diagonally across the street from her car. She'd flown to Chicago to look at a 1960 Porsche Abarth Carrera thinking that she might add to her collection of Porsche racing cars.

The 1,750-pound car was the 19th of 21 built by Abarth for Porsche and had a 1.5-liter, twin-cam, twin-ignition engine. For its day, the car was very fast. The race car was exactly as the owner had stated – the right front fender and nose needed repair and it hadn't run in 11 years. Neither bothered Janis since, if she bought the car, she intended to have it shipped to Porsche's U.S. Restoration facility outside Atlanta.

The owner had passed away and his family's lawyer had the car appraised. He wanted more than top dollar for the race car. Based on her conversations with a representative from the factory restoration facility, repairing it so it could be raced would cost between $75,000 to $100,000.

In the end, the lawyer would not budge from his asking price of $175,000. Janis gave him her phone number and the price she was willing to pay and left.

Rather than take the direct route back to the Palwaukee Airport where she landed her TBM 850 turboprop, Janis parked the rental car on a quiet residential street, and looked at the house in which she grew up. Despite the foot of snow on the ground, she could see that the dark green trim and the gray paint had been maintained. And, just like her childhood, a Volvo station wagon was parked in the driveway.

Janis hadn't been inside the house since she walked out with what possessions she could fit in her 1967 Volvo 123GT. After the graduation ceremony on the Madison campus of the University of Wisconsin, she headed west into the unknown.

There was no college graduation celebration, no dinner, no smiling faces. She saw only tears flowing down her mother's cheeks as both her parents told Janis not to return until she changed her radical political and social views.

The day before graduation, she closed out her savings and checking account which gave her $2,489.67 in cash. Most of which she had earned as a waitress in one of Madison's nicer restaurants. As Janis walked to her car, her father handed her a cashier's check for $9,648.52. It was what was left of the money he had set aside to pay for her college education.

Janis' thank you was genuine, but the hug was awkward. Running your only daughter out of the house on rails, Janis now believed, was harder on her parents than her. At the time, she wanted out and felt the separation was good riddance.

In the ensuing years, she drove by the house several times, but never went in. What could they talk about? Each time Janis replayed the same conversation in her mind.

Mom or Dad – "Janis, have you changed your social and political views?"

Janis – "Yes, I have. Now, I am a capitalist with a portfolio of over three hundred and forty million and I live in Dallas."

Mom or Dad – "That is a change. How'd you make your money?"

Janis – "I was a freelance assassin for about twelve years."

She was about to go through the next question when Janis saw her mother and father leave the house. Her mother was using a cane and holding her father's arm as they walked down the steps to the Volvo. They were still erect, but grayer. Her dad was 81 and her mother 79 and in June, they'd be married 63 years.

The tears flowed down Janis' cheeks as she toyed with meeting them. Afraid of the conversation, Janis started the Malibu and slowly drove past to get a closer look at her parents, wondering if this would be the last time, she'd see both alive.

The ache in her chest and tightness in her stomach was hard to ignore. Janis wondered if they ever thought about her. Maybe the time had come to re-introduce herself to them?

FRIDAY, MARCH 15ᵀᴴ, 2002, 9:26 A.M. LOCAL TIME, HAVANA

A soft tap on the door frame caused Ordonez to spin his chair around. He'd been staring absentmindedly from his third-floor office at the traffic on Calle A in downtown Havana and enjoying the refreshing breeze coming from the water.

Hector Ruiz stood in the doorway holding a bundle of folders. Ruiz looked emaciated but really had a small, wiry frame. "*Buenos días,* Coronel Ordonez, I brought you the requested folders. There is a dozen who meet your criteria from *Estados Unitos* and three countries in Europe. Unfortunately, some of the files are not up to date."

"Excellent. *Gracias.*"

Ordonez smiled as Diaz put the folders on the center of his desk. As he walked out the door, Diaz wondered if Ordonez realized he knew more than what was in the files.

Experience, Diaz learned while he was at the school in the Escambray Mountains, suggested females were better assassins. They tend to be more cold-blooded and have less of an ego. Women blend in more easily during the first part of the mission – surveillance – and the last and most crucial part, escape.

Within seconds, he had two stacks – one with the files of eight men and one with four women. One woman was an American which immediately made her attractive. Another was a Basque, a third was an Algerian living in France, and the fourth was a German. In his stack of male candidates, Ordonez had a American, two Spaniards, a Frenchman, a German, an Egyptian, and two Syrians.

He started studying each file and making notes. Of the men, only the German male met his requirements – fluent in English and Spanish, an expert marksman, and 'common' looking.

Ordonez started on the files for the women. The one for Julia Amy Lucas was very intriguing. He held up the picture and remembered he'd watched her shoot. The file said her control was Enrique Payá. In her training jacket, he read the detailed report on how she killed a Russian GRU officer who was an expert in hand-to-hand combat in a match. Officially, it was an accident, but the report said the man was known to be a bully and liked to hurt people. Unlike the other files, this one had only one photo and no negative.

The file noted that the woman's cover name was Juanita Serrano while at the camp. Another entry said she was married to an American Naval Aviator shot down over North Vietnam and who was listed as missing in action. Julia Amy Lucas came to the camp highly recommended by the Students for a Democratic Society's Action Wing (SDS/AW).

Interesting. Ms. Lucas' association with SDS suggests she doesn't like the U.S. government. Ordonez poured a fresh cup of coffee from the pot behind his desk. After adding several chunks of raw sugar, he wrote down the string of known aliases in the file. She was born Julia Anne Lucas. When she moved to California after graduating from the University of Wisconsin, she changed her name to Janis Anne Williams. When she married, she became Janet Anne Pulaski.

Even more interesting. Even before we trained her, Ms. Lucas was creating false identities. *Why?*

She had to execute another human to graduate from the Cuban assassin course. Her assignment was Lieutenant Colonel Ramirez, who had been convicted of killing an incompetent general Ordonez served under in Namibia. Seeing her, the colonel stood up and shouted 'long live Cuba' just before Serrano/Lucas/Pulaski shot him in the head.

Fantastic! Payá's write-up got him excited.

Pulaski left Cuba with a valid Canadian passport under the name of Jennifer Bertrand.

Excellent. Has it been renewed?

Under relationships at the camp, there was an entry that her only friend was a West German named Monika Arnsdorfer. The file noted both Monika and the Lucas woman shunned relationships with men and were suspected lesbians.

O.K. she likes women. The more he read, the more the Cuban colonel believed this Serrano/Lucas/Pulaski is *la bandida* he wanted. Ordonez wrote five notes on a separate sheet on his pad:

1. Get file on Monika Arnsdorfer
2. Find out if Lucas/Serrano/Pulaski husband was one of the American pilots brought to Cuba for "further interrogation"
3. Get files on any Cuban operations in which Serrano was used
4. Talk to Enrique Payá
5. See if Bertrand passport is still valid

MONDAY, MARCH 18ᵀᴴ, 2002, 10:46 A.M. LOCAL TIME, TEL AVIV, ISRAEL

Even after Aliyah returned to work, she continued her daily physical therapy sessions, graduating from crutches to a single crutch to a cane to no aid. During the winter, Aliya's hip would ache, telling her a cold front was coming. While waiting for a couple of Tylenol to work their magic, she massaged her upper thigh and hip before returning to the work on her desk.

The raid postmortem conducted while Aliyah was in the hospital confirmed her assessment that in Sohmor, the Israelis walked into a well-constructed trap. Mossad leaders promoted Aliyah and made her the head of the intelligence fusion group tracking terrorists considered to be a threat to Israel. Best of all, Eitan Kohan was informally reprimanded for overlooking warning signs on the tips leading to the raid and now worked for her!

On her second day back at work, Aliyah was awarded Israel's second-highest award for bravery, the Medal for Courage. What she didn't know until given the award was that her bravery and leadership saved the lives of the squads that landed just after her *Yanshuf* crashed.

An Al Aqsa Martyrs Brigade suicide bomber blew himself up in Jerusalem on March 2nd, killing 10 including six children and wounding another 50. The attack led to a meeting with the leaders of Shin Bet, Mossad, the Ministers of Defense and Justice, and the prime minister's chief of staff. Since her group was tracking terrorist groups, Aliyah was at the table, not sitting in the back as a staff member.

Aliyah waited until there was a pause in the discussion on how the attacks could be prevented before suggesting, "We can expand our target list to include the leaders of Hezbollah, Hamas, and any other organization that says it will attack Israel."

The PM's chief of staff immediately responded by saying this would be an escalation and could put the leadership of Israel in danger.

Aliyah politely replied, "Sir, we are all in danger. We are at war, whether we want to admit it or not. We should re-evaluate who we target and the method of retaliation."

The Minister of Justice looked at her. He was known for his hardline positions. "Aliyah, explain what you mean?"

"First, we can't continue to react on a tit-for-tat basis after each attack. Let my group develop the criteria to identify which leaders of terrorist groups that should be targeted and rank them in order of importance. Based on the target's rank, determine whether we assassinate the individual, hire a reliable proxy, or do nothing. We've used proxies to kill Nazis wanted for war crimes, and this is no different."

The room remained silent for a few moments before the Minister of Justice spoke. "I'll take the idea to the prime minister.

If he approves, you will lead a working group to develop the criteria and identify who will provide oversight."

THURSDAY, MARCH 21ST, 2002, 10:09 A.M. LOCAL TIME, MAGDALENA, ITALY

Before he left Dubai for Milan, Ghulam shaved his heavy, dark beard, confident his facial hair would grow quickly when he returned to the Arab world. Physically, Ghulam looked like most Middle Easterners, dark hair, olive-colored skin, and not tall at 170 cm (~5' 7") and slim. He weighed 70 kilograms (~154 lbs.). A beard, he believed, made him much more noticeable to Western authorities who used profiling to identify potential terrorists.

It took Abd al Bari Ghulam three days to fly to Milan from Beirut. The first leg of his circuitous route was to drive from Beirut to Damascus to catch a Syrian Air flight from Damascus to Cairo where he spent the night. Leg two took him from Cairo to Dubai on Egyptair and another night in a hotel. From Dubai, he flew on Emirates to Milan's Malpensa Airport the main international airport serving Italy's second largest city.

Once he was in Milan, Ghulam drove around Malpensa, looking for location within a half mile or so from the end of the airport's runways. On the second day, he found a clearing in a wooded area off the Via Brugheria that gave a clear view of airplanes taking off from Malpensa's Runways 35 Left and 25 Right.

The grass and weeds in the large clearing came up to Ghulam's knees. Looking back, he could see the side-by-side trails Faiz Hasnawi and he left in the tall grass. Hasnawi and his teammate Sa'id Darbi who remained in the small Fiat van parked on the Via Brugheria, were graduates of the al Mughabi Corps training program in a camp near Bargah, Iran. They flew on Iran Air to Tehran before transferring to a Qatar Airways flight to Doha and then connected with another Qatar flight to Tunis. From there, they flew on Tunisair to Milan.

In the large clearing, Ghulam listened as Hasnawi watched airplanes climbing out from Malpensa Airport and discussed how he would conduct his attack. To Abd Al Bari Ghulam, Hasnawi and Darbi were just names on a Hezbollah background investigation completed before they were allowed to travel to Iran. Now both were tasked with their first mission.

Before he was dropped off at Milan Red Line's Pero Metro Station, Ghulam again asked the pair to describe their escape plan. Before going into the station, Ghulam ducked his head into the small van to wish both men good luck.

FRIDAY, MARCH 22ND, 2002, 10:38 A.M. LOCAL TIME, MILAN, ITALY

At 10:22 a.m., Ghulam dialed 112 from a pay phone near the Duomo di Milano cathedral. Feigning excitement and fear, he asked the operator to connect him with the *Polizia di Stato* (State Police). He said it was urgent since he saw two men unpack what he thought were guided missiles in a small clearing northwest of Malpensa Airport. He gave the officer the names of the roads, an accurate description of how to find the field, and a fake name.

With that task accomplished, Ghulam entered the Milan office of the *Canale Italia* network and handed the receptionist a small envelope. He told her that their news editor would be interested in what was on the CD. His next stop was Milan's *Stazione Central* where he took his suitcase from a locker and bought a first-class train ticket to Turin.

At about 10:17 a.m., Faiz Hasnawi lifted the Russian-made 9K34 Strela-3 (NATO code name SA-14 Gremlin) surface-to-air missile launcher to his shoulder and pointed it toward the sky in the direction of the northern end of Malpensa's Runways 35R and 35R. Standing a few feet away, Sa'id Darbi was looking through a pair of 10 X 50 binoculars and said he could see the American Airlines logo on the rudder of the 767 that just took off.

Hasnawi squeezed the trigger, and the 10.3-kilogram Strela-3 came out of its tube with a whoosh. It left a corkscrew trail of white smoke as it spiraled toward the heavily loaded airliner at 400 meters per second. Sa'id was handing Faiz the second missile launcher when Italian police officers burst onto the field yelling for them to drop the missile.

Faiz tossed the unfired Strela-3 to the side and grabbed his Ak-47s. Kneeling, Faiz emptied a magazine in short, aimed bursts, dropping two Italians. Sa'id panicked as he unslung his AK-47. He sprayed an entire magazine at the Italians and his bullets went high and wide.

From behind trees, the eight unwounded Italian police officers returned fire with their Beretta 12 submachine guns. Sa'id died when his chest was stitched with four 115 grain, nine-millimeter bullets. Faiz was lying on his side, reloading his third magazine, when several 9mm bullets hit him in the head.

On board the airliner, four passengers screamed as they saw the approaching missile. In the cockpit, there was little the pilot could do other than pray. The 767 was at maximum gross takeoff weight, and the best the pilots could hope for was that the missile would destroy an engine and they would be able to land back at Malpensa.

Neither Faiz nor Sa'id nor any of the Italian police officers saw the Strela-3 streak by the Boeing. The g forces from the rapid acceleration to 400 meters per second cracked the line connecting the nitrogen bottle containing the coolant for the seeker that helped it differentiate jet exhaust from the sky. With no nitrogen, the Strela's seeker could not find a target. The missile continued past the 767 before it ran out of fuel and plunged into an empty field.

That evening Ghulam watched the evening news in his hotel room in Turin. Five minutes were devoted to the attempted shootdown of the American airliner. The report included a clip from the CD showing Faiz and Sa'id standing next to eight olive drab cases containing Strela-3s. A caption said the video was taken in a warehouse inside the European Union.

The video was made two months prior on a set at the al-Masai Corps training center in Iran. The message that Hezbollah had shoulder-fired surface-to-air missiles in Europe was confirmed by the one fired and the one captured. Ghulam hoped European police forces would spend millions of Euros looking for the fictitious stockpile of missiles while Hezbollah watched and learned.

Ghulam never had a second thought about deliberately sacrificing Faiz and Sa'id. He was more concerned about when they would die than if they would be killed. To him, they were soldiers martyred in the holy war against America and the Israelis.

MONDAY, APRIL 1ST, 2002, 11:29 A.M. LOCAL TIME, HAVANA

In the *Dirección de Inteligencia,* answers often came slowly. Of his four questions, only one had been answered. Again, the old archivist who brought him Monika Arnsdorfer's file said she was recruited while a student at the University of Cologne. Her radical beliefs and faith in socialism as the solution for society's ills brought her to the *Dirección de Inteligencia's* attention. She was born Karin Egger and was 20 when she arrived in Cuba to become a forger. She had a severe accident in 1970 while climbing a rope during physical training exercise. Karin was sent back to Germany with a check for 200,000 Deutsche Marks (1970 average exchange rate was $1 = 3.65 Deutsche Marks making this payment worth approximately $54,794.52) and a stern warning to maintain the cover story that she had an accident while hiking. No further contact was made with Egger until 1976 when she was asked what she thought about a terrorist organization called Red Hand. She showed no interest, and the file was closed.

A note in the file said she was friendly with an American named Luna Serrano. Either the writer did not know who Luna was or was instructed not to enter any other information.

The phone rang as Ordonez closed the file. A clerk from the foreign ministry was calling to say that Jennifer Bertrand's passport was renewed in 1980 and again in 1990 using a Calgary address rather than the original location in Toronto. It was not renewed in 2000. The caller reminded him that Cuba did not have a consulate in Calgary or in Western Canada.

With two questions answered, Ordonez sensed bureaucratic resistance. Frustrated, he called the man who approved the project and agreed to set up a meeting with the head of the *Dirección de Inteligencia.*

THURSDAY, APRIL 4TH, 2002, 9:16 A.M. LOCAL TIME, TEL AVIV

Besides the noticeably visible security, Mossad's headquarters was a modern-looking office complex in Yafo, north of Tel Aviv. From the air, the five square buildings near the Gliliot Ma'arav Intersection of Routes 2 and 5 were shaped like an arrowhead pointing northeast. Inside, the facility was a labyrinth of hallways and closed-off areas, accessible only to those with the necessary clearance and access codes.

No one had clearance to roam freely around the building, even the head of the Mossad, Efraim Halevy. The average-looking man entered Aliyah's small office on the third floor, and seeing him, Aliyah stood up. Halevy closed the door and asked her to please sit down.

Halevy pushed his black-framed glasses up his nose. "Aliyah, your decision tree and its criteria to determine which targets will be handled by Israel and which will be farmed out to carefully vetted contractors has been approved."

Mitsuyan!!! Aliyah smiled and nodded. The Hebrew word *mitsuyan* loosely translates to "perfect" in English.

"The next step is selecting those contractors. I presume you have given that some thought."

Aliyah opened a file drawer next to her desk and pulled out the folder she was given in Buenos Aires by DeMedina. "Yes, sir, I did. I'd like to start with those Mossad used before. This file was given to me by retired *Commandante-mayor* DeMedina the last time I was in Argentina. He and I worked closely together on my first assignment in Buenos Aires. He is a tribal member and I trust him completely. The documents in this file are on a woman he believes was hired by Mossad, and he believes killed at least six wanted Nazi war criminals in Argentina. The trail to finding her starts in our archives."

Halevy pursed his lips and nodded. "If we have information on this woman, you'll get it!"

THE SAME DAY, 10:19 A.M. LOCAL TIME, HAVANA

Ordonez wasn't often invited to the top floor of the *Dirección de Inteligencia's* headquarters. On the organization chart, he was one level below the head of the agency's direct reports. In other words, he was two rungs from the top. Ordonez did not want to move up any further to where one could quickly get sideways with the Castros or one of their close friends. A word from the close-knit group that ran Cuba could put him at the wrong end of a firing squad.

Ordonez listened as the head of the *Dirección de Inteligencia* ticked off notes as he spoke. First, American Lieutenant Pulaski was not brought to Cuba for interrogation.

Second, Enrique Payá was murdered in Miami, and the killer was never found. Payá's operational files are off-limits to him. Nonetheless, he will have a cleared researcher look through them for references to Serrano/Lucas/Pulaski and other known aliases.

Third, assuming helpful information is found, Ordonez would be issued a Columbian passport to travel to the U.S. to search for this mysterious American assassin. His cover would be looking for long-lost relatives. In the meantime, he was to look for other candidates.

Ordonez walked out of the meeting thinking, you idiot, there are no other viable candidates.

SUNDAY, APRIL 7TH, 2002, 2:26 P.M. LOCAL TIME, BERLIN, GERMANY

Even though the attack in Milan failed to bring down an American airliner, Ghulam viewed it as a success. His next move was letting the Europeans see more of Hezbollah's man-portable surface-to-air missile inventory. He believed this would reinforce their belief that every airliner taking off or landing at a European airport was at risk.

Ghulam traveled by train from Turin to Marseilles, France. Now that he was inside the European Union, he did not have to show a passport crossing the French/Italian border. Nor did he have to worry about having his briefcase or luggage inspected.

While his bosses preferred that he travel unarmed, Ghulam carried a Walther PPK in a caliber the Germans called nine-millimeter *kurz* or short that the rest of the world knew as .380. The pistol was small, so he could carry it in a holster at the small of his back or in his coat pocket.

Other difficult-to-explain items in his briefcase were the envelopes containing Egyptian, French, Lebanese, and Syrian passports, driver's licenses, national identity cards, and credit cards, all with his picture but different names. A competent investigator would quickly discover all the credit card bills were paid from the same account at the Export Development Bank of Iran.

After a day in Marseille, Ghulam boarded the high-speed train to Paris. There he disappeared into the poor, primarily Muslim neighborhood of Sevran to visit an eight-man Al-Musawi Corps team at their safe house. He wanted to ensure they were ready for the mission he planned to assign to them.

Ghulam's next stop was Berlin. He booked a first-class seat on a high-speed train. Nine and a half hours later, he hailed a cab at the Hauptbahnhof on Europlatz to take him to a hotel in Berlin's central business district catering to road warriors. Confident he wasn't under surveillance, al Bari headed out for dinner.

Ghulam liked the German capital. It had large Muslim neighborhoods populated by refugees from the West Bank, Gaza, Lebanon, Syria, and Iraq. They joined those who came in the 1950s from Turkey and Yugoslavia as "guest workers" to work in German factories.

After 15 years of good behavior with no criminal history and if recommended by their employer, a Gastarbeiter (guest worker) could take the written and oral German citizen tests that required fluency in German. If they passed, they became German citizens and swore allegiance to the Bundesrepublik.

Rather than assimilate into society, the sizeable Muslim communities in Germany stayed segregated to retain their religious identity. Over time, the residents imposed their own version of Sharia law on their streets and ignored those of the host country.

Poverty made the Muslim communities a fertile recruiting ground for al Qaeda, Hezbollah, and other Islamic groups. For Ghulam, they were a place he could hide teams and equipment.

Today, Abd al Bari's first stop after making several detours to check for a tail was a small shop in what used to be East Berlin. At one time, it was a bakery until the native Germans moved out when their new neighbors didn't buy their breads, cookies, and cakes.

The procurement arm of Hezbollah scooped up the building through one of its many shell companies. An astute investigator who took the time to peel back the layers of corporations that bought the building would discover the actual owner was the Iranian Revolutionary Guard Corps. The old bakery had small inset loading dock in the back that shielded it from view was another reason the bakery shop was a perfect location for a safe house.

A block from the shop, Ghulam dialed a number on a mobile phone he'd just bought at a kiosk in the train station and activated. After exchanging passwords, the man who answered said he would be waiting when he knocked on the door.

Inside, the stainless-steel tables where the bakers once kneaded dough were removed, and in their place were eight olive-drab crates. East German Army markings identified the contents of each as a 9K32M Strela 2M shoulder-fired, surface-to-air missile known by its NATO designation, SA-7 Grail.

The missiles were built in the early 80s and stolen from East German stocks when the country collapsed. Thought by many as obsolete, to Ghulam, they were ideal for enhancing his message.

At the back door, Ghulam looked up and down the narrow alley between the two rows of apartment buildings. Satisfied, he wished the eight men well and said instructions on their first mission would be coming soon.

Half a block from the bakery, Ghulam donned a pair of latex gloves before unlocking the lobby door to an apartment building. Rather than take the elevator, he climbed the stairs to the sixth floor of the seven-story structure. Another key opened the door to apartment #2, which faced the street.

Three large metal cases sat in the middle of the living room floor of the unoccupied and sparsely furnished apartment. Ghulam pushed a table against the wall under the window to position the commercial-grade video camera on a tripod facing the bakery's entrance. Then, he connected the cable to a computer and inserted the CD. A quick test made sure the set-up was working.

Ghulam plugged a device into the computer that let the computer connect to Berlin's telephone network. The black screen with green lettering asked for an access code, this one with 16 letters and numbers. Another stream of commands was entered before he was presented with a dialog box asking for his access code. Ghulam typed in the 16-digit code and pressed the return key. One by one, sharp black and white pictures from the cameras hidden in the walls and ceiling of the bakery appeared on his computer screen.

Camera #1 showed the store with unused display cases where baked goods were once sold. Camera #2 was a wide-angle view of the dough preparation room with the eight olive-drab crates. On his laptop, they looked dark gray. Camera #3 was in the living room of the upstairs apartment, and camera #4 was another view of the dough preparation room facing the back door.

Satisfied everything was in order, Ghulam called the Berlin office of the *Bundeskriminalamt,* the German equivalent of the FBI. In halting and grammatically poor German, he told the operator he'd seen two men loading olive drab crates with East Germany Army markings into a building.

The women asked him to repeat the address and for his phone number before asking him to wait. A man came on the line and Ghulam repeated what he told the operator and offered more detail on the men and the crates. The man said thank you and again, asked him for his name and phone number. He gave a nearby address but not where he was, the number for the burner phone, and a made-up name.

Satisfied that the Germans might raid the bakery, Ghulam noted the time he hung up so he could determine the police response time. With nothing to do but wait, he ripped open a package of dried fruit and started nibbling.

Eighteen minutes after he hung up, a black sedan slowed as it passed the bakery and continued down the street, made shiny by the rain. Ghulam turned on the recorder when he saw it enter the alley. Three minutes later, a black Mercedes van parked in a vacant spot 20 meters from the bakery, and heavily armed men spilled out the back and ran to the front door.

Within seconds of each other, the front and back doors were smashed open. Immediately after the flash bang grenades exploded, men carrying Heckler & Koch MP5 SD sub-machine guns and wearing Kevlar body armor stormed into the bakery.

Two of his men came down the stairs toward the storefront, spraying bullets from their AK-47s. They were sent sprawling by well-aimed bursts from the German GSG9 team.

He watched two al-Musawi soldiers use the corner of the bakery oven and the old refrigerator as concealment and cover. They emptied their magazines before they were killed. In less than 60 seconds, the attack was over.

The men of GSG-9 stepped back while the stack of missile crates was inspected by the bomb squad. Satisfied there wasn't a trip wire attached to the top two, the lids were cracked open to ensure a bomb was not inside before being pulled off. Ghulam watched as the Germans methodically examined and photographed each SA-7 launcher before placing it carefully back in its crate.

Outside, green-clothed police officers began to cordon off the area and fan out into the apartment buildings to ask questions. Ghulam put the CD recording of the raid into his briefcase and picked up his umbrella. He left the apartment building before the German police entered. The recording equipment were considered disposable. The Germans would have difficulty finding the buyer since they were stolen months ago. A block away, he dropped the latex gloves in a trashcan. He was confident that if the Europeans weren't convinced Hezbollah could bring their airline network to a halt after what happened in Milan, this should.

To watch a live GSG9 raid, the eight men were expendable along with the missiles that were worth losing due to their age and technology.

MONDAY, APRIL 8TH, 2002, 10:07 A.M. LOCAL TIME, TEL AVIV

From the hallway on the way back from the bathroom, Aliyah heard the phone ringing in her office. The caller asked her to go to a secure conference room at the far end of the third floor.

When she entered, Aliyah was surprised to see the head of the Mossad, her boss Yitzhak Reznik, and a man she guessed was in his 70s but did not know. When she sat down, Aliyah opened her notebook, and the older man, who had not been introduced, spoke. "Do not write this down but listen very carefully. Only a few people know what I am about to tell you and is not to be shared with anyone outside this room."

"I understand." Aliyah closed her notebook.

"After Eichmann was executed, Israel gave the American, British, Soviet and West German governments a list of Nazi war criminals we wanted arrested and tried. Accompanying the list were thick dossiers of evidence. None were taken into custody. In 1970, Israel decided on a different approach. Kidnapping à la Eichmann was too risky, and the PM allowed us to kill as many of those on the list we could."

Aliyah nodded. The old man sipped a cup of tea. "The Prime Minister, the Defense Minister, and the Justice Minister approved each assassination and who, either Kidon or an outside contractor, would carry out the mission."

Kidon is bayonet in Hebrew and is the name of an extremely secretive Mossad special operations group. Aliyah was aware of its existence but did not know any of its members.

"At the time, Mossad was focused on those individuals and organizations that directly threatened Israel. Nazis war criminals are old news except to Jews, so we found reliable people to carry out these missions. A Cuban, Rafael Periente, who was a friend and had escaped from Castro, helped us find a very reliable asset. Last I heard, he lives in Brazil, but I do not know if he is still alive."

The older man swallowed hard as he searched his memory banks. "Rafael told us about Raul Moya who came highly recommended by our friends in the CIA. At the time, Moya had an asset who was a

Cuban trained American woman Moya called *La Estrella Roja de la Muerte,* and I do not know her real name. After Moya was killed in 1982, Rafael told me he believed this woman lived in a town named after a horse of some kind near Palmdale or Bakersfield, California."

The older man turned and picked up a beige folder from the table. "In here is Rafael's last known phone number and address. It also has my notes and the names of the Nazis we used this contractor to kill in Argentina, Chile, Paraguay, and Europe."

Aliyah put the offered folder in her lap and took the man's hands in hers. "*Mitsuyan.* Thank you very much. If she is still alive, I will find her."

Halevy looked at her. "Find as in contact, not recruit or hire. That may come later."

"Understood."

THE SAME DAY, 12:19 P.M. LOCAL TIME, FRANKFURT, GERMANY

Al Bari's work in Berlin was done, and it was time to fly back to Lebanon. He started by booking a seat on an EgyptAir flight to Cairo before taking the train to Frankfurt and Rhein-Main airport. After spending a night in Cairo, he'd fly to Damascus. Having been in Europe for almost a month, he was less worried about being caught than when he arrived.

At the Frankfurt *Hauptbahnhof* (main train station), Ghulam found a locker large enough to take his duffle bag containing his extra passports, 10,000 Euros, the PPK, its four spare magazines, and two boxes of ammunition.

With the key in his pocket, he took the train to Rhein-Main airport to check in for his flight. Al Bari didn't pay any attention to the casually dressed man sitting on a bench with a briefcase next to him. Inside was a camera focused on those who bought tickets on EgyptAir.

Every hour or so, this man changed locations with his female partner to photograph passengers checking in on Pakistan

International Airlines and Iran Air flights. Each evening, they sent the encrypted digital photos to Tel Aviv.

TUESDAY, APRIL 9TH, 2002, 9:17 A.M. LOCAL TIME, MEXICO CITY, MEXICO

Hector Ordonez flew from Havana to Bogota, Columbia and then to Mexico City, where he spent the night before boarding a flight to Miami. Rather than wake up early, he reserved a seat on a late morning flight so he could enjoy what Mexico City had to offer.

While standing at the Aero México check-in counter, the trained intelligence officer scanned the world around him. Nothing appeared to be amiss. Boarding pass in hand, Ordonez headed toward security. The Cuban missed the man near an Aero México banner advertising flights to Cancun, who took his picture and dialed a number on his mobile phone.

The man cupped his hand over the mouthpiece as he spoke in the noisy terminal. "I am certain that Colonel Hector Ordonez from Cuban *Dirección de Inteligencia* will be on board Aeroméxico Flight 422 to Miami. I do not know what name he is traveling under, but I recognized him from when he worked in Venezuela."

The man on the other end was in the U.S.'s new National Counterterrorism Center in Alexandria, VA. He called the FBI office in Miami and sent notes to the file the CIA maintained on Colonel Hector Ordonez. The FBI was ordered to follow Ordonez to determine why he was coming to the U.S.

THE SAME DAY, 6:09 P.M. LOCAL TIME, RIO DE JANEIRO

Aliyah thought getting to Rio from Tel Aviv was a beating. The shortest route was Tel Aviv to London on El Al and then a British Airways flight to Rio. Even with her small stature, being crammed into a coach seat for 19 hours was painful. Her left leg, which hadn't bothered her in months began aching an hour out of London. Two Tylenol only dulled the throbbing, so Aliyah took a hydrocodone tablet.

Even after spending a night in a hotel, Aliyah felt jet lagged and groggy as she drove down the street twice and then walked past the house on the far side of the road looking for surveillance. Adrenalin took over as she walked up to the front door, hoping it was the Pierente's home and they wouldn't slam the door in her face.

Before leaving Tel Aviv, she called, and when a woman answered, Aliyah asked in Spanish if Rafael Pierente still lived there. The woman hung up. Aliyah dialed a second time and told the woman she worked for the Israeli government and would like to talk to Rafael about Raul Moya. She hoped to meet Rafael Pierente when she knocked on the door.

"Who is it?"

"Aliyah Skylar from the State of Israel. I am the woman who called." She spoke in Spanish, knowing Pierente was Cuban.

The response came in the same language. "Do you have identification?"

Aliyah held up her passport in front of the peephole. "This is one, and I have another." She then held up her Mossad identification folder with her picture and Hebrew text. She heard the door start to unlatch, and a woman with white hair streaked with black opened the door.

As she entered, a man ordered her to stop. Aliyah turned and saw a man in his 70s pointing a pump shotgun at her. He gestured with the barrel for her to move into the house. In the living room, he pointed at a single chair. "Sit." He didn't need to say the word 'there.'

Aliyah did as she was commanded. She didn't see the Browning Hi-Power pistol the woman aimed at her back.

"Put your identification on the table."

The woman handed her passport, and Mossad identification folder to the man she hoped was Rafael Pierente. He looked at them for a few minutes.

"Are you from the consulate here in Rio?"

"No. I just flew in from Tel Aviv."

"Why?"

"To ask you questions in person about Raul Moya. I understand you worked for him."

"Who told you that?"

"Moshe Löbel. He is well and sends his regards. He also said you can't read a map worth a damn."

Pierente smiled and relaxed noticeably as he placed the shotgun across his lap. The personal reference to when he helped Löbel ferry an airplane to Panama after the Bay of Pigs fiasco and got lost was key piece of information. Only Löbel would know the story. "That was a long time ago. Please sit."

Aliyah sat on the couch, and the man sat in a chair with the shotgun in his lap. "Did you work with Raul?"

"I did." Rafael Pierente looked into Aliyah's eyes. "So, you are Mossad?"

"Yes."

"Why are you here?"

Aliyah pointed to her backpack. "I would like to show you some pictures. May I?"

Pierente nodded, but the shotgun barrel did not move. It would take only an instant for the Cuban native to aim the gun at her and pull the trigger.

She held up one of DeMedina's photographs, "Do you recognize this woman?"

Pierente looked at one picture and then the other. "I met her."

"*Mitsuyan.* When?"

"May 1982, if I remember. She was here to do a job for Raul around the time he was killed. I am pretty sure that she is no longer active."

"Why do you want to know about her?"

"I cannot tell you."

Pierente guessed that the Israelis wanted to hire her, assuming she is active. "Do you remember her name?"

"I do. She registered in one hotel as JayLynn Nance and in another as Jamie Symonds. I delivered photos of her target, an American CIA officer turned traitor named Gary Savoy. This is how I know. The Cubans and the Americans were searching for Savoy, and both put a bounty on his head. After I found him, I called Raul, and he got the contract from the CIA. This woman took it."

Aliyah struggled to contain her excitement. "Do you, by chance, have any other photographs of JayLynn?"

Pierente leaned the shotgun against the chair and motioned for her to come with him. The older man walked stiffly as he led Aliyah down the stairs. Off to one side, she could see a darkroom where prints once hung from lines strung across the rafters. Pierente waved and said, "old technology." He led her to a large, chest-high gun safe. He spun the dial left and right before turning the brass-colored handle. Inside, Aliyah could see rifles and pistols as well as ammunition cans.

Rafael pulled out a file and opened it on a nearby workbench that smelled from gun oil. Inside were cellophane sleeves with black and white negatives. "Raul always had me take covert pictures of my contacts."

He handed her three photos showing the woman's face. On one, she could see she had a black eye and a bruised cheek. "This is the woman. I am sure that JayLynn Nance or Jamie Symonds is not her real name."

"Do you have a phone number?"

"No. She always called me. She spoke excellent Spanish with a Cuban accent."

Aliyah hugged the man. "*Mitsuyan!!!* Thank you so much. What you have given me is a mitzvah."

CHAPTER 4

IT IS BETTER TO BE LUCKY THAN GOOD

T he center of the FBI world revolves around its J. Edgar Hoover Building at 935 Pennsylvania Avenue, Northwest in the U.S. capital. There, six blocks from the White House, two men bent over a second-floor conference room table as they spoke into a flesh-colored speakerphone.

One was the Assistant Director for the FBI's Intelligence Branch and his counterpart in the FBI's National Security Branch. At the other end of the call were the CIA's Assistant Director of its Counterintelligence Division and the Assistant Director of the Counterterrorism Center.

The topic was operationally and bureaucratically complex and politically charged even seven months after 9/11. The National Security Branch and the Counterintelligence Branches had overlapping responsibilities for the surveillance of foreign intelligence officers. Ordonez was a colonel in Cuba's *Dirección de Inteligencia* which made his visit of interest to both the CIA and

FBI. Ordonez was in the U.S., so the FBI had jurisdiction and scheduled the call.

As soon as they were alerted, the CIA began working the agency's sources in the Cuban exile community to learn why Ordonez was in the U.S. They were about a half a day behind the FBI in starting and neither agency wanted to compromise its sources. What brought the participants together were the questions the FBI sources said Ordonez was asking.

When informed about the topic, the head of the CIA instructed the two men in the conference room that they needed to be candid and truthful with the FBI. However, even in the post-9/11 world, they were to only provide answers to what was asked.

Question #1 – who is or was Gary Savoy?

CIA answer. When Savoy was killed, the Department of Justice had issued a warrant for his arrest for treason and conspiracy to commit murder. When he was charged, Savoy was the head of the CIA's POW/MIA desk and had been passing classified information to the Cubans. His prior assignment was as a CIA case officer who spent a dozen years helping UNITA. When he turned up dead in Rio, the CIA closed Savoy's file.

What the CIA officers did not tell the FBI was that Savoy was afraid of what would come out of a CIA internal investigation into his leadership of the POW/MIA desk. In 1982, he adamantly stated there were no living Americans left behind in Southeast Asia at the end of the Vietnam War. When a Vietnamese drug lord tried to ransom six American POWs, Savoy tried to convince his superiors that the drug lord was trying to scam the CIA out of the $12 million ransom fee. Proof of life photos ended his credibility on the subject. It led to the CIA opening an internal investigation Savoy was certain would lead to some of his actions in Africa. Savoy was afraid the agency would learn he stole millions from the agency and passed secrets to Enrique Payá, a colonel in the Cuban *Dirección de Inteligencia*.

Question #2 – who was Raul Moya?

CIA answer. Moya flew for the rebels during the Bay of Pigs invasion. Shortly, he began working for the CIA as a contract pilot in Laos. In 1970, while flying a B-26 for Air America, he was badly injured in a crash. The CIA helped him set up International Logistics, a company that moved cargo worldwide for the agency.

Question #3 – was International Logistics a CIA front operation?

The FBI Special Agent in Charge had a copy of the police report from the investigation of a fire in Moya's apartment in the Little Havana neighborhood in Union City, New Jersey. Moya's apartment had hardened steel doors, government-issued file cabinet safes, bulletproof glass, and other expensive security features. Inside the flat, investigators found Moya's charred remains along with those of four former members of the Soviet GRU. One was stabbed to death, the other three along with Moya died from gunshot wounds. Moya was shot twice with a 9 x 18mm Makarov rounds and the Russians by .380 bullets.

CIA answer. No. We helped Moya get established and he had other customers besides the CIA.

The CIA officers looked at each other. They had four files on the table, all pulled from the agency's archives. One contained the invoices from International Logistics and the agency's records and equipment given to the firm. No names were mentioned, but there were invoices that billed the agency for undefined "special services."

Another folder was the CIA's personnel file for Raul Moya. The third, but not the thickest, folder contained the results of the agency's classified internal investigation of Gary Savoy. After Savoy was killed, the file was sent to the archives.

The thickest had what the agency learned about Enrique Payá after his diary was dropped off at the U.S. embassy in Bonn, Germany by a woman presumed to be a U.S. citizen. How she acquired it was unknown. The CIA officers were authorized to use the intelligence from the translated diary to answer a question, but they could not disclose the source or the treasure chest of detailed insight about Cuban operations that were revealed. At the time, the agency knew nothing about Colonel Payá other than from debriefings during which former Vietnam POWs identified him as one of the most brutal interrogators they encountered. The agency was stunned to learn how often Payá had entered and stayed in the U.S.

Question #5 – Why did Ordonez risk coming to the United States?

CIA answer. We don't know and were wondering the same thing. What does the FBI know?

The senior of the two FBI agents said, "We think he is looking for an American woman the Cubans trained as an assassin in the early 1970s. When active, she was known as *The Red Star of Death*. Ordonez suspects she worked for Moya. Do you have any idea who this woman is or was?"

Both CIA officers glanced at each other. "Special services" encompassed a wide range of overt and covert operations that the details of Moya didn't provide to the agency. They answered with the truth. "No."

"Do you have any idea where the woman executed her contracts?"

"No, we do not." Another truthful answer.

"Good, if they were CIA-sanctioned hits on U.S. soil, it could become a major problem."

The quick response was, "We know."

"O.K., so here's what we're doing. The FBI is tailing Ordonez to see what we can learn. So far, he has not committed a crime other than entering the U.S. under false pretenses, i.e., a Columbian passport. It is not worth the paperwork to arrest him. We'd like to set up a call in a week. Maybe we'll know more by then. Or, if something breaks, we'll call immediately."

"Sounds like a plan."

Before the two men could leave the secure conference room, the Director of the CIA entered. After hearing the questions asked by the FBI, he ordered, "I want you to put a small, dedicated team together immediately to dig under every rock tasked to learn as much as they can about Moya, Payá, and Savoy, and this woman. I want to know who she is, who hired her, and what she did. And, if you can, find out where she is today. My hypothesis is the agency used her often, and I'll bet a large sum of money several of our overseas friends also hired her. I want answers. And I want them in a hurry, so we know what we are dealing with. The blowback will be very ugly if this gets out."

THE SAME DAY, 11:51 A.M. LOCAL TIME, PALMDALE, CA

Even though she'd flown through 10 time zones and spent 33 hours en route since leaving Israel, Aliyah was keyed up when she walked off the plane at Los Angeles International. Sleep and rest would come later.

After leaving the National Rental Car facility, Aliyah bought a map at the first gas station she came across on La Tijera Boulevard. The station had a Rand McNally Road map of Southern California, so she knew to take Interstate 405 to Highway 14 toward Palmdale which is where Löbel thought was near where the Nance/Symonds woman lived.

In Palmdale, she stopped at a 7/11 where she bought maps of Palmdale, Bakersfield, Tehachapi, and Mojave. Hungry, Aliyah went into a Mexican restaurant across the street from a dojo that offered classes in four martial arts.

Looking at the storefront, she wondered if the instructors knew *krav maga*, the Israeli technique known for its focus on quickly defeating an opponent with the least risk to the practitioner. Before she was wounded, Aliyah had qualified as an expert in *krav maga*.

As she munched on chips and salsa, Aliyah ran her finger down the map's index of towns searching for one with a horse in its name. Tired from the flight from Rio to LA and then driving two hours, Aliyah was annoyed when a blob of salsa fell on the map. When she wiped it up, she saw the name Stallion Springs, and her irritation instantly changed to excitement. Adrenalin pushed the fatigue from her body.

Best she could figure the town was 50 miles away. Aliyah couldn't finish eating, pay her bill, and get out of the restaurant fast enough.

TUESDAY, APRIL 16ᵀᴴ, 2002, 1:37 P.M. LOCAL TIME, MIAMI, FL

The chubby Ordonez was enjoying a cup of café Cubano confident his cover was holding. This was his second trip to Miami and now he knew why its Latin vibe attracted Payá.

He wondered how often his hunt for *The Red Star of Death* would bring him to the U.S. Several times he was tempted to walk into the local FBI office and defect. His fear of what the Cuban government would do to his wife and children held him back.

The man he was supposed to meet was late. No surprise, he was a Latin. In Cuba, nothing ran on time. Ordonez thought he should shorten the sentence to 'nothing runs,' but that is a statement that, if spoken aloud in Havana might lead into a windowless room with people with no sense of humor.

Luis Guiterrez stopped on the sidewalk and found Ordonez at a table off to the side. As soon as he sat down, Guiterrez leaned across the table and said in a low voice, "My friend Alejandro Gomez is on his way, and he was one of Payá's contacts and a cousin of Raul Moya."

Ordonez nodded, wondering if these men were working both sides. The Cuban American community was well penetrated by the FBI, the CIA, and his own agency. If he were to bet which firm had the best contacts, he'd bet on the CIA, and this meeting could be a setup. Why? Most Cubans living in Miami hated Fidel Castro.

More café Cubano was served, and the plate of cassava – fried yucca chips – and dip was refreshed. They laughed about their answer to whether the Cuban national baseball team could beat a U.S. professional baseball team in a seven-game series. Their agreed-upon answer was no since most Cuban players would have defected before any series was over. They were still laughing when Gomez pulled out a chair.

After Gomez's café Cubano arrived, lunch was ordered, Ordonez asked, "Did you work for Raul Moya.

"Occasionally. In those days, I was a customs broker at DHL and helped Moya with paperwork."

Ordonez didn't react. "Do you know what was in those shipments?"

"The paperwork said some type of machinery. What was really in the crates, I don't know other than it wasn't illegal drugs. They cleared customs, and we were never fined nor arrested. Why?"

"Just curious. Alejandro, do you know if International Logistics was involved in any other types of operations?"

"Besides cargo and the occasional airplane sale, no."

"What do you mean by airplane sale?"

"Sometimes Moya bought and sold airplanes that didn't have all the proper maintenance or licensing paperwork. Raul had a friend who now lives someplace in South America with a crew of crackerjack mechanics who could make the airplanes airworthy. They also would complete the necessary paperwork to make them legal."

"Are they still in business?"

"I don't know. Last I heard, Raul's friend had a repair facility on Robert Marinho Airport outside of Rio in the mid-1980s."

"Do you know the name of his friend?"

"Yeah, Rafael Pierente. He is a good man who was very loyal to Raul. I don't know if he is still around."

"Is he Cuban?"

"Yes. He left before your boss took power."

Ordonez nodded and said nothing as the waitress put their dishes in front of each man. It provided the necessary break to change the subject, and Ordonez now had a lead which made the trip worthwhile.

Across the street in a nondescript van, the two FBI agents nodded and turned off the recorder when the group broke up. Three pairs of agents in separate cars followed Ordonez to his hotel in South Miami. Others were detailed to get intelligence on Guiterrez and Gomez to determine if they should be questioned.

THE SAME DAY, 12:46 P.M. LOCAL TIME, TEHACHAPI, CA

Aliyah was exhausted when she checked into the Best Western Motel on Main Street in Tehachapi. She collapsed on the bed and slept for 12 hours until her bladder started screaming, "empty me!"

At the Four Seasons Café on Main Street, she had eggs and orange juice before heading out CA Route 202 to Stallion Springs. She drove around the small community for two hours, unsure what to do next. She was, as the Americans say, close but no cigar.

Back in Tehachapi, she walked into the German bakery on West Tehachapi Boulevard and bought a glass of freshly squeezed orange juice and a nut roll. Aliyah almost dropped the juice when she saw the woman she knew as either JayLynn Nance or Janice Symonds walk into the shop talking to another woman.

JayLynn was dressed in jeans, cowboy boots, and a red plaid shirt. Both women carried briefcases. They sat at the next table with their drinks while they waited for their lunches. A few feet away, Aliyah looked at the book she started on the plane to LA as she listened to the conversation. This is beyond *mitsuyan!*

The woman she recognized was JayLynn was called Janis, not JayLynn by the other woman. The other woman asked, "Janis, how was your trip to Dallas?"

"Judy, great! I got back last night. The house is almost ready to move in. Painting is done; the three coats of polyurethane on the new hardwood floors are dry, and the appliances were put in yesterday. The pool equipment and heater for the spa were replaced and the piping flushed. The pool should be filled by the time I get back. All I need is furniture! The only work left is finishing the gym in the garage. That should be complete by the time the movers get there. It is going to be very nice when it's finished."

"Janis, when are the movers coming?"

"Thursday morning. At three this afternoon, the car carrier picks up the Porsches. Everything in the house is packed, so all the movers have left to do is load the boxes and the furniture and go. I'm hoping the movers leave by Thursday afternoon so I can fly back to Dallas that night. If not, I'll check into a motel in town and leave Friday morning. You can have someone from the shelter for battered women pick up my Yukon at the house when the cleaning crew comes in next Monday. I'll leave the keys, title, and registration on the kitchen counter. And don't forget to send me a receipt for the Yukon so I can list it as a donation for tax purposes."

"No problem." Out of the corner of her eye, Aliyah watched Judy pull a sheet of paper out of her briefcase. "Janis, I've got an offer."

"Judy, that's great. What is it?"

"Remember I am legally bound to bring it to you, and it might be the start of negotiations."

Janis forced herself not to sound impatient as she repeated her question. "What is it?"

"Three point nine five million."

"Not in the ballpark. What do you suggest?"

"I spoke to the other realtor, and he wants you to come back with a counter. The buyer is the ex-wife of some Hollywood producer who grew up on a ranch in southeastern Colorado. She wants to move back to the country and has the money. It is your call."

"I don't want to negotiate with myself, so tell them they need to up their offer. You know I want to walk away with four point seven five after your commission. If they're not willing to come up with more money, we wait for another buyer."

"Got it. Do you want to sign the contracts to maintain the house and the grounds now or just before you leave?"

"I'll sign them now and get it out of the way."

Aliyah waited until the two women left and followed the woman in jeans in the silver Yukon. The two-lane road had double yellow lines so passing wasn't an option. She stayed back 100 feet before she drove past the entrance to the ranch, went half a mile, turned around at the intersection of Stallion Springs Drive and Banducci Road and drove back. If the Symonds woman suspected that she was being followed, there was no indication. Aliyah wondered if she'd gotten complacent in the years since she 'retired.'

The Israeli slowed as she checked the number and found a spot near a water pumping station to pull off the road so she could call the Mossad officer at the Israeli consulate in LA. Gal Pundak didn't know the details of Aliyah's mission and his instructions were to provide whatever she was asked.

This was a classic case of "it is better to be lucky than good!"

"Gal, if I know an address of a house, how do I find out the owner's name?"

"That's easy, go to the city or county tax office. They should have the names of the homeowner since they are public records. Why?"

"I can't answer that question. Thank you."

The maps on the passenger seat would tell her how to get to Bakersfield.

THURSDAY, APRIL 18TH, 2002, 8:58 A.M. LOCAL TIME, HAVANA

The past hour for Ordonez was uncomfortable but not career-threatening. He was sure that the head of his department didn't want to explain to Raul Castro or his brother Fidel why a colonel in the *Dirección de Inteligencia* defected.

Ordonez began with a disclaimer saying that there is always a chance that the CIA or the FBI may have planted the information which fed his boss's paranoia about the CIA and FBI. Tensions eased when he described what he learned in Miami that dovetailed with what he already knew before he left. Some blanks were filled in, but not enough to keep going.

He concluded by saying, "I still do not know the name of the woman or where she lives, but I do have a name in Brazil who may. My conclusion is that we should not waste our time chasing a ghost, and we should look for other resources to use."

Ordonez was surprised by his supervisor's response. "That is not a decision you get to make, and people above both of us will decide and will tell me. Then I will let you know."

Ordonez suspected that the decision would be made by either Raul or Fidel himself. He wondered if he would regret his recommendation that Cuba search for the *la bandida* known as *La Estrella Roja de la Muerte*.

THE SAME DAY, 9:03 A.M. LOCAL TIME, BAKERSFIELD, CA

Aliyah drove straight to the Kern County tax office on Truxtun Avenue in Bakersfield rather than go to the city office in Stallion Springs. She was worried that a clerk might warn the Nance woman. On the way, she rehearsed the story she would tell. When she looked at the clerk, something in her brain said that this middle-aged woman had seen all the bullshit stories in the world. What she planned to say went out the window.

Aliya held up her passport and Mossad ID card. "Ma'am, I work for the Israeli government, and I am trying to find out who lives at this address. They may be relatives of Holocaust victims and eligible for reparations."

"What's the address?"

Aliyah slid the sheet of paper on which she had written the address in Stallion Springs. The woman made a face. "Give me a minute."

Her heart pounded as she watched the woman type on her keyboard. Then she wrote on a piece of paper and came back. "This is what I can give you without a court order, and your government should know that."

Aliyah looked at the paper. Under the address, the woman wrote:

Bought by Jamie Symonds, June 1977
Sold to Janet Pulaski, December 1978
Sold to Janis Goodrich, June 1982

Mitsuyan! She tried to contain her excitement and before she could say, "Thank you," the clerk looked over her shoulder and said, "Next."

FRIDAY, APRIL 19TH, 2002, 8:53 P.M. LOCAL TIME, PARIS, FRANCE

Ghulam stopped a few steps from the stairs leading out of the St. Paul metro station in the Marais district of Paris to get his bearings and check for surveillance. Spring was in the air, and the trees were leafing out. The map in his head said he was three short blocks north of the Pont Marie in a quiet part of Paris' 4th Arrondissement. If he was interested, he could visit the National Picasso Museum a few blocks away.

Crossing Rue de Rivoli, Ghulam headed north on Rue Paveé to the Rue de Rosiers where he spotted two small Citroen 2CV panel trucks. One was in the livery of a non-existent florist. It was parked in front of one with the name of a fake plumbing company on the side.

The driver of the florist van recognized al-Badi who bobbed his head and the driver responded by starting the vehicle. The driver of the plumber's van did the same.

Ghulam retraced his steps down Rue Paveé to where he could see the entrance to Agoudas Hakehilos. In about 10 minutes, worshippers would begin leaving the Hector Guimard-designed synagogue. Constructed in 1913, Parisians viewed this building as one of Guimard's better designs. In the 1960s, art historians began to acknowledge Guimard as one of the best practitioners of the Art Nouveau style of architecture.

Ghulam put his briefcase on the roof of a parked car. He motioned to a young man who looked overdressed for a warm April night as he walked into the stream of congregants coming out of the synagogue. He set off three kilos of SEMTEX plastic explosive on the top step. Thousands of 1/4 inch diameter ball bearings shot out in every direction shattering windows up and down the street. Car alarms were set off by the concussion.

Seven members of the Agoudas congregation disappeared in a pink mist as their bodies were shredded beyond recognition. Others with dozens of steel balls embedded in their bodies fell bleeding. The blast and ball bearings shattered windows up and down the street.

Parisians ran to the scene to help while the van with the florist markings parked diagonally across Rue Paveé 10 meters south of the synagogue entrance. The plumber's van did the same 10 meters to the north, blocking the street. Four men exited each van. Two ran toward the synagogue's destroyed door shooting anyone they saw.

Inside the sanctuary, Henri Camondo stepped out from behind a pillar, ripped the AK-47 from one attacker's hands and used the butt to knock him to the floor. He shot the second attacker with the gun before killing the man from whom he took the weapon. Camondo, a French paratrooper home on leave organized a defense as two other men stripped the dead attackers of their weapons and ammunition.

Peeking around the shattered doorway, Camondo knew a classic street barricade defensive position when he saw one. An RPG streaked toward the first ambulance entering the Rue Paveé. Doors blew off the vehicle as it exploded in a ball of flames. A police van coming from the other direction meet the same fate.

Behind Camondo, those in the congregation still inside filed out the back entrance to what they hoped was safety. From where he stood, Camondo's only protection was the wall as he dialed 112, the Parisian equivalent of 911. At first, the operator didn't believe him before turning him over to a supervisor who thought he was luring more gendarmes into a trap.

Frustrated, Camondo described what he saw – six men armed with AK-47s and RPGs in a mini-fort on the street. Finally, the supervisor agreed to send a squad through the back door of the synagogue.

Ghulam peeked around the edge of a doorway where he had taken cover, thinking so far, so good. Many Jews and French policemen were dead, and he assumed the two men who went into the synagogue were dead.

The first GIGSN – *Groupement de sécurité et d'intervention de la Gendarmerie national* – unit cautiously came around the corner from the Rue di Rivoli in two stacks of six. As soon as Ghulam's men spotted them, they opened fire. The disciplined GIGSN team split into pairs behind cars and returned fire.

Two policemen pushed Ghulam toward the Rue de Rivoli to get him out of danger. He grabbed his briefcase, and as he left the doorway where he was watching the attack, two police sniper teams entered the building.

Walking away, Ghulam listened to the rattle of gunfire. At first, it was intermittent and increased in volume before stopping as fast as it started. He saw paramedics from ambulances stacked up on the Rue de Rivoli who were held back by the police rush forward.

Rather than go into the Metro at the St. Paul station, Ghulam strode down the Châtalet station where he boarded a #14 Purple Line train and rode it to Saint Lazare. There he transferred to the #2 Blue Line and got off at Place Pigalle in the heart of Paris' traditional red-light district. His hotel, the Villa Royale at 2 Rue Duperré, was across the street from where he exited the Metro station. While French police and emergency aid workers were sorting through the carnage, Abd al-Badi watched his recording of the gunfight in his hotel in Montmartre.

All the Paris newspapers and the offices of CNN International, BBC, Sky News, and France 24 had received a note and a videotape showing al-Musawi fighters training at an undisclosed base. The note claimed the attack was the work of the Al-Musawi Corps and warned more were coming. Later that night, as he switched back and forth between the networks, it was clear his strategy was working.

MONDAY, APRIL 22ND, 2002, 7:30 A.M. LOCAL TIME, DALLAS

Every time Aliyah moved, she'd get a whiff of her body odor which was a pungent reminder that she needed a bath. It filled the car and was noticeable each time she opened the door to get back in.

She'd been living in the rented Chevy Malibu for the past four days as she followed the United Moving Van eastward from Stallion Springs. When the two drivers stopped for a few hours at a truck stop in Kingman, AZ, she found a corner where she could watch it.

At a Flying J truck stop in Moriarty, New Mexico, Aliyah slept in the car's back seat. When the van's big diesel engine rumbled to life at 0530, Aliyah went into the truck stop to take a quick pee and buy breakfast. When she returned to the Malibu, the tractor-trailer truck was heading down the entrance ramp to Interstate 40.

Cokes, coffee, and No-Doz kept Aliyah awake as she kept the truck in sight at distances from a few hundred yards to a half a mile. When it stopped, she stopped. The good news was the truck's range either driven by the driver's bladders or gas tank was about the same as hers and the Malibu's. Only once did she have to stop before the truck did and it was a panicked 20 minutes as she drove at 90 plus to catch up.

The moving van stopped at a Pilot Travel Center of I35 and TX 170 Sunday night and got underway just before six on Monday. Aliyah tailed it through the morning rush hour traffic to a modern-looking house in Dallas. Aliyah watched the woman she saw in Tehachapi greet the movers.

"*Mitsuyan.*" Aliyah snapped pictures with the Nikon D1X digital single lens reflex through the F2.8 ED AF Mark III 80 – 200mm zoom lens. Satisfied that the woman would be there for a few hours, she wrote down the address and headed off to find a hotel and a much-needed shower. Later in the day, she returned and took more pictures of the woman.

Tomorrow, Aliyah planned to visit the Dallas County tax office to learn the buyer's name and return to the house. Hopefully, she would take more pictures before flying home to Israel – mission accomplished. She had found *The Red Star of Death*.

After a nap and a call to Reznik, Aliyah asked the hotel concierge where she could go to have some fun and meet other women. The young man handed her a card for a club named Mary's.

Just after eight-thirty, Aliyah picked an empty seat at the bar and ordered a glass of the house's red wine. She settled back in the chair to survey the club that was several times the size of those she'd visited in Tel Aviv.

Aliyah was sipping her wine and looking out over the crowd when a woman pulled out the empty chair next to her. The woman spoke to the bar tender as if she were an old friend, saying, "Hi Shelli, the usual."

Aliyah forced her jaw to keep from falling on the floor. It was JayLynn Nance a.k.a. Jamie Symonds a.k.a. Janis Goodrich a.k.a. and many more aliases she didn't know.

Rather than say nothing, Aliyah smiled, "Hi, my name is Aliyah Skylar."

The attractive woman turned and said, "Hi, my name is Janis Goodrich. First time here?"

Aliyah looked into the hazel blue eyes, knowing they were those of an attractive, middle-aged woman and a cold-blooded killer. "Yes."

"Cool. Talk to Shelli, she knows everyone!" Shelli smiled at the compliment as she filled a glass with two shots of Glenfiddich 18. Janis looked toward the door and waved at a woman just entering. As she stood up, Janis put a $20 bill on the table and took in the attractive woman with dark, olive skin and shoulder length black hair sitting next to her. She nodded in approval before she said, "Have a great night."

CHAPTER 5

WEAK LEADS

Finding *The Red Star of Death* and meeting her had Aliyah flying high. Three questions kept running through her mind. One, would she be allowed to contact her? Two, were other agencies trying to recruit her? Three, was Janis Goodrich willing to come out of retirement?

Her elation was tempered by what she saw on TV. First, there was the report on the Friday night attack in Paris. The body count was 32 plus nine members of the Al-Musawi Corps, and another 53 were wounded.

Second, she learned the Pestalozzi synagogue in Berlin was attacked on Saturday morning. From what she read in the newspapers and from the Paris consulate, the Al-Musawi Corps changed their tactics slightly. This time they stationed a sniper on the roof of a nearby building to pick off the two German policemen outside the door before the suicide bomber went inside. The sniper and nine more jihadists were killed, along with 28 congregants and two German police officers.

At Newark, when Aliyah checked in for the flight to Tel Aviv, the ticket agent handed her another one, a hotel reservation, and a note from Reznik:

Meet me in Berlin. The trail starts there.

A dog-tired Aliyah was escorted to a back room in the Israeli embassy. Reznik introduced her to another grim-faced Mossad officer she did not know who was sifting through a pile of pictures. Reznik was a no-nonsense, career Mossad officer who, like Aliyah, joined the agency right after his compulsory military service. Now 60, Reznik still stood ramrod straight but was one of those whose clothing looked as if he had just gotten out of bed. Aliyah was sure there was not a stylish article of clothing in his closet.

Reznik looked up and said, "Welcome back to the salt mines."

Mossad's director of its counterterrorism section started with what they knew about the French attack. One security camera showed a man setting a briefcase on the top of a car and then adjusting it. Later he is seen picking it up and walking out of the frame.

The French provided enlargements of the photos and a detailed description but no name. They also included details of the weapons, fingerprints, photographs of the attackers, statements by witnesses, and a timeline.

The Germans were still sifting through the wreckage, searching for traces to tie the bomb back to its designer, and had given Mossad what they knew. Unlike Paris, they found a briefcase with a camera and a CD recorder inside. They were trying to identify the fingerprints and where the equipment was bought.

Aliyah made notes as she sifted through the documents. Reznik held up the pictures of the man he called 'the observer.' "Aliyah, since you are so good at finding people, your job is to find this bastard. Once we identify him and the men who ordered these attacks, the Prime Minister will decide how we will respond. They cannot be allowed to continue."

Aliyah nodded, not sure Reznik was finished, and he wasn't. "I have asked for permission to recruit your new American friend." Smiling, Reznik added, "Identify this man who likes to watch and, in your spare time, come up with a plan to convince this American to come out of retirement."

FRIDAY, APRIL 26TH, 2002, 1:49 P.M. LOCAL TIME, WASHINGTON, D.C.

Special Agent William Smith III's prior assignment was in the FBI's organized crime unit. Before that, he spent five years chasing bank robbers. Now, 15 years into his FBI career, the son of a St. Louis cop was working on what he thought was a make-or-break career assignment. In his mind, his accomplishments of the past were just that, in the past.

If he failed, Smith III would go back to what he thought was the point of the FBI's sword, an FBI field office as an investigator. If he succeeded, he would be promoted and take another step up the FBI ladder. To Smith III, either outcome was a win.

His new mission – lead a team of four agents dedicated to finding and arresting the woman known as *The Red Star of Death* who had managed to evade the FBI for 20-plus years. The FBI's renewed interest in *The Red Star of Death* directly resulted from the *Dirección de Inteligencia's* sudden interest in the woman.

Three stacks of folders on unsolved murders between 1970 and 1985 were arrayed on the table of the large conference room that had become his team's office. One stack had hits on Mafia kingpins, and another included files on assassinations of high-profile businessmen. The third contained those that fell into neither category.

On the whiteboard, Smith III's team wrote the common threads they'd uncovered so far. His gut said the key to finding the woman was in the miscellaneous stack.

One folder contained the police report and forensic analysis from the killing of a Vietnam POW in Chicago. The Navy was tight-lipped about why they thought he was killed, and that alone got his attention. The body had a .380 bullet in the forehead, and the killer left a video camera and tripod on the scene. The report assumed the assassin took the tape. The agent who wrote the report hypothesized the killer had forced the victim to make a confession.

Another was the report on Raul Moya's death. U.S. military thermite grenades in file cabinets started the fire to ensure all his files were destroyed. The Russian killed by stab wounds had a dislocated knee and a broken tibia the examiner concluded could have been caused only by a blunt object such as a baseball bat.

Investigators found three Makarov pistols and empty cartridges with dents in the primers all over the apartment, which suggested a gunfight. Two slugs from one of the Makarovs were pulled from Moya's remains. The gun that fired the .380 caliber bullets was not found.

Smith III concluded there had to be a sixth person who was an expert in hand-to-hand combat and used a .380 pistol. Who was it?

The third report that caught Smith III's attention contained details of the murder in Miami the CIA identified as Enrique Payá, a colonel in the *Dirección de Inteligencia*. He was found by his girlfriend with a .380 bullet in his head. The report hypothesized that the lock was picked. The only fingerprints in the apartment were Payá's and his girlfriend's. When he was found, Payá had been dead for several hours, and the apartment was not ransacked.

Smith III now believed he had two significant clues. One, the killer preferred .380 pistols. He made a mental note to ask the FBI Firearms/Toolmarks Unit to compare the slugs. Second, he or she was an expert in martial arts since the charred remains of a bat were not found in Moya's apartment.

SUNDAY, APRIL 28TH, 2002, 8:30 A.M. LOCAL TIME, DAMASCUS

Hezbollah's Damascus offices were in a run-of-the-mill office building not far from the headquarters of Syrian Military Intelligence on Umayyad Square. As part of the group's agreement with the Syrian government, Hezbollah was responsible for protecting its people. Senior leaders entered the building in their cars via the underground garage. Due to the nice weather, Ghulam decided to walk from his hotel today rather than driving.

Ghulam was sure the CIA, MI6, the Mossad, and/or the French equivalent to the CIA – the Directorate General External Security – photographed him as he opened the door. Without being obvious, he made sure he didn't face the street.

As far as photographs went, Ghulam was partially correct. It wasn't just the British, French, Israelis, or the Americans who were interested in who came and went. The Russians were as well, and they were embroiled in a brutal war in Chechnya with Islamist separatists. Some senior officers inside the FSB and GRU suspected the Iranians and their proxies in Hezbollah were helping the Chechens.

It would take a day or two before the film would arrive at Mossad headquarters and be processed. Once prints were made, they were scanned into its facial recognition system.

The Israeli software came from a U.S. Defense Advanced Research Products Agency project called FERET or Face Recognition Technology. Once it was made available to commercial developers, several Israeli firms acquired licenses, enhanced the application, and helped Mossad create a database of known and suspected terrorists. Minutes after the photo was scanned, the annotation noted the times Abd al-Bari Ghulam entered and left Hezbollah's Damascus office.

THE SAME DAY, 10:12 A.M. LOCAL TIME, DALLAS

Janis stopped on her way back to the house from the workout room, which was the old living/dining room in the apartment in the garage building. She was carrying a net on a long pool to skim leaves out of the pool dropped by the large trees that shaded the backyard and the large patio. In the morning, spooning the leaves out of the pool was something she was now doing every other day.

The ringing of the doorbell, wired to ring in the back and inside the house, surprised Janis who was not expecting visitors. Her sweat-soaked t-shirt clung to her body over the sports bra, and she could feel the wetness in the waistband of her panties and gym shorts.

Back in Stallion Springs, there was a gate half a mile away from the front door, and visitors had to press a button to announce their presence. A video camera showed her who was there, and she could open the gate remotely.

Here in Dallas, the video cameras hadn't been installed and she kept a Walther PPK/S by the door along with three Heckler and Koch USP 9mm compact pistols stashed around the house. The German-made pistol made famous by James Bond was held in the small of her back as she stood on the side and cracked open the door. Her visitor was Darla Joyce.

"Good morning, I hope I didn't wake you."

"Oh no. I've been up for hours. Come in and excuse the mess. I just finished working out."

Darla's clothing suggested she was on her way to work. "I stopped by to see if you were interested in coming to dinner at my house next Saturday."

She held up her hand. "Before you answer, it's formal, i.e., cocktail dresses, and the men wear coats and ties. It's a Highland Park thing. Anyway, my husband invited his partners and several of your neighbors. Some are single either by choice or death of their spouses. It's a good crowd."

"You mean I can't come dressed as a tomboy."

Darla chuckled. "I am assuming you do have a dress or two."

"I do, and they're even unpacked."

"The men will love you, and the married women will hate you."

"Why?"

"It's not often that men get to talk to a woman who drives vintage race cars, flies her own airplane, and likes to shoot."

Janis laughed. "I don't want to be the witch blamed for breaking up marriages, so if I am going to be a threat, maybe I shouldn't come."

"Oh no… That's not what I meant at all. There will be women who want to meet you."

She just told me that several women there will be bi, or lesbians like me. And rich ones at that!

"What time?"

Darla held out a sheet of paper. "Here's my home address. Drinks start at seven, and dinner is at eight. Why don't you come at six-thirty? My husband is dying to meet you, and I can give you a who's who in the zoo."

Janis nodded. "Cool. Thanks for thinking of me. I'll be there."

TUESDAY, APRIL 30TH, 2002, 6:09 PM. LOCAL TIME, TEL AVIV

An attack in Marseilles with the same MO as those in Paris and Berlin had Mossad on edge. All were claimed by Hezbollah or a known Hezbollah-controlled group, and more were threatened. Requests for information were coming in daily from European intelligence agencies and the CIA.

Aliyah had to identify the mystery observer, and the pressure was palpable. As she stared at the picture of the mystery observer, Aliyah's mind raced. She'd seen him before. But where?

On a hunch, she went to the woman who headed the archive that kept the original photos. The woman had a photographic memory that could quickly recall faces and match them to their files. Aliyah laid the picture on her desk. "Have you seen this man before?"

Noya looked older than her 42 years, studied the picture for a few seconds, and sucked air between her teeth. Then, she held up her hand before she spun around and opened a file drawer. Out came a thick folder with photos and notes with the time, date, and location the picture was taken and, if known, the subject.

She flipped through the stack of photographs and compared one to the photo given to her by Aliyah. She slid it across the desk. "This is the same man. Wait, we have more. Do you want a digital image or the actual photograph?"

"Show me what is in the computer."

Noya tapped on her keyboard and waited. The computer whirred, and a progress bar started across the screen before two rows of small thumbnails appeared. Each had a date and location the photo was taken.

"Come look. This one was taken a few weeks ago." In the background, Aliyah could see he was in line to check in for an Egyptair Berlin to Cairo flight. The photo, taken on April 8th, also showed the man's flight number.

Mitusyan!!! After thanking Noya profusely, Aliyah couldn't wait until she got to her office. Once there, she dialed the number of the Israeli Ministry of Justice liaison for the Bundeskriminalamt and gave him the info. He said the manifests had to be filed with German

Immigration service. Hopefully, there will be a match, and they will have his name or alias in his profile.

DALLAS, SATURDAY, MAY 4ᵀᴴ, 2002, 9:57 A.M. LOCAL TIME

On Thursday, Janis bought a simple, black knee-length cocktail dress with a shallow V neckline at Neiman Marcus. She planned to wear it with a single strand of a mix of white and black 10-millimeter pearls with matching earrings. On her right hand, she would wear a four-carat oval diamond ring with small chips amounting to another carat around the band. For this crowd, it should be enough bling to compete with what she expected other women to wear.

At the beauty salon recommended by Staci, the stylist trimmed her hair, so it was short but not shorn on the left side and flopped over on the right down to her ear. It looked good, and while sitting there, Janis decided to wear three-inch heels to the Joyce's. As much as she hated wearing high heels, this was one of those occasions that required them.

Rather than take her new Yukon Denali she bought in Dallas right after she closed on the house, Janis drove her 1999 Porsche Turbo she bought new. Her high-heeled shoes went on the passenger seat so she could enjoy feeling the ribs on the rubber pads on the gas, clutch, and brake pedals through her stockings.

Three minutes after the appointed time, Janis rang the doorbell at Darla's home. She wasn't surprised when a middle-aged woman wearing a simple black dress opened the door. Suspecting she was Darla's housekeeper; Janis spoke in Spanish. "*Buenos noches, soy Janis Goodrich.*"

The woman smiled, hearing her native language spoken effortlessly replied in Spanish. "Good evening, I am Angela, you must be Ms. Goodrich. Mrs. Joyce is expecting you. Please, I will take you to them.

Janis nodded. "*Gracias.*" Janis followed Angela, not knowing what to expect.

A very tall, football player-sized man filled the living room. Janis remembered that Darla said her husband Don spent five years in the NFL as an offensive tackle before wrecking his knee. After rehab to prove he could still be a starter, he retired and went to law school.

"Hi, I'm Don."

Janis's hand disappeared into Don's. A quick assessment was that she barely came up to his boobs and was half as wide as this giant man. "I'm Janis."

"Hi, Darla calls you a man's dream come true."

Janis's quizzical look told him to explain.

"Men dream about meeting a woman who loves fast cars, collects and shoots guns, and flies her own airplane."

She giggled at the comment. *I had one man, and that was it. He spent nine years in Vietnam as a prisoner of a drug lord. During that time, he was declared MIA and presumed dead. By the time he was rescued, I had moved on, and no more penises in my life.*

"Oh my, look at you! So, this is what happens when the tomboy dresses up."

Janis recognized Darla's voice and turned to see the realtor holding two glasses of red wine. She spun around on the ball of her right foot to model the dress, and Janis held up her left foot. "And I'm even wearing heels!"

Darla handed Janis the glass of red wine. "I know you like shiraz. You look stunning, and thanks for coming." Darla took a sip of her wine, and Janis could see Darla's eyes smiling. "In some ways, you're the guest of honor, so we can officially welcome you to Highland Park." Darla quickly went through the guest list that, according to one issue of D Magazine Janis bought at a grocery store, were many of Dallas' rich and powerful.

"Don, I have a business question for you?"

Don Joyce was a partner of Baker, Feldman, Joyce & Partners, one of Dallas's larger law firms. The 200-attorney firm had offices in Austin, Houston, New York, Washington, and London. "Shoot."

"Does your firm have attorneys familiar with German tax and trust law?"

"Our London office has a relationship with a German firm based in Frankfurt. Why?"

"I want to gift my former partner's parents five million Euros, and I don't want the German tax man to get a bite."

Don nodded. "I'll call the guys in London on Monday morning and set up a call with the firm in Frankfurt we use to help with German law. Then, I'll call you back to tell you what can be done."

He was about to say something when the doorbell rang. The guests started arriving. Janis struggled to remember them all. What surprised her was that of other guests, only eight were couples. The other five were single, well-dressed women in their 50s. All gave her the once over, and several nodded approvingly.

One man, an executive in a private equity firm, said he'd heard she had a plane. Janis responded with a simple, "I do."

"Where is it based?"

"Jet Aviation at Love Field."

"Is it with a management company, or do you have your own flight department?"

Janis smiled and guessed where this was going. "I'm the pilot and flight department."

It was clearly not the answer the man expected. She suspected he wanted to compare jets as if they were comparing penises. Thankfully, he looked at his nearly empty highball glass and went for a refill.

At dinner, Janis was seated next to the Joyces. On her right was a good-looking man she guessed was in his late 40s. He re-introduced himself right after he sat down after holding out her chair, "Hi, I'm Jason Winthrop. Is that your 996 Targa in the driveway?"

Surprised that the man used the model number rather than the more commonly used Porsche 911 Turbo, Janis answered, "It is." *Those that know the car also know it only comes with a six-speed.*

"I like the Targas."

"Me too, but I left the top on tonight, so I didn't mess up my hair."

The man laughed. "I have a new Carrera 4S, and I'm parked right behind you. Darla tells me you have several Porsches, including some vintage race cars. What are they?"

Janis decided the man was doing more than just making conversation. "I have five more. One is a 1965 356SC coupe I had completely restored five years ago. My 1965 Porsche 904 GTS was raced by the factory at the Targa Florio where it placed fifth in 1965.

The car was sold to a Belgian racing team who kept it a few years. When I bought the car in Germany in 1985, it hadn't been driven in five years and was sitting in the back of a race car shop collecting dust. Porsche Motorsport North America restored it for me."

"Oh wow, that is fantastic."

Janis' mind clicked to a précis of her favorite. "My 1966 Porsche 906 did well at Le Mans, the Nürburgring 1000, and the 24 Hours of Daytona. I acquired it in 1989 and had it also restored by Porsche Motorsport North America."

Winthrop nodded approvingly.

Janis went on. "My two pride and joys are a 1960 Porsche 718 RS-60 and a 1960 Porsche Abarth Carrera. The RS-60 was the next to last one built and the Abarth Carrera is serial number 1019. Both are drivable. For all my cars, I have big thick notebooks on each with documents, the details of the restoration work and high-quality photos."

"This is unbelievable. Where are the cars now?"

"In my garage."

"Do you drive the race cars?"

"I do. When I lived in California, I raced the 906 and sometimes the 904 in vintage races. To learn how to drive, I went to Bondurant's school at Sonoma Raceway, then raced a Formula Ford and then a Porsche 911 for five years. Amazingly, I made it to the national runoffs every year, where I placed in the top three each time."

"Did you ever think of turning pro?"

"I had several offers but decided against it. I liked the camaraderie of SCCA and didn't like the business aspects of going pro." *I really didn't want the publicity of being a female driver and the scrutiny into my background that would come with the profession.*

"I understand."

"Jason, what was your first Porsche?"

The Porsche dealer franchise holder took a sip of his wine, wondering how much he should say. "I don't buy many, and the ones that I do are those that I think will appreciate in value over time. For example, I have a 1973 Porsche 911 RS with the Touring package that was one of only 1,580 built."

Janis' look told Jason he had left out an important fact. "Sorry. My family owns Audi, Volkswagen, Acura, Honda, and Porsche dealerships in the DFW Metroplex, and I run the Porsche store."

After the main course was served, Jason asked, "Would you mind exhibiting your cars at my Porsche dealership and maybe at the Dallas and Fort Worth car shows? I'm pretty sure Porsche will support it."

"Do you have any mechanics trained to work on the cars?"

Jason chuckled. "Honestly, no. Our guys focus on the current models, and I'm afraid they would just screw one of the older cars up. If we have a customer with an older Porsche or a race car, we send them to local specialists we trust who know their way around the cars."

"Thanks for your honesty."

He reached into his pocket and handed her a business card. "Call me during the week, and I'll give you the names of the shops. We can also talk about showing your cars."

"Will do."

Talking to a man who genuinely loved cars made dinner pass quickly. Before dessert was served. Janis made a quick trip to the bathroom, and as she came out, Darla grabbed her bicep and led her to where five women were standing. Her eyes had a mischievous look. "I want to make sure you spend some time with these women. I kept you apart on purpose until now, and when you talk to them, you'll know why."

They all smiled at Janis. One woman held out her hand. She was wearing a dark gray, sleeveless dress, black three-inch heels with straps that went around her calves and ended just below her knees.

"Welcome to Highland Park. If you don't remember, I'm Heather Hazelwood." She held Janis' hand and slid her fingers into Janis'. "We're Darla's lesbian and bi friends, and she suspects you are one of us."

Janis was taken a bit aback by the outright comment. She didn't say anything, so Heather still held Janis' hand. "Here's the deal. We're all single. Ashley and Jenniffer are bi, Barbara, Gail, and I are all girls all the time." As Heather mentioned the woman's names, she nodded at each one. "Here in Highland Park, we're in the land of the bible thumpers, and being gay doesn't fit the Baptist model even though there are more bisexual women in this town than you think. We're discrete, and Texas is unlike California, where you can be open about your sexual preference."

Janis laughed at Heather's directness and nodded noticeably before she spoke. "Man, that's the truth."

"We, and a few others here in Highland Park, get together for lunch every week or so. Sometimes we go out, and other times we eat at someone's home. Want to join us?"

"Cool, I mean, sure."

Heather released Janis' hand. "Wonderful! We'll get your email address and phone number from Darla and send you an invite."

Barbara, standing next to Janis, slid her hand down Janis' back and gently caressed her ass as she whispered in her ear, "We all think you are fucking hot."

MONDAY, MAY 6TH, 2002, 2:31 P.M. LOCAL TIME, TEL AVIV

When Aliyah arrived in her office, she found a yellow phone message slip clipped to her phone saying to call this person as soon as possible. It was signed by Reznik. She called Reznik and asked for any history. All he knew was that the call came from the Israeli Ministry of Justice representative at the embassy in Washington D.C., who passed on a request from the FBI. More he didn't know. When she asked for advice, Reznik said to tell the truth if it didn't compromise any current, planned, or past Mossad operations.

Her wall clock said the time was 2:00 p.m. in Israel. With Daylight Savings Time in effect in the U.S., it was 7:00 a.m. in D.C. Aliyah was expecting an answering machine when she dialed. It rang once, and a man answered. "Good morning, Bill Smith, Special Investigations."

Aliyah leaned back in her chair and, with one hand, bunched her shoulder-length hair as if she was going to put it in a ponytail. "Good morning, sir. My name is Aliyah Skylar, and I was given a message from the Israeli Ministry of Justice to call you."

Bill Smith III was surprised by the quick response. "Ms. Skylar, are you based in D.C.?"

"No, sir. I am in Israel. How may I help you?"

"Are you familiar with the case of Andreas Eisenbrun?"

"If you are referring to *SS-Brigadeführer und Generalmajor der Waffen-SS* Gunter Eisenbrun, who was wanted for war crimes and lived in Pittsburgh, then yes. The Israeli government wanted the U.S. to extradite him to Israel to be tried for war crimes." As Aliyah spoke, she used the correct German pronunciation of Eisenbrun's rank and equivalent to an American lieutenant general.

"Yes. Ms. Skylar, where does your knowledge come from?"

"For several years, I worked on our desk that tracked Nazis wanted for war crimes."

"Then you know he was murdered within weeks after Israel's extradition request was denied."

"Yes, Mr. Smith, I know the judge's ruling well." Aliyah forced herself not to say that she disagreed with the judge. Eisenbrun's attorney claimed that his client could not receive a fair trial in Israel.

"Ms. Skylar, are you with the Ministry of Justice?"

Aliyah stopped herself from saying, "Does it matter?" Instead, she forced herself not to be testy or curt, "What agency I work for doesn't matter. How can I help you?"

Smith III took her evasion as an admission that she was Mossad. "Please allow me to be direct. Do you know if the Israeli government ordered his murder?"

Aliyah knew the answer, and Eisenbrun was on the list Söbel gave her. "No, I do not. "Mr. Smith, why are you asking?"

Smith III was recording the conversation for the FBI's records. He guessed Skylar was, at best, a mid-level manager. Later, if the Israelis were involved, their government could say she was telling the truth since she was not involved with either the decision or the hit.

Smith III had read the Israeli government's statement that Eisenbrun's murder prevented him from standing trial so the world could see the war crimes he committed. He took a deep breath. "I have reason to believe Eisenbrun was murdered by an American woman known as *The Red Star of Death,* and the FBI wants to bring her to justice. I thought the Mossad might have information that might help in this matter."

"Mr. Smith, Eisenbrun was murdered over 25 years ago. Why is the FBI suddenly interested?"

Smith III decided to tell a fib. "We believe this woman is active again, and we don't want her to murder anyone else."

Aliyah was glad the FBI agent couldn't see her mouth the Hebrew equivalent of bullshit. "Do you have any other questions?"

"No, thanks for calling me back."

Aliyah couldn't hang up fast enough as her mind raced; she forced herself not to panic. Shit, shit, shit... The American FBI is looking for Janis Goodrich. Reznik needs to know, and we need to get her out of the U.S. if we want to use her.

THE SAME DAY, 12:38 P.M. LOCAL TIME, RIO DE JANEIRO

Roza Pierente was grilling *picanha*, a steak seasoned primarily with salt, on the deck behind the house. The smell reached Rafael, who slowly put down the phone in the living room. He knew what he had to do.

In the basement, he slid a sheaf of documents from the safe he had not shown Aliyah into a large manila envelope. He wrote a short note on a blank sheet of paper before sealing the envelope and writing Aliyah Skylar's address on the front.

Package in hand, he grabbed the shotgun, loaded it with six shells, pumped it to chamber a round, and added one to the tube magazine. As he emerged from the basement, Reza, his wife of 30 years, saw the shotgun and demanded. "Who called? What is going on?"

"Keep this handy. A contact just called to warn me that the *Dirección de Inteligencia* is looking for me. They are offering 25,000 American dollars to anyone who can give them our address. It is time to leave Brazil, and I am going to mail this at the post office and call that Israeli woman for help. Under the law of return, we can emigrate to Israel."

Reza, who raised his children while he worked on the airplanes flown by Raul Moya, nodded sadly. She suspected this day might come.

"Do not let anyone in the house. Go pack one bag with clothes for four or five days and anything of value you want to keep. We will take a cab to the Israeli consulate when I return."

The post office was only a few blocks away. On the way, Rafael passed a DHL office and decided even though it was much more expensive, it was much more secure. Once the package was in their hands, he left a message on Aliyah's phone with the tracking number. At the post office, he mailed the DHL receipt to Aliyah, so it was not in his possession.

One hundred meters from his house, the hair on the back of Rafael's neck stood up when he saw a man standing by a black sedan, casually smoking a cigarette. Even though he wore black slacks and an open-neck blue shirt, his dress and manner screamed military.

Fearing the worst, Rafael crossed the street and walked past his house. The Browning Hi Power semi-automatic pistol was in his belt; the suppressor and a spare magazine were stuffed in a back pocket. Calling the police was out of the question. There was no time to lose, and he didn't trust them. The Cubans could have already bribed them.

The only way to get Reza out was the direct one. Surprise, he believed, was his best weapon. The only decision he had to make was whether he would go in the front or back door once he passed the driver.

A provocatively dressed young woman walking down the sidewalk interested the man by the car more than an old man did. The gate to the side yard creaked as he opened it, and Rafael cursed himself for not oiling it more frequently. Inside his backyard, Rafael screwed the suppressor onto the Belgian-made 9mm pistol.

He heard voices, and Reza say loudly, "go to hell." Slowly, he turned the key in the lock. He heard the soft pop of a suppressed pistol being fired as he entered the kitchen.

Reza's pain-filled wail sent him moving. In the living room, he counted three men. Rafael pumped two bullets into the chest of the nearest one, and he hit the second one in the stomach before missing the third man with his fourth shot. It gave his opponent time to fire a shot into Reza's chest. Rafael aimed his pistol at the shooter, and they both fired simultaneously.

Rafael's shot was higher than he aimed. The 9mm copper-jacketed bullet hit the man in the base of the neck and blew out his spine. He felt the man's bullet bury itself in his chest. Rafael immediately knew he was badly, if not fatally, wounded. He staggered over to his wife, who looked at him with glassy eyes. "I don't think we are going to make it to Israel. I love you."

Reza's head slumped over, and Rafael dropped to his knees. He was dying, and he knew it. He held Reza's hand and recited in Hebrew, "Hear, O Israel: The Lord our God, the Lord is one." When he finished, life went out of his body.

TUESDAY, MAY 7TH, 2002, 10:38 A.M. LOCAL TIME, LANGLEY, VA

Harvey Reeder did not like working at a desk. Covert operations were his specialty, and he'd returned to CIA headquarters after six years in the Middle East, mainly in Jordan, Lebanon, and Egypt. Being in the U.S. was a nice break, but he wanted back in the field.

At five foot ten and 170 pounds, when Reeder grew a beard, he looked like an Arab and spoke Arabic fluently. He attributed his skin color and dark hair to his great grandfather, who came from Romania. According to his family legend, when Stefan Radulescu arrived at the Galveston, Texas, port of entry in 1907, the immigration officer wrote his last name as Reeder on the form. Family legend held that the immigration officer told his forebear in a thick Texas accent, "In America, you are Steven Reeder."

Reeder liked to do his own dirty work, sometimes with the sanction of the agency and, other times, for his own self-preservation. Only twice was there any blowback, and each time he said to his superiors, "It was my decision. I was there; you weren't. Hunting bad guys is dangerous work. If you don't want me making decisions like this, I'll find something else to do."

Reeder joined the CIA after spending six years in the U.S. Navy as a SEAL. As a newly promoted lieutenant commander, he realized his days in the field as a "shooter" were over, and he would be directing others for the rest of his career. He preferred to be in the field, so Reeder resigned his regular Navy commission. The agency's clandestine service welcomed him and filled Reeder's need for action.

Reeder avoided long-term entanglements with women. They would come when he retired sometime in the far distant future.

What he was handed early last week was right up his alley when he was told. "Find this woman known as *The Red Star of Death* before the FBI does. When you do, give her a choice. Work for us as a trainer, or an assassin, or both, and we'll keep you out of the clutches of the Department of Justice. The word blackmail was not used in his brief but was implied.

On his desk was everything the CIA knew about the woman, including a list of whom the agency thought she killed. He wondered how many hits were CIA-sanctioned and how many weren't but done anyway in the interest of national security. He was also given an outline of what the CIA suspected the FBI knew.

Reeder agreed with his bosses that national security was far more important than getting a conviction for murdering scumbags. Left unsaid was his boss's worry that if the FBI arrested her, the law enforcement agency would find a way to embarrass the CIA.

The "how" he found this woman was up to him. The only caveat he was given was don't kill her.

CHAPTER 6

DINNER BREAK

After the bright yellow DHL envelope from Rafael was checked for an explosive device and dusted for fingerprints, it was delivered to Aliyah's office. She stared at it thinking its contents might answer why Rafael didn't return her call.

Carefully, she slit open the end and let the contents slide onto her desk. There were negatives, more photos of Janis Goodrich, and two sheets of paper folded three times.

On the paper was a list of Moya's contacts in Mi6, the CIA, the French *Direction Générale de la Sécurité Extérieure* (Director General of External Security), along with those in the Stasi, the Soviet GRU, and KGB. The name Moshe Löbel caught her attention. No wonder he was called in. He knows whom Mossad tasked Janis to take out.

Scrawled across the top was the date the package was sent and the note:

> The Dirección de Inteligencia is looking for me. Why? There must be a leak. Please find it. If I make it to Israel, I will help you.

Aliyah could only take it one way. Rafael was scared. She called the consulate in Rio and asked if the Pierentes had arrived. When she was told no, Aliyah asked if they could bring them to the embassy to start their trip to Israel under the Law of Return. The Mossad agent said he would check after she gave him the Pierente's home address.

Two hours later, the Mossad officer called back to say the police reported that their house was ransacked and both Pierentes were killed. There was blood from three other males but no bodies. Aliyah closed her eyes as she hung up the phone, sick to her stomach. If she had been in the office when Rafael called, she might have been able to send help. The turmoil in her belly increased her resolve to meet Janis and maybe hunt down the Pierente's killers, whom she was sure were Cubans or men hired by the Cubans.

The list sitting in front of her was intriguing. It had names, positions, phone numbers, and information on how to contact each person. The question rattling around in Aliyah's mind was who else besides the FBI and the Cubans were looking for Janis Goodrich. And why?

I know what she looks like, have seen her in person, and I know where she lives. Do the Cubans and FBI?

It was time to fly to Dallas. To go, she needed Reznik's authorization.

FRIDAY, MAY 10TH, 2002, 4:30 P.M. LOCAL TIME, LANGLEY

Bill Reeder wondered who else in the agency had access to the file in the center of his desk. In it, were separate sheets for each sanctioned hit contracted to International Logistics. There was no master list, just individual documents giving the fee paid and the date the sanction was issued and executed. A two-word code at the bottom of the page provided another layer of secrecy. At this point, he didn't think he needed access to the protected data.

Looking through the typewritten sheets, Reeder concluded that if the same woman carried out these assassinations, her tradecraft was beyond excellent. Since neither the FBI nor Interpol had a name or a photo reinforced his conviction that the woman was, besides being very, very good, smart enough to quit.

Also in the folder was the FBI's analysis of the rubble of Moya's apartment. Moya was identified through his dental records, and the other four were identified as Russians based on their fillings.

That led Reeder to the printout of International Logistics' phone records acquired by the FBI as part of its investigation. It showed clusters of calls to/from exchanges representing Bakersfield, Boston, New York, L.A., Miami, and Palmdale area codes. The note attached to the printout said phone companies re-issued numbers canceled by subscribers, and many on the list were pay phones. Still, Reeder believed there was valuable information in the records, but he didn't know what.

He sat back in his chair and tented his hands under his chin. If I were her, where would I want my base? Do I want it in a city where I could hide amongst the crowd? Or, out in the open where I could see the bad guys coming?

Me, I like to see the bad guys coming. That led Reeder to the California numbers. On a hunch, he dialed a number used several times, and it was a Holiday Inn in Palmdale. Reeder hypothesized that she used the hotel to dial 800 numbers which wouldn't show up on the room bill, or to take calls. And would make them harder to trace.

He tried another number. It was an answering machine for a dojo in Palmdale. Reeder didn't leave a message but thought it would be an ideal place to make or take a short call. It would also explain the reference to martial arts skills mentioned in the FBI's report on Moya's death. He wrote down the dojo's name and decided to call back for the address.

Reeder was about to leave when the administrative assistant assigned to help him handed him the transcript of his call with the FBI earlier in the day to go with the others he was given. His impression of Bill Smith III was that he was an excellent agent and was letting his training as a crime investigator drive his search. He skimmed the transcript before locking it and the other documents in the safe in his office.

Smith III, you dummy, to find a very successful assassin, you need to think like one. The FBI trains you to find criminals, not individuals who are taught to be invisible. They pay attention to tiny details that could get them caught and whose egos are assuaged by a job well done, not recognition. That's why I have the advantage since I was once one, and now, I am looking for one.

Reeder decided to let his mind process what he had learned today and go home. He had a date with a woman of Vietnamese descent he met while waiting for his car at the Mercedes dealer. Binh Pham wasn't wearing a ring, and Reeder started a conversation. She was the daughter of a Vietnamese refugee and an immigration lawyer for a prominent D.C. law firm. Smiling, Binh handed Reeder her card, saying she worked out of her home on Fridays. If that wasn't an invitation, he didn't know what one was. He called her cellphone that afternoon and asked her out. Tonight was the night.

SATURDAY, MAY 11TH, 2002, 10:36 A.M. LOCAL TIME, DALLAS

When Janis moved into the house, the front flowerbeds needed rebuilding. She had the landscape company she hired to take care of the lawn turn them over and add compost and manure to prepare them for spring planting.

Now, it was time to plant the flowers. Despite the shade from the trees, the 80-degree Fahrenheit temperature made it a sweaty, physical, and dirty task Janis enjoyed. Once they were in, the landscape company could maintain them, but she wanted to do the planting.

Now, with the empty plastic tubs in a pile, Janis stretched as she arched her back and looked at the house's exterior. It looked as lovely as the inside.

Janis had her hands on her hips when an S-class Mercedes pulled into the driveway next door. Old habits die-hard. Janis felt for the pistol in the back of her shorts as she studied the car to determine if it or its occupant was a threat. As far as she could tell, no one had been home since she moved in. Obviously, the driver was either her neighbor or associated with the owner.

A dark-haired woman she'd never met before rolled down the window and said, "Hi…."

Maybe it was her neighbor. Janis waved and said, "Hi…."

The car door opened wide, and a slim woman taller than six feet emerged wearing jeans and smiling. "Hi, I'm Emily Stone, the girl next door.

Janis walked over, pulled off her gardening gloves, and held out her hand. "Cool. I'm Janis Goodrich, your new neighbor. It is nice to meet you. Pardon my dirty hand." Seeing the rows of plastic shopping bags full of groceries in the back seat, Janis added not knowing why, "May I help?"

Emily picked up several plastic bags. "Sure, if you don't mind, you could bring in the bags on the back seat, and we can get to know each other since we are neighbors."

Janis followed Emily into the house and put her load on a counter. She rinsed her hands in the sink. Emily took two glasses from a cabinet over the counter. "May I get you a glass of water or a Coke or something?"

"Water would be wonderful?"

"Ice?"

"Please." Janis's eyes darted around searching for signs of children or a significant other. Darla thought her neighbor was single.

Emily stuck the glass in the door and waited for several ice cubes to clang down before filling it with water. She handed it to Janis and then made one for herself. "Again, Janis, thanks."

There was something that Janis liked about Emily. "No problem." She took a sip and didn't want to eat alone for a change. "How about dinner tonight?"

"As in a dinner date? Or are we cooking?"

"Either way, but if I had a preference, a date. I could go for a steak and have never been to Bob's, and I hear it is terrific."

"Well, if you want a steak, the best place to go is Pappas Brothers. I'll make a reservation for seven-thirty. Come over at six-thirty, and we can have a glass of wine before we go. I'll try to get a table for seven."

"Done. I'll drive and even wear a dress."

Emily giggled. "While I was away, the grapevine said a tomboy moved in next door."

Janis didn't mind the term. She'd heard it all her life and held up her glass as an acknowledgment. "Guilty as charged. Haven't seen you since I moved in, where were you?"

"Palm Springs. I flew out to see my parents, and the trip turned into six after my mother broke her hip. She's back on her feet and should be fine once everything heals."

"That's wonderful. I'll see you in a couple of hours. I've got some more stuff to do around the house."

"Me too."

THE SAME DAY, 8:32 P.M. LOCAL TIME, DALLAS

Janis rang the doorbell five minutes early and didn't know why. She wore a simple black dress over her bra and panties. To dress it up, she wore a diamond pendant with an eight-carat stone she bought in Amsterdam in 1989.

She heard a voice from a speaker, "Janis, it's open." She listened to a clunk of a deadbolt retracting and metallic sound of metal sliding as the door latch opened. Janis turned the knob, opened the door, and heard Emily say, "I'm in the kitchen pouring wine, and I hope you like a fruity Shiraz. It is what I had open."

"I love them." She held up the glass and said, "New friends," as she leaned over slightly so they could clink glasses.

"By the way, welcome to Highland Park."

Janis took inventory. Emily was rail thin and probably around six-four, with dark, shoulder-length, chestnut-colored hair, average size boobs, and a wonderful smile. "Thanks. So, what did you hear about me?"

Emily giggled. "Your fifty-ish, retired, well-off, single, came from California where you had a ranch. You like fast cars, are a pilot, and have a gun collection. The most important part to some in Highland Park is that you are not a native Texan."

"I'm not the high society type."

"I heard that, too. For many reasons, I'm not part of the Dallas in-crowd either. What did you do?"

"I was in the security business, and let's leave it at that."

"Ohhhhh, very mysterious."

Emily explained since there were no tables available at seven, she booked one for seven-thirty. While waiting to be led to their table, Janis looked around the restaurant and felt a soft hand caress her lower back and the top of her ass. She looked up, and Emily had a guilty smile on her face.

Emily had split from her husband after he had an affair and had been single since. Her marriage lasted less than five years.

After making millions developing land into hospitals, several years ago Emily's parents retired and moved to Palm Springs. She stayed in Dallas, where she worked as an attorney. Two years ago, she got tired of the rat race and decided to live off her nest egg and trust fund. It was, she said, far more fun to volunteer at the Children's Hospital in Dallas.

At a stoplight on the way home, Emily put her right hand on Janis' thigh she shifted the Porsche. "How about a nightcap at either your house or mine?"

"Mine, since I asked you out."

"Done. You even know where to go."

Janis parked the Porsche in the back and led Emily to the back door. After she opened the sliding tour and motioned to enter, she looked up at Emily, who bent down. Janis had to stand on her toes as they kissed and began exploring each other's mouths.

Inside, Emily saw the array of expensive single malt scotches on the bar and asked for Janis' favorite with a single ice cube. Janis poured two fingers of MacAllan 25 for both and didn't put any ice in hers.

"Emily, how'd you know I was gay?"

"Heather Hazelwood." She leaned over and kissed Janis. "And the rest will be history."

TEL AVIV, MONDAY, MAY 13ᵀᴴ, 2002, 10:01 A.M. LOCAL TIME

Frustrated was the best word to describe how Aliyah felt, and it was a classic case of hurry and wait. It seemed that no one else in the

Mossad sensed the urgency to recruit Janis Goodrich/JayLynn Nance as much as she did.

For the umpteenth time, she tried scripting the conversation she would have with Janis Goodrich. Whenever she looked at what she typed, she thought it was garbage and started over. Version control in the file name said she was on attempt number six.

A clerk from the mailroom knocked on the door, and Aliyah forced herself to hide her annoyance as she signed for the envelope from the Berlin embassy. She dumped out the contents, three photos, and a sheet of paper saying the traveler was Hassan Mahoud, the flight number, and the Turkish passport number.

Excited, she logged on and ran the name through the database. Aliyah impatiently tapped her desktop with a pen while the system compared the ones and zeros in its files. When the progress bar stopped, Aliyah was staring at the face of Abd al-Bari Ghulam.

THE SAME DAY, 4:48 P.M. LOCAL TIME, SAN DIEGO, CA

Ghulam's Turkish passport identified him as Azra Malas from Ankara. The Turkish passport of the man sitting next to him in the car said his name was Uday Entezam from Istanbul. Neither said much as they waited in the long line on the Mexico side at the Otay Mesa border crossing point between Mexico and San Diego. Their passports had valid U.S. entry visas and Turkish driver's licenses ready to hand to the officer, along with the vehicle's rental agreement.

Their cover was they went to Tijuana for two days. The truth was that they landed in Mexico City and flew on an Aero México flight to Tijuana where a contact waiting for them in the baggage claim area gave them the keys to a rental car picked up in San Diego. The rental car contract listed Ghulam/Entezam as the drivers.

Once in the U.S., Ghulam drove to a house in Anaheim in what was known as Little Arabia. That evening, four more men arrived in pairs, confident they had not been followed.

TUESDAY, MAY 14TH, 2002, 10:13 A.M. LOCAL TIME, PALMDALE

On a hunch, Reeder decided to start with the Palmdale martial arts dojo, hoping he'd get lucky. It was a long shot, but someone might remember a woman with a black belt.

Inside the door, he found a small waiting room and an office off to the left. On the right was a door to a large workout area with a polished wood floor with pads. Several boxing dummies hung from the ceiling, and one wall was lined with mirrors.

Off to one side, he watched an instructor show an elderly woman how to use her cane as a weapon. She was one in a small class of senior citizens.

A deep male voice interrupted his spectating, "May I help you?"

Reeder turned around to see a short man who looked as if he played a Mexican character in a low-budget Western movie. "Hi, I'm Harvey Reeder." He held up his CIA credentials, hoping to impress the man. "I'm looking for a woman who may have practiced here."

"Do you have a name?"

"No."

"May I ask why you are here? You're CIA and are not supposed to investigate American citizens inside the United States."

"I'm not investigating. I'm trying to locate someone who may have practiced here. We're interested in hiring her.""

The Hispanic man crossed his arms as if to say, convince me.

Reeder knew a roadblock when he saw one. Thinking a little truth might help, he offered. "Look, she's an American citizen in her early to mid-50s and has black belts in several disciplines. I just don't have a name. Or a description."

"Sir, that's agency bullshit. I was a Green Beret for twenty-two years. No name, no warrant, no help."

Reeder decided to turn on the charm. He pulled out his wallet and showed him his UDT/SEAL association membership card. "I spent 10 years in the teams before I joined the CIA to be in the field and not push a desk." *As in some pencil-pushing asshole sent me out here on this asinine fool's errand.*

"As much as I'd like to help you, I owe it to my students to keep their names and addresses confidential. I'll be an open book if you come back with a name on a warrant or a court order. Without either one, I can't help you."

Reeder started to say, can't or won't but didn't. Instead, he nodded and said, "I understand. Thanks for your time."

He left convinced the woman he was looking for came to this dojo. After he visited the remaining ones on his list, Reeder was certain.

His mind debated if he should break into the dojo and go through its files, but he wasn't desperate enough to commit a crime. *Breaking and entering is not my forte. And besides, if I hired someone, for whom should I tell them to look?*

Instead, Reeder stopped at a gun store to ask if there was someplace nearby where people went to shoot outside of the rules imposed by insurance companies on indoor ranges. He was given a map to a location in the desert on Bureau of Land Management (BLM) land near the junction of State Highways 58 and 14.

Reeder had a Heckler & Koch USP 9mm Compact pistol he brought with him in his checked luggage and a box of ammunition. He bought 300 rounds and several silhouette targets where he was told about the BLM land. At another, he purchased a metal stand. Tomorrow, he would go there, fire a few rounds, and see if anyone showed up. Who knows, he might get lucky.

WEDNESDAY, MAY 15TH, 2002, 2:23 P.M. LOCAL TIME, WASHINGTON, D.C.

Special Agent Smith III thought he was making progress. After spending an hour session with an FBI profiler, he was confident the woman known as *The Red Star of Death* came from a loving, stable family and was college educated. The profiler suggested that the woman was probably a student athlete who was very competitive and, if she wasn't the best player on the field, was driven to do what was necessary to be one of the top players on the team. The woman, the profiler believed was also an expert in one or more martial art disciplines.

Smith III was also told that *The Red Star of Death* had above average intelligence and spoke English and probably at least one other language. Given what the FBI knew, the woman was most likely in her early to mid-50s.

Unfortunately, the profile confirmed what he already knew but didn't provide any new info. Smith III needed a name and had no idea where he would get it.

He was convinced the CIA and Mossad knew more than they told him. Smith III also wondered if one or both were looking for the same person. If the CIA employs this woman and the FBI wants to arrest her, the politics are off the chart.

Smith III was between the proverbial political rock and the hard place. Telling his superiors that he couldn't find this woman was an admission of failure and would bring cold stares. He was in a professional box and had to find a way out.

FRIDAY, MAY 17TH, 2002, 10:19 A.M. LOCAL TIME, LOS ANGELES

The rain was coming down in sheets, driven by a 30-knot wind. Even though the loading dock at the Cedars-Sinai Hospital off Beverly Boulevard was sheltered from the wind, it was slick with water. Both guards stayed in the shelter of their small booth to stay dry and looked at each other in surprise when a gray van backed up in front of their booth. No deliveries were expected, and one guard came out of the shelter to find out what they were delivering. He was shot with a suppressed pistol.

Seeing his partner go down in a spray of blood, bone, and brain, the second guard dialed 911. Before he could say a word, a bullet entered his head, causing him to jerk. The handset flew out of his hand and banged against the bloody Plexiglas.

Four men, each with an AK-47, twelve 30-round magazines, a Glock 17 9mm pistol, and four 15-round magazines, entered the building. They jogged, single file, toward the large meeting room where Cedars-Sinai hosted receptions and fundraisers.

Emily Stone sat next to her parents and her brother on the dais. All were smiling. The hospital was giving her father an award to say thank you for the fund-raising and construction of its new cancer center.

The president of Cedars-Sinai was partway through his remarks when the four terrorists burst through the door, shouting *Allahu Akbar*. Their first targets were the exposed people on the podium. Three bullets from an AK-47 stitched across Emily's chest. She slumped over and was dead when her mother and father died. Her brother took two bullets in the stomach and went down next to the hospital president, whose sightless eyes stared at the ceiling.

People screamed as the attackers systematically hunted down the audience, who cowered behind and under tables. As their AK's clicked empty, the attackers reloaded.

The first policeman arrived less than a minute into the attack. From behind the entrance door, he shot one of the attackers. In return, bullets from a long burst stitched the sheetrock wall he used for cover and blasted chunks of concrete out of the wall behind him. He cowered with his hands over his head. When the bullets stopped flying, he stuck his hand around the door and fired wildly until his pistol was empty.

A second police officer, a woman, came around the door, spotted one of the attackers, and fired two shots. Both hit the attacker in the chest. Uday Entezam fired back, and one of his bullets hit the officer in her leg, sending her to the floor, trying to staunch blood flow. As she fell, her Beretta 92F went clattering across the terrazzo floor.

Uday waved at his partner, who was yanking spare magazines from the torso harnesses of their dead comrades. He tossed two to Uday, who pointed to a side door, and it led to another hallway where people were running from the gunfire.

Of the two, Uday wanted to escape more than he wanted to kill more infidels. They were headed to a side door when four police officers came around the corner with AR-15s at their shoulders. All fired simultaneously, and Uday felt the first bullet hit him in the hip below his Kevlar vest. The second smacked into one of his loaded magazines carried in a pouch on his chest. He didn't feel or hear any others after the third went in his eye and blew the back of his head off. He also didn't see his partner hit six times and die.

Outside, Ghulam waited in a Ford Expedition in a handicapped spot until the shooting ended. Convinced that none of the attackers survived, he drove to a motel in San Diego where he'd already booked a room.

DALLAS, THE SAME DAY, 6:02 P.M. LOCAL TIME

Right after Janis closed on the house, she drove out to Motorsports Park in Cresson, Texas, a small town southwest of Fort Worth, and bought a membership on the spot. Out back, her Porsche 906 was lashed down on the 20-foot-long flatbed trailer hooked up to her Yukon. Tomorrow, Janis planned to tow the car to Motorsports Park and spend the day driving it.

Jason Winthrop gave her the names of the three shops his dealership refers owners of older Porsches to for service. Classic Porsches was the logical choice since they had a group of mechanics on staff from teams that raced Porsches.

Tomorrow, Classic Porsches had a half dozen cars scheduled to be at the track on Saturday and Sunday. To support its customers with Porsche race cars, the shop's mechanics would have the firm's trailer loaded with spares in the paddock. Janis, like the other Porsche race car owners, paid the shop a flat fee for preparing the cars, labor at the track, and technical support. Any parts needed that day were extra.

She planned to leave on the two-hour drive after rush hour and stay at the small hotel near the track on Friday and Saturday nights. With her Yukon and trailer on the side of the driveway, there was enough room to get her Porsche Turbo around the Yukon and trailer if she needed to go someplace.

While looking through the kitchen window at her bright white 906, Janis turned on the small TV in the kitchen to catch the weather forecast for Saturday. On Thursday, the long-range forecast indicated the weather was supposed to be overcast, but no rain.

Rather than the local anchor, Janis saw a Los Angeles ABC affiliate reporter standing in front of LA city hall. He said the press conference on today's terrorist attack at Cedars-Sinai would start in about two minutes. *Terrorist attack? Is Emily safe?* Her dad was getting an award which is why she went.

Curious, Janis turned on her big Sony TV in her living room in time to listen to the mayor describe the carnage at Cedars-Sinai. All four attackers plus 12 more in the room died. Of the 21 wounded, 11 were in serious or critical condition.

Janis's mind went into overdrive. Emily was at Cedars-Sinai. From their first dinner until Emily left yesterday, the pair were like long-lost lovers who couldn't get enough of each other. It was sex and more sex, rest, and make love again. Now some goddamn terrorists may have killed her.

Emily didn't answer and Janis left a voicemail, hoping not to sound panicked or worried. Janis called the track and left a message saying she was not coming. Every hour, Janis checked CNN, Fox News, and each local news channel to learn when the victims' names would be released. Fearing the worst, she called Emily after dinner and again before going to sleep. Both calls went to voicemail.

SATURDAY, MAY 18ᵀᴴ, 2002, 2:30 P.M. LOCAL TIME, NEWARK INTERNATIONAL AIRPORT

The crowd outside a bar in Terminal A blocked half the hallway to the concourse. Few people talked as they watched replays from the Cedars-Sinai's security cameras. As the images were played, the police chief provided details on what happened.

Aliyah and Moshe stood quietly in the back of the crowd. Both were sickened by what they saw, but it was not the first time they saw the results of a terrorist attack. By May 1ˢᵗ, 2002, there were already 24 attacks in Israel by Hamas, Hezbollah, or Fatah-supported groups that killed 144 Israelis and injured another 961. And this didn't include the recent attacks in Europe.

While walking toward the gate, Aliyah turned to Moshe. "Everything has changed, and my instinct says, given her history, Ms. Goodrich may want to kill the bastards who did this."

CHAPTER 7

THE RELUCTANT RECRUIT

SUNDAY, MAY 19ᵀᴴ, 2002, 9:46 A.M. LOCAL TIME, FLORIDA STRAIT,

During the night, rain hammered the 110-foot *U.S.S. Knight Island.* The Coast Guard ship corkscrewed in the churned-up six-foot seas. The combined pitching and rolling made some of the crew uncomfortable, but the seaworthy cutter was never in danger.

The front passed, and dawn revealed a few puffy clouds dotting the clear blue sky. The wind was now under 10 knots and not enough to create white caps.

On board the 168-ton Coast Guard patrol boat, the daily routine for the 18 sailors and two officers was well underway. They left their berth at the St. Petersburg Coast Guard Station three days ago with orders to patrol the western end of the Florida Strait looking for refugees and smugglers. On platforms above the bridge, lookouts scanned the deep blue water around the cutter.

Through their powerful binoculars, in calm waters, the lookouts could see a man's head a half-mile away. Their visual horizon was five to seven miles, and the ship's radar could detect small objects up to 25 miles away.

Petty Officer Third Class Angela Husband, an electronics technician by training but now standing watch on the forward starboard lookout station, slowly scanned her 90-degree sector. The object appeared and then disappeared. She lowered the binoculars, then searched the area again and saw nothing, so she continued her sweep aft.

Husband's brain said something was out there, so she returned to where she thought the object was. Nothing.

Another slow scan. The raft crested a swell and stayed there long enough to see human beings. Husband keyed her mike. "Bridge, starboard lookout. There is a raft 30 degrees off the starboard bow about a mile out. Looks like three people, and I can't tell if they are alive or dead."

"Bridge, aye."

On the bridge, Lieutenant Junior Grade Luciana Perez had been in command of *Knight Island* for four months and issued two commands. The first turned the ship toward the raft. The second used the cutter's main communication system to broadcast to order the crew to ready the Zodiac for launch.

Knight Island had a small crane aft of the bridge to lift the Zodiac and lower the inflatable boat into the water. Once the cutter was on its new heading, Perez scanned ahead of the patrol boat for the raft. From her station, Husband kept providing directions until Perez spotted the raft, now about 10 degrees off its starboard bow.

None of the people on the raft were moving, which, unfortunately, was not uncommon. On Knight Island's previous two patrols, they rescued five living and six dead Cuban refugees. Most of the people the cutter rescued set out for the Florida Keys without sufficient food or water. They drifted until they either died of exposure, thirst, or starvation or made landfall.

Perez commanded. "All ahead dead slow." The quartermaster repeated the command, and the patrol boat slowed noticeably. There was no doubt as to what the next order would be.

One hundred yards from the raft, Perez and Husband saw what they thought was a hand move. Neither woman was sure whether it was caused by the raft rolling or the person was alive.

Perez's soft but authoritative voice boomed when carried by the ship's main communication system. "Boat away. Potentially three survivors."

Husband didn't have to look aft to see the crew release the tie-downs and swing the orange Zodiac out over the side before the crew clambered aboard. Once in the water, they'd start the motor and release the cables connecting them to the hoist.

"All stop."

The quartermaster, a young black woman whose last name was Jones grew up in Harlem. With a high school diploma and determined to escape the ghetto, Chrystal Jones left her apartment with $40 in her wallet. Her two most valuable possessions – her high school transcript showing that she graduated in the top 10 percent of her class and her diploma were in a folder in her backpack. Chrystal didn't say goodbye to her mother, who was passed out on the couch from whatever drug she was taking and hadn't seen the man supposed to be her father in years.

She was confident of her future as she left the rundown apartment building with the only clothes, she thought were decent stuffed in her backpack. The days of being ostracized by other students who wanted to party instead of studying were over. Party meant drugs and sex. In Chrystal's mind, being excluded from that crowd was good. She wanted to make a new life as far from Harlem as possible.

From military recruiters who set up tables at her high school, she learned she could join the military if she met four criteria. One, she had to be clean, i.e., no drugs; two, no criminal record; three, no children; and four, had a high school diploma. The first person to greet her at the Armed Forces Recruiting Station was a young African American Coast Guard Petty Officer First Class Operations Specialist. He listened to Chrystal's story and her fear of going home, it was one he'd heard many times before. With the recruiting station commander's blessing, he allowed Chrystal to live with his family for three weeks until her background check was completed. Then she would receive orders to report to the Coast Guard's boot camp in Cape May, New Jersey.

Jones finished operations specialist A school at the Naval Training Center, Great Lakes and reported to *Knight Island* the day before the ship deployed, repeated. "All stop, aye."

She loved standing watch at the helm of the cutter, which put her in control of the ship. Yes, she got commands from the officer of the deck. Still, for the first time in her life, she was in control of something important other than staying alive and away from drugs, gangs, and men who wanted to have sex with her.

Chrystal loved every minute of being in the Coast Guard. She had money in her pocket and shipmates who respected her for what she did and how well she did it. One day, Chrystal believed she would make chief and command a Coast Guard boat.

From where Chrystal stood behind the ship's wheel, she could see the Zodiac bounce through the waves. When she reported on board, Perez looked at the woman's evaluations from A School and said, "We'll put you right into the bridge watch rotation."

Jones watched the Zodiac slow, and the sailor in the bow grabbed hold of the raft bobbing up and down. The long six-foot swells made it hard to see what was happening. The speaker on the bridge came alive. "Skipper, we have one body and two barely alive. We're bringing the living survivors back to the ship first and will go back for the corpse."

Perez picked up the mike. "Skipper, aye."

Chrystal watched the two men in the Zodiac lift one, then a second person on the Zodiac before the bowman pushed off. The Zodiac raced toward *Knight Island*. Based on her training, she played out what would happen next. The survivors would be taken to the ship's small dispensary, where the cutter's medical technician would examine them and administer what care he could. If they were in terrible shape, the ship would call for a helicopter to airlift them to a hospital in Key West.

Stokes litters were lowered to the Zodiac, the survivors gently loaded onto the wire-framed litter, and quickly hoisted aboard. As soon as the two survivors were on board the Knight Island, Jones watched the Zodiac go back to the raft.

Chrystal tried to imagine what it would be like to handle a corpse that had been in the sun for days. In the ghetto, death was an everyday event, and the bodies were quickly carried away. Hence, she never saw one except in a casket. As a teenager, someone from her high school was shot or died from a drug overdose almost every week.

With the Zodiac stowed and tied down, Skipper Perez ordered, "Come port to one-zero-zero and make turns for 12 knots."

Chrystal repeated the command and eased the ship's throttles forward to set its twin diesel engines rpm to propel the patrol boat through the water at the ordered speed. The Coast Guard cutter didn't have the old engine telegraphs of years gone by, but procedures on

THE RED STAR OF DEATH

the bridge hadn't changed. The difference was that on *Knight Island,* Seaman Chrystal Jones moved the throttles connected to the engines without human intervention. As soon as the ship began to move, Chrystal turned the wheel slightly to steer the bow onto the new course. "Skipper, ship is steady on new course, one-zero-zero, turns for 12 knots."

Perez turned to her new helmsman, pleased with the precision of the woman's work, and smiled. "Captain, aye."

Five minutes later, the "bitch box," as it was known on Coast Guard and Navy ships, came alive on the bridge. "Skipper, this is Davidson."

Everyone on the bridge knew who Davidson was. Officially, he was Petty Officer First Class James Davidson and *Knight Island's* Medical Technician. In the other services, he would be known as a Corpsman.

"Skipper, aye."

"Sir, the survivors are in really bad shape and need more medical attention than I can provide. We have a male whose Cuban national identity card says he's 55, a woman who's 53. The body is another male, aged 36. They've been in the water about six days, and I recommend a helicopter medevac, ma'am."

"Will do. I'll call it in."

"Yes, ma'am. There's one more thing. The man, Hector Ruiz, is clutching a pouch that he will not let me have. He wants to give it to the CIA as his proof of his value to the U.S. According to Garcia who is here translating, the guy used to work in the archives section of the *Dirección de Inteligencia.* He wants to talk to the CO of the ship."

Perez turned to the officer of the deck, another operations specialist who was an E-6, a.k.a. petty officer first class. "You've got the con."

Lieutenant Junior Grade Perez waited until she heard an acknowledgment before climbing down the ladders from the bridge to the main deck and then down the first deck and the dispensary. Born in Miami to parents who fled Cuba, she'd heard stories about the *Dirección de Inteligencia,* and none were complimentary.

She held Ruiz's hand and spoke in Spanish. "Mr. Ruiz, I am Lieutenant Perez, captain of the U.S. Coast Guard Cutter *Knight Island.* How may I help you?

"I have intelligence your CIA would like to have. Just before we left, a Colonel Ordonez requested the file on an American woman who Cuba trained as an assassin in 1970. I believe my government wants to find and hire her."

"Do you know the name?"

"When she was recruited, the woman's name was Jamie Amy Lucas. This is a copy of her file."

Ruiz' head fell back on the pillow, and he closed his eyes. Davidson looked at the monitors and shook his head. "He's gone."

Perez looked at the two other men in the dispensary. "This doesn't leave the room. I'll write up what I just heard, and both of us will sign it. Meanwhile, I'll figure out to whom *Knight Island* needs to send a classified message. In the meantime, do what you can to save the woman, and I'll get a helicopter on the way."

THE SAME DAY, 10:27 A.M. LOCAL TIME, DALLAS

On the way from DFW Airport to their hotel Saturday night, Aliyah drove Moshe Löbel by Janis' house to show him where she lived. The Yukon Denali with the white race car could be seen from the street, and the house lights were on.

They drove by the house for the first time at eight in the morning, and the SUV and trailer had not moved. Just after 10, after watching the house for 30 minutes, they decided it was time. While they waited, Aliyah's last conversation with Reznik before she left kept running through her mind, "Do what is necessary to recruit this woman, even if it means sleeping with her."

Aliyah took Reznik's orders to have two meanings. First and foremost, recruiting Janis Goodrich was important to Israel and to Mossad. His last words kept rattling around her head. He had given her permission to have sex with a woman and she wondered why.

From a religious perspective, Reznik would be considered a very orthodox Jew, many of whom did not approve of homosexuality. Aliyah believed Reznik fell into that camp and rationalized his comment as a way of telling her that for the purposes of this mission, he approved of her sexual preference.

No one within Mossad ever asked her if she was gay even in her annual security reviews so his knowledge probably came up during the vetting process. If they did, she would have told the truth.

Aliyah and Moshe had their Israeli passports and Mossad identification folders in hand when Aliyah rang the doorbell. It took two attempts before a weak voice called out from the speaker box.

"Who is it?"

"My name is Aliyah Skylar, and with me is Moshe Löbel. We're from the Israeli government and would like to talk to you?"

"Why?"

"It is important that we talk, but not while standing outside your front door. If you wish, I can give you a names and phone numbers you can call in Tel Aviv who can verify who we are."

"Bullshit. Go away."

"Please, Miss Goodrich, we need to talk. Give me fifteen minutes, and if then, if you don't want to continue, we'll never come back."

"Who is the man with you?"

"Moshe Löbel. He and Rafael Pierente were friends. Rafael was murdered a few days ago, and Moshe knew Raul Moya well."

It was then that Aliyah noticed the camera above the entrance. "Just a minute."

Neither heard the door unlatch. Only a voice from behind them. "Open the door and walk straight to the living room and stop. Do not look at me. Disobey, I will put two bullets in each of you within seconds. You're now inside my house and if I say I was in fear for my life, no jury in the state would convict me if I killed you. Understand."

Both Aliyah and Moshe nodded and said, "Understood."

"Good, start moving."

As they stopped at the steps to the sunken living room, the voice behind them said. "Mr. Löbel, step outside and face the trailer. Do not turn around or attempt to look at me. Take off your shirt and your trousers. Ms. Skylar, take everything off except your bra and panties. I need to ensure you are not armed or wearing electronic devices. Put the briefcase down on the table. We'll get to that in a minute."

The Israelis complied.

"Good." The scars on Aliyah's left hip and leg, along with those made by the mortar fragments, were noticeable. "Aliyah, open the briefcase and walk to the far side of the pool."

The Israeli woman did as she was ordered. In Aliyah's briefcase, Janis found a few papers, a pad, and a thick manila envelope. "What's in the brown envelope?"

"The material we want to discuss with you?"

"Are you Mossad or Aman?"

Aliyah thought it was time to lay their cards on the table. "Mossad. Our titles are not important. You worked for us through Raul Moya, and we're here to ask if you will help us again. I promise you, the Israeli government, and more importantly, Moshe and I will not turn you over to the FBI or the CIA."

"Why not?"

"Because we need you."

"Why?"

Moshe interrupted. "I am uncomfortable discussing this partially dressed and out in the open."

Janis replied sharply. "That's my call. So again, why?"

Aliyah turned her head, so her chin was on her shoulder. Still, she could not see the American. "Before he retired, Moshe selected the Nazis war criminals we wanted to be killed and gave the information to Raul Moya. My job is to find terrorists outside Lebanon and the West Bank and kill those who threaten Israel. We want your help."

Janis flipped through the two passports and Mossad ID folders, looking for signs of forgeries. Finding none, she memorized the ID numbers.

"Get dressed."

Aliyah turned around, and what she saw what not what she expected. The woman was wearing a soiled T-shirt, her face was drawn, and her hair was disheveled. It was clear from her bloodshot eyes she either hadn't slept a lot recently or had been crying. This was not the Janis Goodrich/JayLynn Nance she expected to meet.

Inside, Janis pointed to the couch and sat opposite them. She had a Walther PPK/S pistol in her right and which lay on her lap. She put two seven-round magazines on the end table within easy reach.

"I apologize for my rude welcome and that my house is a mess. A close friend of mine was killed in the terrorist attack in Los Angeles." She paused and looked at her watch. "O.K., your fifteen minutes has begun. What brings you to my front door?"

Aliyah could hear hostility in her voice. On the coffee table was a single glass with a trace of the golden liquid on the bottom and an empty bottle of Macallan 25. She decided to be consolatory. "Janis, and I am assuming that is your name, I am sorry if we disturbed you at a bad time, but I think what you Americans call the punch line is this. Mossad wants to hire you. We will, if needed, give you Israeli citizenship and protect you from any law enforcement agency trying to arrest you."

"Why would I need that?"

"I think you know."

"Who's looking for me?"

"We are convinced the FBI has re-opened their investigation and wants to arrest you for several killings on U.S. soil. We suspect the CIA wants to bring you out of retirement, either willingly or by blackmail, and we know Cubans are looking for you as well, but we do not know why. Is that enough?"

Löbel held up his hand and leaned forward. "If the CIA or the FBI knew who you were or where you lived, you would be in jail or at a CIA safe house. The fact that you are not tells me they have bupkis on your whereabouts, at least for the moment."

Janis made a face and was not going to agree or admit to anything. "That's an interesting theory. Why me?"

"We know you are *La Estrella Roja de la Muerte*." Aliyah's spoke the last words in her impeccable Spanish.

No translation was needed. Janis knew what the words meant, and Moya created the moniker. "So, you think I am this person." Janis was careful not to use the female pronoun."

Aliyah looked at Moshe and then nodded noticeably. "Yes, we do. May I show you why?"

The Israeli woman pointed to the briefcase as if to say, "May I?" The photos taken by Rafael were on top of the stack, and she put two on the table. "Rafael took these and gave us one of your aliases."

Janis remained impassive. There was no doubt that the photos were of her and should have suspected Pierente might be taking them. She was in a hurry to retire and live with Karin and had, obviously, gotten careless. Janis was not going to give away anything even though her past had just re-emerged after 20-plus years. "Hypothetically, what does Mossad want me to do?"

Aliyah nodded once emphatically before she started speaking. "My office ranks terrorists based on their threat to Israel, and the Prime Minister decides whether or not to sanction them. If he does, we carry out the mission by ourselves or, as we did with the Nazis, hire a contractor like you."

"Give me an example."

"Sure. May I?" Aliyah pulled a photo from a folder in her briefcase and spun it so Janis could see the man's face. "This is Abd al-Bari Ghulam. He goes by a lot of names, but he is Lebanese. We believe he is the mastermind behind the recent attacks on the synagogues in Germany and France and probably the one at Cedar Sinai in Los Angeles on Friday."

Janis picked up the photo and stared at it. She was looking at Emily's killer or the man who ordered the attack that took her life. She forced down the anger growing in her booze-filled stomach. Her hangover was dissipating quickly. "Tell me about him."

"He started as a soldier for Hezbollah and spent a year in Iran setting up a training camp. If we were in Tel Aviv, I could show you pictures of the camp that trains the commandos that carried out the attacks. He also spent a year at American University in Washington."

Janis looked at the woman opposite her. She had dark eyes that bored holes in you. In stature, Aliyah was probably a few inches shorter than she was. Her pitch-black hair was braided in a ponytail that rested on her left shoulder and breast, and Aliyah wasn't wearing a wedding or engagement ring. Aliyah had dark, olive-colored skin that was common to those from the Middle East. "Go on."

"With the help of the Germans, we traced Ghulam to Germany, and the French have him on camera watching the attack in Paris."

Seeing no reaction, Aliyah stopped speaking. A question forced its way to her mouth. "What was the name of your friend killed in the attack in LA?"

Janis winced visibly and wiped her eyes which were starting to moisten. "Emily Stone. She died along with her mother and father, and her brother is in the hospital but should survive."

"I'm so sorry. I've heard that the Stones raised millions for hospitals in Israel."

Janis nodded. "I heard about the attack Friday night, and they released the names of those killed late yesterday. When I saw Emily's name, it hit me harder than I could have imagined. Those bastards had no right to kill innocent women and children."

Aliyah's tone was very sympathetic and genuine. "We Israelis feel the same way."

Janis nodded and changed the subject. She didn't regret opening a small window into her soul. Her gut and her brain liked Aliyah. "What happened to your left leg? You have shrapnel scars all over your body."

"I was hit by two AK-47 rounds in my pelvis during a raid in Lebanon that went bad. The other scars are from mortar fragments from the same action. In cold, damp weather, it aches a lot." Aliyah didn't know why she added the comment.

Cool. A fellow warrior.

Seeing Janis nod, Aliyah continued. Her training said she needed to build a relationship. "Before the raid, I warned the planners that I thought we were walking into a trap, and as it turned out, I was right. Months later, we learned the planner was Ghulam. Six Israelis died unnecessarily that night."

She knows the cost of failure. "So, this is personal." Janis meant it both as a statement and as a question.

"Yes and no. Israel is always under attack by Arab terrorists who will not stop until our country has been destroyed. From that perspective, killing men like Ghulam is my work. Like you, Ghulam murdered my friends, so this is personal."

"And you Moshe. Why are you here?"

The older man laughed. "I am here as credibility and can answer questions about Raul and Rafael that Aliyah can't. I came to convince you we are really from Mossad."

"What is Rafael doing these days?"

"He and his wife were murdered by the Cubans a few weeks ago. Before he was killed, he sent us all his records from his work with Raul and us."

"Moshe, what do you do for the Mossad?"

"Before I retired, I led the section that hunted Nazis wanted for war crimes. When the Allied nations stopped trying Nazis that embarrassed their new West German friends, Israel took matters into its own hands. We started killing the ones who committed the most heinous crimes rather than trying to extradite or kidnap them.

Sometimes we did it ourselves, sometimes we hired people like you It was simpler, easier, and still sent a message that there was no place on earth these bastards were safe."

Janis ignored the reference to her past and put the pistol down on the side of the chair. "Are you hungry?"

"Famished?" It wasn't a lie from Aliyah. Her stomach was growling, and they'd talked for almost an hour.

"Good, we can keep talking over lunch. I'm starved."

THE SAME DAY, 3:39 P.M. LOCAL TIME, DALLAS

Aliyah and Janis did most of the talking during the afternoon, and Moshe listened. He had pointed questions about the "how" Janis worked, and both he and Aliyah stayed away from the "what." The hits both knew the Mossad hired Janis to carry out through Moya were off-limits.

Moshe now understood why Janis was never caught. She was careful, creative, and paid attention to the little details that got people in her profession arrested or killed. It was clear that Janis followed hard and fast rules from the moment she decided to take on a contract until she was safe at home.

Each answer was carefully stated as a hypothetical example of how Janis would operate. Never once during the afternoon did Janis admit to killing anyone.

Both Israelis truthfully answered Janis's questions believing that if Janis suspected they were lying or playing games, the conversation would be over. They would never get a second chance.

After answering a question about tradecraft, Janis changed the subject, "You know this is not about money."

Although Aliyah didn't know the type of race car on the trailer, and it, the Porsche Turbo and the house all suggested Janis had money. "We suspected as much, but we intend to compensate you quite well."

Janis smiled as she shook her head. "We're still far from my agreeing to do anything for Israel. All we have talked about is terrorists and how I would take them out if I was in Mossad's shoes. Right now, you're still selling, and I'm still skeptical. Let's take a break. How about a swim? Moshe, you can swim in your underwear or go nude. Aliyah, bra, and panties work. Or I can give you a bathing suit that may fit, or we can all go naked."

Moshe was adamant. "I'll pass. No one wants to see me in a bathing suit or naked."

"Aliyah? Do I have to swim alone?"

"No, I'll join you if you have a suit that fits me."

Taking a dip gave Janis time to process the conversation and splashing around in her pool was another way she could step away from the grief that had been consuming her ever since she learned Emily was killed. Getting into the pool also had the benefit of giving Janis a good look at Aliyah's body.

Her dark skin that lightened around her breasts and crotch caused stirrings in Janis' body she could not ignore. Her head said, "Be careful." Her crotch said she wanted Aliyah.

There were way too many things to work out. Revenge for Rafael's and Emily's deaths was foremost in her mind. Sex would come later.

In her bedroom, Janis put the pistol on the dresser and suggested Aliyah toss her clothes on her bed. At the same time, she pulled out several two-piece bathing suits from a drawer in the closet. "One of these should fit you."

"I'll take the red one."

Janis handed her the suit, and Aliyah dropped her jeans and panties on the floor before lifting them up with her right foot so she could place them on the bed. It gave Janis a good look at her crotch and the scars. The Israeli was lucky she didn't lose her leg.

The American did the same. The shorts and pants went down first, and then on came the bottom. Janis noticed that Aliyah's eyes were focused on her shaved groin. *I think you might like a taste of it.* "Towels are in a chest out by the pool."

Outside, Moshe was already stretched out on a lounge chair.

Janis dove in, followed by Aliyah. The floating thermometer said the cool and refreshing water temperature was 75⁰ Fahrenheit. Aliyah waded to where Janis was standing in chest-deep water. "Aliyah, do you have a significant other back in Israel?"

"Do you mean do I have a boyfriend or lover?"

Janis smiled broadly. Aliyah's breasts were lovely. Small, round and had the same dark olive skin that covered the rest of her body that turned her on.

"Neither. Some think I am married to my work."

"Would you and Moshe stay for dinner? I'll grill some steaks I defrosted yesterday and planned to grill out at the racetrack."

"I would." Aliyah turned to Moshe, and there was a dialog in Hebrew.

Janis held up a hand as if to say stop. "Look, if we are going to work together, speak a language I understand, so please choose either English, Spanish or German."

"I'm sorry. I just told Moshe we were invited for dinner, and I wanted to accept. He said he was tired and wanted to back to the hotel and to call him later to check in."

"Is that all?"

"He will also call Israel and let them know we made contact and are talking."

"Good."

THE SAME DAY, 5:13 P.M. LOCAL TIME, DALLAS

While Aliyah took a shower after they came out of the pool, Janis picked up the living room. She was ashamed of the mess she made after hearing Emily was killed. Getting drunk was stupid and totally out of character.

Aliyah came out with a towel wrapped around her head and nothing on below. "May I borrow a hair dryer?"

"Sure. I'll get it. When you're done, we'll make dinner."

Janis let her hand run across the top of Aliyah's ass as she fished out the hair dryer. The Israeli didn't move.

"When you're done, I'll shower and change."

"Why don't you take one now?"

Janis took the meaning to be neither one of us had anything to hide. "O.K."

Janis peeled off her bathing suit, draped it over the sink, and took out a pair of panties and a bra from the dresser. She could feel Aliyah's eyes on her as she went into the closet for a pair of shorts and a golf shirt.

While she showered, Janis saw Aliyah studying her in the mirror. While Janis toweled off, Aliyah motioned her to the chair in front of the make-up table.

"I love your hair. Let me dry it for you."

Aliyah did it expertly and used her free hand to caress the back of Janis's neck. Her touch gave Janis goosebumps and her vagina got wetter by the minute as she debated which of the two Alpha women in the bathroom would make the first move. Then Janis decided, I will.

As Aliyah put the dryer down, she gently squeezed and caressed Janis's shoulder. Janis held Aliyah's hand as she stood up and faced the Israeli. "Are you…"

"Always was and will always be." Aliyah kissed Janis softly.

"Hmmmmm." Janis kissed her back, and Aliyah responded by opening her mouth. "This could be very complicated."

After a long, passionate French kiss, Aliyah whispered. Her tone was sensual and soft. "How?"

Janis' tone was soft and husky, "If I decide to help you."

"So, are you going to help me?"

"Cum or professionally?"

Mitsuyan! "Both."

"Aliyah, let's work on cum first and keep talking about the second."

CHAPTER 8

ENEMIES MAY BECOME BEDFELLOWS

J anis' body clock rang just after six saying get up; let's go for a run and work out. She looked at the sleeping form next to her and began kissing the closest breast and caressing the other. Aliyah's nipples hardened almost immediately, and she moaned and opened her legs as Janis's fingers caressed her labia. "Mmmmm, I like that."

"I'm going to work out in my private dojo, do you want to come?"

"Sure."

Janis rolled out of bed and pulled on a pair of panties followed by jogging shorts and a sports bra, the first clothing she'd had on since before dinner last night. She pointed to the drawers with underwear as if to say, pick what you want. Aliyah chose a pair of shorts and a sports bra.

Janis had an old Nordic Trak cross-country ski machine, an elliptical, a rowing machine, a bike, and free weights in what used to be the bedroom of the small apartment. The old living room had padded mats on the floor, and a heavy punching bag hung from the ceiling in one of the corners.

As she stretched, Janis pointed to the machines. "Pick one. I'm going to do katas for about an hour, and my body needs it. Then we can have breakfast."

"What are we doing today?" The recruiting process wasn't over, and Aliyah was going to keep trying until she had an answer, one way or the other.

After last night, she was very optimistic about two things. One, Janis was going to work for Mossad, and two, she may have found the lover she'd been searching for all these years.

"We're going to a gun club. When was the last time you fired a pistol?"

Aliyah thought for a second and realized it had been a long time. "Not for a while. When are you going to give me your answer?"

"Later today. We'll have a late lunch with Moshe and talk some more. Today, we'll see how good you are with a pistol."

Yesterday, Janis deliberately didn't open the gun vault, thinking it wasn't appropriate, and didn't want to show the array of weapons she owned. On a tour of the house, Aliyah asked what was behind the large steel door.

Janis said, "It's my vault." And her tone suggested she didn't want questions about what was in the vault.

This morning, she gave Aliyah a quick tour of the antique Winchester rifles that were not hanging on the wall in her office. As she dialed the combination, Janis pointed to the fireproof file cabinet in her office. It held the provenance for each firearm, pictures of her shooting it, the target, and the day she fired it. The cabinet also held all her documentation on her race cars.

Janis pulled up on the chrome handle and then opened the door. The smell of gun oil wafted into the office as a walk-in gun vault was revealed. It was, Aliyah, believed, much bigger than the closet in her bedroom in her apartment back in Israel.

On the racks, there were antique Winchesters and Henry rifles, along with Remington, Colt, and Smith and Wesson pistols dating back to the Civil War hung along one wall. All of which were in 80 percent condition or better and fully functional.

On the other long wall, Janis had more modern rifles, several of which were equipped with large scopes. In the back, there were a dozen different pistols. Lining the floor were olive drab ammo cans, each marked with the type of ammunition they contained.

Janis handed Aliyah an H&K USP 9mm Compact and a Smith & Wesson M&P 9mm Compact and asked her to choose. Aliyah liked the American-made weapon. From a safe in the garage, Janis took a metal ammo can filled with 9mm ammunition, targets, and a roll of blue masking tape. The pistols, tape safety glasses, ear protectors, went into a shooting bag she put behind the seats of her Porsche Turbo along with the ammo can.

Aliyah watched as Janis effortlessly drove the high-performance car through the morning traffic. Emotionally, she was confused. Sex with Janis was the best she had in a long time, and she wanted more, a lot more. Getting emotionally involved with Janis could be professional suicide and might even get her killed.

Before closing the door to the Porsche at the Dallas Gun Club, Janis rested her elbows on the car's roof. "Aliyah, we're about to enter a man's world. They let me join, thinking I'd come a few times, get bored and leave. Wrong. I practice here every week and compete in the men's division of their tournaments. I do quite well even when the competition includes professional shooters. The male members here today will ogle us thinking they might get either of us into their bed. We're going to have an audience, so I hope you brought your A-game. I've reserved one of the combat ranges for two hours. Trust me, we'll draw a crowd."

Janis placed seven targets in a row and then used three-foot sections of 2 X 4s to mark where she wanted to shooter to stand. Markers on the side of the revetment provided a distance reference to help her place the targets at five, seven, 10, and 15 yards from the 2 X 4s. Once the targets were in position, the pair loaded six magazines for each pistol.

Janis pointed at the two targets side by side and seven yards away. "Warm up first, and then we'll have some fun. You go first."

Aliyah positioned her feet shoulder width with her left foot slightly ahead of the right and crouched slightly with the weapon close to her chest and the barrel tilted down. She extended her arms and squeezed the M&P 9mm Compact's trigger. A hole appeared in the ring with an X, a.k.a. the 10-ring. A second shot punched a hole about half an inch from the first, and 10 rounds later, there was a three-inch diameter group of small holes around the X.

Pleased with herself, Aliyah turned to Janis, who nodded, took up a similar stance, and fired. The rounds came out quickly, and Aliyah watched as the barrel was quickly back on target after each shot. When the H&K locked open after 12 rounds, a ragged one-inch diameter hole had replaced the X.

After two magazines, Janis asked if she was ready to try tactical drills. Aliyah nodded, "of course." Out of the range bag came a timer.

"Have you ever used one of these?"

"No."

Janis held the timer so Aliyah could see its display and controls. "Press this button, and you get a tone that signals the shooter to start. When the last round is fired, you press it again, and the screen says how long it took. The timer is accurate to hundredths of a second."

The course of fire Janis set up – five targets, three bullets per target, two magazines – required a combat reload. The lowest time and the most rounds in the center of mass are defined by the eight, nine, or 10 rings, and the head won. If there was a tie, the winner was determined by the most headshots.

Behind them, a dozen men watching a respectful 20 yards away. Shooting elsewhere on the pistol range had stopped.

Janis nodded toward the men. "The audience has arrived. When we leave, a couple of the single guys will hit on us. Do you want me to go first?"

Aliyah nodded and took the timer. "Shooter ready?"

When the timer went off, Janis ran toward the first target, her arms extended, and the pistol pointed down. As her foot touched the ground behind the first 2 X 4, she squeezed off two rounds at the center of the silhouette target and one in the center of the head. The shell casings were still in the air as Janis began moving to the next 2 X 4, seven yards from a target. Again, the first shot rang out as she was coming to a stop. The two body shots were in the center of mass, less than an inch apart on either side of the X, and the third was dead center in the head.

Janis dumped out the magazine that contained six rounds between the third and fourth targets. She took a deep breath once she stopped moving, focused on the target 15 yards away, and squeezed off all three rounds. The last piece of brass had yet to hit the ground when she began jogging to the final target, which was the closest, at three yards. All three were headshots.

Janis put the pistol down on a table. "I'll go tape the holes. We add a second for each shot outside the center of mass or head."

Aliyah's run was strong, and only one shot was outside the eight-ring when she returned to the table where they had the spare magazines and ammunition. When Janis congratulated her on a great run, Aliyah shook her head. "Not like yours."

"I do this drill and others like it every week because I want to ensure that I hit what I aim at. Stray bullets cause problems."

There's a message in there. Aliyah nodded, and Janis handed her two loaded magazines. "Go show the guys how it is done!" The Israeli wasn't sure if this was Janis' way of letting her show her skills or telling her that she needed to practice with a pistol if they were going to work together or both.

THE SAME DAY, 2:39 P.M. LOCAL TIME, CARACAS, VENEZUELA,

Angel Gardez had not chosen the role into which his supporters pushed him. The economy was contracting despite the country having the world's largest oil reserves, and there were shortages of everything – fuel, consumer goods, medicines, clothing. The only "thing" that was plentiful were the attempts by the Chavez government to squash dissent. Gardez was, until Chavez was elected president, one of the National Assembly's more liberal members and one of the leading opponents of Chavez's dream of a national police force.

He was proud of Venezuela's progress toward democracy and human rights until Chavez was elected. As a lawyer and a prosecutor, Gardez earned a reputation for rooting out corruption. Several times, he successfully prosecuted several Chavez cronies and earned the enmity of the country's president.

Now, as a member of the National Assembly, Gardez was one of Chavez's most vocal critics. Chavez, he believed, was trying to become another Castro, and he didn't want that to happen. It was bad enough that Venezuela was close to becoming a police state.

He was getting out of the car to go into his office when Gardez heard zzzziiiiipppppptttt followed by a smack. He turned to the sound. The last thing he saw were flakes of concrete falling from a circular hole as another 151.2-grain bullet from a Russian-made 7.62 X 54mm rimmed cartridge hit him in the back of the head and blew his face off.

THE SAME DAY, 3:07 P.M. LOCAL TIME, DALLAS,

When they returned from the gun range, Janis excused herself to compose her thoughts. Several had been randomly running through her head, and now was time to organize them.

Janis was afraid of being blackmailed into again being an assassin and hunted until she was jailed or killed. She was enjoying retirement that was, thanks to the CIA, the FBI, and the Cubans, about to end. Janis didn't want to lose her freedom. While she might trust individuals in the CIA, she didn't trust the CIA as an organization that followed the changing policies of presidents.

Now, she had a choice, and liked the Israelis who were narrowly focused on national survival. They were prepared to do what was necessary to ensure their country's and Judaism's survival in a kill-or-be-killed world. They try to maintain the moral high ground even when operating in the shadows. Working with them intrigued Janis.

While they waited for Janis, Moshe warned Aliyah that Janis might be playing her. Aliyah disagreed.

The casual mood from the morning became more serious as Janis led the two Israelis to her dining room to hear the verdict. Neither Israeli was sure what Janis would say. She looked at Aliyah and then Moshe, but mainly at the woman she'd slept with.

"I am about to give you my requirements for working together, and some are not negotiable. So, here goes."

Both Israelis smiled as they nodded. Aliyah had a lined pad in front of her on the table.

"First, Aliyah and I work together to identify, plan and execute any operation. If I am disabled, everything else stays in place. If physically and mentally able, I will become an advisor and coach. Second, I can veto any assignment and will not take on political assassinations anywhere. Third, Israel will grant me citizenship and provide me with legal protection for any action taken against me by any country for my past and future work outside Israel. As an Israeli citizen, Israel will provide healthcare if I am injured on an assignment. Fourth, Israel will allow me to continue to manage my portfolio in a tax haven. In other words, I want to be exempt from Israeli taxes. I will continue to pay U.S. taxes unless I lose my U.S. citizenship. Fifth, Israel will negotiate an agreement with the Department of Justice that U.S. federal, state, county, and city law enforcement agencies will not investigate or attempt to arrest me. Call it a pardon, immunity or whatever. This agreement **must be** signed by the U.S. Attorney General or his designated representative before I start work, and my identity **must r**emain a closely guarded secret within Mossad and the CIA."

Aliyah looked at Moshe who had been keeping the head of the Mossad informed since they arrived in Dallas. Moshe put his hand on Aliyah's forearm as if to say, let me answer. "First, Aliyah and I are delighted you want to help us. I think the Israeli government will agree to your conditions with some clarification. The guarantee that the U.S. government will not come after you may not be possible."

"The agreement is critical. Without the agreement, I will constantly be looking over my shoulder for the CIA and FBI and the friends of the bad guys' Aliyah, and I go after."

"To me, immunity will be the biggest issue to solve." Moshe took a deep breath. "Pardon me, but may I ask how large your portfolio is?"

"Large enough to be very attractive to any private bank in the world. The First International Bank of Israel would welcome a chance to have me as a client. They have a relationship with Pictet et Cie, one of my bankers."

Moshe persisted, knowing the size would make the deal easier to sell.

"Janis, what are we talking about? A couple million, maybe twenty? Can you give me an approximate number? It will help."

"Use three hundred and forty million in liquid investments as a working number, and it is on the low side. That number doesn't include the value of my gun collection, the Porsches out back, this house, or my airplane." Janis didn't mention the three bank deposit boxes, each with five million in cash and valid credit cards and passports from different countries that are kept current.

Moshe put his pen down as he forced himself not to react. He looked at Janis. "Do you have any suggestions on how to convince your CIA to help us?"

Janis smiled, knowing this could be the most likely deal breaker. "I do. I am sure the head of Mossad can call Director Tenet at CIA at any time to discuss what I have to offer. In addition to the material I have on CDs that have details on my activities, I will agree to three, four-hour debriefing sessions. This will give them insight into the individuals or agencies who hired me and should be worth its weight in gold to the CIA. So, to get a valuable asset that both agencies can use to eliminate Muslim terrorists, I think they would be more than open to this kind of an agreement."

Löbel's tone was grim. "You know, someone in the Department of Justice may object."

"I suspect the intelligence value of what I know would trump the Department of Justice's need to put me behind bars. Right now, the CIA only knows what contracts it sent to Moya but not the other contracts I took from him. This intelligence costs them nothing other than a piece of paper from the Attorney General to get access to me which comes through the Mossad. This is what consultants call a win-win deal."

"Are you willing to meet with the head of Mossad and others in Israel to finalize our arrangement?"

"Of course. I assumed that would be necessary."

Moshe nodded. "Excellent. Aliyah and I have work to do. Would you mind if we called Israel from your office behind closed doors?"

"Please, feel free to do so. I'll sit outside."

"Thank you."

When the two Israelis came back onto the deck, Moshe said, "I've got things started. My boss, as do I, think the CIA and your DOJ will need some convincing."

Janis didn't want to probe on what was said. "I didn't think it would be easy. I'll bring something we can use to convince the CIA of the agreement's value. When are you leaving to go back to Israel?"

"Tomorrow. We will take a morning flight to Newark or JFK and catch an El Al flight back to Tel Aviv."

"Great, then we can have dinner."

Moshe looked at both women. "I think the two of you would prefer to have dinner alone, and I will make reservations and call Aliyah."

"I'll make sure she makes the flight."

"Excellent. See you in the morning."

THE SAME DAY, 4:49 P.M. LOCAL TIME, PALMDALE

It was in the 90s and one still needed sunglasses when Reeder put his new margarita under the umbrella's shade. His chair gave him an unrestricted view of the pool deck to watch women come and go.

Last night, the hotel's concierge suggested a local hot spot saying professionals who worked at Edwards for contractors and single, female officers from the Air Force Base hung out there. The club was, he was told, a good mix of young and old, and this being California, of all sexual persuasions. The young man was right, and when Reeder walked in this morning, he handed the concierge a 20-dollar bill.

Reeder wondered if the brand-new Air Force lieutenant colonel and a test pilot stationed at Edwards found him or he found her. The woman knew what she wanted, and Reeder was delighted to oblige. After breakfast and another love-making session, the CIA case officer returned to his hotel to think about the next steps in his search.

His cell phone next to the margarita buzzed. At the other end was the CIA watch officer in their Miami office, who put the names, Ordonez, and Reeder, together and called. He'd known the former SEAL when they were both on active duty.

Both needed to be circumspect since Reeder was not using a secure phone. "Bill, it's John Henry. Start looking for a Julia Amy Lucas. The source is a guy from Ordonez's firm. I'll run the name through the databases, so our friends on the other side of the river won't know why or who was asking. The results will get to you in a day or so."

"Thanks, John Henry." Friends on the other side of the river went by the initials FBI.

Reeder looked at the phone. I am staying in Palmdale for another day or two, and I'll see if the lieutenant colonel would like a second date. Maybe, Palmdale isn't so bad after all!

Reeder went back to his room to change. Rather go through the list of dojos, he returned to the one he thought had the most promise. The sign on the door said it closed at 2100 on weekdays.

"I see you are back."

Reeder turned around, again surprised the man got close to him without him knowing. He must be slipping.

"I am. Does the name Julia Amy Lucas ring a bell."

"Should it?"

"It would if you knew the names of your students."

"Do you have a warrant or a court order?"

"No."

"When you have one, I will tell you if it rings a bell. As I said, get a warrant, and then I'll look. If not, don't come back. If you do and do not have a warrant or a court order, it will be the third time, and I will assume that you are looking for a U.S. citizen in the United States. If I remember my civics lessons, that is a job for the police, not the CIA."

Reeder knew a no when he heard one. His earlier thought about breaking if he didn't get any help immediately evaporated, and it was not worth the risk.

WEDNESDAY, MAY 22ND, 2002, 8:30 A.M. LOCAL TIME, LANGLEY

This was not Harvey Reeder's first time in Greg Nasher's office. The plush carpet and nice furniture in the head of the CIA's Special Activities Division was a step up from the cubicles assigned to case officers and field agents. Both came into the agency at the same time. Reeder elected to stay in the field while Nasher gravitated to working 'inside.'

As he waited for Nasher to finish a telephone conversation, Reeder polished the script that he would use to lay out his idea. He'd been given 30 minutes, although he was told the director wanted him out in 15.

"Here's my idea that I didn't want to explain over a non-secure phone. We, and by that, I mean the FBI, the Dirección de Inteligencia, and the CIA are looking for this female assassin who at one time was known as Julia Amy Lucas. Neither agency has a clue as to where she is. We and I suspect the Cubans want to bring the Lucas woman out of retirement to do their bidding. That leaves the FBI as the odd man since they want to put her in jail. If they do, neither the Cubans nor we benefit."

Reeder stopped and looked at his friend, who nodded, saying go on.

"So, we should contact Ordonez and make a deal. We pool our resources, find this woman, and encourage her to work for both of us. I don't think she'll be swayed by patriotism, so we make it very lucrative. We have the legal wizards who can figure out how to make the arrangement work."

The man on the other side of the table knew by 'encourage' Reeder meant blackmail and threaten if needed.

"Interesting. How do you propose we proceed?"

"The CIA has an office dedicated to working with other intelligence agencies. They're not squeamish about talking to anyone in the interest of the U.S., even our enemies. Operations can take the project on if they don't want it."

Nasher rubbed his chin. "This is an intriguing idea. Let me run the concept up the flagpole, which will take a few days."

"What do you want me to do in the interim?"

"Hang around D.C. and stay out of trouble until I call."

THE SAME DAY, 9:18 A.M. LOCAL TIME, DALLAS

After Janis returned from DFW, her house seemed empty, almost joyless without Aliyah. The Israeli woman brought a spirit and love for life she hadn't experienced since Karin's passing. It was headed in the right direction with Emily, but they only had a few days together, and now Emily was gone. Janis realized she needed someone in her life to love and who wouldn't freak out about her previous life. Aliyah, in many ways, was perfect.

Since clearing up what she thought were all the loose ends by killing Payá, Janis believed she was permanently out of the assassination business. By living quietly with Karin, Janis hid in plain sight.

Apparently, recent events changed everything. Janis understood the motives of the players who have surfaced so far. The Cubans wanted a tool to create mischief in Latin America and occasionally help the Kremlin. The CIA and Mossad wanted an asset, and the FBI wanted to make a splash with an arrest.

Being a freelance assassin was not a life Janis was eager to re-enter. In the 20-plus years since she was active, surveillance cameras made staying invisible harder, and computers could sift through reams of data finding links that humans couldn't.

La Estrella Roja de la Muerte was older, wiser, and smarter about the world. Still, time and technology, Janis thought, may have passed her by.

As she sat by the pool sipping her coffee, Janis reflected on her past two lovers. When she stumbled on Karin purely by chance in a lesbian club in Cologne in 1982, they had not seen each other since they were in Cuba in 1971. She was attracted to the blond German girl in Cuba, and Karin became the love of her life.

Then, she met Emily. There was fire between them from the moment they met. Now, Emily was taken by an act of terrorism before a serious relationship could develop. That attack led to Aliyah standing on her doorstep.

This was, Janis believed, more than just a coincidence. She was not religious, but maybe God was watching out for her when he sent Aliyah.

It was a strange and more religious and spiritual thought than Janis ever believed she could have. Her parents were Catholic, and she rejected Catholicism and Christianity long ago.

As a little girl, Janis asked a nun how Jesus could die for her sins when she was only eight and hadn't committed any? How did he know what I was going to do? The answer "because he is the son of God" didn't make sense to her then or now.

In the eyes of the church, I killed for money and made love to women, which makes me a sinner. Therefore, I am dammed and will go to hell. What nonsense!

Catholicism's focus on death and the afterlife always bothered her. She'd caused enough death to believe that when you were dead, you were dead, and that was the end. There was nothing more; if you were lucky, your family and generations who followed remembered you.

It's been 30-plus years since I've seen my brothers, sister, or parents. To them, I was twenty-two when they disowned me for my radical social and political views I had long ago abandoned as naïve and irresponsible. Do they ever wonder what happened to me?

Janis shook her head to shake the memories out of her conscious thoughts. Her work as an assassin was clinical. The targets were given to her, and the job was simple – find, kill, escape, get paid, lay low, and wait for the next assignment. The rush from the act of killing had long since faded away. It was a job, albeit a dangerous one, but nothing more.

What the Israelis will ask me to do will be a matter of national survival, and it will be killing for a purpose, not just money. That I like.

Her mind shifted to the list of things she needed to do before leaving for Israel. She called Jason Winthrop, and he readily agreed to put the 906 still on the trailer on his showroom floor for a month. When she returned, it would be rotated with the 904, the RS-60, the Abarth Carrera, and maybe the 356SC.

She wasn't worried about her portfolio. It was managed by a wealth manager at Pictet et Cie in Geneva, who deposited $50,000 each month in her Wells Fargo checking account. The $100,000 jumbo CD whose interest was also dumped into her checking account, would stay at Wells Fargo.

Satisfied all that was left was to make reservations to fly to Israel, Janis went for a run. She needed it to work through the details of her next steps.

THURSDAY, MAY 23RD, 2003, 10:06 A.M. LOCAL TIME, HAVANA

Clipped to the copy of Venezuela's largest newspaper by circulation – *El Universal* – was a copy of the *Dirección de Inteligencia's* official report on Gardez's assassination. The paper had pictures, a detailed story on the incident, and an opinion piece blaming Chavez for Gardez's killing.

He compared the newspaper accounts to his agency's report to what he knew about *La Estrella Roja de la Muerte's* skills and methods. Ordonez concluded the analyses in the *Dirección de Inteligencia's* agents' report were unmitigated bullshit. The more he studied the document, the more he was convinced the person who determined the hit was the work of *La Estrella Roja de la Muerte* was dumber than dirt.

Report in hand, Ordonez walked into the head of the operations division and sat down. The man glanced at him and continued giving instructions to a woman standing in front of his desk.

The woman glanced at the chubby but still handsome Ordonez as she walked out without saying a word. The director waited until the two were alone. "You know Ordonez, you need an appointment to come into my office. So, this must be important. What's on your mind?"

"How stupid do you think *La Estrella Roja de la Muerte* is?"

"Leadership thought blaming it on her was a good idea."

By leadership, Ordonez knew Hector Gonzalez was referring to the head of the *Dirección de Inteligencia* and/or the Castro brothers.

"Tell me why you don't like it?"

"One, the idea that blaming the shooting on *La Estrella Roja de la Muerte* as a means to flush the woman out is ridiculous. Since we know she is an American, Chavez will blame the assassination on the CIA. Gardez was a vocal opponent of Chavez, so that argument doesn't pass the smell test."

"What else is wrong?"

"Two, the assassin needed two shots. *La Estrella Roja de la Muerte* never needed more than one per target. Second, the police have the rifle. Never has *La Estrella Roja de la Muerte* left the weapon behind. Anyone who knew her MO will immediately conclude that this is not the work of *La Estrella Roja de la Muerte*. Third, they got a vague description of the shooter, which never happened before."

Gonzalez tented his hands under his chin and looked at Ordonez. The man's points were valid. The *Dirección de Inteligencia* was told to carry out the operation and plant the story that it was *La Estrella Roja de la Muerte*. He was not involved in planning the hit. "So, you think this was a mistake."

"If you think this will make her come out of hiding, I do. She is probably someplace laughing over a glass of wine. Next time, if generating a lead on this American woman is one of the goals, get someone involved who has read her file rather than some political asshole."

THE SAME DAY, 7:46 P.M. LOCAL TIME, ON A TRAIN IN THE U.K.

Ghulam enjoyed traveling by train. There was much less scrutiny and if one booked a first-class ticket, there was more working space, comfort, and privacy.

He was sipping his tea and watching the lush green countryside roll past the window as he thought through the next attacks. The trip from Manchester to London's Euston Station gave him three hours to decide if the next two should be carried out in sequence or simultaneously. They would be bigger, bloodier, and send a strong message to Israel's allies that they needed to stop supporting the Jews.

The men and weapons were in place, and the bombs were being built. He had to wait until the right time to give the order to prove to the infidels that no place on earth was safe from the Al-Musawi Corps and Hezbollah.

CHAPTER 9

REVELATONS

Janis was dumping food into the garbage that would spoil while she was in Israel when she heard the doorbell ring. On the monitor for her security system, she saw a young woman wearing a knee-length skirt standing a few steps back from the door. Her long jet-black hair was tied in a ponytail on the left side of her head.

Since she was not expecting visitors, Janis grabbed a Walther PPK/S, one of several pistols stashed around the house, and went to the door. "Who is it?" Janis stood behind the concrete wall.

"Stephanie Stern. I am one of Emily Stone's cousins."

Janis unlocked and opened the door while she held the pistol behind her back. Stephanie was probably in her 40s, with average size and build. "I'm sorry, but I was not expecting anyone, and I apologize; my house is a mess."

"We're sorry for not calling, but we just got to Dallas. My mother, Emma, and I would like to talk to you for a few minutes. She's in the car."

"Sure."

Stephanie waved at the car, and a woman in her 70s got out. The stranger could have been Emily's twin sister. She walked to the steps and held out her hand, "Hi Janis, I'm Emma Stern."

Janis pointed to the living room. "May I get either of you something to drink?"

Emma shook her head before she and her daughter sat down on the couch. "No, thank you. We'll only be a few minutes." Emma took a deep breath and started talking. "Emily's father was my brother. Emily and I were very close. I was the 'fun' aunt if you know what I mean. I never told her parents that Emily confided in me when she was 13 that she thought she was gay. She tried to be straight. Then, after the divorce, she told her parents. Her husband was unfaithful, which is why they split, and Emily was happy that she could now be herself."

Janis didn't say anything. This confirmed what Emily told her and confirmed that her parents had trouble with her sexual preference.

Emma sat on the edge of the couch, looking at Janis. The pained expression on Emma's face indicated how painful and uncomfortable this conversation was for both women.

"Then, the day after she met you, Emily called me to say she believed she'd met her true soul mate. She was so excited, and I know the two of you spent time together before Emily went to California."

"We did. We talked Friday morning before the ceremony; that was the last time I spoke to Emily."

"Yes, Friday was horrible. We were all so scared. Stephanie and I were lucky we weren't shot."

"And, your husband, is he alright?"

"I'm a widow, and my husband died of a heart attack four years ago."

Dummy, you should have looked for a ring. She has a huge diamond on her right hand, just like I do.

"I'm so sorry."

"Thank you, it was very hard for the first few months, but I think Stephanie and I have learned to accept what happened."

Janis could see the hurt behind the woman's eyes. There was nothing she could say or do to alleviate the pain, so she said nothing.

"Anyway, Emily wanted us to meet right after this ceremony."

I didn't know that. Neither of us had seen Mount Rushmore, and we were planning to leave this week or next. Instead, I'm going to Israel to hunt down the bastards who planned the attack that killed Emily.

Emma started crying and shaking her head as if to get the image out of her brain. "One of the horrible things Stephanie and I had to do was identify the bodies in the morgue since we were the only relatives not in the hospital."

Janis came over to the couch and put her arm around Emma to console her. She was afraid that anything she said might sound trite. Janis had grieved until Aliyah arrived. Now, she'd transitioned to warrior mode – cold and ruthless. *Emotions had to be set aside.*

"Janis, please excuse me, I didn't mean to lose my composure."

"Emma, it is alright. We all suffered a terrible loss. I wish I'd known Emily longer." *I loved it when she wrapped her long legs around me and pulled me close.*

The older woman nodded several times and dug into her purse. "Emily was wearing this when she was killed. Every day since she met you, Emily would call, and I could tell she was very happy. I think she would want you to have this to remember her by."

Emma Stern held out a small jewelry box. "Please, take it."

Inside was the Star of David Emily wore with blue sapphires on the six points. Janis' jaw dropped slightly, letting out a soft gasp. "Mrs. Stern, this is beautiful, but I am not Jewish."

"We know. Wear it occasionally in Emily's memory."

"Thank you, I will do that." *I am about to become Emily's avenging angel. And that is very cool.*

After the Stern's left, Janis sat in her living room for an hour looking at the six-pointed star. The excitement of the hunt and the rush of pulling the trigger, knowing an evil person was about to die, was back.

Thinking about the contracts she had the most satisfaction in completing were those that killed Nazis wanted for war crimes that, for political reasons, governments decided not to prosecute. The enemies have changed, but not the mission.

Janis was puzzled by her sudden mysticism and sense of purpose. This was not about trigger-pulling, making money, and getting away.

What she now felt was much different. Hunting terrorists for the Israelis had captured her heart and penetrated her soul. She now had a reason to kill. As she admired the Star of David, Janis wondered if she should become one of the chosen people.

CHAPTER 18

THE DEAL

The Shura Council, which runs Hezbollah, met in a simply furnished room in its headquarters in Beirut. At one end, there was a tray with pastries and tea. At the other end of the room, a telephone sat on a small table and was not plugged into the wall outlet.

Ghulam had been "invited" to appear before the Shura Council to answer questions on the attack in Los Angeles, it's first on U.S. soil. The council members listened patiently to his description of how the attack was planned and carried out. Ahmad Busaid, the most senior man in the room, waited until Ghulam was finished before asking what lessons could be applied to future attacks.

Without hesitating, Ghulam said. "There are three …"

Lesson 1 – we can bring men into the U.S. easily through Mexico. Those who speak passable English and have good documents can drive through the border checkpoints into Arizona, California, New Mexico, and Texas.

Lesson 2 – except in Southern California and Arizona, major targets are far from the border. If this route was chosen, attacks must be carried out in Los Angeles, Phoenix, or Dallas.

Lesson 3 – America has many targets ideal for mass killings. Sporting events and concerts have minimal security.

Ghulam stopped speaking and looked around the room. At the head of the table, Busaid looked at him and asked. "So, what do you propose?"

"An attack in Israel, in Europe, and the United States on the same day. To carry out the American attack, we move an eight-man team through Mexico and into either California or Texas. We have men in Europe, and I will pick the targets and dates."

Talal Hamiyah, who coordinated terrorist attacks from Hezbollah-sponsored groups nodded in agreement. "This is the right strategy."

Farhad Madhavi, the Iranian veteran of the Iran-Iraq war and who ran the Al-Musawi training camp, spoke. "Abd al-Bari, we need six months to a year to train men in the Al-Musawi Corps that you are throwing away like candy wrappers. Maybe we should try something else."

"Like what, Farhad?" In the camp, he was known as "Colonel No." Madhavi had never heard a new idea he liked.

"Like focusing our attacks directly on Israel. Iran has given Hezbollah the rockets and the artillery. Why don't we rain death and destruction on the Jews?"

Ghulam remained respectful as well as determined. "We will succeed in destroying Israel only by putting pressure on their allies. Once their aid slows, we can destroy Israel. If we do not attack them outside Israel, the Jews will continue to attack us."

"You, Ghulam, are too pessimistic. My government and I believe a long war will exhaust Israel if executed properly, and the Jews will sue for peace. In a few years, we can wipe them out."

Busaid leaned forward and spoke before Ghulam could respond. "Colonel Madhavi, how many men do we have in the camp who are ready?"

"Two hundred and twenty."

"And how many are in training?"

"Approximately two hundred?"

"And how soon will they be ready?

"Within two months."

"And how many men do we send to you each month?"

"Fifteen to twenty."

"So, colonel, if my math is correct, we can have four hundred and twenty commandos ready in two months and send you fifteen to twenty every month. So, if we lose eight each month, we will still grow. Am I not correct?"

"Yes, you are, but… "

Busaid cut him off. "We have a waiting list of volunteers, and our goal is to create a force of at least five hundred commandos. We are, by any standard, well on our way. So, Ghulam, proceed with your plans. When you have a schedule and a list of targets, come to me, and we will determine how to proceed. Thank you. May Allah be with you."

THE SAME DAY, 1:30 P.M. LOCAL TIME, TEL AVIV

From her seat next to a window in first class, Janis noted that the Swiss Airlines MD-11 was over land for just a few miles before it touched down with a thump at Ben Gurion Airport in Tel Aviv. While the plane was taxing to the gate, the senior flight attendant in the first-class section came to Janis' seat and said pleasantly, "Ms. Goodrich, please get your bag and come with me."

When the door was opened, a grinning Aliyah Skylar stood on the jet bridge next to a man from the Israeli Border Police. The officer said, "Ms. Goodrich, *shalom,* and welcome to Israel. Please come with me, and our immigration process will take just a few minutes."

VIP treatment. How cool!

After Janis tossed her bag in the trunk of Aliyah's Volkswagen Jetta, Aliyah wrapped her arms around her new American friend and French kissed her. "Welcome to Israel. I missed you, and tonight, I will properly welcome you to my country."

"I can't wait."

On the way to her flat, Aliyah turned to Janis. "Why did you stop in Zurich?"

"I had to talk to my Swiss banker and sign some papers." It was only partly true. Yes, she signed some papers, but the real purpose was to take a set of CDs out of her safe deposit box.

Aliyah started caressing Janis's thigh when she put her hand on Aliyah's. "So, what's on the schedule?"

"Tomorrow starts with interviews with Mossad security experts to begin the vetting process. You're meeting the head of First International Bank of Israel's private bank at two. Thursday, you are meeting Efraim Halevy, the head of Mossad at nine. In the afternoon. Friday and Saturday are our weekends, and I can start giving you a tour of Israel."

"What about the agreement with the CIA?"

"We're working on it. The CIA didn't say no, and they didn't say yes. They like the idea of having you as an asset, but they don't like you being under Israeli control. Moshe thinks your Department of Justice will do what the CIA asks. That is one of the things that Efraim Halevy wants to talk to you about."

Aliyah zipped into a parking spot, and as Janis got out of the car, she could see the royal blue of the Mediterranean. "Come, we can see the water better from my apartment."

Before Janis could take in the view, Aliyah was all over her, and she was just as horny. Clothes and hands went everywhere as they stripped. Janis moaned in pleasure from Aliyah's touch as she kissed Aliyah's lips and neck and ran her hands all over her lover's body. Clothes started to litter the floor.

THE SAME DAY, 9:09 P.M. LOCAL TIME, MAAMELTEIN, LEBANON

Ghulam decided to celebrate Busaid's blessing to proceed. He never married, although once, he was infatuated with a fellow university student that ended when she moved to France. After Ghulam joined Hezbollah, he didn't want the emotional baggage that came with a girlfriend or wife and family. He feared a clever enemy could use a family to get to him.

To care for his needs, he frequently turned to the oldest profession in the world. In Lebanon, prostitution was legal, and there were many clubs in Maameltein, about 20 kilometers along the coast road north of Beirut where he could go. The government had strict rules the clubs followed or risked losing their license. One law required all the women must be foreign nationals allowed into the country on an "artiste" visa once they had a contract with a club.

Another regulation was the women must be in the club between eight p.m. and five a.m. No sexual acts could be performed in the club. Dates were made at the club, and the "guest" would go to the woman's apartment at the appointed time the next day.

The process was inconvenient but legal. Call girls and streetwalkers operated outside this framework and were chased by the police. If caught, both the hooker and the john were arrested, which was an embarrassment Ghulam wanted to avoid.

His favorite club was Excalibur, where he was a regular, and the madam knew his preferences. A bottle of champagne appeared at his table, followed by a scantily clad, very blonde Ukrainian woman. After drinking a glass of wine, they settled on 2 p.m. tomorrow afternoon.

WEDNESDAY, MAY 29TH, 2002, 11:46 A.M. LOCAL TIME, TEL AVI

The beach was less than two kilometers from Mossad headquarters. Walking took 20 minutes, driving less than 10. Since time was of the essence, Eitan Kohan drove. He followed Yunitsman Street past the roundabout and found a parking spot on Ariel Sharon Road that paralleled the Mediterranean coast.

Walking toward the row of benches, Eitan carried a small paper bag with his lunch and a book. He looked like anyone wanting to eat his lunch on the beach. Along the way, Eitan put a stick of chewing gum in his mouth.

The gum taste was gone by the time he sat on the specified bench, but Eitan kept chewing and looked around. Not seeing anything or anyone suspicious, he took the gum that was now tasteless out of his mouth and pressed it onto the thumb drive he took from his lunch bag. Accidentally on purpose, he let a napkin fall on the ground. When he bent over to pick it up, Eitan pressed the thumb drive into the corner where the slats of the bench joined the legs. Mission accomplished, Eitan picked up the napkin, finished eating, and drove back to Mossad headquarters.

Within minutes of Eitan's departure, a man with a long, dark beard sat on the same bench to eat his lunch before he plucked the USB flash drive from its hiding place. The one-gigabyte memory device went into his trouser pocket.

On Ariel Sharon Drive, the bearded man flagged a passing cab that took him to his hotel, where he downloaded the flash drive onto his computer. Each file was opened and encrypted before being attached to an email and sent to an address in Beirut.

With his work done and his need to stay in Tel Aviv over, the bearded man drove to his home in the West Bank town of Ramallah. Thanks to Eitan Kohan, Hezbollah has insight into the inner workings of the hated Mossad.

THE SAME DAY, 12:50 P.M. LOCAL TIME, TEL AVIV

Lunchtime shoppers were coming out of the Petah Tikvah mall when two women wearing maternity dresses entered the Basel Street entrance. To the casual observer, they looked as if they were due any moment. They sweated in the heat, not from carrying an infant encased in amniotic fluid but from five kilos (11.02 lbs.) of ball bearings packed into two kilos (4.41 lbs.) of SEMTEX.

The soldiers standing guard at the entrance waved the pregnant girls into the mall. Once inside, the women headed to different concourses.

Outside, a man started a stopwatch to time 13 minutes from the time the women disappeared into the mall's entrance. When the hand touched zero, he pressed the button on the aluminum box and was gratified when he heard two muffled explosions.

Five blocks away, Aliyah and Janis were at the door of the headquarters of the First Israel International Bank when both heard the booms. Aliyah grabbed Janis's arm. "I know this is cold, but we need to go inside. There's nothing we can do. By tomorrow, Mossad will know what happened, who the bomb maker was, and how it was set off."

Janis nodded and went through the revolving door. *We will find and kill the fuckers who ordered the bombing.*

THURSDAY, MAY 30ᵀᴴ, 2002, 11:48 A.M. LOCAL TIME, TEL AVIV,

Janis stayed at Aliyah's apartment until it was time for her appointment with Halevy. The break from Aliyah gave her time to again think through questions she might be asked. When Janis gave the cab driver the address Alyiah had written on a slip of paper in Hebrew and English, the cab driver gave her an odd look, but didn't say a word.

At the entrance, Janis showed her passport, and after her purse was inspected, the officer took her phone, saying it would be returned when she left. A security officer led Janis, now wearing a badge clipped to her blouse, and Aliyah to Efraim Halevy's office. She sat in the center of the couch facing the head of the Mossad, who sat in an armchair.

Reznik and Löbel took seats at opposite ends of the C-shaped couch that backed up against a floor-to-ceiling window. Drapes kept the sun out, and Aliyah was 'banished' to a chair at the conference table.

The pleasantries and welcome to Israel ended when Halevy asked Janis why she decided to help the Israelis, not the CIA. The discussion went back and forth until Halevy again changed the subject. "Janis, we're ready to agree to what you asked, but to be blunt, the CIA needs more convincing. Your Attorney General needs more details about the intelligence you will provide so they can determine the value before giving you immunity."

Janis nodded and pointed to her purse. Janis told the security guard that she would give the CDs to Mr. Halevy. An eyebrow was raised, and a note was made in the log, but she was allowed to keep them. "May I?"

Halevy nodded, and Janis pulled out two CDs. "These CDs have documentation on everything I did. It starts with a video about what I remembered about my training in Cuba. It ends 11 years later with the contract to kill Gary Savoy. I scanned all the documents I was given for each contract and then destroyed the originals. For each hit, there is a video of me recorded by my friend Karin Egger describing the contract, my research, surveillance of the target, the hit itself, and my escape. The CDs took us the better part of two years to complete. Much of our time was spent finding copies of newspapers and magazines documenting the results. I have the master, and besides this copy, there are four others in safe places around the world."

She put the two plastic CD cases on the coffee table. "I will give this copy to Mossad and give the CIA their own set as part of the agreement."

Halevy softly rapped the CDs on his leg. "Let's go into my conference room and take a look."

The time on the clock, Janis noted, was 9:36 a.m. The CDs were organized by year and with a folder for each hit. Halevy selected folders at random and asked questions. Janis's Rolex President said it was almost twelve when Halevy popped out the CD. "When did you finish gathering the material contained in the CD?"

"December 1985. I don't remember the exact date. I do remember we flew to Europe a few days after we finished to spend the holidays in Germany with her parents and to go skiing in Austria." Janis did not believe Halevy needed to know that they stopped in Zurich to put the master and three copies in her safe deposit box at Pictet et Cie. Another was given to the law firm in the same town that acts as her agent, so the information is protected by attorney-client privilege. A fifth was kept at a law office in Washington D.C. of a firm recommended by Moya that specialized in espionage cases.

"How much of this can I share with the CIA?"

"At this time, only enough to convince them that I am *La Estrella Roja de la Muerte* and can provide insight into Moya's other clients who hired me. I'll agree to three, maybe four half-day debriefing sessions with the CIA, no other agency. They only get access to me if they agree to the conditions I set forth when I met with Moshe and Aliyah in Dallas which bear repeating. The U.S. must grant me total immunity for my past actions in the U.S., and no local, state, or Federal law enforcement organization is to know about the agreement with the CIA. This also means that the FBI and all Federal, state, and local law enforcement organizations agree to never open or re-open any of their investigations into my activities. They will also cancel all domestic warrants and Interpol notices. By the way, the U.S. Attorney General does this all the time, so this is not new. For this, the CIA receives one copy of the CDs for their use on the condition that they cannot share them with any other intelligence agency. Please don't use my real name when you talk to them."

Halevy nodded his head. "I understand, and this will be a big help." He looked at the clock on the wall, "As soon as my contact gets into the office, I will call him. Meanwhile, if they would like to talk to you, are you willing?"

"Sure, as long as we speak on a secure phone and don't use my name."

"We can do it from my office." Halevy looked at Aliyah. "Please stay in Tel Aviv so you can come in on short notice."

THE SAME DAY, 8:29 A.M. LOCAL TIME, WASHINGTON, D.C.

Bill Smith III thought the report was significant enough to schedule a conference call with the CIA before the regularly scheduled one on Friday. He wondered if they received the same information from their contacts.

What triggered Smith III's call was an Interpol Purple notice issued by the *Cuerpo de Investigaciones Científicas, Penales y Criminalísticas*. It originated with the Venezuelan police force asking for details on methods of operation, procedures, or hiding places used by an assassin known as *La Estrella Roja de la Muerte*.

According to the report, Venezuela's national police agency received a tip suggesting she killed Angel Gardez. Smith III had, through the FBI's international police liaison office, asked for and, surprisingly enough, promptly received a copy of their report.

Reeder picked up his mobile phone after three rings. He sounded as if he had just gotten up because he did. "Reeder."

"It is Bill Smith. Did I wake you?"

"You did. Late night. What's up that can't wait until Friday?" The woman he slept with left at about six, and Reeder went back to sleep.

"Did you see the Interpol Purple notice from the Venezuelans looking for info on the woman known as *The Red Star of Death?*"

"No, not yet. What did it say?" The notice should be on his desk when he arrives. Reeder was now fully awake and went into the kitchen of the condominium he owned in the unincorporated town of McLean, which was in Fairfax County, Virginia, to make coffee.

Smith III summarized what was in the report. After saying he'll fax it directly to his office, he asked, "What do you think?"

Reeder may have been slightly hung over, but this was better than tomato juice, oxygen, or aspirin. His mind was on the job at hand. Reeder rattled off reasons why he thought the report was bogus. They were similar to what Ordonez told his boss.

Then, he added, "If I remember correctly, she never killed a politician, which means this is a new category target for her. So, riddle me this, batman, why suddenly did she come out of hiding?"

"Harvey, the only reason for coming out of retirement I can come up with is a pile of money. So, let's assume this is real, who is paying the bill, Castro, or Chavez. Chavez has money and motive."

"Agreed. My question is, why did the Cubans or the Venezuelans use an outsider? Chavez has his own secret police to do his dirty work."

"Good question. Thanks for the insight." As Reeder stirred his coffee, he thought the deal with Ordonez, if it happened, would give the agency and, by definition, him more insight.

FRIDAY, MAY 31ST, 2002, 10:03 A.M. LOCAL TIME, LANGLEY

Reeder wasn't told why he was summoned to Nasher's office just to be there at 10. As he came in, Nasher waved him to a chair next to the desk, suggesting this would be a friendly meeting, not an ass-chewing.

"Here, look at this."

Reeder looked at the paper that had what the CIA had on Julia Amy Lucas. It was a series of name trees beginning in 1970. There were almost 10,000 women with the same name. When agency analysts narrowed it down to women between 50 and 60, the number dropped to under 5,000. Eliminate those who didn't live in California; the list was less than 2,000.

Nasher pulled the printout back. "This is where we are, and we are going to stop."

"Why?"

Nasher looked up to make sure the door to his office was closed. "The Cuban deal is off. The Cubans were very interested, and as of this morning, the Director said we're out. The Cubans have been notified."

"Again, why?"

"Because we got a better deal, and you have a new assignment."

Reeder's head snapped back in surprise. "What kind of deal?"

"This morning, the Director talked to his counterpart in the Mossad. On the phone was the woman known as *La Estrella Roja de la Muerte,* and we – the CIA and Mossad – agreed on an arrangement that gives us full access to what the woman knows. She has some CDs that the agency will find very useful, and she will be an asset we can task. I don't know the other details of the deal."

"What about the FBI?"

"They're going be told today in no uncertain terms to shut down their investigation. Apparently, the Attorney General approved and signed the deal, which gives her immunity and a blanket pardon for any past crimes in the U.S. So, here's where you come in. You, Mr. Harvey Reeder, will be on the debriefing team. We get three 4-hour sessions with her and possibly a fourth. Make them count. Once they are finished, Walt Bishop as the Deputy Director, Middle East Operations will be her control."

SATURDAY, JUNE 1ST, 2002, 9:56 A.M. LOCAL TIME, TEL AVIV

Friday afternoon and evening were spent in Halevy's conference room going back and forth over the wording in clauses with U.S. Department of Justice lawyers and CIA officers. It was after 10 p.m. Tel Aviv time when a marked-up draft was agreed upon and initialed by Janis, the CIA, and the Department of Justice. Advising Janis was an American who was a Federal prosecutor before he immigrated to Israel and now worked for the Israeli Ministry of Justice on extradition cases.

It had also been reviewed by Brett Carlson, her attorney in D.C., on a need-to-know basis. Before Carlson was read in, the Attorney General and CIA insisted he agreed to additional confidentiality requirements. He signed them along with an agreement that any discussions he had with Janis on this matter were covered by attorney client privilege.

A smooth copy would be ready for one final review on Monday before it was signed by the attorney general, couriered to Tel Aviv, and signed by Janis. Once the DOJ agreement was executed, Janis would sign her contract with Mossad.

When they went to bed around one a.m. on Saturday morning, Janis was exhausted and needed a break.

Janis' body clock still said around six that it was time to get up. She stepped out on the small balcony and was greeted by an overcast sky and light rain. With the temperature in the 20^0 Celsius (68^0 F) and perfect for a run along the beach. Then, as Aliyah suggested, they would go shopping.

The rain coming down was cool and had a slight taste of salt. For the first time in a long time, Janis felt totally at home and peaceful. The feeling was coming from deep inside and was something she never felt before. By the time she walked dripping wet into Aliyah's apartment, she was ready for what the future would bring.

SUNDAY, JUNE 2ND, 11:40 A.M. LOCAL TIME, TEL AVIV

The Ramat Aviv mall surprised Janis by its size. Other than the signs in Hebrew, it looked like the North Park Mall in Dallas and had a wing of stores offering designer clothes and accessories. The prices converted from shekels to dollars were much higher than in Dallas.

They just turned away from looking at displays at a store with designer – read expensive – shoes and handbags when Aliyah suddenly started running toward a young woman wearing a light blue abaya. In her hand was a small cylinder with a red button and she was only 10 feet away.

Aliyah screamed, "Everyone, get down!!!" as she grabbed the woman's wrist, as they slammed onto the gray and black terrazzo. She rolled on the woman's chest to pin the woman's arms with her knees. The cylinder with the red button connected to a wire lay out of reach on the terrazzo floor.

In the background, Janis heard yelling and screaming from those who suspected a bomb. Two police officers came running and spoke rapidly into their radios before they pinned the woman screaming invectives in Arabic to the floor.

Outside the mall, a man sitting in a car looked at the aluminum box in his lap. The three green lights showed he was transmitting, but nothing happened. He calmly cycled the on/off switch. The green lights said everything was in order, and he again pushed the button to set off the bomb. Nothing.

When he heard the police sirens, the man drove back to his apartment in Jaffa. His bosses in Beirut will know what happened when the Israeli press announces a suicide bombing was thwarted and a bomber arrested. Meanwhile, he needed to figure out what went wrong.

A member of the bomb squad disarmed the suicide bomber and helped her to her feet so the vest could be removed before she was taken away.

Janis stood off to the side, and once Aliyah finished giving her statement, they went back to her Jetta where Janis put both hands on Aliyah's cheeks. "That was very, very brave. How did you know it was a bomb?"

"By the way the woman acted. When she walked into the mall, she expected to die. The bomb had a radio-controlled detonator that didn't work for some reason, so she had to use the handheld one and maybe changed her mind."

"Why didn't you just do what I did and dive behind cover?"

"We were too close. I knew that if the bomb went off, I would be shredded by the ball bearings packed into the plastic explosive. It was either prevent her from setting it off or die. The choice was clear."

Aliyah kissed her friend sitting in the passenger seat. "Tomorrow, we'll know more. Right now, I need a drink and a good fucking. Later, when I have time to think about it, I'll be petrified!"

SATURDAY, JUNE 8TH, 2002, 7:26 P.M. LOCAL TIME, HAIFA

After dinner, the Skylar clan decided to go to a nearby park where the grandkids could play, and the adults could watch or join in the fun. Once there, Golda Skylar pulled her daughter aside. "I hear you are dating someone."

"*Eema,* who told you that?" Aliyah used the Hebrew word for mom and suspected the source was her older brother Elon. He was a senior vice president in First International Bank of Israel's investment bank.

"I have my sources. So, who is she?"

Aliyah assumed her mother already knew some details, but not all. "An American. Would you like to meet her?"

"You know the rules; you cannot bring your girlfriends to family gatherings where there are children."

"Maybe we could meet someplace for dinner the next time she is in Israel." Aliyah wanted it to be in a public place to minimize the chances of an explosion.

"No, if she is staying in a hotel, she'll enjoy a home-cooked dinner. You tell me the day, and I'll make something special."

Aliyah didn't want to tell her mother that Janis was staying with her. "*Eema*, promise me you will be nice."

"I will do my best."

CHAPTER 11

FIRST JOINT OPS

On the way to her parent's apartment, Janis watched the cool, calm, professional intelligence officer melt into a blob of nervous anxiety. As she listened to Aliyah explain "the rules," the primary one of which was no displays of affection, one would have thought they were going to her execution. Aliyah reminded Janis, "My *eema* doesn't speak much English. With her Yiddish, limited English, and your German, you should be able to have a conversation. If not, my dad or I will translate!"

Yuri Skylar was all smiles when he opened the door. The history professor and archeologist hugged his daughter. When introduced to Janis, he took her hand in both of his. "*Shalom.* Welcome to our house."

Aliyah went into the kitchen and brought her mother out. To Janis, who was good at reading people, Golda Skylar was tense, almost angry.

"*Shalom.* Welcome to Israel. I have wanted to meet you."

Janis believed Golda was sincere but could feel hostility from the woman. The questions from Golda came in bursts, one of which was how she made her money? Janis patiently explained that she was a security contractor who solved difficult problems and invested her fees well.

Janis changed the subject to Yuri's childhood in Ukraine and how he became an archeologist. She was fascinated by his work excavating and exploring Masada.

Around nine, Aliyah said she had an early meeting. When Janis shook hands with Golda, she got a curt nod and a cold stare.

On the way back to her apartment, Aliyah prattled continuously on a random group of topics. It was, Janis' thought, her way of letting the tension melt away.

MONDAY, JUNE 17TH, 2002, 10:27 A.M. LOCAL TIME, NABULUS, THE WEST BANK

The temperature of 28°C (85°F) was made hotter by the bright sun. Rather than providing some cooling, the light breeze blew dirt around in little swirls. There was enough grit in the air for Abd al Bari Ghulam to taste between his teeth. Glare from the bright sun required sunglasses and kept the blowing dust out of Ghulam's and Bakir Issawi's eyes. Issawi ran Hezbollah's bomb-making school near Beirut.

They were at a Fatah Al Aqsa Martyrs Brigade's factory that made suicide vests and car bombs. The Iranians facilitated the visit with a rival group to demonstrate a technology that Iraqi insurgents successfully used against the Americans. Hezbollah's Iranian contacts believed Fatah may have the solution to the failed attack on the Ramat Aviv Mall.

The workbench was hidden under a galvanized roof at the back of a large courtyard bordering a farmer's field. This location was chosen so that a blast wouldn't destroy the main building if there was an explosion.

On a large table, one man was using a wooden rolling pin to flatten bricks of SEMTEX into one-centimeter-thick rectangular sheets. Another man pressed steel balls in neat rows into the plastic explosive. The sheets, Ghulam was told, were sewn into the vest before the detonator was wired to the switch.

Now that they'd seen the vest, their guide Hassim showed them a disassembled mobile phone. The receiver was wired to a detonator. As soon as the phone began to ring, the detonator went off with a loud bang.

While Bakir made notes and a sketch, Ghulam smiled that from a cell phone, he could set off bombs all over the world.

None of the men in the building saw the Israeli Hermes 450 unmanned aerial vehicle orbiting at 3,000 meters (9,843 feet). As the Shin Bet internal security officer studied the incoming images, he decided to keep the facility under surveillance to see what developed before deciding on either a raid or an air strike.

TUESDAY, JUNE 18TH, 2002, 1:26 P.M. LOCAL TIME, SIDON, LEBANON,

Six stake trucks rumbled up to a small warehouse on the inland side of the coast road. One by one, they backed up to the open door, and Hezbollah soldiers used forklifts to unload the heavy crates and pallets stacked with olive-drab-colored boxes. If the canvas covers were removed, an observer could read the markings that would tell him that they contained fin assemblies, rocket motors, and warheads for 122mm Katyusha rockets.

The unloading went on for almost three hours. When the last truck was unloaded, Ghulam ordered the garage door closed and four Hezbollah soldiers stationed on the loading dock as guards.

A Lebanese Christian saw the trucks as he drove past on his motorbike. Two miles south on the coast highway, he stopped, turned around, and again drove past the warehouse. Each time, he used a small camera to take pictures. Back in his apartment, he transferred the images to his computer and emailed them to a friend in Tel Aviv.

WEDNESDAY, JUNE 19ᵀᴴ, 2002, 7:58 P.M. LOCAL TIME, TEL AVIV

Even though most people eat shakshuka – poached eggs on top of a spicy tomato sauce – for breakfast or lunch, Aliyah made it for dinner. She and Janis ate on the porch, and since Aliyah did the cooking, Janis did the dishes. She was cleaning the last item, a cast iron skillet with a paper towel, when Aliyah's phone rang.

"Hi *Eema!*"

Janis turned off the water and dried her hands when she saw Aliyah's face go from happy to surprise as she tried to control her anger. Forcing herself not to say something she'd regret later, Aliyah listened. When the call was over, she gently placed the phone in its cradle and steadied herself by putting both hands on the counter. Janis put her arms around her lover from behind and rested her chin on Aliyah's shoulder. "What was that about?"

"The short answer is that my mother is pissed that you are a *shiksa*. She said being a lesbian is bad enough but is furious I am dating a non-Jew."

"She has a right to be upset. Your mother is a very traditional woman. If you wish, I will move out, and we can have a platonic relationship."

Aliyah, I've been there. My parents disowned me right after I graduated college, and I have not spoken to them since, nor do I know if they are alive or dead. Until Karin, I didn't have a deep relationship with anyone, something I don't wish on anyone.

Aliyah turned around; her eyes glistened with defiance and determination. "No, you are not moving out. This is her problem, not mine. Hopefully, over time she will come around."

THURSDAY, JUNE 20ᵀᴴ, 2002, 2:36 P.M. LOCAL TIME, TEL AVIV

After lunch, Yitzhak Reznik asked Aliyah to bring Janis to a secure conference room. On the table was a thick file folder. "Janis, Aliyah, it is time to put you to work. Your first target is Hamid Kirdar. He collects 10 to 15 million Euros each month for Hezbollah from Arab-owned businesses in France, Belgium, and Germany. The cash is deposited in accounts controlled by Hezbollah. Before he went into the collection business, he was the brains behind attacks in Germany and France in the 80's and 90's. We gave what we know to the French and Germans who have done nothing."

Reznik pushed the file toward the two women. "Kirdar has subordinates who identify businesses and negotiate the fee. In America, it is called extortion. Sometimes Kirdar is brought in to close the deal or put the fear of God into the business owner. He brings the cash back to Berlin, where he deposits the money in local banks before transferring it to Hezbollah's account in Byblos Bank. Kirdar travels by train with one or two bodyguards, we presume they are armed. We have his address in the Berlin suburb of Neukölln, and our sources say he will be back in Berlin by the weekend. Your job is to kill him. How is up to you. This is a test to see how you work together. Let me know what travel documents you need as soon as possible."

Reznik left the pair in the room, and Janis pulled a pad of lined graph paper close from her purse and uncapped a Waterman fountain pen. The medium-width point made a scratching sound as she wrote.

Curious, Aliyah leaned over. "What are you writing?"

"Eight simple rules that I never violated, nor will we." Finished, Janis spun the pad around. "Read these and commit them to memory."

1. Leave no witnesses.
2. Never buy or take possession of the weapons we plan to use before we need them.
3. Always avoid face-to-face contact with anyone in the chain that tasks us.
4. Select only those assignments with manageable risks.
5. Always allow time for reconnaissance and study. Do NOT be rushed into a hit.
6. Assassinations of political figures are off-limits, as are some countries.

7. Always have a plan B, C, and, if needed, the outline of a plan D, for the hit and escape.
8. Always have at least two spare identities for each operation.

There was pain in her voice when Aliyah spoke. "We just violated rule number three by meeting with Reznik."

"Exactly. From this day forward, you and I must use the rules as a guide from when we begin planning a hit until we are safe at home. Any more violations, and we abort. Now you know how I stayed alive and out of jail."

From the file Reznik left, Janis parsed the documents and data on the target into five categories – history, habits, photographs, location, and logistics. When she finished, Janis had five pages of notes and three photos. "All we need now is a map of Berlin, documents, and tickets. Once we finish our reconnaissance, we'll ask for the weapons we need."

THURSDAY, JUNE 20TH, 2002, 6:18 P.M. LOCAL TIME, BERLIN,

Janis flew to London on British Airways and changed to an Air Berlin flight as Julie Hammond, an American from Los Angeles. Aliyah traveled as Riva Botvinnik from Botsani, Romania which was near the Ukrainian border. She flew in on a Lufthansa flight to Frankfurt with a connection on the same airline to the German capital. When Aliyah entered the baggage claim area, Janis was waiting. "Good trip?"

"Yes."

Neither said much in the cab ride to the hotel other than Aliyah noted the dreary rainy weather. "Do you know long it is going to rain?"

"No."

Once in the room, Janis allowed Aliyah to kiss her and gently pushed her away. "Mission first, fucking later."

Aliyah made a pouty face. In the meeting with Reznik, she watched Janis' transition instantly from a loving, caring partner into a ruthless, detail-oriented, cold-blooded killer.

Janis spread a street map of Berlin on the bed. "Kirdar's apartment is a few blocks from the Neukölln U-Bahn station. About fifteen thousand Palestinians live in the neighborhood, so this is a perfect place for him to hide. Let's go take a look."

Niqabs, hijabs, abayas, and burkas were not uncommon sights in Berlin. Their hotel was used by wealthy Arab businessmen, some dressed in traditional white dishdashas, others in suits. Women walking in niqabs, and hijabs were commonly seen in the five-star hotel.

Janis wore a conservative, black full-length abaya with a light gray embroidered band around the chest and the bottom. The neck portion of the gray niqab was pulled up over the bridge of her nose. Aliyah, who was wearing a dark blue full-length niqab did the same.

They entered another world when they emerged onto the street at the Neukölln U-Bahn station. Neither looked out of place. Al-amira style hijabs, like Aliyah's were the most common, followed by dark-colored burkas and abayas.

Walking toward the apartment complex in the light rain, they searched for surveillance cameras and found none. Inside Kirdar's apartment building, one could walk right to the elevator. Satisfied, Janis nudged Aliyah, and they crossed the street to a café where they enjoyed a cup of coffee and watched the entrance.

Aliyah watched as Janis's eyes took in everything. The American bent over and whispered softly in English, "Giggle after I tell you we are going to the leasing office."

The Israeli did as she was told. Janis put down the cup and nodded as a signal to leave.

The rain had stopped, which made the umbrellas unnecessary. Kirdar's apartment was in Building #2 of 4 in the development. Each apartment had a small porch that overlooked the park in the center of the complex, filling an entire block.

"Don't look up… Kirdar's apartment has more than one light turned on, which means either they are on timers, or someone is home. Knowing how expensive electricity is in this country, I'll bet someone is home."

Janis nudged Aliyah and pointed to the leasing office. "Let's go in there and ask about an apartment. I'll say I've been recently widowed, and you are my friend who just left the West Bank to come to live with me, which will explain why you don't speak German. I want floor plans and hope she can show us a two-bedroom apartment like Kirdar's. I'm going to keep the conversation in German. If she asks why I don't speak Arabic, I'll tell her I grew up in Mainz, where my father was a Gastarbeiter for Opel. That will also explain my Bavarian accent."

After a short discussion, Latifa Haddad, the complex's sales manager, made a phone call. She stood up. "Come, let me show you a two-bedroom flat on the sixth floor of this building. The tenant moved out last week, and I must apologize, the apartment has not yet been cleaned or any needed repairs made."

Aliyah scanned the lobby for security cameras as she followed Haddad and Janis. The tour of the empty apartment was detailed and thorough. Haddad pointed out that all the two-bedroom apartments had the same exact layout. From the living room window, Janis could see the lights in Kirdar's apartment were now out.

Haddad led them to the roof and showed them the gardens. Tenants paid an annual fee to use the three-by-five-meter boxes from April to October.

While the gardens were interesting and surprised Janis, using the roof as an observation post was out of the question. There was no way they could control who might come up.

Back in the office, Haddad gave Janis a folder with a complex diagram, floor plans for the one, two, and three-bedroom apartments, highlights from the contract, pricing, and a business card. She apologized that it was not in Arabic.

Back in their hotel room, the two women pulled off their damp garments and hung them in the bathroom. Pointing to the apartment floor plans on the bed, Janis said. "About six, we go back wearing different clothes and try to get to Kirdar's floor. Then, we have dessert at another café down the street, not the one we had coffee at, but another. I want to see Kirdar before we make our next move."

Aliyah nodded. She was about to help her lover commit murder which was both exciting and terrifying at the same time. Yet, Janis acted like she was going to a grocery store.

They were 20 meters from Kirdar's building carrying shopping bags with different Berlin department store logos when Kirdar walked out of the building. Staying about 50 feet behind, they followed him into a restaurant. During their dinner, the spoke softly in German, occasionally giggling when they made guesses about the sizes of the penises of the men in the restaurant.

After he finished his meal, the restaurant's owner gave Kirdar an envelope as he left. On the sidewalk, Kirdar stopped to light a cigarette. Janis put enough Euros on the table to cover their dinner and a nice tip and followed Aliyah out the door.

After following Kirdar to his apartment building and into the elevator, Janis put out her hand as if to say stop. She pushed the number six and turned to Aliyah, "Something's odd. This is way too easy."

When the elevator door opened on the sixth floor, Janis stuck her head out, saw no one, and stepped back in. She pushed four and the one for the ground floor. When the elevator stopped on Kirdar's floor, Janis again stuck her head out. She saw a man sitting in a chair at the end of the corridor in front of Kirdar's apartment door. He waved and said good evening in Arabic. Janis nodded and let the elevator go down.

Back on the street, they walked arm in arm toward the U-Bahn station. "This is an assassination, not a raid. I do not want to fight our way in. We go in quietly, kill Kirdar and leave. Later we go back to see if the man is still sitting there."

"Why can't we just kill the guard and then knock on the door?"

Janis turned to face Aliyah, "What if he gets a shot off? And, even if he doesn't, what will you do with the body or bodies? We get away because they don't find out we've killed Kirdar for hours. Remember, getting away and leaving no evidence is more important than the hit itself."

Aliyah nodded. She was learning that reading about how to do an assassination was a lot different than planning and executing one.

THE SAME DAY, 10:56 P.M. LOCAL TIME, BERLIN

Later that night, a different man sat in the chair outside Kirdar's door suggesting the bodyguards rotated shifts. The intelligence analyst in Aliyah wondered what else was the bodyguard and Kirdar protecting?

To Janis, the new bodyguard meant at least three men had to be killed, maybe more.

Experience told Janis there was no way of knowing who was in the apartment. They had to assume everyone inside was armed and had three choices. One, kill Kirdar and his bodyguard on the street. Janis rejected the idea immediately – too many potential witnesses.

Choice two was a sniper shot from another building. While doable, the approach required she that wait in a hide on a roof for Kirdar to appear. What if someone came up on the roof? And she would need armor-piercing bullets to reduce the deflection caused by the glass.

The riskiest was the best choice. – a direct assault that gave Janis and Aliyah the element of surprise. From the floorplans, they knew the layout of the apartment. Janis believed that surprise and fast, accurate shooting would carry the day.

As they got in the elevator, Janis looked at Aliyah. "Remember, once we enter, there's no hesitation. We kill everyone inside – men, women, and children. No witnesses. Are you ready?"

Aliyah nodded. Janis could tell her lover was scared, and so was she. Janis didn't like gunfights that took time, were loud, and the results were unpredictable.

Under their abayas both wore Kevlar vests front and back that would stop pistol, but not rifle rounds. They leaned on each other and giggled loudly as if they had too much to drink.

The man in the chair looked up and didn't pay attention until the pair was within three meters. He hissed. "Go away, women."

Aliyah staggered toward the guard and stumbled into his lap. Distracted, he did not see Janis getting ready to hit him with a blackjack she made from stockings and pebbles she bought at a pet store until it was too late. The blow crushed his temple and killed him.

While Aliyah looked for his wallet, Janis propped the man up in the chair. They used his belt looped under his armpits and around the back of the chair to keep him upright.

Aliyah rapped on the door to Kirdar's apartment. When the door started to open, Janis shoved it hard. Surprised, the man fell backward, pulling the door open.

Once inside, Janis fired one 9mm round from her suppressed Browning Hi-Power into the man's head. Another man, sitting on the couch, shouted a warning and reached for a weapon, and he didn't have a chance. Double taps from Janis' pistol shoved him back onto the couch, dying from a destroyed heart. She fired third to his head to make sure he was dead.

Kirdar heard the shouts and came out of a bedroom with a quizzical look. A single shot to the head ended his life.

Both women quickly searched the apartment and found no other occupants. Aliyah took the hard drive from Kirdar's computer and put a ledger she found in the apartment into her backpack. Two minutes after they approached the guard, Aliyah and Janis walked out of the building.

In the U-Bahn station, they went into two stalls in the ladies' room where Janis, still wearing latex gloves, fieldstripped the pistols and put the parts in four different plastic bags. The gloves went into a fifth bag. Each dropped a bag in a different trashcan at the Neukölln Station. Another two bags went into garbage cans at the Möckernbrüke Station, where they transferred from the Blue U-7 line to the Green U-1 line. After getting off at Uhlandstrasse, the last stop on the Green Line, the pair dropped the last bag into garbage cans on the street.

Both peeled off their clothes in their hotel room, and Aliyah filled out the form before the garments were stuffed in a hotel laundry bag. "Aliyah, I'll drop the bag off with the concierge and tell him we need them back by noon tomorrow. Then we are going to take a bath and make love."

MONDAY, JUNE 24ᵀᴴ, 2002, 8:06 P.M. LOCAL TIME, DALLAS

When Janis propped herself up in bed, she'd been back in her house for almost two days. Part of the escape plan was that Janis would fly back to the U.S. via a connection in London, and Aliyah would take a circuitous route back to Israel.

She opened *Pathways Through the Bible* by Mortimer Cohen, one of four books on her night table. And, as she underlined passages and made notes on the Composition notebook with five squares to an inch graph paper, Janis felt she was back in college.

Every night since Janis returned from her first trip to Israel, she read from one of the books. She started with Martin Goodman's *History of Judaism* and now was well into *Pathways*. As she read, Janis made notes and wrote down questions.

The other two books – *Essential Judaism* by George Robinson and *A History of the Jews* by Paul Johnson – were yet to be opened. The books were there so she could learn about Judaism which helped Janis understand what made Jews and Israelis tick. She'd joined a conversion class at Temple Shalom because she wanted to become one of them.

WEDNESDAY, JUNE 26TH, 2002, 7:56 A.M. LOCAL TIME, LANGLEY

For D.C., it was a typical late June day, with the temperature in the mid-80s with 65% humidity. The hot and sticky weather matched Janis' prickly mood as she dressed for her first CIA debriefing session.

A pantsuit and comfortable shoes were the order of the day. Some would call her mannish haircut with short hair on the left side and long on the right with a noticeable part in the middle very dyke ish. The longer hair fluttered in the light morning wind as she walked up the steps into what she told Aliyah was "the lion's den."

Janis had spent the 24th and morning of the 25th in Dallas preparing for the debriefing. Her TBM-850 touched down at Dulles International Airport just before sunset on June 25th, three hours, and 15 minutes after she pushed the single engine turbo prop's throttle forward.

A young man, she guessed was college-age, looked inside to see if anyone else was aboard before driving the golf cart with Janis and her bag to the terminal. After signing for the rental car and the fuel order, Janis checked into the Tyson's Corner Marriott to spend the night.

Before leaving the hotel, Janis called the number she was given and described what she was wearing. She was reminded by Betsy Quist not to check in or show any identification.

As she walked into the lobby of CIA headquarters, a middle-aged, slightly overweight woman with gray hair held out her hand. "Hi, I am Betsy Quist; you must be Ms. Elizabeth Harris. Mr. Bishop and the team is expecting you."

Elizabeth Harris was the cover name assigned to her by the CIA. Her real name appeared only on the legal documents she negotiated earlier. Once signed, they were filed under her cover name as if she was in the Federal government's witness protection program. Janis' original was with her lawyer in D.C., and a certified copy was at the Swiss law firm she had used in the past.

"I am. Nice to meet you." *I really don't want to do this.*

Betsy handed Janis a badge and pointed to the guard desk. "They need to inspect your purse, and do you have a cell phone?"

"Yes."

"I'll take it and give it back when you leave."

Janis suspected Betsy knew why she was at CIA headquarters.

Waiting in the room when Janis arrived was Bill Reeder. He held her hand longer than necessary, and Janis felt he was inspecting his next conquest. Based on where the video camera and microphone were set up, where she was to sit was obvious.

Next, to enter was Rachel Simms carrying her laptop and the CDs couriered to the CIA. Accompanying the CDs, was a formal letter documenting the transfer and warning the CIA that any attempt to copy the CDs would render them useless. Nonetheless, she suspected that the agency may try.

Simms introduced herself as a senior analyst. Jim Green, another analyst specializing in debriefing defectors, came in a minute later. He was followed by Walt Bishop, who explained the ground rules and left after saying he would be her control once the debriefing was finished. His departure set off alarm bells in Janis' brain.

Janis felt cold; it wasn't the air-conditioning. The set-up was clinical, and suspected Simms and Green would try to find inconsistencies in everything she said. Session two would be tomorrow, and session three was, as Bishop said, TBD – to be determined.

Reeder looked at Rachel Simms, who nodded, causing Janis to think, *let the inquisition begin.*

Simms spoke first. "Let's start with timing, Ms. Harris. When did you start pulling the material in the CDs together?"

"I can't give you the exact date, but it was sometime in 1982 after I decided to retire. We worked at on the project several days a week."

"Who's we?"

"My lover Karin Egger and me. She passed away on November 11th, 2001, from uterine cancer."

Rachel Simms wasn't expecting that answer. She pursed her lips. "I am so sorry." Rachel let a few seconds pass before she asked her next question. "What did you rely on to put the material together?"

"My detailed diary, documents given to me by the buyers of my services, the information I collected in preparation for executing the hit and newspaper accounts. We found some video clips from newscasts. Once the documents were scanned and the source information noted on the file, the paper copies were destroyed."

"Where is the diary?"

"Its location and contents are out of scope as per our agreement. It contains personal data that is not germane. The relevant intelligence is on the CDs." *Nice try, but you will not get my diary since it contains way too much sensitive information about my lovers and me. The last thing I need is a CIA shrink reading it.*

"Have you ever been married?"

"Ms. Simms, the answer to your question is again not within the scope of this debriefing. Revealing it would enable a bad actor to identify me if it were leaked. We're here to talk about what I did, how I did it, and who I believe hired me. If you continue along those lines, then we're done."

Simms made a note on her pad. "I'm sorry. My bad. Why did you retire?"

"Karen came into my life, and I had more than enough money to live comfortably."

"Why did you agree to come out of retirement?"

"The Israelis asked me. It is now clear that one day an FBI agent or someone from the *Dirección de Inteligencia* or CIA would arrive at my front door or Lord only knows who else. Trust me, I was astonished when Mossad came calling, and I believe I can help both the CIA and Mossad now that I am un-retired, so to speak."

"Why didn't you approach us directly?"

Janis laughed. "You've got to be kidding. The CIA often tosses people out into the cold based on the political winds coming from the White House. Trying to get someone in the CIA to believe who I was would have taken days, maybe weeks. Then there is the danger of leaks which still exists and frightens me. Just sitting here is a huge personal risk."

"So, you decided to work for Mossad?"

"Yes, and through them, the possibly the CIA. The agreement I signed gives you access to me, but only if I accept the assignment and the CIA agrees to pay my fee." Janis leaned forward. "Here's the difference between Mossad and the CIA. The Israeli intelligence community comes to work every day knowing that if they fail, the State of Israel goes up in smoke. They die, their families die, and the rest of the world will witness another Holocaust. Living on that precipice gives one a different perspective."

"We at the CIA feel the same way. We're all dedicated to protecting the United States."

"I do not doubt your dedication to our country, but the situation is not the same since failure doesn't have the same dire consequences. In the U.S., if a few operatives are killed, the CIA may receive bad publicity at a Congressional hearing, but life and the world continue. Israel doesn't have that luxury."

Rachel sat back in her chair. "You don't trust the CIA, do you?"

"Miss Simms, the short answer is no. Don't take it personally; I don't trust the politicians and politics that drive the CIA's policies and behavior." Janis paused for a few seconds. "Can we get back to what's on the CD?"

THURSDAY, JUNE 27TH, 2002, 2:46 A.M. LOCAL TIME, SIDON

The loudest sound was the hissing of the water as the two rubber-raiding craft known as Zodiacs that were made from Kevlar moved swiftly through the water. The muffled engines gurgled as the boats, each carrying 12 Israeli commandos from Unit 212 of the 89th Commando Brigade, stopped on the L-shaped spit of land just south of the Lebanese town.

Their target was the Hezbollah rocket factory in a warehouse just off the coast road. Rather than risk collateral damage caused by an air strike, the General Staff decided a raid would be better.

Captain Binjamin Badani looked over the scene through his night vision binoculars from behind the stone wall separating the beach and the road. Born in Yemen, his parents moved to Israel when he was two. A veteran of many raids, Badani's gut said something was wrong but couldn't put his finger on what.

Two hundred yards away, Ghulam was one of three Hezbollah leaders watching the Israelis haul their Zodiacs onto the beach and spread out along the wall. The commander of the Al-Musawi Corps men standing next to him spoke into the mike. "Let them get across the road before we open fire."

As soon as the last pair crossed, Ghulam heard the command, "Open fire."

Two Israeli soldiers fell, and their comrades dragged them behind the sea wall. Tracers from Hezbollah machine guns laced the night sky, and four more Israelis went down as they retreated to the sea wall. Badani's radioman contacted *I.N.S. Romach,* the *Sa'ar* 4.5-class missile boat that brought them to Lebanon. Its 76mm gun boomed, and shells with 6.3 kilograms of high explosive came out of the barrel at 80 rounds a minute.

Ghulam heard the distant boom but did not see the flash. The building next to him shook from an explosion. And then another before the machine gun fire from the Al-Musawi Corps men stopped. He turned to Qaid Aziz, the unit's commander, "Tell them to withdraw. We made our point, and no sense in losing any more men."

Aziz shook his head. "No, we have enough men to overwhelm the Israelis, and the Israeli ship will not risk killing their own men once we close with them."

"You idiot. You will get our men killed unnecessarily."

"My men are prepared to die."

No, you will get them all killed, just like I do.

The gap in the fire allowed a third Zodiac with 12 more commandos to land. Those who'd already landed were now on the beach side of the sea wall loading their dead and wounded comrades on the Zodiacs.

Badani scanned the buildings from where they were taking fire. *In less than two minutes, we'll be off this godforsaken beach.*

The shouts of 100 screaming Al-Musawi Corps soldiers streaming from two buildings gave Badani what he wanted – revenge for the ambush. Badani's radioman called the ship to adjust its aim, and the first four 76-millimeter shells exploded amid the enemy.

The Al-Musawi Corps soldiers kept running toward the Israelis. Some shot their AK-47s from the hip, and others knelt and fired even though the 76-millimeter shells were tearing them apart.

From behind the seawall, the disciplined Israelis fired back. Thirty Al-Musawi Corps soldiers made it across the road. Badani's Uzi clicked empty. No time to reload and he drew his Jericho 9mm pistol and shot the attacker closest to him. A second tried to stab him with a bayonet, and he shot him too.

Badani focused on the man in front of him and wasn't paying attention to the world around him. Fighting with his knife in one hand and his pistol in the other, he took on one Al-Musawi fighter after another. It was a world filled with thumps, bumps, grunts, screams, and single shots. He dispatched a fighter nearest to him with his knife, dumped out the empty magazine from his pistol, and reloaded when the world around him went quiet except for the wounded moaning.

The fight was over. Three more of his men were dead, and 10 more were wounded. Badani was the last Israeli to board a Zodiac. As he jumped on board, he looked over his shoulder at the beach littered with dead and dying members of the Al-Musawi Corps. They had been ambushed, and even though it was a victory of sorts, his unit had suffered way too many casualties.

THE SAME DAY, 8:46 A.M. LOCAL TIME, LANGLEY,

The camera and audio recorder were left in the secure conference room during the night. Before they left for the day, Rachel Simms cleaned the table and put the trash outside the room before locking the door.

Once they were notified that Janis was in the building, Simms, Green, and Reeder took their seats and waited for Janis. Bishop was still conspicuous by his absence.

Being suspicious, Janis refused coffee and put a bottle of water she had brought with her on the table. Like the day before, Simms asked most of the questions. Green said very little, and Reeder's brain alternated between admiring her skill as an assassin and wanting to see what she was like in bed. It was a shame she was a lesbian.

Simms asked how Janis selected weapons when there was a soft knock at the door. All conversation stopped while Reeder opened the door to find Bill Smith III standing next to Betsy Quist. If looks could kill, the glares from Rachel's, Janis' and Betsy's eyes would have fried Smith III's brain.

Reeder was not a happy camper whose voice reflected his anger. "Smith, what are you doing here?" He closed the door so Reeder could not see into the room, but those in the room could hear what was said.

"A birdie told me you were debriefing the woman known as *La Estrella Roja de la Muerte,* and the FBI would like to ask her some questions. After all, many of her murders took place on U.S. soil, where we have jurisdiction."

Janis forced herself to keep calm. The FBI was NOT supposed to be here. She was ready to walk out of the room. *Already there is a leak, just as she feared.*

Let's see how Reeder deals with this. Now with Smith III's help, an FBI artist could make a sketch of me.

Reeder said in his most conciliatory voice, "Bill, what is going on in this room is none of the FBI's business. This is a CIA-only meeting, and the FBI was not invited."

"That's bullshit. The FBI has jurisdiction and has a right to interview this woman."

Reeder tried lying. "Sorry, Bill, that is out of the question. Now, you can either leave voluntarily, or I can have our security people throw you out."

"May I give you the FBI's questions?"

"Sure."

"Will you ask them?"

"Only if we think they are appropriate.'"

Smith III flushed with anger as he shouted so Janis could hear, "We're not done with you."

"Oh yes, you are." Reeder grabbed Smith III on the bicep and stuck his head in the door to speak to the group. "Would you mind taking a break until I return?"

When Reeder returned, he smiled and nodded to Janis, obviously pleased with what he did. "I don't think Special Agent William Smith the Third will bother us again. By this afternoon, he may no longer be a special agent. I brought him to the director's office, who called the Attorney General, who called the head of the FBI. It was a very interesting conversation. I listened to the Attorney General make it clear to the FBI Director that neither the FBI nor any U.S. law enforcement agency was to pursue, investigate, question, or speak with Ms. Harris. That includes Mr. William Smith III. So, shall we continue?"

Janis looked at Reeder. "You have a leak. That is not acceptable!"

"Noted. The Attorney General knows who you are. Someone in his office may have talked to the FBI. There's only seven people in this building who know you are here – the Director, Greg Nasher, Walt Bishop, Rachel Simms, Jim Green, Betsy Quist, and me. They will regret it if any of them spoke to the FBI."

"Do you think the FBI will listen?"

"I hope so. If the world learns the bureau violated an immunity deal, there will be hell to pay. Eventually, many people with calmer heads within the FBI will realize you saved the taxpayers the cost of investigations, trials, appeals, and keeping the bad guys in jail."

Janis' stomach was turning when Rachel asked her next question. *The leak must be plugged. Who is he or she, and who is going to do it?*

CHAPTER 12

FIRST FAILURES

TUESDAY, JULY 2ND, 2002, 5:34 P.M. LOCAL TIME, TEL AVIV

Getting into Israel was more straightforward than Ghulam thought. Rather than try to cross from the West Bank, he flew in from Istanbul on a Turkish Airlines flight. From Ben Gurion, he took a cab to his hotel before taking a walk to see if he was under surveillance. He wasn't, and he called his contact in Israel from a pay phone in the hotel's lobby. A car arrived shortly, and Ghulam sat in the front passenger seat with a small aluminum box with two toggle switches and red and green lights.

The driver wove through Tel Aviv, making random turns to ensure they were not tailed before stopping in front of an apartment building. Ghulam nodded to the driver of a well-used, dark gray Toyota Corolla. The driver pulled ahead, and the two cars drove toward the Mediterranean.

The bomb in the Toyota was in two parts. Ten kilos of SEMTEX were in a suitcase on the back seat, along with the wiring to the detonator. In the trunk, four 20-liter bottles of propane were lashed together and connected to a switch on the center console between the driver's and passenger's seats.

Ghulam's driver followed 200 meters behind the Corolla that was following a pre-planned route to the Tel Aviv Hilton. Ghulam hoped the bomb would bring down the front side of the hotel. If the driver couldn't or didn't do his job, he would set off the bomb.

Traffic on Arlozorov Street was heavier than usual. Just before crossing Weizmann Street, the car in front of the bomber stopped abruptly at a traffic light. The bomber slammed on his brakes, and the car behind plowed into the Toyota's trunk, shoving the Corolla into the Renault that stopped short. Steam rose from the Toyota's crumpled hood, and the driver smelled the coolant leaking from the Toyota's radiator. Knowing that the police would arrive shortly, the driver set off the bomb.

The concussion rocked Ghulam's car, and he could see debris flying that landed on the street and on their car. Shattered glass from building windows now littered the sidewalks. A police officer appeared from nowhere and banged on the hood to get the attention of Ghulam's driver. The policeman wanted him to turn on Helsinki Street. Later, he'd learn how many were killed and injured on the evening news.

Ghulam believed the mission was a success – Hezbollah assembled a large bomb in Israel proper that worked as designed. Only a random accident prevented the driver from getting to his target, and he would try again.

THURSDAY, JULY 11TH, 2002, 3:26 P.M. LOCAL TIME, SPA, BELGIUM

The Ardennes are known for its thick forests, rugged terrain, and mineral-rich spas. One of its treasures is the Manoir de Lébioles, a luxury hotel a few kilometers outside Spa. When it was finished in 1910, some called Georges Neyt's new villa the "small Versailles of the Ardennes." Others thought the manicured grounds and stone buildings were the extravagant home of a wealthy nobleman. In 1999, new owners turned the complex into a luxury hotel.

Janis had stayed at the five-star hotel before when she and Karin came to watch the Belgian Grand Prix. She liked the food, the attentive staff, and its remote location.

As a vintage race car owner, driver, and fan, Janis couldn't resist taking Aliyah to the historic Spa-Francorchamps track, where races had been run since the 1920s. As they drove around the portion of the track open to the public, Janis told Aliyah about Dan Gurney who won the 1967 Belgian Gran Prix in a car designed and built in the United States.

The Ardennes is also famous for the Battle of the Bulge, one of the biggest land battles of World War II. On day two, the couple visited the Malmedy Memorial near where Johannes Peiper – a German SS Officer – ordered his men to shoot American prisoners. Eighty-four GIs were machine-gunned to death.

A cryptic message left on June 10th at the Manoir de Lébioles front desk said their meeting was set for "noon on the eleventh." Translation – their targets – Waadi Jalal and Abdul Chakroun – would arrive around noon.

The message prompted an evening trip to the Brussels train station. While Aliyah waited in the car, Janis went to the kiosk where people stored luggage. She showed her passport, and the man looked at a ledger before he gave her a key. She paid the storage fee and left a 10 Euro note as a tip.

On the way to the locker, Janis wiped the key with a pad soaked in alcohol. With the locker open, she stuck her hands inside so no one would see her pull on a pair of latex gloves unless they were paying close attention.

Out came a duffel bag, and as she reset the key, she wiped it again with the alcohol-soaked cloth. The bag went into the trunk of their rental car, and Janis ran a small scanner around the top and sides of the bag to ensure there were no tracking devices installed.

Driving toward Spa, Janis exited E40 at Rommerson and turned off so she could drive to a spot where she could stop on the side of the road. After opening the trunk, she unzipped the bag and made a cursory inspection of the weapons. Satisfied that they were what she requested, Janis returned to the driver's seat and Aliyah handed her lover a bottle of water. "Paranoia?"

"Let's put it this way. In this business, outside of you, I don't trust anyone. That is why I don't take missions planned by someone else – too much risk."

The weapons were taken to their room and inspected again before being put back in the bag. They, along with Aliyah and Janis, spent the night in their hotel room.

After feasting on the breakfast buffet the next morning, the pair stopped in at a bakery and a small grocer in Malmedy where they bought bread and a small grocery store to buy salami, ham, cheese, and a six-pack of bottled water. It all went into their packs.

Janis drove through Spa to the Route de Berizenne. Just after the road made a 90-degree turn to the east, Janis found a place to pull safely off the road. A note in both French and English was left on the dash saying they would be back in the afternoon after hiking in the woods.

A kilometer hike brought them to where they could see a two-story brick house and a barn. Their intelligence said Hezbollah recruits from France and Belgium were brought here to wait while their travel arrangements and documents were prepared for their trip to the Al-Musawi training camp.

Staying well back in the trees but still able to see the building, Janis assembled the rifle, known in the U.S. Marine Corps as the M25 Sniper System. The rifle was a specially modified M-14 with a match-grade barrel, glass bedded stock, special gas piston, bipod, and a large suppressor. The M25 came with a Bausch & Lamb 10 power scope and a card showing how the rifle performed at 100-yard intervals up to 900 yards. Her 20-round magazines were loaded with Cartridge, Caliber 7.62mm 175 grain M316 Mod 0 ammunition specially made for sniping.

While Janis was getting ready, Aliyah focused a 40-power spotting scope on the house's front door. Two hours passed, and they saw nothing – no people, no van, no Chakroun or Jalal.

Waiting was part of the job. Sometimes the target showed up right away; sometimes, it did not. Janis didn't like leaving their car, even though it was parked legally and well off the road. The rental VW was, as a practical matter, their only way out other than walking. Janis felt exposed.

The photographs given to them showed the gravel driveway widened into a large parking area in front of the house. Janis estimated the distance from where their photos showed the van parked to the house's front door was 30 yards. In the time needed to run from the car to the front door, Janis was confident she could fire four accurate shots with the semi-automatic M25. At just over 500 yards, the driveway was well within the range of her ammunition.

Janis slowly scanned the area through her scope. First, she studied the tree line on the other side of the driveway, then the field in front of them, and last, the house. There was a window open on the second floor of the house in which she saw a white curtain flutter.

A glint at the base of a tree caught Janis's eye. "Aliyah, we have company." Janis described the location, and Aliyah slowly moved her 40-power scope, whose greater magnification came with a much smaller field of view.

"Shit. You're right."

"Do you think he's spotted us?"

"I don't know." Janis tugged on the section of pantyhose that she duct-taped to the front of the rifle scope to prevent glint, and Aliyah had done the same to the spotting scope.

"Let's go on the assumption he has. We're going to crawl back 15 yards, move to the right about 30 yards and set up farther back in the woods. My gut tells me there may be a second shooter on the second floor set back from the window and hidden in the shadow."

Janis kept her rifle pointed at the sniper in the trees while Aliyah crawled into a new position between two large trees. Janis followed, and several anxious minutes later, Janis re-found the sniper in the woods.

Aliyah whispered. "Janis, I am pretty sure there is another shooter set up well back from the window behind a dark cloth hanging from the ceiling. I saw the barrel of his rifle move, and I don't think it is suppressed like the one in the woods."

"We've spotted two snipers, and I wonder how many more there are?" Janis paused as she processed what they were facing. "This smells like a trap. Sweep the field and see if men are hiding in the grass. If Chakroun or Jalal show up, we have a decision to make."

"What do you want to do?"

"Not sure yet. Let's see if there are any more shooters. This tells me Hezbollah was tipped off."

After searching the grass for 10 minutes, Aliyah whispered. I don't see anyone in the grass."

"O.K., here's the plan. If the targets show up, I take out Jalal and Chakroun, then go after the snipers. We have the advantage in that our rifle is suppressed, and they won't see the flash. As soon as I start shooting, you slide back, pack up the scope and get ready to cover our retreat. When I finish, we'll leapfrog back to the car. Hopefully, we won't need to see how good you are with the M16A3."

The crunching sound of tires crunching on gravel caused both women to swing their glasses to where a car would emerge from the trees. A black Volkswagen Eurovan stopped where Janis suspected it might.

Based on the waving of the grass, Aliyah called out the wind, and Janis adjusted the scope and pointed her rifle to the front of the van where she would pick up the targets. "They're getting out of the van."

"It's a trap. Neither are Jalal and Chakroun. Get ready to leave."

Janis shifted her aim point to where the sniper in the woods was in time to see a puff of smoke rise from the barrel of his rifle. The bullet smacked into the tree near their original position. She exhaled and made sure her body was perfectly motionless as her right forefinger took up the slack on the trigger. The M25 shoved her shoulder back. Through the scope, she saw a rifle fly up as her target was knocked backward by the impact of the 173-grain bullet.

Neither needed a scope to see the muzzle flash from the house's second story. The bullet smacked into the tree next to where they had been. Janis swung the M25 on the bipod so she could shoot at the house and saw another flash. The bullet thudded into the ground five feet from Aliyah as Janis squeezed the trigger.

A second later, she saw the barrel tilt upward. "Time to go."

The two men from the van pointed in their direction, yelling to a dozen men carrying AK-47s that were spilling out of the van and the house. They split up, half ran down the road, and half went wide around the field.

Janis knelt behind a large pine tree. "I'm going to slow them up, then we'll leapfrog. Get moving!"

She dropped one man in the field and then pivoted to fire at the two men closest to her on the road. Both went down. Trees partially blocked her view of the field, but when she saw a man with an AK-47, a single shot to the chest sent him sprawling.

As Janis ran crouched over and zigzagging through the trees, bullets smacked into the tree trunks and kicked up dirt where she'd been. After a few hundred yards, it was clear that they were not being pursued. At the edge of the woods, Janis put a hand on Aliyah's shoulder and made a patting motion, as if to say, stop and get down.

Whispering, Janis said, "We just escaped from a well-planned ambush and we're not out of the woods yet." She pointed to their car and the grassy area between the woods and the road. "Look for anything out of the ordinary. They may have stationed a couple of shooters out in the field to pick us off if we escaped the trap back at the house.

Aliyah took the 10 X 50 binoculars from her pack and began searching. "What am I looking for?"

"Anything unusual or that doesn't quite fit, such as a poorly prepared hide. Then I'll look at it with the rifle scope." Janis lowered herself to a prone position and rested the bipod on the soft earth. She popped out the magazine, which only had nine rounds left, and replaced it with a full one with 20.

"Janis, there's what looks like a stump of a tree about five hundred yards from us at 11 o'clock and about ten yards from the tree line. An off-color green mound doesn't match the grass, but I can't make out much detail."

It took a few seconds for Janis to find the tree stump, and she adjusted the scope before slowly moving the rifle to find the off-color mound. "It's a hide of some sort. I see a suppressor on a rifle barrel. I will wake them up with a shot into the tree stump."

Unless you were within 50 feet and listening carefully, the average passerby would not hear the soft crack from the suppressed M25. Both women, Aliyah through the binoculars and Janis through the rifle scope saw the wood fly from the impact of the 173-grain MK 316 MOD 0 bullet.

Whoever was in the hide was surprised by the bullet impact. Janis saw a man toss off the netting as he changed positions to reorient his rifle. It was a fatal mistake. Before he could point his rifle in Janis' direction, the second round was on the way. It hit a little off her point of aim. Instead of entering the man's head at the bridge of his nose, it entered his mouth and blew off the back of his head.

A second man tried to grab the rifle but exposed himself, and he, too paid for his life with two rounds into his chest.

Janis waited a few seconds to ensure there wasn't a third man in the hide before saying to Aliyah. "Go to the car, but from about a hundred yards away, unlock it. If it doesn't explode, then walk around it to see if any of the tell-tales we left were missing. Do not touch the car until I get there."

Janis jogged over to the hide where she found a position stocked with food and ammunition for a Dragunov SVD-63 sniper rifle. Both men were dead. She covered them with the netting and walked toward the car.

At the Jetta, Aliyah pointed to the two small slips of paper on the ground. She could see a mark where someone slipped in a shaft to unlock the door. "Aliyah, back off about a hundred feet. I am going to slowly open the driver's door. If the car doesn't blow up, I will pop the hood. My guess is the bomb is either under the driver's seat or in the engine compartment. If it is not there, then it is under the car."

Aliyah nodded grimly and watched as Janis opened the car door and then slowly felt around for a bomb. Finding none, she pulled the latch to open the engine compartment. The clunk was the loudest sound on the empty road.

Janis felt for a wire around the hood. Finding none, she slowly lifted it and nestled in a space near the battery was a brick of SEMTEX. Taped to it was a cell phone. Two wires were clipped using alligator clips to the battery to provide power.

"Aliyah, go up to the hide and see if you can find a cell phone. If you can, bring it here."

While she was gone, Janis took her multi-tool from her backpack and disassembled the rifles, which went back into the trunk of the Jetta. The time it took for Aliyah to jog to the hide, find the phone, and then return gave her time to study the bomb. She wondered if she turned off the phone, would it explode?

Backing away from the car, Janis asked Aliyah to turn off the cell phone she found. No explosion.

The next step – turn off the phone connected to the bomb. Again, no bang, and both women breathed a sigh of relief. Janis used the multi-tool to cut one and the other wire to the car's battery. Her rationale was that she didn't want to risk making a spark by removing the alligator clips.

With a few more deep breaths to calm herself, Janis carefully slid the detonator out of the plastic explosive. Once it was out, she lifted the bomb out of the engine compartment and handed it to Aliyah.

"You can't take this back with you on an airplane, so I think you need to take this to the Israeli embassy and give it to the local Mossad agents. I am sure there is something they can glean from this."

Laughing, Aliyah said, "Sure, I'll walk into the embassy and show my passport and Mossad ID. What do I say? Hi, I'm Aliyah Skylar from Mossad headquarters here in Belgium on a secret mission I can't discuss with you. Hezbollah planted this bomb in my rental car, and you should examine it!"

"Get in the car. You have half an hour before we get back to the hotel to figure out what to do. We're checking out, and you're getting on the next plane to Israel, and I'm going back to the states."

Once they were on the road, Janis didn't take her eyes off the road as she drove as fast as it was safe. "Aliyah, they knew about when we were coming, which is not cool. This means they had inside intel on the operation. So, who within the Mossad knew the details of the op?"

"Reznik, me, and three members of my team. Halevy knew only that we were authorized to make the hit. We had intel from other parts of the Israeli intelligence community and from the CIA. Hence, the agency knew we were interested in Jalal and Chakroun, but nothing more."

"Are you sure there was no one else?"

"No. But I know where to start."

"Good. You're going back to Israel to find the traitor. I'm going to London and back to the U.S. for a week or so to give you time to sort things out in Tel Aviv. Then, I'll rattle Walt Bishop's cage. If there is a leak, Mossad must find the bastard before we take on another assignment."

FRIDAY, JULY 12TH, 2002, 1:52 P.M. LOCAL TIME, LONDON, U.K.

After an early morning flight from Brussels to London, Janis waited in the Admiral's Club for American Flight 79, leaving at 2:00 p.m. London time. Boarding was going slower than usual. She had the last aisle seat – 11L – in the business class section and decided to make a potty stop before the plane pushed back from the gate. Coming out of the lavatory, she locked eyes with a man for a second. Janis was sure she had seen him before but couldn't remember where.

As Janis walked back to her seat behind him, her mind raced as she processed the face. When she sat down, she was convinced that the man was Abd al-Bari Ghulam. She left a short message on Aliyah's phone and was dialing Walt Bishop when the flight attendants insisted that passengers shut off their phones and computers. The call to Bishop would have to wait.

Frustrated, Janis reconciled herself to sitting on an airplane with one of Hezbollah's top leaders for the next nine hours. She rationalized that none of the Islamic terrorist organizations would want to kill one of Hezbollah's top men unless they thought he was a traitor.

On the hike from the jet bridge to immigration and customs, Janis dialed the number she was given by Walt Bishop. He said it would connect her to him no matter where she or he was.

The phone rang once, and a woman answered. Janis gave the code word, and the phone rang twice before Bishop answered.

"This is Elizabeth Harris."

"Hi, what's so urgent?"

"Abd al-Bari Ghulam was on American Flight 79 from London Heathrow to Dallas. I don't know what name he is using, but I am sure it was him."

"Who is he?"

They were on an open line, so she had to talk around the issue. "My friends think he was responsible for the bad events in Paris and Los Angeles."

"Interesting."

"If I were you, I'd want to know why he is in the U.S."

"I'll get people moving on it. Do you know what seat he was in?"

"No, but he was one of the last coach passengers to board. He was in coach, and I was in business. There was no reason for me to walk back into coach, and I didn't want to tip him off."

SATURDAY, JULY 13ᵀᴴ, 2002, 9:46 A.M. LOCAL TIME, PIMA COUNTY, ARIZONA

For men used to living in the dry arid countries of the Middle East, al-Musawi fighters thought following Angel Martinez through the desert of the American Southwest would be easy. Martinez was an experienced coyote who knew how to survive in the desert. For the eight mean he was leading, the trek wasn't easy. They'd stopped in a stand of trees within 100 feet of the road, the eight men were tired, dirty, out of food, hungry, thirsty, and out of water.

When he was contacted by a man who spoke Spanish with a strange accent, Angel said his fee was $20,000 for the 20-mile hike which had to be in his account before they left Mexico. The buyer came highly recommended, but Angle was adamant, no money, no guide.

Martinez was adamant when he said each man, regardless of the cargo he carried, should bring three liters of water and food for three days that didn't need cooking. He would not allow fires at night, and either the men kept up or would be left behind. Temperatures of 110⁰F during the day dictated walking at night and sleeping during the day.

Angel didn't care or want to know what the strange-looking and smelling men carried in their own packs. It was their business, not his.

With the money in his bank account, Angel gave the caller a mile marker south of Sasbe, Mexico. The eight men and the man with the strange Spanish accent were exactly where he told them to be. None saw him emerge from the dry brush and didn't know he had watched them for the past hour.

After the stranger drove off, Angel turned to the eight men and said, "Vamanos. Let's go." Angel didn't know whether they spoke Spanish or English. They would walk for two hours, stop for 15 minutes, and repeat the process four times each night. Each morning, they'd find shade, sleep, eat and, just before dark, start again.

Before they started hiking on the third night, Angel walked out of hearing distance from the group and called the man with the strange accent. The call confirmed the meeting location five miles west of Arivaca, Arizona. The sun was just peaking over the horizon when Angel pointed to a stand of trees from the road called West Pusch Street.

Right on schedule, a dusty Chevrolet passenger van stopped on the road. Confident that the Border Patrol was not nearby, Angel pointed to the van. The leader of the group turned around and looked for Angel. By then, the coyote had disappeared back into the brush.

When he stopped the van, Abd al-Bari Ghulam left the engine running and had the air conditioning on the Econoline van going full blast. After they put their packs in the back, he handed each one a cool bottle of water from a cooler and said, "Welcome to America."

Other than for gas, food, or bathroom breaks, Ghulam didn't stop until they pulled into the garage at a safe house in a city between Dallas and Fort Worth called Irving. They'd covered the 908 miles in 14 hours.

MONDAY, JULY 15TH, 2002, 8:00 A.M. LOCAL TIME, TEL AVIV

As soon as Aliyah walked into Mossad's headquarters, two armed guards escorted her to Noah Dohan's office, the agency's head of internal security. Her briefcase and purse were taken, and as she was patted down, Aliyah wondered if her superiors thought she was a traitor. She consoled herself by rationalizing that if they did, she'd be in an interrogation room, not an office.

A grim-faced Dohan pointed to a chair in front of the desk, and another man who didn't introduce himself sat off to one side. When she was seated, Dohan pushed the start button on a small recorder, noting the time and date, why the recording was being made, and who was in the room. That's when Aliyah learned that the second man was Ezra Elbaz from Dohan's staff.

The palm-sized recorder was placed in front of Aliyah. "Everyone associated with this operation is under suspicion. So, Aliyah, you must tell us every detail. Start with a list of everyone you think might know about this operation and what they were told."

Aliyah nodded her head. While she had nothing to fear, Mossad did not like failure or traitors. Mistakes happen during a mission and are a fact of life, but traitors are another story. It was Dohan job to find them, and internal rumors said many never made it to trial.

The list started with the arrangements Janis, and she made for travel and weapons and with whom they spoke. Those who knew the names of the targets came down to Halevy, who spoke to the prime minister and minister of justice privately with no staff listening to the call to receive permission. Reznik, who provided the official tasking, and Eitan Kohan, who provided the analysis on the targets as one of the agency's experts on Hezbollah.

After her 'interview,' Aliyah found a note on her desk asking her to go to Reznik's office, where his assistant told her to go right in. Sitting at the small table was Efraim Halevy. Aliyah, seeing the head of the Mossad, stopped. "I'm sorry… I didn't mean to interrupt."

A grim-faced Reznik looked at her. "Come in. We were at a stopping point, and I was told your debriefing session went well."

"I hope so. I have nothing to hide."

"We expected that. I want you to take some time off while we investigate. You look like you could use it."

"Sir, I have work to do."

Reznik's voice hardened. "I know you do, but until we find this bastard, everything on your desk can wait. We don't want Janis, or you compromised. So, go someplace. Just let my administrative assistant know where you are."

"May I leave the country?"

"Where are you thinking about going?"

"The U.S."

"To see Janis?"

Am I that transparent? I know he knows we are sleeping together. "Yes, if she doesn't have other plans."

"Good. Go, we can notify both of you with one phone call. Let us do our job."

Mitsuyan!

TUESDAY, JULY 16TH, 2002, 2:46 P.M. LOCAL TIME, LANGLEY

Walt Bishop sat in his office fuming. He didn't know whether to throw his phone against the wall, scream, or do something more destructive. Instead of calling the DFW office with Ghulam's description and detaining him, Al Benjamin, the Immigration and Naturalization Service agent in Dallas, waited until he received the manifest from American Airlines. By then, all the passengers had left the immigration area.

Luckily, an alert customs agent flagged several passengers and photographed them while they were at his kiosk. One was a man with an Egyptian passport named Ekram Farooq.

Benjamin sent the Immigration Officer a Mossad photo of Abd al-Bari Ghulam. The officer called back within minutes, saying Farooq was Ghulam and his destination was Tucson.

Benjamin didn't check with American to see if Farooq boarded the flight or made a hotel or rental car company reservation in Tucson since Bishop's call was an information request. There was no outstanding warrant for Ghulam/Farooq's arrest, nor was he listed in their database as a person of interest. Hence, there was no reason to detain Farooq for an interview.

Bishop wanted to yell into the phone, "You moron. He IS a person of interest, and that's why we are asking about him!" Instead, Bishop said thank you politely and slammed down the phone when he heard a dial tone.

This was the second call of the day that had Bishop shaking his head in disbelief. Earlier, he sent the FBI the same data. Smith III returned his call now that he was back after his 30-day suspension and assigned to the FBI's office conducting background investigations on immigrants with a suspicious history. He said the FBI would only act if the tip came from a vetted FBI source.

Bishop's argument that war crime trials were all based on evidence developed outside the U.S. flew over Smith III's head. He told Smith III that if Ghulam launched another attack on U.S. soil, the FBI would be in the crosshairs when the bureaucratic finger-pointing began.

The CIA officer now had three 'get-out-of-jail-free' cards. One was the documents Reznik sent to the FBI and CIA through official channels. Therefore, the FBI had been officially notified that Ghulam should be apprehended. The second was his notes from his call with Ms. Harris. The third were his notes from his call with Smith III.

Right after Bishop joined the agency, he was sent to Lebanon to help pick up the pieces after the bombings of the Embassy, the Marine barracks, and the Embassy annex. They documented Iran's involvement in creating Hezbollah and was in Lebanon when Lieutenant Colonel William Buckley was kidnapped, tortured, and killed by Hezbollah. Bishop spoke Arabic and Farsi fluently and maintained contact with Iranian intelligence officers he met unofficially in Lebanon. He was considered one of the agency's experts on Iran and its links with Hezbollah.

What also pissed Bishop off was that Ghulam's appearance in the U.S. violated another unofficial and clandestine agreement he made with his contacts in Tehran. Under it, Hezbollah agreed not to conduct any more attacks in the U.S. or allow its operatives to enter the country. In exchange, Bishop agreed to feed them information for a fee.

THURSDAY, JULY 18TH, 2002, 12:07 P.M. LOCAL TIME, DALLAS

Aliyah called Janis as soon as she returned to her apartment. Janis said a ticket for a business class seat will be waiting for Aliyah when she arrives at Ben Gurion Airport. As promised, Janis was waiting at Newark when a smiling Aliyah walked outside immigration, towing a small bag just after 6:30 in the morning

Signature Flight, where Janis parked her TBM the night before, was ready for the four-hour flight to Dallas Love Field. When Janis flared the TBM over the numbers of Runway 13R, the single-engine turboprop settled on the concrete with a gentle thump, and the clock on the instrument panel said it was just after noon. By one-thirty, the women were in bed making love.

Aliyah slept most of the afternoon, trying to recover from the jet lag while Janis puttered around her race cars. After Aliyah woke, both were standing chest-deep in Janis' pool when Aliyah looked at her lover. "How do you deal with the killing?"

"Over time, I learned to treat the killing like a meeting in an office; only the players, the target, and I aren't in the same room. I focus on the act and escaping. Nothing else matters. Once I am home safe, I do a mental dump into my diary, which is a cathartic, cleansing action."

"That's cold-blooded."

"Maybe, but the process kept me sane." Janis took a deep breath. "I don't have a guilty conscience since I was killing people society called bad. Like the Nazi war criminals I took out, many were individuals a government, for whatever reason or reasons, decided not to prosecute."

Janis took a long swig from the coffee cup on the brick floating around the pool and put her arms on Aliyah's shoulders. "Look, let me give you some advice. Dwelling on the killing will eat you up psychologically. Remember, you are a soldier in a war. Don't feel guilty when the bad guys go home in a body bag. It is much better than your friends dying."

Janis saw the pained look on Aliyah's face, and the tears that followed told her that she had struck a sensitive chord. Janis pulled Aliyah into her arms and caressed the back of her neck. "You're O.K. What you are feeling is normal."

Aliyah's voice was hoarse as she whispered. "Killing people goes against everything I was taught growing up."

"Me too. Thou shalt not kill is one of the Ten Commandments. However, Israel is at war with these terrorists. It is either kill or be killed, and I prefer to do the killing."

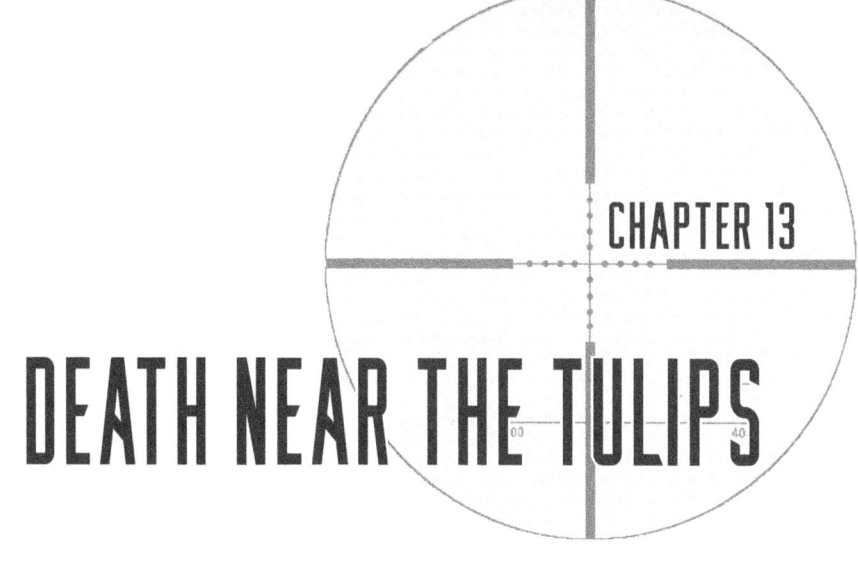

CHAPTER 13

DEATH NEAR THE TULIPS

A s he usually did, the captain of the Arkia Airlines Boeing 757 was hand-flying the airplane as the gear thumped into the wheel wells and the flaps retracted into the trailing edge of the wing. He'd trimmed the jet to climb at 220 knots as he flew the runway heading until he was cleared to turn left to a heading of 085^0 to intercept the 106^0 radial from the Schiphol VOR. The captain followed the Arnem 1G Standard Instrument Departure from Schiphol International Airport. Suddenly, the cockpit filled with the warbling tone from the airplane's missile warning system filled the cockpit.

Both men, reservists in the Israeli Air Force, looked at each in surprise and then at the six-inch diameter screen on the instrument panel. Two small circles told them they were being targeted by two surface-to-air missiles. When the missiles were launched, the 767 had climbed past 300 meters (~1,000 feet).

In the cabin, the 225 passengers had no idea the airplane was in mortal danger. The co-pilot released his shoulder harness so he could crane his head around and spot the missile trails, but the wing blocked his view.

Software in the directional infrared countermeasures system (DIRCM) identified the two missiles as SA-14s, known by their NATO code name – Gremlin. The system detected the missiles milliseconds after launch and automatically began tracking them. Sensors fed the software that aimed the system's mirrors and lasers on the closest Gremlin.

The main improvement of the SA-14 over the SA-7 Grail was that its seeker could better differentiate between a decoy and an airplane. Against a system carried by the Arkia Airlines 757, the upgrade didn't matter.

The pulses of high-intensity light from the 767 confused the missile's guidance system causing the seeker to no longer "see" the exhaust plumes from the 767's engines. Confused, the SA-14 flew off into space. The second missile also went stupid after being confused by the 757's DIRCM system. None of the passengers saw the white plumes passing well behind the climbing airliner.

On the boundary road, Sergeant Erik Haas and Corporal Henrik van der Boor of the Dutch Royal Military Constabulary detachment at Schiphol saw the missiles streak skyward. Haas floored the Volkswagen's gas pedal and turned toward where the missile's smoke trail from the ground rose. De Boor radioed their command center to report what they witnessed and call for reinforcements.

Haas skidded the silver-blue Volkswagen to a stop blocking the road at the edge of a field where they saw two men running to a white Peugeot. One stopped and aimed an AK-47 at the Volkswagen. Bullets stitched a line of holes on the VW's white-striped hood. Haas heard bullets pinging off the engine block and steam hissing from the radiator.

He popped up over the hood and fired half a 30-round magazine from his H&K MP-5 at the front of the Peugeot. The French-made car lurched to a stop with anti-freeze spewing out of the radiator.

Both the occupants of the Peugeot spilled out and ran for cover in nearby trees.

Van der Boor stood up and fired a series of three-round bursts, dropping one of the men. The other man fired a long stream of bullets in his direction. One 122-grain bullet hit him in the shoulder, two slammed into the chest plate in his Kevlar vest, and the third gave him a new belly button.

With his partner down, Haas kept the remaining attacker pinned down until two more patrol cars with four more policemen arrived. The gun battle lasted another three minutes before the second man was killed. Neither missile shooter had any identity papers, and the Peugeot was stolen. While the car was being searched, a helicopter airlifted Van der Boor to the hospital.

Ghulam learned about the failed attack by watching CNN. He did not know why the attack failed and decided the next attack against an airliner would be in the U.S.

THE SAME DAY, 7:46 P.M. LOCAL TIME, TEL AVIV,

Collecting classified material wasn't hard for Eitan Kohan. Getting the documents out of Mossad headquarters was. Every briefcase was searched, and employees were sometimes patted down and screened with a wand. At first, he used rubber bands to strap documents around his thigh or put them in plastic sleeves inside his shirt. When that became too risky, he'd mail documents to a post office box from the post office inside Mossad headquarters.

He used his home printer/scanner/fax to load the documents onto a flash drive and then purged the printer's memory. Nothing went on his home computer. Delivery of the thumb drives at blind drops was made once a month, and Hezbollah deposited money into his Lombard Odier account.

Eitan was tired of being poor. After serving as a battalion intelligence officer, and four years at Shin Bet – Israel's internal security agency – Kohan transferred to Mossad. He viewed his treason as a method to fund a comfortable retirement from Mossad at the end of 2002. He planned to immigrate to the United States or Canada, where he could live modestly on his savings or find another job outside the intelligence community.

When Kohan stepped off the bus in Jaffa, the oldest part of Tel Aviv, he walked past the café twice to check for surveillance. Seeing none, he sat at a table and ordered coffee with cardamom added. The drink was served with a plate of dried fruits and nuts. Kohan waited, ostensibly reading *al-Ittihad,* Israel's oldest Arabic language newspaper.

His contact arrived as Eitan took his first sip, and the waiter returned to take the second order. While they were talking, Eitan slid the flash drive inside the folded newspaper across the table. The other man nodded thank you. To a casual observer, they were two friends having a cup of coffee.

Neither man saw Aaron Gold, who knew Kohan from when they served together in the 932nd Infantry Battalion of the Nachal Infantry Brigade. Gold was about to cross the street to say hello to his former roommate when he saw the man glance inside the paper. Suspicious, Gold browsed at a store window across the street and followed Kohan's contact to an apartment building in the Arab section of Jaffa.

Gold found a nearby pay phone and called his battalion's commanding officer. A car brought Gold to Mossad headquarters within minutes of hanging up, where his statement was recorded.

From a stack of photos taken from Shin Bet's files, he identified Asif Hadrami as the man with Kotan. Hadrami was a suspected member of Hezbollah, thought to live in Nabulus, not Jaffa. An apartment in Jaffa was a new development. Gold was sent home with a warning not to discuss this with anyone.

When Halevy came to work, Reznik was waiting in his outer office with a copy of Gold's statement. Reznik started the impromptu meeting. "Eitan Kohan is probably the traitor. We must answer whether we use him to get to Hadrami and others or do we arrest him now."

It took only a few minutes to agree to the plan Reznik proposed. Step one, give Kohan a new job as a promotion, gathering intelligence to support raids against Hezbollah. Kohan would be fed false data first to confirm he was the source. Step two was to use the disinformation to strike Hezbollah.

Reznik needed a coordinator he could trust to feed the intelligence to Kohan. He looked at the clock as he picked up the phone and wondered if Aliyah was up.

THURSDAY, JULY 25ᵀᴴ, 2002, 9:30 A.M. LOCAL TIME, LANGLEY

To ensure that Aliyah made the daily El Al Newark to Tel Aviv flight, Janis flew Aliyah to Newark. They stayed at the Marriott near the terminal the night before her flight. With Aliyah through security, Janis rode the Signature Flight Services shuttle back to their facility.

Janis called Bishop from a small conference room, wanting to learn what the CIA had learned about Ghulam's trip to the U.S. Bishop had nothing new. He asked if she could stop by in the next day or so to discuss a possible contract.

By TBM 850, Dulles International Airport was an hour and a half from Newark, and the Marriott in Reston was her next stop. In the morning, she drove to the CIA complex where Ms. Elizabeth Harris was expected.

Bishop closed the door as soon as Janis entered. "Are you interested in an assignment from the CIA? It will help your friends in Tel Aviv. If you are, I can run the approval traps."

"I'm listening."

Bishop turned around, pulled a file from the drawer behind his desk, and handed a photo to Janis. "You're looking at Gerd Hofer. His father Hans worked for Mauser, who went around the world selling German arms for the Third Reich. After the war, Hofer senior set up shop in Syria and sold the Arabs all the arms they wanted from World War Two German stocks stashed in odd places. Gerd was born in Damascus and took over his father's business."

"So why is the CIA interested in him?"

"Hofer acquired a large chunk of the East German army's inventory of SA-7s and SA-14s right after the wall fell, along with weapons and ammo the Russians left behind. Where they are stored, no one knows other than every so often; some show up. For example, the SA-14s fired in Holland, and the AKs came from the missing East German inventory."

"Why doesn't the CIA ask the Germans to arrest him?"

"For what? We don't know where the weapons are or have hard evidence that shows he sold them to a terrorist group. Look, the CIA's hands aren't clean. We've bought stuff from Hofer that went to organizations we support. Recently, Hofer threatened to expose our dealings with him. From what we understand, he has all his contacts and his records in a small notebook he keeps with him. We want the book and him out of the picture."

"Why doesn't the CIA do it?"

Bishop gave Janis a surprised look as if to say, isn't it obvious. "Facetious answer. That's why we signed the agreement with you and did business with people like Moya. The optics are terrible if the Germans find out the CIA conducted a hit on their soil, particularly after both the FBI and the CIA asked them several times to investigate Hofer. If you do it, the CIA can deny involvement and say it was an arms deal gone bad."

Boy, I heard that line before when The Broker would offer me contracts. Bishop is using what must be standard CIA phraseology.

"What else do you have on Hofer?"

Bishop showed Janis pictures of Hofer's three-story stone manor house she guessed was built in the 1880s.

"Burglary is not in my bag of tricks. If I get this black book and the location of Hofer's stashes, what will you do with the weapons?"

"Honest answer is unknown until we have an inventory of what he has. The Germans told us that the East German records of what was missing were, and I quote, incomplete. The agency smells a rat."

"I'm not surprised. Has anyone else issued a contract on Hofer?"

"Not that we know."

Janis rubbed her chin as she looked at the surveillance photos of Hofer, a diagram of the house, and a garage that was a separate structure. She'd bet before the war the garage was a carriage house and a stable. "Has the CIA lost anyone trying to get info on Hofer?"

Bishop looked surprised and decided to tell the truth. "Yeah. An asset trying to discover where he stored the weapons disappeared."

"How long ago was that?"

"Summer of 2000. Just after the Second Intifada started. The Al Aqsa Martyrs Brigade and Fatah started using shiny new East German AKs with serial numbers from what we think are from Hofer's inventory."

"Have you shown this material to the Israelis?"

"Yes. Feel free to coordinate with Mossad. He's not a war criminal or leading attacks on Israel so they're not interested. What they have on him is in the file I will give you."

"How soon do you want Hofer dead?"

"No timetable, but we want the book and him out of business sooner than later."

"May I have a few minutes alone to study this material?"

"Sure. How much time do you need?"

"Fifteen minutes. If I accept the contract, I'll tell you what I want to take and what else I need."

"Super, I need to go to the bathroom, and I'll take my time."

Janis looked through the photos and data Bishop left behind. Killing Hofer will be easy; finding the book will be hard. Janis decided to double her price. No pay, no contract.

CHAPTER 14

SOLO MISSION

he setting sun was a bright orange ball on the western horizon. Already, on the desert floor, the temperature was dropping quickly. Coyotes liked the national refuge because the clumps of trees and dry streams provided natural cover. And, almost anywhere, a man could see recognizable landmarks that made navigating without a compass easy.

The Border Patrol didn't have the manpower to station surveillance teams along all the known smuggling routes. Observation points in the cat-and-mouse game were picked based on where agents could watch several routes at once, knowing that after catching one group, the trail would not be used for a few months.

The location Supervisory Border Patrol Agent Jesus Flores picked was under a large rock outcropping. It provided shade all day long and was high enough off the desert floor so he could watch known routes. Flores reached his spot mid-afternoon, several hours before any coyotes would move out with their charges.

Flores felt the heat rising from the rock exposed to daytime temperatures in the 120s that warmed the cold, dry night air.

Sitting on an air mattress, Flores scanned the desert through 8 x 50 binoculars. After dark, he'd switch to a long-range thermal imager. Experience said there was a one in three chance he'd spot a group of illegal immigrants or drug smugglers.

Flores checked in with Jeffrey Ellison, his teammate in another observation position half a mile away. With radio communications established, he checked in with his command center via his satellite phone. With all the required tasks done, Flores could enjoy the desert that came alive at night as animals searched for food.

Flores was sure he saw a pile of brush move in the fading light. When he looked again, there was not one but eight bundles moving in a ragged line. Four carried a tube he estimated to be about three feet long and lashed to their packs. That was very unusual. Drug smugglers carried rectangular bundles.

As he studied the group slowly winding their way through a ravine, Flores noticed all eight had AK-47s. That too, was unusual. He radioed Ellison and gave them the location and direction of movement.

Ellison, a former Army Ranger, needed a few minutes to spot the column. "Holy shit!!!" were the first words he spoke. "They're carrying some type of missile. Saw them in Iraq during Desert Storm. You gonna call it in?"

"Yeah… Let's meet at the baseball boulder, and then we can trail them." The "baseball boulder" was a rounded 50-foot-tall weather-beaten chunk of sandstone between the two men.

The agent in the command center was skeptical and needed convincing, which cost precious time. Flores deflated the air mattress and rolled up his lightweight sleeping bag. Hooked to his load-bearing harness, he had four pouches, each with two 30-round magazines for his M4A1 carbine. Strapped to his right leg was his Beretta 96D pistol in .40 caliber and two extra magazines. He had the night vision goggles on his head and under his pack, his camelback was three-quarters full of water. For food, he had six Klif bars stuffed into one of the pouch pockets in his dark green trousers.

THE SAME DAY, 10:59 P.M. LOCAL TIME, BUENOS AIRES NATIONAL WILDLIFE REFUGE

Before the sun went down, Imad Ayood took compass bearings of the mountain peaks on either side of him. He made a small X where the bearings suggested he was and then compared his position with the GPS. This double-check put him within 100 yards from where he thought he should be. They were right on the route he had planned.

At dusk, Imad waved his hand in a circle and pointed in the direction he wanted the team to go. He let one man pass him before he joined the column in which each man was spaced about 10 feet apart.

Two hours later, Imad held up his fist and whispered, "stop" to the man in front. The group closed-up and prepared to switch loads, so each man alternated carrying the 20-kilogram missiles along with his pack.

With the 15-minute rest over, Imad shouldered one of the packs with an SA-14, picked up his AK-47, and headed north. The others got to their feet and followed.

THE SAME DAY, 11:16 P.M. LOCAL TIME, BUENOS AIRES NATIONAL REFUGE

Ellison and Flores could see the column 200 yards to the west through their thermal imagers. Both agents paralleled the smuggler's course that was roughly due north over ground that both men knew well.

Trained as a sniper and an Army Ranger, Ellison joined the Border Patrol in 1998 after his second enlistment ended. Because of his experience in Desert Storm, Ellison carried eight 30-round magazines for his M4A1 carbine instead of the Border Patrol requirement of four.

Both were sure the column was headed to a rendezvous with a vehicle on South Pusch Street. The asphalt-surfaced road ran west from Arivaca, Arizona, to Highway 286, and paralleled the Arizona/Mexican border 10 miles to the south. It was also known as the Arivaca/Sasbe Road.

At a rest stop, Ellison asked, "What did the command center tell you?"

"They want us to wait until the Blackhawk helicopter arrives just before sunrise. Roadblocks will close the road in either direction, and two 4-man teams will be coming in SUVs. Once the helicopter arrives, we make the arrest."

"Jesus, we've got to keep them from using one of the missiles on the helicopter."

Jesus shook his head. "I didn't think of that."

"I'm betting on a firefight."

The thought scared Flores. Two months ago, when a Border Patrol team tried to arrest a group carrying marijuana, two Border Patrol agents died. These guys were more heavily armed and probably trained soldiers.

SATURDAY, JULY 27ᵀᴴ, 2002, 4:05 A.M. LOCAL TIME, BUENOS AIRES NATIONAL REFUGE

Ayood could see the sky start to lighten on the eastern horizon. Based on his navigation and the GPS, they were 100 yards from a wooded area close to the road that would give them cover and shade. Once there, he would call the number loaded into his burner phone, and by eight or so, they should be in an air-conditioned van and out of this god-forsaken desert.

THE SAME DAY, 4:15 A.M. LOCAL TIME, BUENOS AIRES NATIONAL REFUGE

From where Ellison and Flores lay on a low rise that let them look down on the smugglers, they watched the smugglers shrug off their packs and lean them against the trees. Each man drained at least one bottle of water. A sentry was posted near the road while the others kept their AKs across their laps where they sat.

Their thermal imagers gave the range to the centermost smuggler as 300 meters. Both Ellison and Flores believed the flat trajectory of the 5.56mm M855 round fired by an M4A1 gave them an advantage over the men with the AKs that were notoriously inaccurate beyond 200 meters. As he studied the smugglers through his 8 X 50 binoculars, Ellison heard Flores whispering in the mike and was glad he could barely hear what he said. Sound in the still desert morning traveled farther than one thought, and manmade sounds stood out.

THE SAME DAY, 4:19 A.M. LOCAL TIME, BUENOS AIRES NATIONAL REFUGE

Ayood dug the satellite phone out of a pouch in his pack and was delighted the battery charge was 90%. He waited for the phone to go through the start-up routine and acquire a signal. He tapped out the number written on what was now a sweat-stained piece of paper and pressed the call button. When a voice answered on the first ring, he was sure the man had been up for a while.

"Allo."

"Code is sunrise." Sunrise meant they made it safely to the rendezvous and were waiting for pick-up.

"I'll be there in less than an hour." Ghulam smiled as he hung up the phone, confident that soon, he would have his second, eight-man team and four more SA-14s in the U.S. He was already on 286, two miles south of a small town southwest of Tucson, called Three Points.

THE SAME DAY, 4:21 A.M. LOCAL TIME, BUENOS AIRES NATIONAL REFUGE

Ellison turned his head and whispered. "The son-of-a-bitch just made a call. I'll bet he was confirming their pick-up."

Flores turned toward the Army Ranger, "Agreed. The guys on the helicopter know this will probably be a hot landing. We're to open fire if they try to bring down the helicopter. The Suburbans with eight more agents are supposedly less than twenty minutes away."

"I'm locked and loaded. Make sure you switch your scope to daylight and stay semi-automatic to conserve ammo. You'll go through magazines much faster than you think." Ellison held out a spare magazine for Flores, who took it.

Flores nodded and listened to the radio. "Helicopter ETA is 5:15 a.m.

Ellison had the red dot in his Aimpoint sight, known as the M68CCO Close Combat Optic, on the center of the chest of the man with the phone. At this range, the bullet hits where the dot is placed.

THE SAME DAY, 5:09 A.M. LOCAL TIME, BUENOS AIRES NATIONAL REFUGE

The faint beat of the Blackhawk's blades caused Imad to search the brightening sky. The increasing noise said the helicopter was headed in their direction. He pointed at two of his men. "You two, take a missile up to that clear area by the road. If the helicopter starts to land, shoot it down."

The two men unbuckled the clasps at the end of one tube, dumped out the missile launcher, and scrambled along the dry riverbed to a clear area where they could see the approaching helicopter. The man with the missile rested his AK against a large boulder. He turned on the missile to allow the nitrogen to cool the seeker that would lock onto the helicopter's exhaust. The other searched the sky. Ayood and remaining five took cover in the grove of trees.

THE SAME DAY, 5:11 A.M. LOCAL TIME, BUENOS AIRES NATIONAL REFUGE

Flores rolled onto his side and turned on the electronic bullhorn. He hated making the required announcement because the response could be a hail of bullets in his direction. But, in the U.S., the announcement was a legal requirement.

"Attention, this is the United States Border Patrol; put down your weapons. I repeat this is the United States Border Patrol. Put down your weapons and surrender. You are under arrest."

Imad looked around. He heard but could not see the speaker. He waved at the other men who knelt behind trees. The helicopter was now much closer.

Ellison pointed his M4A1 at the two men out in the open. "Jesus, I've got the missile shooter. If he puts that thing on his shoulder, I'm shooting him."

"I'll wait for you to open fire."

"Good. Don't give away our position."

Flores repeated the announcement and swallowed hard as he turned off the bullhorn. He checked his M4A1, thankful for all the times Ellison took him to the rifle and pistol range to practice.

Flores and Ellison could see the Blackhawk now within a mile. Flores keyed his radio mike. "Keep it coming."

Ellison had the red dot centered on a spot between the man's shoulders. Ellison didn't like the idea of shooting someone in the back. Still, if his shot prevented someone from firing a surface-to-air missile at a helicopter full of Border Patrol agents, he would pull the trigger.

Flores voice broke his concentration. "The two Suburbans got a late start but are on the way, and we are to start the party without them."

The man lifted the SA-14. Before it was halfway up to his shoulder, the impact of the 62-grain bullet traveling at around 2,600 feet per second sent him sprawling and the missile tumbling to the ground.

When the missile shooter's assistant poked his head and shoulders around the boulder, Ellison's M4A1 barked again. The bullet entered the man's mouth before blowing the back of his head off.

Puffs of dirt from a short burst from an AK-47 erupted 20 yards below and to the left of where the muzzle blast from Ellison's rifle kicked up dirt. Hidden between large rocks, Ellison figured it would take a lucky shot to hit him.

Flores watched as the six remaining men fired short, aimed bursts in their general direction, thinking these were not druggies but trained soldiers. But whose?

The Blackhawk circled 500 feet overhead, looking for a place nearby to land. Its crew chief sat in the open door, occasionally firing a burst from his M4A1 carbine. Still, the 70-foot trees prevented him from getting a good view or shot at the smugglers.

Ayood sat with his back against the largest diameter tree he could find and frantically dialed the same number he had called earlier. It rang and rang.

Unknown to Ayood, to the west, the Border Patrol kept traffic from turning east onto the Arivaca-Sasbe Road from Arizona Highway 286. Two Border Patrol Yukons kept traffic from heading west from Arivaca, the small and old mining town with a population of just under 30,000 that was five miles to the east of where Ayood sat. When Ghulam saw the Border Patrol vehicles, he turned around, turned the phone off, and headed back to Tucson.

To Imad, their mission just changed from getting into the United States to killing Americans. Each man had only eight magazines for their AKs. He yelled at his comrades to conserve ammunition and to wait until the Americans came out of hiding before they fired.

The Blackhawk landed on the road's north side, and the eight men were now on the same radio net as Flores and Ellison. They crossed the riverbed and were within 100 yards of where Ayood sat. In the lull, Ellison keyed his mike. "Give Flores and me a few minutes to see how many we can pick off. These guys are soldiers, not druggies. Let me know when you guys are ready to hit their flank."

Ellison got two clicks in response. Ellison looked through his sight for a target. Finding the shoulder and part of a pack, he squeezed the trigger. A man screamed and fell forward away from the tree. For his second shot, the red dot was centered on the man's chest when he squeezed the trigger.

"Five left."

Two clicks.

Another man took a quick look, and Ellison fired a snapshot. Bark flew from the tree. His rifle's bolt stayed back. Not wanting to take a chance on the rifle jamming, he dumped out the magazine, cycled the bolt twice to ensure the weapon was clear, and inserted a new magazine. Reloaded, he let the bolt slam forward and pushed on the forward assist to ensure the round was seated.

Ellison ducked as a burst from an AK-47 stitched the dirt in front of him. Several rounds pinged off the rocks, sending shards into his cheeks. *You bastard, where are you?* Ellison slowly scanned the trees, saw a head pop out, and then went back. *Was it you? Let's find out.*

Ellison adjusted his aim point to the opposite side of the tree where he saw the head thinking if he came out that side, he'd squeeze the trigger. If not, he'd wait.

He first saw the barrel, then a shoulder, and then a torso. The M4A1 bucked against his shoulder, and the man staggered backward with blood soaking his shirt. Next to him, Flores lost his fire control discipline and sprayed the trees wildly, quickly emptying a magazine. Another smuggler stuck a rifle around the tree and pulled the trigger. Through his optic, Ellison could see the AK-47 dancing wildly as the shooter fired all thirty rounds in the magazine.

He heard the transmission, "We're moving in." Ellison glanced toward the road and saw eight Border Patrol agents wearing full tactical gear with M4A1s pressed into their shoulders. Each man already had a target, and the fight was over in seconds.

"All clear! Eight bad guys are down."

Ellison stood up and said, "Jesus, let's go." He was shocked when he saw Flores face down in a pool of blood.

SUNDAY, JULY 28TH, 2002, 2:38 P.M. LOCAL TIME, OTTOBEUREN, GERMANY

Before Janis left Bishop's office, she reminded him she was not getting on an airplane until two conditions were met. One, Mossad formerly approved the operation, and two, half of her two-million-dollar fee was in an account at a bank in Seychelles designated by her.

When the money arrived on Saturday morning, the funds were transferred to a bank in Lichtenstein that sent the balance less their transfer fee to her Pictet et Cie account. In both the Seychelles and Lichtenstein banks, the accounts were for one-time use, i.e., the funds came in, transferred out, and closed. The two countries' bank secrecy laws required a court order that documented evidence of a major crime before details of the transfers could be disclosed.

What drove her decision to choose Frankfurt was the availability of high-performance cars for rental. One agency rented Porsches, Lamborghinis, AMG Mercedes, and Ferraris near the Frankfurt Airport. Speaking German helped when she called to make the reservation.

Janis was picked up at the curb by a company representative in one of the agency's Mercedes sedans they rented. She was offered a choice of a cabriolet or a coupe at the desk and took the convertible. The clerk apologized, saying the Porsche Carrera 2 did not have an automatic transmission. Janis laughed and said she owned several Porsches with manual transmissions.

She'd driven on the Frankfurt-Mannheim Autobahn before, and as usual, it was crowded with trucks. South of Stuttgart, the traffic lightened, and Janis cruised in a line of cars in the left lane going 175 and 180 kilometers an hour (~109 – 112 mph). In front of her was a Mercedes sedan and, at a safe distance behind, a VW Golf GTI.

From the Kirschheim Unter Teck exit, Janis drove as fast as she thought was safe on the secondary roads to the Park Hotel Maximilian Resort and Spa in Ottobeuren. The hotel was less than eight kilometers by road from Hofer's estate outside the small town of Lachen.

The CIA file noted Hofer was a bachelor who came to the Maximilian once a week for a massage and frequently dined in the hotel's five-star rated restaurant.

THE SAME DAY, 11:13 A.M. LOCAL TIME, LANGLEY

Walt Bishop saw the same news reports watched by Ghulam. The classified reports would start reaching him tomorrow. They would provide details about the captured missiles, the men killed, and the name of the terrorist organization claiming credit for the attack. Whatever they said didn't matter. His unofficial agreement with the Iranians that they would not allow Hezbollah or its affiliates to conduct attacks on U.S. soil had been violated in Los Angeles. And now, Ghulam had been spotted in the U.S., al-Musawi fighters killed, and man-portable, surface-to-air missiles captured.

He needed an explanation that would satisfy his bosses at the CIA and didn't have a good one which made him angry. His boss Greg Nasher would demand he has an uncomfortable discussion with his contacts in Iran. He could threaten to stop selling them information, and they might do the same.

Bishop rationalized that the tough conversation would not end the relationship with Iran. They needed the data he was selling them more than he needed their intel. But what if the CIA found out he was selling far more than authorized?

THE SAME DAY, 5:58 P.M. LOCAL TIME, TUCSON

Ghulam wasn't sure if he was more upset about having his smuggling strategy discovered or the eight missiles he lost. The eight members of the Al-Musawi Corps who were killed in a shootout in Southern Arizona didn't matter. They were martyred, but now the Americans knew Hezbollah could smuggle men and weapons into their country from Mexico.

What mattered was that he had to change his plans, and his only easily accessible intelligence source was the American news channels who said the men killed were members of a drug cartel. Ghulam knew they were Al-Musawi Corps and believed so did the CIA.

A senior Border Patrol agent interviewed on camera stated that agents tracked eight men carrying fully automatic AK-47s. One agent was killed in a gunfight west of Arivaca, and there was no mention of the SA-14 missiles.

Ghulam believed the authorities were not telling the American people that the Border Patrol captured eight SA-14s to prevent panic among the flying public. He decided to return to Lebanon and called Air France to book a coach seat from Phoenix to LA and then to Paris. He gave the ticket agent his Turkish passport. Once in Paris, he'd pick the best route to Beirut.

MONDAY, JULY 29TH, 2002, 4:23 P.M. LOCAL TIME, TEL AVIV

Laid out on Eitan's desk was an American Tactical Pilotage Chart G4D showing northern Israel, Lebanon, eastern Syria, Cyprus, and parts of Turkey, Jordan, and Iraq. On the map, Eitan had plotted Syrian missile battery locations, and three possible routes helicopters could use to fly into Lebanon's Bekaa Valley. Pushpins held photographs of a suspected Hezbollah missile assembly facility and its defenses on a giant corkboard on his wall.

The target was a BM-21 (NATO code name Grad) missile assembly facility northeast of the Lebanese town of Rachaiya. Once the three sections – fins, body/rocket motor, and warhead – were loaded in Iran and trucked through Syria into Lebanon, the BM-21 missiles were assembled.

Videos taken by Israeli drones showed trucks being unloaded in Rachaiya. The empty crates were stacked outside and the entrance to an underground bunker where the assembled missiles were stored.

He noted the latitude and longitude of the two closest places where an H-53 full of commandos could land and showed the locations to the team doing the detailed raid and air strike planning. When they finished, the general staff would ask for permission for the raid.

He scribbled details of the missile facility attack and a planned air strike on a truck convoy carrying missile parts from Iraq while in Western Syria. The sheet of paper was carefully folded and stuffed into his wallet.

Finished for the day, Eitan walked out of the Mossad headquarters and headed to his flat. Unknown to him, cameras in his office recorded every move, and his apartment and printer/scanner were bugged. Two plainclothes officers from the Israeli Police force followed Eitan home with orders not to arrest him unless he attempted to leave the country.

While walking to his apartment from the bus stop, Eitan called a number in Jaffa and said he had something extremely valuable to deliver tonight. After negotiating a price twice his regular fee, the meeting was scheduled at a coffee shop in Jaffa at seven p.m.

THE SAME DAY, 7:17 P.M. LOCAL TIME, JAFFA

Eitan did his best to conceal his nervousness by trying to read a book while he waited for his contact to arrive. The delay caused the two police officers in the van across the street to wonder if the meeting would happen.

In the van, the only noise was the soft whirring sound made by the two CD recorders as they recorded a man with a beard sitting at Eitan's table. The officers could see the Arab's lips but not Eitan's. They adjusted the directional mike to filter out the background noise and recorded what was said:

Eitan: Thank you for coming on short notice. The IDF plans to raid your missile assembly facility in Rachaiya and bomb a truck convoy from Iran carrying missile components as soon as it enters Syria.

Arab: And you know this how?

Eitan: I evaluated the intelligence used to plan for the raid and the air strike.

Arab: When will the raid occur?

Eitan: The mission planners recommended the night of August 9th and 10th. My notes are on sheet of paper in this book.

The team leader in the van dialed the cell phone carried by the police officers in the café. "We've got enough on tape. Arrest the Arab right after he goes into his apartment so we can get the book, his phone, and his computer."

THE SAME DAY, 7:39 P.M. LOCAL TIME, TEL AVIV

Badi Hashemi took his usual precautions on a circuitous route to his apartment two streets away to ensure he was not followed. Convinced he was not observed, he went straight to his computer. Right after he logged in, the door to his studio apartment flew open, and six Israeli police officers in full battle dress stormed in. "Badi Hashemi, you're under arrest."

"For what?"

The officer grabbed his arms and pulled him to his feet. Another officer patted him down before lifting the lid to his scanner, revealing Eitan's notes. "Espionage."

Chief Inspector Yosi Gutman, who had just entered the apartment, read the paper. He keyed the mike to his secure radio. "We've got Kohan's notes, and I'm going to pick up Kohan."

THE SAME DAY, 7:59 P.M. LOCAL TIME, TEL AVIV

Gutman's driver drove with siren blaring and lights flashing until he was two blocks from Kohan's apartment building. Four police officers in full battle dress were waiting with orders to arrest Kotan if he left his flat. Gutman was not expecting trouble but wore a Kevlar vest and insisted on knocking on the door.

"Who is it?"

"Chief Inspector Yosi Gutman, Israeli Police. Open the door, now." Gutman stepped aside and held up his hand while he counted to five.

The door lock exploded with the impact of one of the officer's boots. Three others rushed inside and grabbed Kohan, who was in the bathroom trying to flush papers down an overflowing toilet. The documents were pulled out and placed on a towel.

Kohan was pushed to the center of the apartment. "Eitan Kohan, you are under arrest for espionage."

THE SAME DAY, 8:18 P.M. LOCAL TIME, TEL AVIV

Inside the police car, a plainclothes officer sat on either side of Kohan. As soon as the car pulled away from the curb, a black hood was pulled over Kohan's head. He had no way to estimate how long he was in the car but figured the police officers drove him around for at least an hour.

Kohan couldn't see the armed Israeli policeman who eased him out of the car and led him inside the secure detention facility in Tel Aviv. With the hood off, Kohan looked at the smooth concrete walls painted light gray. On one wall there was a steel door next to what he assumed was two-way glass. There was a table and three folding chairs in front of the chair to which he was chained. The only item on the table was a 500-milliliter bottle of water. When he tried to move his chair, it didn't budge since it was bolted to the floor. Overhead, he counted eight lights, only four of which were on. As he sat there, Eitan was convinced he was in a Mossad interrogation room and being filmed.

He let his head drop and closed his eyes, forcing himself to relax. As an Israeli citizen, he was entitled to a lawyer, and that request will be the first words to come out of his mouth.

The turning of the latch caused Eitan to look up. He glared at Yitzhak Reznik as he walked to the table. Reznik placed the two sheets of paper on the table. "Eitan, you are charged with espionage. Each document is a single count. However, the number of counts right now is irrelevant. This one is all we need. Add the other evidence we collected in your flat, and we are confident you will be convicted."

Reznik held up his hand as if to say, do not speak. "In a few minutes, the prosecutor assigned to his case will come in. Earlier, I spoke with Halevy and the Minister of Justice. You are a reserve Army officer, and Israel is at war with Hezbollah, allowing the government to ask for the death penalty. Do you understand?"

Eitan nodded his head.

"Good. You have a choice to make. Either you cooperate fully and provide us with everything you gave to Hezbollah and other terrorists. If you do, then you will spend the rest of your life in prison."

Reznik looked Eitan directly in the eyes as he spoke in measured tones. "Or, if you don't help us, assuming you are convicted and not given the death penalty, we have the option of where to keep you. Since you like the Arabs so much and wanted to help them defeat the country where you were born, we could put you with the Arab prisoners. If we were cruel, we might let it slip that you were Mossad, and if we did, my guess is that you will be dead in less than a week."

Reznik clasped both hands on the table in front of him. "We can ask the judge to commute your sentence and release you on the West Bank so you can be with your Hezbollah friends. Before you think that is a good idea, Israel will have taken action to discredit any information you passed to them. Hezbollah beheads those they believe betrayed them."

Reznik thought he saw a flicker of fear behind Eitan's defiant eyes and stood up. His mission finished. "I thought you might be interested in learning what is in store for you."

"I want a lawyer."

Reznik picked up his laptop and the sheets of paper. "We suspected you might. Good night, Eitan."

TUESDAY, JULY 30TH, 2002, 00:17 A.M. LOCAL TIME, BEKAA VALLEY, LEBANON

From the Israeli Air Force base at Ramat David, about 45 kilometers southeast of Haifa, Rachaiya was 190 kilometers and 15 minutes flying time away in a two-seat F-16D. Spread out in a loose finger four, the F-16Ds from the 109th Fighter Squadron, a.k.a. the Valley Squadron, were at 10,000 meters and cruising at a fuel-saving 450 knots. Four F-15Is, 1,000 meters above and 20 miles to the east, provided air cover.

The back seaters in each F-16D made sure the infrared and laser designator in the Israeli-designed Litening targeting pod was fully operational as they headed north. In the front seat, the pilots scanned the night sky looking for the telltale signs of surface-to-air missile launches as the F-16s S-turned as each pilot kept at least 2 gs on the airplane.

Each F-16 had a specific target. The first F-16 would drop its four 1,000- pound GBU-16 Paveway II laser-guided bombs on the facility's truck park. Dash two, or the second airplane in the flight, would put one 1,000-pound bomb into each of the four revetments where completed missiles were readied for transport. The missile assembly building was the third plane's target for its four Paveway IIs. Dash four, the last aircraft to drop, would aim its two 1,000-kilogram GBU-27 penetrating bombs into what Israeli intelligence believed was an underground storage bunker.

The symbols on their radar warning receivers and the warbling tones in their headsets told each crew that their plane was being tracked by the Syrian Air Force. So far, no missiles have been fired.

As the flight approached Mount Herman, the leader pushed his throttle to full military power but did not ignite his engine's afterburner. The three other pilots added power, and the heavily laden F-16s accelerated to 580 knots.

All four F-16s dropped their bombs and were out of the target area in 20 seconds. The explosions from the truck park and revetments sent ripples of light through the night sky.

Time delay fuses set off the bombs in the assembly facility about a meter off the concrete floor. The intense heat from the burning missile warheads and rocket motors whited out the infrared cameras on the F-16s, making their recordings useless for assessing damage.

The penetrating bombs burrowed into the earth and crashed through the reinforced concrete before the fuses sensed they were in an open area. The sympathetic detonations of stored missile warheads and rocket propellants created a shock wave that shoved the four F-16Ds forward like surfers riding a wave. As they flew back into Israel, the crews felt the pulses from explosions that lit up the sky behind them.

THE SAME DAY, 6:41 A.M. LOCAL TIME, BEKAA VALLEY

Just after dawn, a Searcher remotely piloted vehicle began orbiting the Rachaiya facility at 3,500 meters. The live color feed showed the burning assembly facility and smoke pouring from two holes in the storage bunker and the entrance. Flames inside the bunker were clearly visible, and the gray-black smoke rose past 3,000 meters. Three of the 12 trucks in the pre-strike photos had disappeared, four were on their sides, and the others showed signs of damage. When the first Searcher was replaced by a second remotely piloted vehicle at 10:00 a.m., the missile storage bunker was still burning.

THE SAME DAY, 12:47 P.M. LOCAL TIME, OTTOBEUREN

After sleeping longer than planned, Janis ran for 45 minutes after working out in the gym to help overcome jet lag. She felt refreshed and ready after a full body massage at the spa.

Janis initially planned to have lunch in Ottobeuren but seeing the hotel restaurant's buffet, she decided to eat at the hotel rather than in town. Janis was in reconnaissance mode with a guidebook and digital camera in hand when she was led to a table overlooking the park. When asked if she wanted a menu, Janis replied in German that she would try the buffet.

The 10-meter-long buffet was organized in five sections – salad, cheeses, and cold cuts, rolls and pieces of sliced bread, soups, and hot dishes. Janis made a salad on one plate and on another placed cheeses, hams and salamis, and bread she learned to like on her trips to Germany with Karin.

Heading toward her table, Janis spotted Gerd Hofer resplendent in a dark suit and a red and black striped tie, being seated. A man she assumed was his bodyguard stood discretely by the door, more interested in the people in the lobby than those in the restaurant.

Even though he was dressed in a suit and kept his hands clasped at his waist, the bulge under the bodyguard's right arm suggested he was armed.

Hofer and Janis made eye contact and flashed her best, "I'm available smile." Seeing her target before she started her surveillance was an unexpectedly pleasant and surprising start. It was also a red flag.

Janis ate with the opened guidebook next to her salad plate, glancing up every few seconds to watch Hofer and check on the bodyguard. On one glance, Janis saw the maître d' nod vigorously after Hofer spoke with him.

The allure of the array of pastries on a separate table, particularly those made with chocolate, was overwhelming. Janis rationalized that since the pieces were small, she'd try several. She debated which ones to take when the maître d' approached and spoke in German. "Fräulein Mitchell, Herr Hofer would like to know if you would join him for dessert?"

When he spoke, the maître d' nodded subtly toward Hofer as if she was supposed to know who Herr Hofer was. His deferential tone suggested Herr Hofer was important, at least in Ottobeuren.

Since she spoke German to the waitress, Janis assumed the maître d' was told. When she sat down, the waitress asked for her room number, and the man called the front desk, who gave him her name – Jocelyn Mitchell – an alias she hadn't used since 1981.

"Please tell Herr Hofer I would be delighted to join him."

The maître d' nodded and went to Hofer. Based on the conversation length, Janis suspected there was more to the discussion than her impending arrival. When the maître d' returned, he told her a selection of pastries and coffee would be brought to the table.

As she waited for the maître d' to hold out her chair, Janis thought this may make it simpler to get into his lair. Getting away unhurt and unnoticed was always the challenge.

Hofer stood up as Janis was seated. His closely cropped dark hair was graying on the sides. Hofer matched the photos she was given by Bishop and was about six feet tall, average build, and guessed he weighed about 190 pounds. Janis sensed an air of arrogance that told people when Gerd Hofer came into the room.

"Thank you for joining me. It is not often that the hotel has a lovely wealthy American woman as a guest." Hofer spoke German and was told Janis drove the Porsche cabriolet in the parking lot. Karin often said that most Germans thought all Americans were wealthy.

Janis nodded at the compliment and answered in Hofer's native language. The CIA said he spoke Arabic, Swahili, English, and German. "I'm on holiday, and I'd never been to the Allgäu so I thought I would spend a few days in this part of Germany." *So far, so true and good.*

"Where did you learn to speak German?"

"I had a close friend who was German from a town near Munich, and she taught me German, and I taught her English." *That is not precisely true, but close enough. I keep in touch with the Eggers and plan to call them when I am finished here.*

"Ahhhhh, that explains the Bavarian accent." Hofer smiled as if a round peg was put in a round hole. *Alles was in Ordnung.* Everything was in order. "Is it Mrs. or Ms. Mitchell?"

Janis smiled demurely and fluttered her eyelashes. "It's Jocelyn, and I am not married." Another truthful answer. *I'm also not interested in sex with men.*

"So, how long are you going to stay?"

"Two or three days. The hotel is lovely."

"How long are you staying in Germany?"

"Another week or so, and then I will decide whether or not to fly home or go to Zurich to take care of some unattended business." *Or, until I kill you. I am sure a question about work I do is coming.*

"What kind of work do you do?"

"I don't. I retired a long time ago." *True, until I un-retired in May. Here we go. Now the fun will begin.*

"What kind of work *did* you do?"

"I was a security consultant. Confidentiality agreements require me not to say much about what I did."

Hofer nodded as his mind processed her answer.

Maybe I told him too much. My gut is waving red flags. Much of what Bishop said about Hofer didn't compute, but that was often the case.

She never had perfect intelligence nor met her targets socially before killing them. Her brain said to be very careful, even consider walking away.

Hofer changed the subject. "Do you like the mountains?"

"I do. I like to hike and enjoy picnic lunches in the fresh air in the summer. And I like to ski." *Karin was an avid skier, and I took up the sport. We averaged 40 – 50 days a year, and most would consider me an expert. I can ski almost anything, including moguls and deep powder with confidence.*

Hofer nodded as if her answers were filling in blanks in a form. He looked at his watch. "I'm sorry, I have a conference call in 40 minutes and must return to my office. Perhaps we could have dinner tonight or tomorrow at my house and continue the conversation? I could have my chef cook a special dinner."

"I am sure your chef is wonderful, but I would prefer a restaurant for the first date." *Meaning I am not going to give you or your chef a chance to put drugs in my food. Even then, he could take me to a place where my food could be drugged or poisoned.*

"Fair enough. I will leave a message at the front desk as to what day and time I will pick you up.

Hofer, I plan to turn you down and meet you on my terms.

WEDNESDAY, JULY 31ˢᵀ, 2002, 8:19 A.M. LOCAL TIME, BEIRUT

When Ghulam entered the conference room, there were grim faces and very little talking. The past few days had not been good for Hezbollah. Hassan Nasrallah, Hezbollah's Secretary General didn't use any notes as he went through the failures.

A missile storage facility was destroyed. Half of Hezbollah's inventory in Lebanon went up in smoke. They managed to infiltrate a suicide bomber into Israel, but the attack killed only one instead of hundreds.

In the U.S. a whole team was killed and eight precious SA-14s were presumed captured even though the Americans had not mentioned the missiles. And last, their source within Mossad was arrested.

Priority one was to determine if their network in Israel was compromised and, if so, take measures to prevent penetration by the Israelis. However, operations against the Jews and their infidel allies will continue. According to Nasrallah, building another assembly and storage facility was priority two.

When he finished, Nasrallah looked at Ghulam at the far end of the table. "So, Abd al-Bari, tell us of your plans?"

With that, Ghulam described the attack he planned to carry out in Dallas to bring the war to American soil and kill hundreds of Americans. Nasrallah nodded in acknowledgment when he told Ghulam to proceed with the attack in America first, followed by ones in Germany and Belgium.

CHAPTER 15

INTO THE WOLF'S LAIR

THURSDAY, AUGUST 1ST, 2002, 8:21 A.M. LOCAL TIME, OTTOBEUREN

After waking up and going to the bathroom, Janis picked up the sheet slid under her door that listed the events at the resort and today's weather. It noted that the high would be 22°C (~73°F), with rain beginning after midnight. Thinking it was a perfect time for a run, Janis put on a pair of nylon running pants, a sports bra, and a t-shirt. The small fanny pack around her waist held her driver's license, credit cards, passport, and 300 Euros in bills. She took a 500 ml bottle of water from the cooler in the room and headed out.

The Park Hotel Maximilian Resort bordered a large park, so as she did the day before, Janis started down the path, thinking she could run several laps before working out in the gym. If Hofer was serious, she'd have a note inviting her to dinner when she returned.

Janis was enjoying the runner's high as sweat started to soak her clothes as she ran northeast toward the small lake. There, she planned to turn south and run along Kindlemanstrasse for 500 feet before turning right down onto a path that led back into the park.

Hearing the clicking sound of a bike chain not correctly aligned, Janis turned and saw the source 100 feet behind her.

Without slowing her pace, she strode over the curb onto the grass along the little used road.

Her sense of danger caused Janis to again turn toward the biker who aimed a dart gun at her. Janis put up her hand as she started to jump to the side, and the dart glanced off her hand and stuck in her shoulder. Fighting the drug's effects, Janis ripped the dart out of her skin and felt someone cradling her. She was vaguely aware that she was being lifted into a van when she passed out, thinking this was a shitty way to die.

THE SAME DAY, 9:48 A.M. LOCAL TIME, LANGLEY

Walt Bishop had never been invited to a meeting in a room in what he, and others, referred to as "mahogany row." The nickname referenced the wood paneling in the offices and the floor where the agency's senior leadership had its offices.

Before he left his office, Bishop buttoned his collar and slid the knot of his tie to nestle it between the wings of his shirt's collar. His sport coat was left unbuttoned because, if he managed to suck in his gut to fasten the buttons, he was afraid they would pop off if he relaxed his stomach.

At the table, Bishop saw the Director of the CIA, the National Security Advisor, the head of the FBI, and the head of the National Security Agency. Bishop, not being a "principal," sat in a chair along the wall next to the only other staffer in the room – an FBI agent.

Apparently, someone connected eight dots – Abd al-Bari Ghulam, Gerd Hofer, and the four SA-14s captured in Arizona – which made them the agenda items. The CIA director turned to Walt and asked, "You got the lead on Ghulam from a credible source. What do you think?"

"Sir, I'd bet my life on the source."

"Did you pass on the info we got from the Israelis to immigration?"

"I did as soon as I received it."

The Director of the CIA turned to the head of the FBI, "Do we have an APB out on Ghulam or whatever name he is using?"

"No. We could not verify the credibility of the tip. All we received was a phone call from our CIA liaison saying go after this guy. The FBI needs more if we want the arrest to stand up in court."

The head of the CIA shook his head. "Maybe we should change the policy. We're fighting a war against terrorists and need to adapt."

The FBI director was also a lawyer. When he spoke, his tone was terse, "The FBI will not violate the law or the Constitution just because we think this guy is a bad actor. Give me some evidence on which to base an investigation on so we can find and arrest the bastard if he is in the U.S."

After listening politely, the Director slid a folder containing a sanitized version of what Mossad passed to the CIA across the table to the Director of the FBI. Any reference to the material's source was eliminated. "This should give you enough."

The FBI director looked at the material. "This should give us enough to open a formal investigation. I assume that none of this can be used as evidence in court."

"Find the bastard, and then we'll ask the sources if they will testify. They just might."

As soon as Bishop returned to his office at Langley, he made two calls. One was to the satellite phone Janis carried. His message said that her cousin Walt had some information about a new family member. If anyone listened to the message, it would sound innocent. His second was to a number in Lebanon to let them know that Ghulam was now a priority target of the FBI.

THE SAME DAY, 4:06 P.M. LOCAL TIME, OTTOBEUREN

The satellite phone buzzed several times and went silent. No one heard the tone because the phone was inside the foam-lined safe in Janis' room bolted to the wall in the closet.

Raimond Harz, one of Hofer's two bodyguards, searched Janis' room at the Maximillian Hotel and didn't find the satellite phone. Nor did he hear the phone beeping as it attempted to tell its owner that a message was waiting. Not wanting to make it look like a burglary, Harz tried several four-digit combinations he deduced from Janis' passport. None worked so he left the safe alone.

Finding nothing else of interest, Harz left five minutes after he used the master key he was "loaned" in exchange for a 500 Euro tip to the bell captain. Had Harz gotten into the hotel's safe, he would have found the jewelry Janis had brought along with the phone. When he searched Janis' luggage, Harz didn't find the compartment in the base of her roller bag containing a sealed envelope with a second identity.

Motion started to wake Janis as she was carried by someone who smelled like a man who smoked, so she remained limp. Janis guessed that they thought she'd be out longer than she was. She was still groggy and let her head hang down as her wrists were duct-taped together behind the chair.

Once her hands were taped, a man with smoker's breath pushed open an eyelid. She forced herself not to let her eyes focus or react to the ashtray smell. The man with bad breath spoke to someone else in the room. "You'll be able to talk to her in 30 minutes."

Her head was clearing when Janis heard a door close and slowly opened her eyes without raising her head. She was in the center of a room with concrete walls. At one end, she spotted a gurney with leather arm and leg straps hanging down.

That explains why they didn't tie my legs to the chair. They're going to either use pain or drugs on me. This is not cool!

On the far side, metal-on-metal sounds told Janis the man in a white coat was placing implements in a tray she could not see. A Nazi flag hung above the door, and under it was the bodyguard she saw with Hofer in the hotel. She sensed his eyes were focused on her.

I'm in Hofer's lair, and he will torture me. I need to get out of here, NOW!!!

Janis used her fingers to get to the ribbon knife she kept in the back of her jogging shorts for such an occasion. Once out, the sharp made short work of the duct tape. The blade could cut her badly in a fight, making it a weapon of last resort.

The man in the white coat was the one she presumed was going to torture her. His clothing reeked from cigarette smoke and gave away his presence in front of her. It was now or never.

When he bent over, Janis snapped her head back and felt the back of her head slam into his chin. As he staggered back, she stood up and drove her shoulder into his chest, pushing him straight at the guard. Rather than get out of the way, the guard drew his SIG Sauer P220 9mm pistol from his shoulder holster and hesitated, not wanting to shoot the man in the white coat.

The man in the white coat grunted as Janis slammed him into the bodyguard, who grunted and lost his grip on the pistol. It clattered to the floor. Janis bent her fingers, so the tips were under the knuckles and drove her right hand into the throat of the man with the white coat. He gasped and staggered away, leaving Janis' face to face with a six-foot-tall, 200+ pound man. Besides having a height and weight advantage, he was probably stronger, a lot younger, and not recently drugged.

In the dojo, the mantra she was taught was to follow the three D's – deny, disable, and destroy. Deny meant keep her opponent at bay. Disable was just that, hinder or cripple him or her so he or she could not hurt you and then decide if you must execute the third D, destroy. In other words, finish the fight by either killing or eliminating your opponent as a threat. Janis was already into the disable mode and didn't want to grapple with the bigger man but had to keep him from his pistol.

Instinct took over. While the man may have been well-trained, Janis put him on the defensive with a rapid series of punches to his gut and side. He fended off a blow aimed at his head but could not stop the kick to his groin. Janis felt the top of her foot crush his balls. The man's eyes rolled back in his head as he doubled over, gasping. Janis slammed the bottom of her foot on the side of one knee, snapping it like a dry tree limb. The bodyguard went down, his face contorted from pain. Janis pounced on his back, put one hand on his chin and the other on the back of his head, and twisted. The bodyguard's spine snapped with a soft pop.

Janis went over to the doctor, who was still struggling to breathe. He backed-up to lean against the wall for support and waved a scalpel as a weapon. "You'll never get out of here alive."

"Why not?"

"All the doors are locked and have codes for which you need special badges."

The man in the white coat started to reach into his jacket. Janis swatted the hand with the scalpel to one side with her left hand and hammered her right fist into his temple. She felt the bone give way. The man in the white coat fell over, and his hand released a folder with a badge.

Janis picked up the P220 pistol and checked to see if a round was in the chamber before she rolled the bodyguard over to find his badge and spare magazines. The cold steel sent a chill up her spine as she slipped the SIG Sauer pistol into the waistband of her jogging shorts. Janis grabbed the bodies by the forearms and dragged them across the smooth tile floor to a corner so the door would shield them from view when it was opened.

Next, she looked for security cameras and didn't see any. If they were there, they were well hidden, and she didn't have the time to find them. Janis rationalized that Hofer probably didn't want what went on in this room recorded.

At one end of the table, someone had neatly laid out the contents of the small pouch she was using to carry her documents when she was kidnapped. Janis put the badges and spare magazines into the compartments and went to the other end of the table. There, Janis found a syringe loaded with diazepam, a.k.a. valium. Enough would knock someone out. Too much would kill.

While Janis was rummaging through the wallets from the bodyguard and the man in the white coat, she heard the click of an electronic lock and the door cracked open. A familiar voice spoke, "Heinz, is our friend awake yet?"

Janis waited until Hofer was inside the room. "She is, and this is not the way to treat a lady on the first date!"

Hofer let the door close with a Germanic thunk and took two strides into the room. He didn't see Janis, who was behind the door. Hofer turned to the sound of Janis voice and saw the 9mm P220 leveled at his chest. "*Hände Hoch!*" Hands up.

Hofer complied. "Are you going to kill me?"

"Maybe. Why did you have me drugged?"

"Ahhhhh… At first, I thought you might be an interesting date. That was before the front desk clerk told Heinz that you had a massage. My bodyguard gave the masseuse 200 Euros, who described the scars on your body. From their description, I was sure they were made by bullets or knives. So, I became curious. In my business, one has to be careful."

"You could have asked."

"But I would have had to get you in bed to do that."

"I would think a man of your charms would be confident that he could seduce me. Take off your coat and empty your pockets onto the gurney."

Hofer did as he was told, exposing a pistol in a shoulder holster. He put the gun, a Walther PPK, two spare magazines, a mobile phone, several sheets of folded paper, a Palm personal data assistant, a key chain, his badge, and some pocket change in a precise, Germanic-looking row. "Take off the shoulder holster." Hofer again complied.

Janis pushed the chair that was lying on its side toward Hofer. "Sit, but before you do, unbuckle your belt and drop your trousers to your ankles."

"Why?"

"Because I said so. Trust me, I'm not interested in giving you a blow job."

"What a waste." Hofer picked up the chair and put it on its feet before he dropped his trousers. For a second, he thought about rushing her, and instinct told him that Janis would probably get off two accurate shots before he could get his hands on her.

"What are the numbers to unlock the phone and the PDA?"

"Why should I tell you that?"

"If you don't, I will do what you were going to do to me. So, what are the numbers?"

"Six, two, eight, one. The numbers work on both devices."

"What do they signify, or are they random?"

"They are my father's SS serial number. He knew Hitler personally."

Now that she knew the basis of his PINs, she could unlock his electronic secrets. To check, Janis entered the four digits on the Palm and the first screen popped up, and the device was 91 percent charged.

Janis opened the folded sheets of paper she took from Hofer's coat pocket. One was a 1978 Interpol Blue Notice with a vague description of a young, blonde woman of average size being sought as a person of interest for a hit she made in Germany. Another was an Interpol Purple Notice looking for information on a hit Janis made in 1980 in

Belgium. Both had the same general description. Hofer also had a copy of the background check from the rental car agency. Reading them gave her chills, and Janis wondered how Hofer got them.

"Who told you I was coming?"

"A friendly bird."

"Don't fence with me. Who?"

"A customer."

"Who?"

"Sorry, you will have to torture me to get that name from me. By the way, I gather you've done this before."

"How do you know that?"

"By your reaction to reading the notices. That's you they are describing, isn't it?"

Janis didn't answer. *Hofer had just become a loose end, and the CIA wanted him dead. Now, so do I.*

"You know, you need a code to open the doors."

Hofer was stalling for time, and Janis suspected more bodyguards were somewhere in the house. The question was, where were they, and when would they arrive?

"Not a problem. I can either have you do it or kill you and take out your eyeball. The tools to do it are right there on the table."

"You're not serious."

"I am as serious as a heart attack."

"Who hired you?"

"There are a lot of people who would like you dead. Tell me, who tipped you off?"

Hofer stared at Janis. His face was impassive, but she could sense fear building in him.

"Was it Walt Bishop?"

Janis was sure she saw a flicker of recognition in Hofer's eyes. The German tried to change the subject. "I could offer you several million or more to walk away, but I don't think you would take it."

"You're right."

"So, Fraulein Mitchell, what happens next?"

Do I interrogate Hofer and see what I can get, or do I just kill him and leave? The book Bishop wants is in his Palm. Her mind said, find out what you can, and her heart said, kill the son-of-a-bitch. Shooting him will make noise and bring others running. So, how do I kill him?

Janis walked behind Hofer, pricked his neck with the syringe with diazepam, and pushed down on the plunger to inject a small amount. "This will help you relax."

Hofer's eyes glazed over in seconds, and his head dropped as he went out, allowing Janis to tie his hands behind his back and wrap duct tape around his chest and the chair. Then, she taped his feet to the chair.

Next, she cracked open the door, and no one was in the hallway of what looked like a basement. When she slid each badge into the slot, the lock clicked open. She gently closed the door and returned to Hofer.

Janis slapped his face several times. Hofer's eyes opened, but she could tell he was having trouble focusing.

"Who told you I was coming?"

"A customer."

"Is he an Arab?

Hofer shook his head.

"An American?"

Hofer nodded.

Hofer was losing consciousness, so Janis slapped him again, hard enough to leave fingerprints on his cheek. "With the CIA?"

The yes sounded more like a hiss. The valium was taking effect.

"Was his name Bishop?"

Another nod and a hissed yes. Hofer's head hung down. He was out. She slapped him several more times to no avail. Hofer was not going to awaken soon. Janis returned to the table, refilled the syringe, and jabbed it into his neck before pushing the plunger down until it stopped. "Good night, Herr Hofer."

Paranoia about being identified drove Janis's next series of actions. On the table, Janis found a bottle of isopropyl alcohol, latex gloves, and a glass bottle of gauze pads. She pulled on a pair of latex gloves, and everything she touched – chair, door handle, syringe – was swabbed down twice to remove any fingerprints. She burned the Interpol notices after dousing them with alcohol.

Next, Hofer's badge, phone, and PDA went into her pouch. Before she headed out the door, Janis put her index finger on Hofer's neck, and there was no pulse.

With her hand on the doorknob, Janis looked around the sterile-looking room to make one last scan to see if she had missed anything. She was about to open the door when she heard the click signifying that someone had just slid his card into the reader.

The door swung open, and a medium-sized man with blonde hair came in. He was wearing an identical suit to the bodyguard she had just killed. Seeing Hofer slumped over in the chair, Raimond Harz hurried over to his boss, letting the steel door close. "Herr Hofer?"

For a second, Janis debated slipping out the door but decided he knew she was here and could recognize her. Therefore, he had to die.

Sensing immediate mortal danger, the blond man started to reach for his pistol and turn around. He was too late. Janis' hammered him in on the side of the face with the SIG's barrel. The man was well-trained, he staggered, blood streaming down his face, and backed up to gain space to defend himself.

The one thing Janis didn't want to do was to have a gunfight at close range in a closed concrete room. One, others might hear it. And two, she didn't want to give him a chance to get a shot off.

With her left hand, she reached for the man's right arm that was coming across his chest to pull his SIG P220 from a shoulder holster. He immediately grabbed her with his left hand, assuming he was stronger. He was right, but the move let Janis jam her SIG Sauer pistol under his ribs and angle it up.

The muzzle blast knocked her hand away when she pulled the trigger, but Harz's body muffled the sound. The 115-grain, 9mm hollow-point bullet ripped open a lung and went through his heart before stopping in his spine. The man's surprised look changed to one with vacant eyes as he keeled over.

Janis searched him quickly and yanked his badge hard enough to break the chain. The badge and his three magazines for his SIG Sauer went into the pouch. With the one in her pistol and the seven she now had, Janis had enough for a brief firefight. Now was the time to escape.

As she moved along the corridor with her back to the wall, Janis was ready to kill anyone she saw. With the pouch buckled around her waist, she had a SIG Sauer in each hand. Janis was, to paraphrase what athletes say after a game, taking the doors one door at a time. As she moved, Janis looked for security cameras and saw none.

At the end of the corridor, Janis slowly turned the handle. The door opened, and she expected to see another corridor. Instead, she saw mowed grass. Janis walked sideways, keeping her back pressed against the wall. Above, Janis could see the windowsills of the upper-story windows and the bottoms of two balconies.

Daylight was fading fast, helped by the overcast sky. Glancing around the corner, Janis could see the garage where all the doors were closed. Beyond the garage were trees through which she was confident she could make it to the road.

As Janis picked her way through the trees, staying just inside the tree line and parallel to the driveway, she wondered if anyone else saw her brought into the basement. Every 20 to 30 feet, Janis stopped, listened, and looked for surveillance cameras and sensors. She found none. Either they were well hidden, or Hofer was arrogant enough not to have any. However, in a place like this, one could never be sure.

At the six-foot-tall, wrought iron fence, Janis waited until it was dark before she climbed a tree. Hanging from a limb, she hand-walked over the fence until she could drop down to the grass that ran alongside the road.

A sign said it was 10 kilometers to Ottobeuren. Janis started jogging and wondered if Hofer's staff had found his body. The overriding questions running through her mind were, had anyone else seen her, and what would they do?

THE SAME DAY, 7:29 P.M. LOCAL TIME, OTTOBEUREN

Each time Janis saw headlights, she jumped into the trees, unsure if it was just a motorist or someone from Hofer's organization searching for her. Along the way, she fieldstripped each pistol and, at random intervals, tossed the parts into the woods along with the bullets and spare magazines. The last to go was the latex gloves peeled off and dumped into a trashcan on the jogging path near the hotel. Rather than go through the lobby, Janis used her room key to enter through the back door.

Just before she slid her card into the lock, Janis paused, wondering if she should have kept one of the guns. As quietly as she could, she opened the door and slid along the wall until she got to where it opened into a bedroom.

Thankfully, no one was in the room. The first thing Janis checked was the safe, and it hadn't been opened, but someone had spun the dial and wasn't smart enough to reset it to the number Janis had selected.

Janis looked in the mirror, surprised that she didn't look totally disheveled. A long hot shower followed.

She had to get out of Germany. Seeing the Eggers would have to wait. Leaving tonight might raise suspicions with those at the hotel who knew Hofer. Before she went to sleep, Janis booked a first-class seat back to Dallas from Frankfurt. She would check out in the morning a day early. Famished, Janis called room service and ordered dinner while she contemplated what she would do about Bishop. He had access to her debrief and might be able to discover her identity. That was unacceptable.

She wasn't sure if she was angrier at herself for being careless or at Bishop, who set her up. Should she tell Mossad and let them tell the CIA so they could deal with Bishop. Or should she take care of him herself? The latter, she concluded was the better option.

THE SAME DAY, 8:49 P.M. LOCAL TIME, OTTOBEUREN

Heinz Berg hadn't seen his boss since he left for the basement several hours before, which was very unusual. When home, Gerd Hofer spent 10 or 12 hours a day in the office making phone calls, either trying to make a deal or finding new weapons to sell.

Berg was Hofer's accountant, chief-of-staff, and the administrative half of the firm. Hofer had the contacts and made the deals. Berg made sure the arms transfer paperwork was in order, collected and moved the money, and kept the books. To keep the German "tax man" happy, Berg kept one set of accounts for their German tax return on a computer in their office. A separate set of computer discs in a bank vault in Switzerland showed Hofer and Associates' real profit.

Hofer paid millions in Euros to the German government in taxes each year. If he were to report his actual income, he would pay millions more. Berg's advice was to file and make it look reasonable to avoid suspicion while taking advantage of every legal loophole. Berg's rationale was that the government would need years to determine his true income.

Berg was in Hofer's palatial office when he received a call from a CIA contact that caused Hofer to go from smiling to very grim in a matter of seconds. After hearing what was discussed, Berg advised him to stay away from the Mitchell woman, get in his jet, and go someplace.

Instead, Hofer insisted he had a foolproof plan to deal with Mitchell. Hofer had a dark side that Berg didn't like that revealed itself in situations such as this one. Berg, not wanting to be part of a kidnapping and murder, stayed in the firm's third-floor offices but could not find a convenient, believable excuse to leave the grounds.

Wondering why Hofer hadn't returned upstairs, Berg went to what Hofer called his "conversation" room. Mitchell wasn't the first person to be taken there to be tortured. That room and most of the basement were off-limits to the household staff.

The first thing Berg saw was Hofer slumped in the chair. In the corner, the bodies of Gunther Wagner and the man he knew as Dr. Stumpf were sprawled awkwardly on the floor. Harz lay in a pool of blood where he died. The Mitchell woman was gone.

Looking at Stumpf's body, Berg thought good riddance. He disliked the man who was a disciple of Josef Mengele.

There was a faint smell of alcohol, and several pieces of cloth were wadded up in the trash, along with some partially burned gauze pads. This suggested the Mitchell woman wiped her prints off everything. He looked for Hofer's PDA and cell phone, and both were gone, along with the badges for all four men. He assumed the Mitchell woman had them as well. Soon, she would figure out that he was part of Hofer and Associates, which made him very afraid.

Berg ran upstairs, thinking now was time to execute the plan he had worked out over the years if Hofer was assassinated or arrested. In the office, he spun the dials to the double door floor safe and pulled out the half a million in 100 Euro notes Hofer kept on hand for "emergencies." They went into an empty briefcase.

Next, he logged in to the company's financial system. He transferred one million Euros into each of the accounts Hofer had set up for his pilots and household staff. With the deposit confirmations printed, Berg wrote each a check for two years' salary and a 30 percent bonus to exceed the layoff requirements of German law. On the confirmations, he wrote down the access codes for each account the employees could change later.

That done, he checked to ensure there was enough money for the outstanding checks he'd mailed earlier in the month and added 100,000 Euros to be safe. The remaining balance was transferred to his account at the Lombard Odier branch in the Bahamas. Slowly, the computer spit out the confirmations on the printer.

Satisfied the recurring bills for Hofer and Associates would be paid for six months, he went to his suite on the second floor of the mansion. Berg took his "go bag" from his personal safe and placed it next to his briefcase. It had 100,000 Euros in cash, his Swiss and Austrian passports in separate envelopes with matching credit cards, national identity cards, and driver's licenses.

With the confirmations he took off the printer in his hands, Berg summoned the five members of the household staff to his office. There, he told them that Hofer and Associates is ceasing operations and Herr Hofer has left and is not coming back. Then, Berg handed them envelopes with the checks and details on their Lombard Odier savings accounts. He also said he would document their departure with the German government showing they were outstanding employees.

After explaining the steps to change the passcodes printed on the sheets of paper, he reminded them "to be careful with the money. A million Euros doesn't go as far as it used to …"

He insisted that they leave immediately, check into a hotel in Ulm of their choosing, and have them bill Hofer & Associates. He would notify them when they could return to pack up their apartments. Berg watched them drive down the long driveway from a window on the front of the house.

Once the cars were out of sight, Heinz began the next stage of the plan – disposing of the bodies. In the stable, he checked the forest-green Fendt tractor to ensure the backhoe and front loader were attached correctly, and the hydraulic lines were not leaking. The diesel engine rumbled into life, and he let it idle for a few minutes to load two bags of fertilizer, one of lime, and another of grass seed, into the bucket.

Berg drove the tractor into the large meadow behind the house and garden, where he used the backhoe to dig a hole five meters long, two wide, and four deep. The dirt was piled neatly off to the side.

Using the same basement door Janis used to exit the building, Berg loaded the three bodies into the front loader. Harz's bloody body was wrapped in towels to absorb the blood and then rolled into a blanket. With all three bodies in the front loader, Berg dumped them in the pit. He climbed down to arrange the corpses, so they were flat before spreading the bags of fertilizer and lime over the bodies.

He used the front loader to refill the pit, and when it was nearly full, he ran the tractor back and forth to compact the loose dirt. He put the sod back that he carefully peeled back when he began digging and pressed it down by the tractor's wheels. To finish the job, Berg spread fertilizer over the grass by hand.

Still running on adrenalin and following his plan, Berg drove the tractor back to the stable and hosed down the front loader's bucket. He was not worried that the four men would be missed.

His next task was to clean out the "conversation room." What he could burn, he put in one bucket, and what had to go in the trash went into a bag that would go into the dumpster. Then he swabbed down the floor with disinfectant.

Berg was sure Reinhard Stumpf, the man in the white coat, didn't have any relatives. Before the wall came down, Stumpf was a Stasi "medical examiner" specializing in torture. There wasn't a need for men like him once Germany was re-united, and Stumpf found himself out of work and money. That's when Hofer found the 50-year-old bachelor and put him on retainer so he could call him when needed.

Gunther and Raimond were orphans and single who were adopted by Hofer's father. Hofer and Associates was their life, and Gerd was their father. He was sure they didn't have any girlfriends since once a week, Berg paid for call girls to come to the mansion and service them.

Sweaty and dirty, Berg took a long shower before taking the next step in his plan – transferring the ownership of Hofer's property to his name. The buy-sell agreements were already stored on the computer along with the power-of-attorney that enabled him to act in Gerd Hofer's name. His contract, also signed by Gerd Hofer, allowed him to commit the company on legal documents such as contracts, loans, tax returns, and more.

With Gerd's encouragement, the buy-sell agreement was already signed but not dated or sealed. Hofer's rationale was that if one needed to sign it in an emergency and the other wasn't around, all they needed was a date and the corporate seal. Berg added the date and applied the corporate seal on the document that sold Hofer's stock in the company to him. Later, he would transfer the funds he paid for the stock to his accounts when he shut the company down. He did the same for all the corporations Hofer had him set up to confuse government investigators. Into one, he put the house and land into the one which owned Hofer's condo in Muisenberg, South Africa called HAOFA – Hofer & Associates of Africa. Once he filed the new deed in his name, they were his.

By two a.m., Berg was exhausted physically and mentally. He thought about checking into a hotel but decided to spend the night. He would begin moving out tomorrow.

CHAPTER 16

UGLY NEWS

FRIDAY, AUGUST 2ND, 2002, 11:28 A.M. LOCAL TIME, SIDON

A s he drove down the coast road from Beirut, Ghulam had mixed emotions. He wasn't sure if he was madder at his father or mother for concealing the seriousness of her illness. He learned how sick his mother was when his father slipped during a phone call when he revealed there was no effective treatment for pancreatic cancer. They just had to wait for the disease to run its painful course.

The drive down the coast road let his mind wander between his childhood memories and the operational problems he faced. His father, Ziad Ghulam, was a Lebanese fish merchant who started with a cart and then opened a small store on Sidon's waterfront. He had expanded the business into a thriving retail and wholesale operation he now ran with Ghulam's younger brother, Chadi.

The store funded Ghulam's education. Originally, Abd al Bari wanted to study engineering but did not like it. His parents paid for a year at American University in Washington, D.C. where he studied history and political sciences, where Ghulam excelled. He graduated from American University in Beirut in 1979.

His father met his mother, Saira, when he came ashore in Sidon in his fishing boat after fleeing Palestine. She was alone, penniless, and looking for work after having just walked to Sidon from her home in Acre.

Ahmed needed someone to help on his boat and hired her on the spot. Some wags said Ziad was the only one who would ever propose to Saira. Still, Abd al Bari and Chadi, believed their parents had a loving relationship.

The influx of refugees into Sidon and the never-ending war with Israel were both good and bad for the family business. People needed food, and fish was cheap.

Saira had left Palestine as a wanted woman. The British and, later, the Israelis wanted to arrest her for murder. She had no love for the Jews, and for her, her choice was either to flee or be arrested.

Abd al-Bari didn't care about politics until his year in the United States. He thought of himself as a secular Sunni until he saw the influence American Jews and Israel had on U.S. policy. When he returned, a Hezbollah recruiter offered more money than his father could afford to pay.

Ghulam rose quickly through Hezbollah's ranks. After he set up a pipeline to bring arms and ammunition into Lebanon, he moved from logistics to operations. He believed Hezbollah's attacks would be even more successful if all the dead were Jews.

Before he opened the door to his car parked near his father's store, Ghulam concluded that a series of even bloodier attacks were needed. They would enhance the message that the Al-Musawi Corps and Hezbollah are a global force to be reckoned with. He had assets in place in three countries. Now, Ghulam had to pick the targets where he could create the most carnage.

THE SAME DAY, 9:46 A.M. LOCAL TIME, OTTOBEUREN

Driving in Germany was one of the things Janis loved about Germany. There were no speed limits on many of the Autobahn's sections. Heading to Frankfurt, the Porsche was loafing along with the top down at 180 kilometers per hour (~111 mph).

While she was enjoying the drive, Heinz Berg was in Memmingen, buying boxes to pack his office. Clothes would go in the back of his Mercedes.

On the way back to Hofer's house, he stopped at the hangar and told the two pilots that they were no longer employed. He gave them the same documents he gave to the household staff before telling them to fly Hofer's Falcon 50 to Jet Aviation in Dusseldorf so the plane could be sold. He gave them a thousand Euros for expenses to get back to Bodensee where they lived.

Back at Hofer Hof, Berg walked through the second-floor collection of exhibits and memorabilia from Gerd Hofer's father on the second floor. The photos, clothes, documents, and artifacts came from his father's relationships with the leaders of Hitler's Third Reich. They were proudly displayed as if they were in a museum. Their very presence made Berg uncomfortable, and he believed someone who would pay handsomely for the collection.

Once the museum and the arms collection in the basement was sold, he would put Hofer Hof up for sale. Meanwhile, he had to find a place to live outside Germany.

FRIDAY, AUGUST 2ND, 2002, 7:36 P.M. LOCAL TIME, MCLEAN

After work Bishop usually unwound by watching TV, renting a movie, or reading a book. He didn't like to cook or eat TV dinners, so dinner was take-out from a local restaurant three or four nights a week. Before Bishop left the office, he decided on what Chinese food he wanted and 15 minutes from the restaurant, he called. The woman who took his order always said his food would be ready in 20 minutes. Bishop couldn't remember when it wasn't ready when he walked in the door.

He put the plastic bag with the container of moo Shu chicken, the pancakes rolled in aluminum foil, and the small container of plum sauce on the floor, and at the same time, he unlocked the door to his two-bedroom condominium. With the Chinese food in his left hand and his briefcase in his right, Bishop walked into the dining area that divided the kitchen from the living/family room.

"Did you bring enough for two?"

Bishop was surprised by the female voice coming from the couch. He turned to see Janis holding a pistol pointed at him.

"When did you get back?"

"Yesterday."

"How did you get in here?"

"My secret." Janis avoided the security cameras at the entrance to the complex. Picking the lock to Bishop's two-bedroom condo was easy. "When I was in your office to talk about Hofer, I got your address from your condo lease renewal sitting on the corner of your desk."

Bishop wasn't worried about being recorded. His condominium was swept routinely for bugs. Unless some foreign agency planted a listening device since the last check, what was said in his condominium would stay there. He tried to ignore the Walther PPK/S pistol pointed at his chest by a woman wearing latex gloves. "Is Hofer dead?"

Janis tossed Hofer's cell phone and PDA on the table. "He is. On the way home, I bought chargers so I could spend time looking through them. They contain lots of fascinating and, for you, very compromising info."

"You don't need the gun, Janis. I'm not the enemy."

Janis made no attempt to hide her sarcasm. "Really! Based on what is in this PDA, the CIA's Inspector General could start asking you some ugly questions." She waved the gun. "When was the last time you talked to Hofer?"

"I can't recall."

"Don't lie to me. You sent me on a mission two days after you called Hofer. Then, after I landed, you two talked again. Who paid me, you, Hofer or the CIA?"

Bishop looked down at the floor. His lack of an answer meant Bishop paid her, and she would not receive the second half of her fee for killing Hofer if she killed Bishop. Once before, Raul Moya reminded a buyer of her services who initially refused to pay the second half of her fee that he would pass the buyer's contact info to her. The payment arrived two days later.

"So, what's the deal between Hofer and you?"

"We used Hofer to buy and deliver weapons, so the CIA didn't have any fingerprints on the shipment."

"What kind of weapons?"

"Mostly small arms – rifles, machine guns, grenades, rocket-propelled grenades, mortars – that kind of stuff. The shipments are based on the threat our friends were facing. Sometimes, he delivered Russian shoulder-fired surface-to-air missiles."

"What else did you tell him?"

Bishop didn't say a word.

"Let's play multiple choice. Choice A – I'm a new asset Hofer could task through you for a fee, and of course, you'd pocket a percentage. Choice B – the Israelis were coming after Hofer for his arms sales to a who's who of terrorist organizations in the Middle East. Choice C – I want you to take her out before she discovers I'm a traitor and either kills me or tells the CIA. Or choice D – you wanted Hofer taken out as a loose end, knowing that eventually, the CIA will learn that you've been selling secrets to Hezbollah, Hamas, and the Iranians. Pick one, Bishop?"

"I didn't tell him anything about you."

Janis pursed her lips, trying to control her anger. "Bullshit, Bishop. I think you picked C and D. You ratted me out to Hofer, you bastard!!! You gave him my description and sent him the Interpol notices, didn't you?"

"No, I swear I didn't."

"Then how did he recognize me?"

Bishop blinked and lowered his head. "I told him you were a threat to both of us and sent him a still from the debriefing." Softly he asked, "Are you going to kill me?"

"Good question." *Of course, I am, but I'm not going to tell you.*

"How much money did Hofer pay you?"

"By your standards, not much. I've got five million stashed away."

"Where'd the money come from?"

"Commissions from Hofer, the Iranians, and their friends."

Janis shook her head. "Let me get this straight. You were profiting from Hofer's arms sales which may or may not have been sanctioned by your employer, AND you were selling intel on the Iranians."

"My deal with the Iranians was a two-way street."

"Bullshit. I doubt they gave you anything useful."

"They gave us mostly low-level stuff that filled in some blanks, and we had an off-the-books agreement that they wouldn't allow Hezbollah to launch attacks on U.S. soil. The Iran desk knew about the deal."

"So, I gather the attack in LA was a surprise."

"Yes, that and the SA-14s they were trying to smuggle into the U.S. We captured four in Arizona a few weeks back and have kept it out of the news."

"You're in deep shit, Bishop. I'd guess you are in way over your head and saw no way out. Having me kill Hofer was one step to getting out of the hole you've dug."

Bishop didn't say a word. By the looks of the apartment, Janis believed Bishop was probably paying alimony to an ex-wife and living on what was left of his government salary. She'd bet his ex-wife didn't know about Bishop's offshore nest egg that he probably wasn't planning to touch until he retired from the CIA.

Hofer's PDA had a series of digits Janis recognized as a numbered bank account at Pictet et Cie under Bishop's name. She thought the CIA's Inspector General would be interested in how often and who made the deposits and the total.

"So, Ms. Harris, what are you going to do?"

"Not sure yet. I don't like loose ends, and I hate people who are not trustworthy. And you, Walt Bishop, are both."

Bishop stared at her with open eyes.

"Why don't you eat? Your food is getting cold."

Bishop nodded. "Want a beer?"

Janis walked toward the table. "No thanks. Please, help yourself. Before you start looking for the PPK/S you had in the kitchen drawer, I'm holding it. The one beside your bed has been unloaded, and I have the ammo."

Nodding as he took a beer out of the refrigerator, Bishop picked up a fork from the drawer, and a plate from the cabinet over the counter. While doing so, Janis ripped open the bag and laid the roll of pancakes next to the opened container of moo Shu chicken. Bishop didn't see the small syringe used to give kids medicine orally. She squeezed the plunger and sprayed the cyanide she took from Hofer's house onto the moo Shu chicken.

"Here, you can eat while we talk."

Relieved that he would not die in the next 30 seconds, Bishop sat at the table and put two thin pancakes on a plate. Each got a dollop of plum sauce, followed by the stir-fried mix of scrambled eggs, chicken, diced scallions, and cabbage on the pancake.

"Tell me when you first met Hofer?"

With that question, Bishop bragged about how often he and the agency used Hofer, thanks to his low prices. Bishop encouraged Hofer to quote a higher number to increase his 10 percent commission.

Janis watched Bishop make and finish a third rolled pancake of moo Shu chicken. When he was done, Bishop took another beer from the refrigerator. While standing there, he asked if Janis wanted any ice cream, and she shook her head.

"Well, Bishop, that's all for now."

"So, are you going to kill me now?"

"No, not yet. But the cyanide in your food will give you a fatal heart attack any minute."

Bishop's eyes got wide with fear. He ran to the sink and stuffed his fingers down his throat to force himself to puke up his dinner. The move was too late. He felt a searing pain in his chest as his heart stopped working. He turned to look at Janis and fell face-first onto the floor. His body convulsed once and was still.

Before she left the condo, Janis pulled Bishop's files from his safe, which she managed to open while she waited, and put them in her soft-sided briefcase. They joined a mobile phone she suspected was only used for his "unofficial" business and his list of Swiss bank account numbers.

Anything Janis touched was wiped down with alcohol wipes taken from her purse. They and the latex gloves and syringe went into a trashcan well away from the apartment complex. Janis was confident that by the time police found Bishop's body, the cyanide would be long gone, and only a very skilled forensic examiner might figure out what killed him.

Deciding to kill Bishop brought Janis back into the world she left 20-plus years ago. She was upset with herself. Killing Bishop was an emotional decision instead of one with her head. Maybe, she should have called the CIA and let them deal with him. But who was she to call? Bishop was her control. And more people would know who she was.

In the end, she decided that she couldn't trust anyone or the process to take out Bishop. That left only one choice, killing him herself.

Shortly after she left Bishop's apartment, Janis was in her TBM climbing through 5,000 feet on the way to Flight Level 180 for the first leg of her flight back to Dallas. Flying helped push Bishop into the back of her mind and let her subconscious process her actions.

When she landed, she still hadn't decided what to do with Hofer's PDA and phone and Bishop's phone and records. How and why she acquired them would lead to questions for which she didn't have good answers. For the time being, they would have to be stored in a safe place outside the U.S.

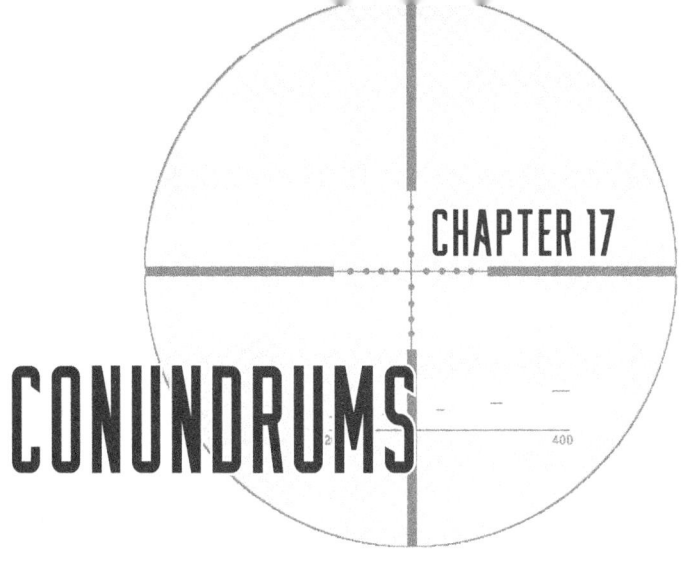

CHAPTER 17

CONUNDRUMS

The temperature had just reached 30° Celsius when Ghulam picked a table in the shade at an outdoor café. The cool, damp wind off the Mediterranean made the air feel cooler. As he sipped his coffee and watched people pass by, Ghulam let his mind mull over the two problems he had yet to solve.

One: where could he get more shoulder-fired, surface-to-air missiles, rocket-propelled grenades, and automatic weapons within the EU, so he didn't have to smuggle them in?

Two: what were the best venues to attack? Abd al-Bari Ghulam believed the list of potential targets handed down by the Shura Council wouldn't create enough carnage – *more* Jews had to die. If his teams attacked synagogues and killed everyone inside, the body count might be in the hundreds. Ghulam wanted to kill thousands.

During their seasons, American football and soccer matches were scheduled every week in major cities in Europe and the U.S. If thousands could be killed in one attack, it would ratchet up the political pressure on the country's government. This made them perfect targets.

Targets dictated weapons and tactics. Without the right weapons, Ghulam couldn't create the desired results. It was time for him to go shopping.

THE SAME DAY, 9:46 A.M. LOCAL TIME, DALLAS

When she arrived home a little after two in the morning, Janis couldn't sleep since her mind kept running through scenarios of what to do with the data from Hofer's phone and PDA. Frustrated that she couldn't doze off, Janis saved, printed, and scanned every page in Hofer's and Bishop's PDAs. From their phones, she created a spreadsheet with the phone contacts and the numbers both men called.

She put her elbows on her desk, resting her chin on her clasped hands as she stared at the printed sheets. Yes, the Israelis could use this data, but so could the CIA. However, killing Hofer wasn't a sanctioned hit by either the CIA or Mossad, nor was killing Bishop. Murdering Bishop also violated her immunity agreement and that could be a problem. So how would she explain how she acquired the files?

Then, there were the files she took from Bishop's condo. Using the usernames, passwords, and account numbers Bishop wrote in one of the folders, he had the money to pay her. A million was withdrawn and transferred to the account she gave him just before she left for Germany.

Clearly, Bishop was off the reservation when he paid for her to kill Hofer knowing she was being set up. Large deposits from one of the accounts in Hofer's PDA showed Bishop and Hofer were in cahoots. Still, she couldn't tell how far into the CIA Hofer's relationship extended. So, what does she tell the CIA?

She tried logging into Hofer's bank accounts, but the passwords didn't work. Rather than raise suspicions by asking for a new password, Janis stopped and suspected someone had changed them after Hofer was killed.

Wondering about what to do kept Janis tossing and turning all night. Even after gulping down two fingers of scotch, she still couldn't sleep. Finally, around four, Janis dozed off and got up at nine.

As Janis thought about what to do, the more complex the decision became. Every possibility other than doing nothing led right back to the answer to one question – how did she get the PDA, Hofer's and Bishop's phones, and their files? Finally, she worked her options down to three choices.

One: Tell the CIA Bishop was a traitor and taking a cut on CIA weapons deals with Hofer. If the hit on Hofer was authorized, the CIA would have a record of her meeting with Bishop, the authorization, and the money transfer. If not, it was proof that Bishop was on his own.

Two: Go to the FBI. They'd love to investigate crimes by a rival agency, particularly the CIA, but that would come back to her, which was an unacceptable risk even with the immunity agreement since she killed him on U.S. soil after the immunity agreement was signed.

Three: Tell the Israelis. Hofer arms shipments would interest Mossad, and they will want to know how I got the information.

The bottom line was that killing Bishop or Hofer wasn't sanctioned by either Mossad or the CIA. She could make a case for killing Hofer by confirming that she believed Bishop was acting in his capacity as her control. When she found out differently, as an independent contractor, she could no longer trust Bishop, so she took matters into her own hands rather than take the problem to the CIA.

She felt as if Hofer's PDA and phone were staring at her as they sat on her coffee table. Maybe they weren't used to that much inactivity.

WEDNESDAY, AUGUST 7ᵀᴴ, 2002, 11:33 A.M. LOCAL TIME, BEIRUT

Ghulam found the two phone numbers he wanted from a file on previous transactions. Both started with 49, the country code for Germany. He heard three rings before the answering machine picked up. Ghulam left a message in Arabic and English, knowing Hofer spoke both.

He then dialed Hofer's mobile number. Again, the phone rang three times, and a voice said in German and then English, "please leave a message." He did so in Arabic.

In the past, when he left a message for Hofer, the German called back within two days, and now he had to wait.

THE SAME DAY 5:48 A.M. LOCAL TIME, DALLAS

Janis was asleep when she heard a phone ringing that didn't sound like hers. On a hunch, she went into her office, and the "message waiting" light on Hofer's phone was blinking. The screen said the call originated from a number with a 961-country code. She listened to the message but didn't understand a word, suspecting the man was leaving a number in Arabic.

She flipped through the PDA and found the name Noorani which had the same number that called the phone. Janis looked at her Rolex and added seven hours before she dialed a number from memory. It was 6:48 a.m. in Tel Aviv.

"Good morning, Janis. You're up early. What's going on? Are you horny?"

"Yes, but that is not why I called. Aliyah, I need you to listen to a phone message that I'm pretty sure is in Arabic. It came from a number in the 961-country code."

"That's Lebanon. What's the number?"

Janis read number to Aliyah, and she repeated it to make sure that she had it right. "O.K., I'll check the number out. Now, play the message back with the volume full up. Hopefully, I will be able to understand what he is saying."

Janis held Hofer's phone about two inches from hers and pushed the keys to replay the message.

"When did the call come in?"

"Less than ten minutes ago. Why?"

"Did this person call you?"

"Not exactly."

"Janis, what is going on? Noorani is an alias used by Abd al-Bari Ghulam, and he wants the phone's owner to call him back."

"It's a long story. I've got some intel you need to see or discuss but not on the phone."

"Give me a hint."

"I can't, not on this phone."

"Is it worth a trip to Tel Aviv?"

"Yes. I'll call you when I know when I'll land."

"Do that. Meanwhile, I'll see what else we have on this number."

Janis packed her make-up and enough clothes for a week. By 5:30 a.m., she was airborne in the TBM, climbing to Flight Level Two-One-Zero, and cleared direct to Newark Airport. She had a first-class seat on the non-stop flight leaving that afternoon, landing in Tel Aviv just before seven Tuesday morning

THE SAME DAY, 13:03 P.M. LOCAL TIME, ZURICH, SWITZERLAND

The park between General-Quisan Quai and the lake known as Zurichsee was crowded with office workers enjoying the summer sunshine. Berg's walk was part exercise and part change of scenery to give him time to plan his next step knowing one misstep and he could wind up in jail or dead.

Berg had known Hofer since they were officers in the Bundeswehr's 12th Panzer Division. At the end of their commitments, they went their separate ways. Hofer went into his father's arms business, and Berg went to school to become a chartered accountant. When Hofer senior died, Gerd Hofer called Berg.

The deal was simple – run the financial side of the business, and in a year or two, you will be rich. Hofer's offer was quadruple his current salary and included a suite in Hofer's house for which he didn't have to pay rent. The job had other perks, such as he could use the corporate jet for vacations. And his current job was very boring. "The job offer was …" Hofer said, quoting from the movie The Godfather, "… a deal he could not refuse."

Initially, Berg's primary job was to make sure that the financial statements would pass muster if scrutinized by the German Federal Central Tax Authority. To maintain the proper paperwork trail, Berg slowly took over the administrative functions of the business, the most important of which was the documentation used on the arms shipments. The expenses, shipping documents, and invoices had to match what was on the company's books. This necessitated two sets of books, one the German government could inspect and the one kept in a safe deposit box in Zurich.

Hofer was dead and had no heirs. Berg rationalized he could let Hofer's money grow and eventually become unclaimed property confiscated by the German government. Or he, as the sole surviving executive and shareholder of the company, could take company funds and Hofer's investment portfolio. As the sole shareholder and executor of Hofer's estate, Berg had every legal right to take over Hofer and Associates, Hofer's investment portfolio, and do what he wished. That was what he was doing.

Berg wanted to shut the arms business down. To do so, he had to sell the inventory – *all* of it. The sooner the better.

The transfers, he told the cautious Swiss banker as he opened new accounts at Hinduja Bank and Pictet et Cie, were simply a business decision. He neglected to mention that Hofer was dead.

The forms he signed and showed the Swiss bankers certified that the money being deposited was earned legally. He had paper trails for the weapons they acquired and sold. Whether or not they fully complied with the International Traffic in Arms Regulations was a matter for a court to decide. Since Hofer had never been arrested, he suspected that the German government didn't want to prosecute him.

The day before he drove to Zurich, Berg went to the Commerzbank branch in Memmingen and emptied both corporate safe deposit boxes. One had 500,000 Euros, 200,000 Swiss francs, 100,000 British pounds, and 200,000 U.S. dollars.

The second box had what Hofer called their "escape identities." Berg's were Eberhard Bauer and Giljs Aartsen and were now in his new Swiss safe deposit box at Hinduja.

Bauer was Swiss, and his passport, national identity card, driver's license, and credit cards indicated he was a resident of Zurich. When they were issued, the address was a flat Berg had rented to qualify for the passport but did not renew the lease.

Giljs Aartsen's papers showed he was born in Eindhoven and had dual Dutch and South African citizenship. His South African passport indicated he lived in Muizenberg, a suburb of Cape Town. The address was for a condominium Hofer bought as a place to work while handling arms shipments to rebels in Africa.

Now that he had almost 30 million Euros in Swiss banks set up to generate a healthy return, Berg planned to start his search for an apartment in Zurich. Before he got in bed, he listened to Ghulam's message on the Hofer and Associates answering machine.

Berg decided to return the call in the morning, so he had time to think about what to say. Would he tell Ghulam and Hezbollah that Hofer was dead? If he did, would they deal with them? That was the real question.

CHAPTER 18

MORE QUESTIONS THAN ANSWERS

E ach time Janis arrived at Ben Gurion, she was treated as a VIP and deplaned before all the other passengers. Aliyah and an immigration officer escorted her to a kiosk, stamped her passport, and the pair left the airport.

Before they got in the car, they had a quick kiss. Aliyah took an envelope out of her purse and offered it to Janis. "I've been waiting to give these documents to you in person."

Janis took the #10 envelope. "What's in here?"

"Your Israeli passport with visas to pretty much anywhere, Israeli citizenship papers, Israeli national identity card, and Mossad ID folder. I used a Mossad cover address so that anyone inquiring will talk to a Mossad agent who will alert the right people."

Janis fanned the envelope to move the documents to one end before she ripped it open. She flipped through the passport and looked at the cards. "Thank you. The pictures are better than I expected."

Aliyah sensed something was driving Janis, who didn't say anything until Aliyah was well into Tel Aviv's morning rush hour traffic. "Aliyah, three things brought me to Tel Aviv. One: Walt Bishop set me up to be waxed. Two: Bishop and the arms dealer Gerd Hofer were business partners. Hofer was selling weapons directly to Hezbollah, and Bishop profited from it. I don't know if the CIA knows the extent of Bishop's arrangement with Hofer, but I suspect they don't. Three: Bishop was selling classified info to Hezbollah and the Iranians, and I don't believe it was disinformation. I have the documents that, if they don't prove Bishop was a double agent, they will give an investigator a place to start."

"How do you know all this?"

Janis turned away and looked out the passenger window. Aliyah didn't re-ask the question since she suspected the answer.

"Aliyah, I need help, and that's why I called. There's something else going on. Bishop wasn't pursuing Ghulam, and the CIA cannot operate in the U.S., so his hands were tied. With a major terrorist operative in the U.S., one would think the CIA and the FBI would be moving heaven and earth to get local law enforcement agencies to search for him. But they weren't."

"So, how does this affect Israel?"

"You want Ghulam for the attacks he planned against Israel and Jews in Germany and France. I want Ghulam for what he has done to mine. Bishop said something to me that was very, very strange. He said terrorism and an occasional terrorist attack in the U.S. is good for the CIA. We'll talk more when we get to your office?"

Aliyah gave Janis a quick glance and a smile. "Who said we are going to the office? We have needs to be taken care of, and you probably want a shower."

Janis stroked Aliyah's thigh. "Let's go to Mossad headquarters so I can tell Reznik and you the entire story so analysts can start digging. Then, I'll be tired from the trip, and we can go to your flat and fuck each other's brains out."

"Is it that serious?

"It is."

THE SAME DAY, 10:06 A.M. LOCAL TIME, ZURICH,

Since he feared someone would target him with a car bomb, Berg flagged a cab near his apartment for the ride to Zurich's Kloten Airport. He walked to a bank of payphones in the open area where the airlines issued boarding passes and checked luggage. With a roll of Swiss francs in his pocket, he dialed the number in Lebanon.

When someone answered, he asked in English for Fuad Noorani. "This is he." Ghulam responded in English, knowing that Noorani was the name that Gerd Hofer knew.

"Good morning, this is Hans Berg. I am Gerd Hofer's business partner. Mr. Hofer asked that I return your call. I am sorry that it took so long."

"Where is Mr. Hofer?"

"He is seriously ill and is taking a few weeks off." *As in dead.*

"I see."

Even from a public phone, Berg wondered if calls to Lebanon were being recorded. He'd already researched what Noorani bought. "If you are looking for the same items in our catalog you purchased before, we have them. And, in fact, Mr. Hofer is willing to empty our warehouse at a bargain price if you take our entire inventory."

Ghulam didn't answer for a few seconds. He'd knew Berg's role, but they had never met, and Hofer was always willing to negotiate. *Does 'empty the warehouse' mean they are getting out of the business? Or does he think they are about to be seized? Or is it a trap?* "Mr. Berg, what do you propose?"

"You look at what we have left, and if you like it, we negotiate a price, and you take possession at our warehouses."

He wants to show me the weapons, get the money, and I am responsible for moving them. Assuming this is true, I like everything about this other than the meeting.

"Mr. Berg, where do you want to meet?"

Noorani is interested. Where would be a safe place? The fewer borders the man must cross, the better. "Dresden is the closest airport to our inventory. Please let me know when you will arrive?"

"I will. What number should I use."

Berg anticipated this question. "My mobile number is best. We are renovating our offices, and the main number may not be available at all times." *That is not exactly true. Once the weapons are gone, Hofer & Associates is going out of business. By the end of the week, I'll be in my new flat in Zurich, living under the name of Bauer. I have two new mobile phones from different providers, and the number I just gave you will only be used for this transaction.*

THE SAME DAY, 2:56 P.M. LOCAL TIME, TEL AVIV

Aliyah took Janis to a secure conference room in Mossad headquarters. It had a large table and a floor-to-ceiling whiteboard on one wall, which gave them space to spread out the documents from Hofer's PDA and Bishop's condominium. Aliyah constructed a timeline of Hofer's and Bishop's interactions for the past four years. This established the two men had a long-standing commercial relationship. They also identified the times when Bishop sold info to the Iranians.

Neither Janis nor Aliyah could decipher three groups of digits on Hofer's PDA. At first, Janis thought they were latitudes and longitudes. Those locations were in the middle of the Indian Ocean, so that assumption was wrong.

Yitzhak Reznik came in to see what brought Janis to Israel and brought with him a man named Avram, who came from Unit 8200, the Israeli version of the NSA. As he laid Hofer's and Bishop's phones next to each other on the table, the young man smiled at the two women who were old enough to be his mother.

Avram held up one of Bishop's phones. "Walter Bishop made regular calls to Lebanon and Syria with this phone. He has the home and personal mobile numbers of a who's who of generals in the Iranian Quds Force, the Al Aqsa Martyrs Brigade, Hezbollah, Islamic Jihad, the Al-Musawi Corps, Fatah, and Hamas. The numbers were called regularly."

He picked up Hofer's phone. "This too has many that are of interest to us. Fuad Noorani as Abd al-Bari Ghulam, who spoke with Hofer on many occasions in the past three years. I've cataloged all the calls and the call patterns on this thumb drive that I will leave with you."

The two men left, and with the door closed, Reznik looked at Aliyah and Janis. "The question is not how Bishop got these numbers, but why he had them and what the conversations were about. They could be sources, or he could be a traitor. Either way, the CIA should be told."

I offered to help the CIA and was almost killed in a well-laid trap by a traitor. This won't happen again.

Reznik's voice brought her back into the room. "What else do you have?"

Janis slid a piece of paper across the table. "We're not sure what these are. At first, I thought they were latitudes and longitudes, but if you plot them, they're in the middle of the Indian Ocean."

Reznik looked at them for a few seconds. Then, his training as an artillery officer took over. "These are grid squares. I'll get someone to convert them to latitude and longitude. Janis, why are they important?"

Janis handed him a spreadsheet compiled from the data on Hofer's PDA. "These are inventories of the weapons Hofer either had in his possession or had access to, and each is tied to one of those numbers."

"My guess is the grid coordinates are the locations of his storage facilities. I'll get someone on it right away." Reznik studied the sheet, then he looked at Aliyah and then Janis's drawn and fatigued face. "I think the CIA needs to know they have a rat on their hands. Janis, you look like hell. Aliyah, take your friend someplace so she can get some sleep."

Aliyah smiled. "With pleasure."

As soon as Janis and her roller bag were inside her apartment, Aliyah put both hands on Janis's cheeks and kissed her. "Make love first, sleep later."

Janis's hands were on Aliyah's rear, pulling their crotches together, and she was breathing heavily. "I missed you so much," popped out between kisses and sighs.

"I missed you, too," came out of Aliyah's mouth between moans of pleasure.

Janis pulled off her light turtleneck, and Aliyah unhooked her bra. The Israeli woman's mouth went right to Janis' left breast, and she let her tongue linger on the hard nipple. "I love your breasts."

"They're too small."

"No, they're not. They're just the right size." Aliyah's pulled down Janis' skirt.

Janis's panties were already soaked, and so were Aliyah's. As Janis caressed Aliyah, the Israeli led Janis by the hand to the bedroom.

THE SAME DAY, 3:09 P.M. LOCAL TIME, LANGLEY

Rachel Simms replayed the voicemail about Walt Bishop again. This was the fourth time. Each time she heard it, Rachel added to her notes. The caller had details that only someone who knew Bishop well would know. So, was Bishop really a traitor? If true, the call was enough to start assessing the damage. Or was Bishop just enriching himself by skimming money from sanctioned operations? Or both?

Rachel headed to Greg Nasher's office, the agency's Director of Operations. When she started working at the CIA, Rachel worked for Nasher and was sure he would see her without an appointment.

When she knocked, Nasher waved her in, and she found two men standing in his office with grim faces. The DO, as Nasher was known, asked, "What's up, Rachel?"

Rachel didn't know who the other men were, so she didn't say anything. Instead, she tilted her head, and the DO took the hint. The other two men stepped outside. "Sir, I'm here about Walt Bishop. This morning, a voicemail on my direct line from a Sue Ellen Dorf told me that Bishop was dirty. The message said Bishop was making money on deals he steered to an arms dealer named Gerd Hofer.

Hofer is suspected to be one of the main arms suppliers to Hezbollah and other terrorist groups."

"Who is Sue Ellen Dorf?"

"I don't know. Whoever made the call was using one of those boxes that distort your voice, so we'll never know. She also said Bishop authorized unsanctioned hits and has current contacts the CIA probably doesn't know about with the Iranians and other terrorist organizations. This Dorf woman implied that Bishop had sold them classified information."

"Shit. This past Tuesday afternoon, when Bishop didn't return Betsy's calls, she asked our security unit to go to his condo, where they found him. He'd been dead for several days."

"Was he murdered?"

"We don't know yet. According to the Fairfax County Sheriff's office, there's no sign of forced entry or a fight. The apartment wasn't ransacked, and they found two loaded Walther PPK/S's not registered to anyone."

The DO went to the door and asked the two men to come in. Both were from the CIA's Inspector General's office and were assigned to work with the local authorities to determine what happened to Walt Bishop. It took Rachel two minutes to describe the voicemail.

When Rachel returned to her office, she pulled out her notes from the Elizabeth Harris debrief. She deliberately didn't point out that if Bishop was murdered, it didn't fit Harris' MO. He wasn't shot.

THURSDAY, AUGUST 9TH, 2002, 11:29 A.M. LOCAL TIME, RIESA, GERMANY

Berg was dressed like a chauffeur – black suit, white shirt, red and blue striped tie – and held up a small sign with his last name. Ghulam waved an acknowledgment.

Unknown to Berg, Ghulam's gesture was also a signal for his men to follow in another car. The additional security was in case Berg tried to kidnap Ghulam or lead him into a police ambush.

They drove to a former Soviet Army base outside Riesa, 30 kilometers northwest of Dresden. When the Soviet 9th Tank Division left Riesa for Smolensk, Hofer acquired the property and the contents from the East German government in the chaos following the collapse of the Democratic People's Republic of Germany. The East German generals were happy to take money for the stocks of weapons and ammunition left by the Soviets.

Berg noticed the same Opel kept appearing in his rear-view mirror. When he mentioned they were being followed, Ghulam admitted they were his men.

The drive from Dresden's Klotzsche Airport to an exit south of Riesa took 28 minutes and then another 11 before Berg stopped at a gate in a fence.

Thirty meters (~98 feet) into the stand of trees that blocked any view of the facility, the gravel road turned 90^0 to the right and went past an unmanned guard station. Fifty meters later, in front of a large pillbox, the road turned 90^0 to the left past a second concrete pillbox before exiting the trees. Berg parked in front of the second of six bunkers, each 50 meters (~164 feet) long, 10 meters (~32 feet) wide, and 10 meters tall. All were covered with grass making them hard to see from the air.

Ghulam waited in the car while Berg walked to a box on the exposed concrete face, undid a latch, and pressed his index, fore, and middle fingers on the pad. A light glowed green, and Berg entered his eight-digit passcode. The green lights went out telling him that the security system was turned off, and the fuses to the explosives planted to provide a nasty surprise for anyone who broke in were disabled. Berg pulled down a large lever at a different control panel a meter away. A mental clank indicated the pins on the door had released, and he pushed a large green button under the word "*Öffnen*."

The steel door grumbled and began to move. When the gap was about two meters wide, Berg pressed the red button, stopping the door. He waved for Ghulam to come over as he went inside to turn on the lights.

"Mr. Noorani, if I remember correctly, you bought SA-7s, SA-14s, and RPGs from us along with small arms. We don't have any SA-7s left and very few SA-14s. But we do have twenty-four of an improved missile called the SA-16. Known by the NATO code name

Gimlet, the SA-16 has a better seeker that cannot be as easily fooled by infrared jammers. In this bunker, we also have RPG-7s and a few RPG-29s, which I believe you already have."

"May I see an SA-16?"

Berg nodded sharply and led Ghulam down the bunker, past a row of RPG-7s in wooden crates to a waist-high stack of olive-green boxes. He popped open the latches and lifted the lid revealing an SA-16, complete with the instruction manual, battery, the tube containing the missile, and the sighting system.

"Go ahead, Mr. Noorani, pick it up. The missile won't fire unless the battery is installed."

Ghulam put the missile to his shoulder. He spun around and aimed at a light at the end of the bunker. Then, he brought it down and cradled the weapon in his arms thinking if they had these instead of the SA-14s, maybe they would have shot down the airliner outside of Amsterdam.

"How many of these did you say you have?"

"Twenty-four."

"How much for each?"

"If you take all 24, 50,000 Euros per SA-16."

Ghulam nodded and did not react. "What else do you have to show me?"

"Machine guns, RPGs, AK-47s, Dragunov sniper rifles."

"Do you have RK, PK or RPD machine guns?"

"We have all three. How many do you want?"

"Depends on the price and the terms. Can you show me?"

"All the ones we have are, as the Americans say, new in the box. Come with me."

Ghulam followed Berg to another bunker after he closed and locked the door. He went through the same process to open the blast door, revealing a bunker half full of munitions. From a previous trip, Berg knew precisely where the weapons were amongst the stacks of cases. Some were unpainted wood; others were others in brown and olive green.

Berg pointed to one stack. "Those are all PKs. Pick a box."

Ghulam pointed to the third one down in a stack of four. Two of his men lifted the cases and put them on the floor. Berg held out a large pry bar. "Sorry, but this is the only way to open these."

The levered-off lid revealed a brand-new 7.62mm PK machine gun wrapped in oiled paper, a spare barrel, a sling, and a bipod. The serial number and the markings on the crate indicated it had been built in 1985.

"I can show you some RPDs if you would like. They are over there." Berg waved toward the entrance where they came in.

"No, this is good enough. How much are these?"

"Depends on the quantity and how much ammunition you want. I have thousands of rounds already in belts."

"I would like to buy everything you have, but I need to consult with Beirut. My problem is that I need some delivered here in Europe and some shipped to the Middle East."

Berg rubbed his chin as he tried to contain his excitement about the idea brewing in his head. Berg reached into his coat pocket and handed Ghulam the complete inventory.

He waited until Ghulam finished looking at the numbers before speaking. "I have a proposal. You want the munitions and probably need a secure place to store them. How about if Hofer and Associates sells you everything in these six bunkers for fifteen million Euros. As part of the deal, I will sub-lease the land with the bunkers to you for six months. You take the weapons out on your schedule. After six months, the land comes back to me unless you want to buy it."

Ghulam looked at the list again. Fifteen million Euros was very reasonable and gave Hezbollah an arms stockpile in the heart of Europe. "How long do I have to decide?"

'Forty-eight hours. I'll make it simple. You transfer the money as you have in the past. Once the money is in our account, the arms are yours, and I will send you the current codes and instructions on how to change them." *I then move the money to my new accounts and disappear.*

Ghulam looked at Berg. Money was not the problem, he just wanted to make sure he understood the deal before he okayed the purchase. "I will call your cell phone to give you an answer as soon as I can."

THE SAME DAY, 3:11 P.M. LOCAL TIME, TEL AVIV

The windowless conference room Aliyah and Janis were using at Mossad headquarters was littered with papers, maps, and photographs. Empty coffee cups and plastic containers with the remains of the breakfast they carried in at 7:00 a.m. littered the table. They went back and forth with ideas as they fleshed out a plan that they thought might catch Ghulam. After briefing Reznik on their concept of operations, Janis agreed to stay in Tel Aviv until either the project was blessed or, if requested, changes made.

At a small restaurant overlooking the beach near the Dan Hotel where they had lunch, Janis watched Aliyah wince noticeably as she sat down. This was not the first time she'd seen Aliyah grimace. Several times while they were making love, she felt her recoil in pain. "What's wrong?"

"Nothing."

"Bullshit. You're talking to the woman who regularly has her hands all over your body. What's up?"

"My left leg and hip are bothering me. I should go see a doctor."

"You will go Monday or as soon as possible, and I'll stay in Israel if you need surgery. There are some places I'd like to see as part of a course I am taking and the books I'm reading."

"What course?"

"On Judaism and its history."

"*Mitsuyan!* Why?"

"I want to know more about your country, Judaism, and what makes Israel tick. In a few weeks, you will find out more."

Aliyah reached out for Janis's hand and leaned across the table. "You know, I am an expert interrogator, and I will get whatever you are hiding out of you before you leave."

"No, you won't."

"Bet?"

"Yup. I know what you plan to do. You'll get me orgasmic and, ultimately, get me to tell you when I can't take the pleasure any longer."

"That's just one of my interrogation techniques. I have others."

"Other than drugs, what kind of tricks do you have?"
"You'll see."

THE SAME DAY, 4:48 P.M. LOCAL TIME, ZURICH

Berg walked out of the leasing office smiling. One more box was checked off in his plan to disappear into a well-funded retirement. He just signed the rental agreements for a three-bedroom apartment near the heart of Zurich's central business district. The flat came with a space in an underground garage and state-of-the-art security.

To enter the lobby, tenants used an electronic card. Once in the elevator, tenants slid the same key card into a slot and entered a six-digit code that let them go to their floor. They had to enter a different code plus the floor number if they wanted another floor.

He paused on the sidewalk when the mobile phone with the number he gave Noorani phone rang. He was expecting a call back from an auction company who wanted to visit Hofer Hof on Monday to evaluate "the museum" and determine if the contents were worth taking to an auction. "Allo."

"Noorani here. We'll do the deal, but only want to pay ten million Euros."

Berg grinned as he stepped into a doorway, away from the street noise and for privacy. Negotiations had begun. He could sell them for 10 but agreeing to their offer was not good form. "Fourteen million."

"Eleven-five."

"Thirteen-five."

"Done. The money will be in your account by close of business Monday."

"When it is confirmed, I will send you the codes."

"We would prefer if they were hand delivered."

"I prefer a courier or lock box at a train station." Berg didn't want to meet either Noorani or his men, and he was too close to being very wealthy and didn't want to be killed.

"Courier." Noorani rattled off an address of a hotel in Dresden and gave Berg the date he wanted the package delivered. Berg read the contact details back to confirm the information.

Hofer's Falcon 50 jet was sold earlier in the week for two and a half million Euros. Now Berg only had three things to sell – the house and land, the firearms collection, and the museum before he could go quietly into the sunset.

LANGLEY, THE SAME DAY, 1:25 P.M. LOCAL TIME

Even though she was five minutes early, Rachel Simms was the last person to walk into the conference room. She recognized the Director of the CIA and Grant Hershey, the investigator from the CIA's Inspector General's office with whom she worked, but not the other two men. At the CIA, it wasn't unusual to be in meetings and be given only first names – knowing they may be covers.

One introduced himself as the medical examiner from Fairfax County where McLean was located. The other was a forensic scientist from the CIA.

Rachel listened carefully while the two men explained their findings. When they were done, she asked, "If there was cyanide in Bishop's blood, isn't that clear evidence he was assassinated?"

The ME looked at Rachel, who, at age 55, was trim and still quite attractive. Gray hair now formed streaks in the sandy brown hair of her youth. Practicing martial arts daily or in a dojo kept her fit. Age, so far, had been kind to her.

Marriage, on the other hand, had not. By her forty-fifth birthday, Rachel had been divorced twice. Husband number one walked out after three years, saying Rachel was married to the CIA. Rachel was tired of him, and he was tired of her. Sex with hubby #2 was a rare affair. When she could coax him into the act, he'd get himself off and never tried to satisfy her. Once he left, a vibrator, a dildo, her fingers, and a growing collection of porno videos became her best friends.

One-night stands didn't interest Rachel, and she wondered if she was like Queen Elizabeth I – married to her country and work. On a whim, she bought a tape with a man and two women and watched the woman-on-woman scenes repeatedly.

This tape led to a collection of lesbian videos, and Rachel realized she was more than bi-curious. She wanted to have sex with a woman but hadn't worked up the courage to visit a lesbian bar, of which there were many in the DC area. She rationalized her reluctance thinking that if the agency discovered she was gay in a routine background investigation, it would view her as a security risk.

The ME clasped his hands on the table as if he was about to give a lecture. "Ms. Simms, the amount of cyanide in Bishop's blood was below the level that would indicate cyanide poisoning. We tested his blood three times, and the results were the same each time. Cyanide leaves the blood quickly; after four days, we can only speculate on how much cyanide was in his blood. Our conclusion was that Mr. Bishop had a heart attack. Our autopsy showed Mr. Bishop had two partially clogged arteries, heart disease, and signs of a previous heart attack. Medically speaking, unless Mr. Bishop had the blockages removed, it was only a matter of time before Mr. Bishop had another major heart attack. And, since there were no signs of forced entry or a struggle, we must rule the cause of death as a heart attack."

Rachel nodded. She'd seen the police report. Bishop's two-bedroom unit was searched, and no hidden compartments were found. In the safe, police officers found a key to a bank safe deposit box. In it were Australian, Jordanian, and Omani passports with Bishop's picture, credit cards, and $300,000 in cash. None of the documents were issued by the CIA, and their existence convinced CIA investigators that Bishop was a traitor, and this was his "go-stash."

With the discussion on the cause of death over and the medical examiner gone, Rachel stood up, ready to leave, when the CIA Director asked her to remain. Hershey hesitated, thinking there would be some discussion; the Director said, "Grant, this doesn't concern you or Bishop."

Grant Hershey nodded, and when he left, Nasher closed the door and looked at the female CIA case officer and analyst. "Rachel, you've been around the agency a long time. How bad did Bishop hurt us?"

"Not as bad as Aldrich Ames. Bishop got a couple of our agents in Lebanon killed and fucked up a half dozen covert operations. I don't think we've identified all the losses, and I also believe he was working on his own."

"I'll keep Hershey on it until we know as much as possible." Nasher paused and slid a folder in front of him. "Different subject. I've looked at your personnel file, and your performance in the agency has been stellar. Why do you think you haven't been promoted?"

"Sir, two reasons. I like being an analyst, and I don't think I can kiss ass well enough to be an executive."

Nasher sat back and laughed. "I've never heard that answer before."

"Sir, it's the truth. My analyses are not spun to an agenda and are well supported by facts. The guys above me can slant my work how they want, but the more they spin, the farther it gets from ground truth."

"Well, Rachel, I like unvarnished fact-based analyses. Earlier in your career, you were a field officer involved in covert operations. Why did you become an analyst?

"Husband number one wanted me home more, so to keep him happy, I became an analyst. I like the work it, but miss being in the field."

The Director picked up a piece of paper. "I'd like you to take Bishop's slot. All I need to do is sign this form, and the job is yours. I'll have the paperwork expedited, but the process will still take a few days. Your first task will be to finish the postmortem on Bishop, and you'll be the Harris woman's control."

Rachel looked down at the table and was smiling when she looked back up. "Sir, I'd be delighted to be your new Deputy Director for Middle East Operations on one condition."

"And that is?"

"When I raise the bullshit flag, I won't embarrass you, but you must promise you'll listen with an open mind."

"Rachel, not having to separate the feces from the nuggets by myself will be a welcome relief. You're on."

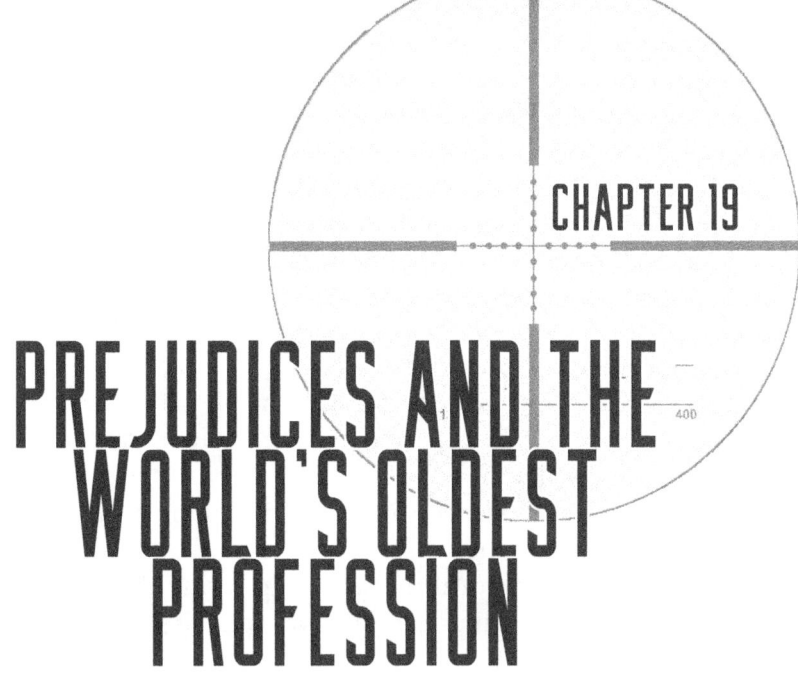

CHAPTER 19

PREJUDICES AND THE WORLD'S OLDEST PROFESSION

Saturdays are quiet days in the signal intelligence world in the Middle East since the sixth day of the week is the Sabbath in Israel and its neighbors. Most businesses, other than restaurants and some retail shops, are closed. Nonetheless, intelligence gathering continues just at a slightly slower pace.

The Israeli government's organization chart shows Unit 8200 as a subordinate of Aman, Israel's military intelligence organization. Unit 8200 is the Israeli equivalent of the U.S. National Security Agency. Smaller than the NSA, Unit 8200 is known for its skill, tenacity, and focus on gathering actionable intelligence on threats to Israel.

Maya Aranow was one of 20 soldiers on watch in a bunker on Mount Hermon, monitoring intercepts. She had been in Unit

8200 since completing basic training. In high school, Maya was the youngest of four children and an indifferent student who wasn't challenged. Her analytic skills on tests given to high school students led her to be assigned to Unit 8200.

When a mobile number on the watch list made several calls from Leipzig, Germany to a number in Beirut used by Hezbollah, she noted the times in her log. Maya made sure that, if possible, the call was recorded. On the second call, the originating number appeared familiar, and she found that phone made calls to the same number in Beirut from Dresden, Germany, on Thursday and Friday. While she waited for the computers to find out if they recorded the transcripts, she dialed the number given to report activity on this phone.

When Maya heard the recording saying if this was urgent, to call a different number, she was surprised when a woman answered. "Allo."

"Good Shabbos. This is Maya Aranow on an unsecure line. We just sent you data on telephone calls from numbers that interest you."

Aliyah knew exactly what Maya meant. She thanked her and went back out on her apartment's balcony where she kissed Janis on the back of the neck. "I must go into the office for a few minutes, and I'll call you later, and then we can figure out what to do for dinner."

Janis slid her hand up Aliyah's shorts. "I know what I want."

"I'll be dessert."

"And the appetizer."

Aliyah cursed the traffic that seemed heavier than usual for a Saturday and mused that she never made a traffic light when she was in a hurry or late. What should have taken 15 minutes, she noted as she handed her purse to the guard, today, took Aliyah 22.

More than curious, Aliyah logged onto her computer. Finding Ghulam was going to be difficult, but the one thing she learned from studying the attacks in France, the U.S., and Germany was that Ghulam liked to watch the carnage.

On the log, one number stuck out. Out of curiosity, she dialed the number, listened to the recording, and hung up, smiling. Ghulam had called a whorehouse.

Another number recorded on his phone in Lebanon didn't match the others. Just out of curiosity, Aliyah called it, and it too was a brothel.

Abd al-Bari Ghulam, you frequent whorehouses, and that's a weakness we may be able to exploit. I know why you called Hofer's phone, and I suspect I know why you are in Germany. Unfortunately, I don't have permission to kill you, at least not yet.

THE SAME DAY, 8:46 A.M. LOCAL TIME, RIESA, GERMANY

The white van with the pink T logo of Deutsche Telekom on the sides was parked off the road. The vehicle's nose was within two meters of a telephone pole, and the three technicians put out the obligatory pylons and triangle. The orange pylons were placed two meters behind the front and rear bumpers, and the triangle was put on the road 20 meters from the back of the truck to warn oncoming traffic.

Two technicians checked to see if any cars were coming before they climbed the fence and headed into the woods, checking for security sensors. Finding none, they scaled a utility pole along the road to the bunkers and installed a day/night video camera. Sensors would alert the camera if vehicles were detected.

Next, they climbed each grass-covered bunker and mounted a camera and a sensor on top of each one. Electrical power came from the power lines connecting each bunker.

Once set up, they tested the installation that enabled the cameras to transmit imagery to a receiver mounted on the top of the telephone pole just outside the complex, which was connected to the phone lines. If the cameras detected a vehicle, the receiver "made a call" to a monitoring station set up in an office suite and manned by Mossad agents.

THE SAME DAY, 9:16 P.M. LOCAL TIME, TEL AVIV

The light from the setting sun gave everything on the balcony a red hue. The small table between Janis and Aliyah was host to their empty dishes. Dinner was a tomato, olive, and cucumber salad and pan-fried chicken breasts seasoned with a Yemenite spice mix of cumin, black pepper, turmeric, and cardamom called *hawaij*.

When the American's phone rang, Aliyah was stroking Janis' thigh with one hand and sipping a glass of a sauvignon blanc from the Golan Heights with the other. The ringing sound poured a bucket of ice on their romantic mood. Before she answered, Janis said, "Don't move. I'll get rid of whoever is calling."

Janis walked into the apartment to get away from the street noise. Aliyah followed Janis waited until her lover said, "Hello." From the front, she pulled down her lover's shorts and began kissing her crotch. Janis responded by caressing Aliyah's neck and struggled to stifle a moan.

"Ms. Harris, this is Rachel Simms. I am sorry to bother you on a Sunday afternoon. Am I interrupting something important?"

How the hell did you get this number? Oh shit, she gave it to Bishop. Nothing other than my lover doing her level best to make me have an orgasm while I am talking to you.

"Rachel, what can I do to help the CIA?"

Hearing the name of the agency, Aliyah got more aggressive. "This is a personal call and has nothing to do with the CIA."

Oh, that's interesting. Rachel, you're married to the agency, and there's not a sliver of light between you and the CIA.

"What's going on?" Janis hoped she didn't sound cold.

Rachel took a deep breath. *I know better than to ask where Janis is.* "Do you plan to come to D.C. in the near future?"

Janis tried to push Aliyah's head back but couldn't. She had both hands on her butt, her panties were already down, and Aliyah was making it hard for Janis to think, much less keep from moaning in pleasure.

"No, but I can be there later this week or next. Why?"

"I'd like to take you to lunch. Just girl talk."

"I didn't think the CIA allowed just girl talk."

"Trust me, our conversation will have nothing to do with work."

"Let me see what I can figure out. Can you give me a number I can call tomorrow so we can pick a date?" *Why do you want to meet with me personally? Is this a trap?*

"Sure. Do you have a pencil handy?"

No, but I am about to have a mighty powerful orgasm. Thankfully, there was a pen within reach and a scrap of paper. Janis wrote down the number Rachel specified was for her personal mobile phone.

Once Janis hung up, her mind switched from business to the sensations flowing through her body as she had a knee-buckling orgasm.

MONDAY, AUGUST 12TH, 2002, 9:50 A.M. LOCAL TIME, OTTOBEUREN

Berg could hear the crunching of wheels on gravel as he hurried down the wide staircase with its red and black carpet that ran down the center of the steps. His visitors announced their arrival at the front gate via the intercom. By the time they parked their black Mercedes E-Class sedan at the front of the house, Berg was standing on the front steps.

He checked to make sure his Walther PPK pistol was in his right coat pocket, and two spare magazines were in the left before he opened the door. Why he was not sure, but it seemed to be an intelligent thing to do.

Berg waited while the two men climbed the 10 steps to where he stood with his hands clasped behind his back. When the older of the two visitors reached the wide, granite landing, Berg held out his right hand. "Herr Fischer, I presume?"

Fischer vigorously pumped Berg's hand twice in the traditional German manner. "Yes, I am Herr Fischer from Fischer und Sohn, and this is Herr Dieter Hoffman, a member of our appraisal staff."

"Please come in." For some reason, Berg was expecting someone in his 60s, not a man about his age. These two looked as if they were right from an SS poster – blonde, blue-eyed, tall, well-groomed, and dressed in dark suits with red and black striped ties. All that was missing was the red armband with the black swastika in a white circle.

Berg led the two men to a drawing room off the entrance foyer on the first floor, where he had coffee and tea in insulated sterling silver pots. Both visitors helped themselves.

Fischer und Sohn had a worldwide reputation as an auction house that sold memorabilia, firearm collections, and antiques. Their headquarters was in Munich, with satellite offices in Zurich, Berlin, London, New York, and Zurich.

Berg provided a more detailed description than he did on the phone of what was in the house and the basement. When he finished, Fischer nodded saying that, assuming everything was genuine, he thought they would be able to get top dollar for both the memorabilia and the historic weapons.

On the way up the staircase, Herr Fischer touched Berg's arm. "Herr Hofer and my father and all our associates have similar backgrounds. At the war's end, my father started our business as a way of helping his friends generate enough money to survive. We found there was a great deal of interest all over the world in their memorabilia."

Berg interpreted what he just heard as both Fischer's and Hoffman's fathers were members of the SS. He pointed to a table outside the door to the museum. "Herr Fischer, this notebook has a complete inventory of what is on this floor. When we are finished here, I will take you to a basement room where we have what Herr Hofer preferred not to display. If you wish, I can give you a tour or wait until you walk through yourself."

"Please come with us. Today, we are gathering enough information to make a rough estimate what the collection is worth so we may recommend options. Before putting anything on the market, we must make our own inventory and check each item's provenance. This will enable us to certify everything is as it should be."

Berg nodded and led the way through the museum. When the three men walked out, Fischer nodded emphatically, "Most impressive, and all the provenance is here. There is a strong market for this material assuming it is genuine. Shall we go downstairs?"

The rhythmic tapping of their soles on the concrete was the only sound as they walked down the cement floor toward a vault door opposite the one for the "conversation room." Fischer and Hoffman remained a respectful distance while Berg spun the combination lock. When tumblers clicked, signaling they were all aligned, Berg pushed down on a spoke of the brass wheel.

Inside, Berg turned a light switch, and fluorescent lights flickered as they came on. He held out two pairs of white gloves. "This collection has weapons dating back to Fredrick the Great. In this room, there is at least one used by the Prussian or German military since 1742. Each one is in perfect working condition. Herr Hofer has never fired Mauser rifles and pistols from the Franco-Prussian War, World War I, and World War II. He also has two dozen very rare and never fired *Sturmgewehr* 44s. All have very low serial numbers and are just as they came out of the factory. There are machine guns in here, but no cannons or grenades. The file cabinet in the back has our documentation on each weapon." He held out two sets of white cotton gloves. "So, please put these on if you intend to handle any firearm."

Fischer's head swiveled back and forth as he surveyed the rows of gun racks and wooden cases. Fischer nodded and pointed to the back wall. "May I look around?"

"Of course. Herr Fischer, until we have signed a contract, I cannot give you a list of the firearms. The collection also has ammunition from the Franco-Prussian War and both World Wars in the original boxes. They are stored in a bunker away from the house."

Berg followed a few steps behind Fischer and Hoffman. Occasionally they would stop, look at a firearm and then move on. When they were done, Fischer gave Berg a smile that signaled satisfaction. "I think we have seen enough. Let us go upstairs and talk options."

On the way to the first floor sitting room, Berg apologized by saying that he had let the staff go since the house would be sold once the collection and the antique furniture were gone.

Fischer poured a cup of coffee for himself and then one for Hoffman before he sat on one of the armchairs made during the reign of Kaiser Wilhelm II. Berg sat opposite the two men on a small couch.

"Herr Berg, I would like to suggest we hold three auctions since our buyers are interested in different items. One would be for the museum. There are collectors all over the world who, if they knew I had this collection under contract, would be standing in line. For the firearms, I would sell them in four groups: antiques up through 1914,

World War I, World War II, and automatic weapons. All should earn a premium due to their condition and provenance. Last, if interested, we could also sell the antique furniture, which, given their excellent condition, would bring a premium."

Fischer took a sip of coffee and then continued. "We can sell them publicly as individual items or as collections at an auction site. If Fischer und Sohn were to hold a public auction, my fee is 15 percent, and we would add 15 percent to the buyer's bid plus any moving and storage expenses. Each group would take days to sell off. There is always a risk that some items will be left over, and we can discuss how to dispose of them if you choose this route."

The "sohn" in Fischer und Sohn put his coffee cup down deliberately on the table. "The other option would be a series of private sales. We would still take pictures and document the provenance, much of which Herr Hofer has done, and I call customers who would be interested. Again, the material would be sold in groups. In a private sale, we do not have the expenses associated with an auction. My firm takes 10 percent of the sale price and another 10 percent from the buyer. In a private sale, you have the option of the buyers inspecting the material and taking possession here at Hofer Hof."

"Herr Fischer, how much is the museum and the firearms worth?"

Fischer pursed his lips and then clasped his hands on his stomach. Ever since he walked into the museum, he'd been wrestling with the answer to that question. He decided to be conservative and reduced what he thought the material inside this house was worth by 20%. "From private buyers, I think we could get between seven and eight million Euros for the museum and furniture. The firearms would bring another 15 to 20 million, net of our fees."

Berg struggled to contain his excitement. He knew the firearms were valuable, but not that much. He'd already taken a "few" for his private collection and deducted them from the inventory. "Herr Fischer, assuming we sign an agreement, how long does it take to complete the sale?"

"Ahhhhh, another very good question. Within days, Herr Hoffman and several associates will arrive to take inventory and pictures and examine the provenance. I would plan on at least two weeks before we could finish. Then, we will go back to our archives and other sources to establish a value for each item. That will take at least another week or two. From this process, we can provide an itemized and accurate estimate of the collection's value. For a public auction of this size collection, we will have to rent a secure facility and move the material there. For planning purposes, I'd estimate six to eight months from the contract date to the end of the public auction and my firm handing you a check."

Fischer poured himself another cup of coffee, dropped in two lumps of sugar and a dash of cream before he continued. "Assuming you elect to sell them privately, I will start making calls tomorrow to generate interest. A private sale, from when we get bids to when you receive a check, and the artifacts are picked up, maybe a month. Normally, we pack and ship to the owner's specifications from here. Some buyers, however, will insist on using their own movers."

"Which auction will give me the greatest return, private sale or auction?"

"Ahhhhh, that is the heart of the matter. If we go to a public auction, you may make ten to fifteen percent more but assume the risk that not everything sells. Plus, you pay the moving and storage fees. In a private sale, we insist the buyer takes everything in his lot and they pay for packing and shipping."

"Do you have a sample contract I can review?"

"I will do you one better. I have one prepared for you to sign. When our inventory and valuation are complete, we add them to the contract as an attachment."

Fischer pulled the contract out of his briefcase. "All you have to do is check which option you prefer, private or public auction. Please shred the document if you decide not to do business with Fischer und Sohn. Do you have any other questions?"

"No. This has been very informative. I will contact you after I read the contract and decide what to do."

The men shook hands, and Berg ushered them to the door. Once he let them out the gate, he went to his office. The contract was only a half dozen pages. Most of the clauses were exemptions protecting Fischer und Sohn if the material was not genuine. When he finished reading the contract, he decided on a private sale. The artifacts would be gone sooner, and in the end, he believed he would net more money. He'd sign and date the contract tomorrow and call Herr Fischer.

TUESDAY, AUGUST 13TH, 2002, 9:46 P.M. LOCAL TIME, DRESDEN, GERMANY

Before Germany's new prostitution law sponsored by the Green Party was passed, the profession was legal and taxed. Men and women in the industry were required to be routinely examined and tested for sexually transmitted diseases. As of January 1st, 2002, under the new law, sex workers had the same rights and pension benefits enjoyed by those in other industries. Ghulam liked Germany because it had none of Lebanon's absurd regulations governing brothels and prostitution.

Leipzig, like other large German cities, had a selection of brothels. The paler and blonder they were, the more Abd al-Bari liked them.

After meeting with Berg, Ghulam drove to Leipzig and checked into a hotel near the central train station and on the edge of Volksmardorf, the Muslim neighborhood on the city's east side. From there, he orchestrated his next move, which started tomorrow at 8:00 p.m.

Abd al-Bari was ushered into a small sitting room at the brothel on Dessauer Strasse. After speaking to the hostess, an attractive, older woman, several girls entered, one at a time. He specified a natural blond, and none wore panties under their flimsy robes.

Ghulam picked Katrina, who said, in heavily accented English, that she was from St. Petersburg, Russia. She led a grinning Ghulam down the corridor to her room, where classical music played in the background, and a violin sat on a stand in the corner.

Ghulam stood and listened to the unfamiliar music. Katrina said, "The music is Chopin's violin concerto in C minor."

"Oh...." Ghulam didn't have a clue as to who Chopin was or what a violin concerto was. He pointed to the violin. "Do you play?"

"I do."

"Would you play something for me?"

"Sure." When Katrina picked up the instrument, Ghulam sat on the bed and watched her persona change from willowy, sexy blond prostitute to a concert violinist. Katerina played for a few minutes and then abruptly stopped.

Ghulam took her hands in his. "Why are you not in an orchestra?"

"I was until it ran out of money. Now, I make a living using my God-given talents as a woman. It is steady work that pays as well as the orchestra, and every day, I practice and go to auditions. The company that owns this place gives me an excellent reference."

Katerina looked down at her client's hands. The fingers were long and slender, almost feminine, and they were in her mind, those of a doctor. Gently, she placed her hands on Ghulam's shoulders and pushed her groin toward his face. "Are you ready?"

Ghulam nodded.

"Blow job first, and then fuck?"

Another nod and Katerina unbuckled Ghulam's belt and pulled down his pants while he undid his shirt. What he didn't see was as Katerina fondled his balls, she put a condom in her mouth. Within seconds, she slid the condom onto his erect penis.

He struggled to restrain himself, and Katerina knew when a man was ready. She nudged him to encourage him to lie down and asked, "Me on top or you?"

"You."

When Ghulam was finished, Katerina rolled off and with practiced expertise, slid the semen-filled condom off and dropped it into a trashcan next to the bed.

After kissing her finger and placing it on Ghulam's lips, Katerina pulled on her robe and panties. When she led him back to the lounge, he had been in her room for less than 20 minutes, and 70 percent of the 200 Euro fee would be in her account by the morning. Ghulam was her third client of the day.

WEDNESDAY, AUGUST 14ᵀᴴ, 2002, 7:36 A.M. LOCAL TIME, TEL AVIV

Aliyah was sipping coffee, looking at the Mediterranean from the balcony of her apartment, and watching for Janis. When she spotted the American coming up the street from her run along the beach, Aliyah would begin making breakfast.

While she was looking down the street, her cell phone rang. "Allo."

"Aliyah?"

Aliyah recognized her mother's voice. "*Eema,* what's wrong? Why are you calling so early in the morning?"

"Is that woman there?"

Aliyah could tell from the icy tone a storm was brewing. The hurricane probably started Saturday night when Janis and she met her mother and father for dinner at a local restaurant. Her mother was polite since she was in a public place. "No." *The less said, the better. I wish Janis would open the door now, so I don't have to listen to the tirade I am about to get.*

"She's *goyim.*" Her mother used the Yiddish word for a non-Jew, and her negative tone said it was derogatory. "The only reason you are seeing this American is her money, and she has lots of it."

"*Eema,* religion, and money don't matter to me. I'm seeing her because I like her." *And it is my job.* Then Aliyah added, "We're not about to have children!"

"Don't make fun of me. Aliyah, I love you with all my heart, but if you are living with a *shiksa* or, worse, marry one, I will assume you are dead and start saying Kaddish for you. Please don't do this to me."

Kaddish is the Jewish prayer for the dead.

Aliyah took a deep breath. She'd had enough and pushed back. "*Eema,* I am not doing this to you. You are doing it to yourself. If you disown me, you will never see me again. And I don't think that's what *abba,* Elon, or Ariel want. You are the one who is pushing me away."

"Do not mention that woman's name in my presence ever again unless you are about to tell me you are no longer seeing her. And, if you are still seeing her, I don't want either of you in my house. DO YOU UNDERSTAND?"

I am sure my father doesn't know you are calling me. While he disapproves of my sexual preference, he told me several times that he accepts me as a lesbian. "Yes, *Eema,* I do. Shalom." Aliyah wanted to get her mother off the phone before she said something she would truly regret and hoped her mother's anger would pass.

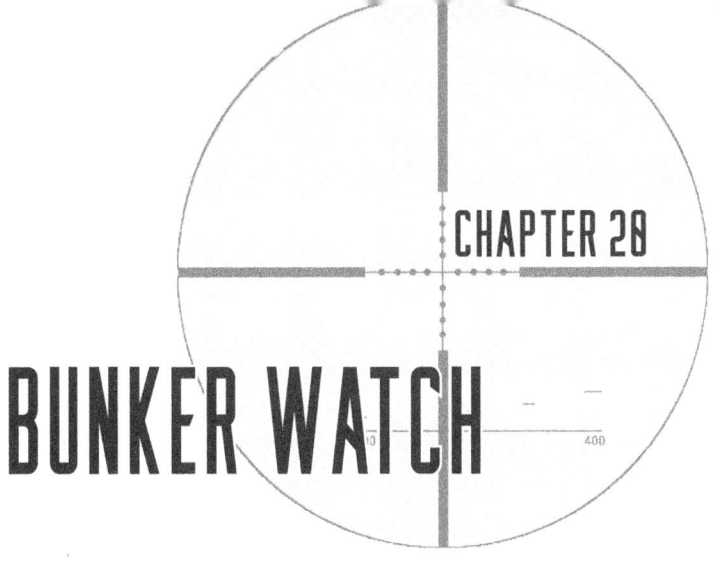

CHAPTER 28

BUNKER WATCH

THURSDAY, AUGUST 15TH, 11:20 A.M. LOCAL TIME, RIESA, GERMANY

The yellow and red DHL package arrived at the Leonardo Hotel right on time. Ghulam signed for the package at the front desk, and within half an hour, he was on his way to Riesa to meet an eight-man team based at a safe house in Munich. While driven to the former Red Army base, he called a second team hiding in Mainz.

Each team brought cots and sleeping bags that they set up set up in the back of the bunker with a bathroom and a working shower. The 16 men would provide security and stay until the trucks hauling the intermodal containers arrived on Friday.

Having both teams together was a risk, but Ghulam had no choice. Once the trucks left, his role in acquiring the weapons was over, and he could go back to orchestrating attacks.

Ghulam opened the bunker door closest to the entrance and then changed the codes based on Berg's detailed, easy-to-follow instructions. His first order of business was to verify the inventory. Everything Berg promised was in the bunkers plus a pleasant surprise, i.e., 100 kilos of SEMTEX.

THE SAME DAY, 11:22 A.M. LOCAL TIME, DRESDEN

In the office suite Mossad rented, the agent on duty was reading a book when the computer buzzed informing him that the cameras in Riesa had turned on. Seconds later, he watched Ghulam unlock the gate at the end of the access road. Each time a van entered; the agent noted down the license plate number.

Guards were now posted at the bunker near the entrance and patrolling the grounds. When the first CD was full of live videos, the computer switched to a second recorder so the operator could change CDs.

By mid-afternoon, the agent counted 16 armed individuals on the grounds. When he had three full CDs, his partner drove them to the Israeli embassy in Berlin. There, a copy was made and put in the diplomatic pouch that went back to Tel Aviv and Mossad headquarters.

BERLIN, FRIDAY, AUGUST 16TH, 2002, 2:38 P.M. LOCAL TIME

In a conference call with the Israeli ambassador to Germany, the Foreign Minister, the Minister of Justice, and the head of Mossad decided to show what the Israelis had collected about the weapons to the German Justice Ministry. The purpose of the meeting would be to encourage the Germans to act, i.e., seize the weapons and arrest the members of the al-Musawi Corps.

Alon Schiff, the Israeli Ministry of Justice representative, assigned to the Israeli embassy in Berlin, called Adolf Weber, his liaison officer in the German Ministry of Justice. He promised to show them evidence of an illegal arms depot in Germany, members of a known terrorist group guarding the depot, and sales of those weapons to known terrorists.

Weber invited two experts on illegal arms sales – Kurt Jung and Uwe Schneider – to the meeting. Schiff, who had been a prosecutor before he accepted the assignment in Berlin, outlined his case. Weber's response was that Hofer's organization had acted legally and filed all the required arms sales paperwork.

Schiff opened the thick folder he had put on the table. He looked at Jung, whose title indicated he was the more senior of the two Germans. "Herr Weber, this is a list of the arms sales of Hofer and Associates made to Hezbollah and the documents that support them. When one compares the serial numbers on the arms where they were captured and where they were supposed to go based on Hofer's legal filings, they do not match. And that, sir, is a violation of German law, to say nothing of the international agreements on arms sales."

Jung sat back and crossed his arms, not willing to accept the Israeli's evidence. Schiff was not finished.

Schiff spoke easily in German. His father was one of several hundred teenage children smuggled out of Germany in 1936. In 1948, his parents returned to Germany to piece together what had happened to his family. They stayed for 15 years before returning to Israel, where Schiff was born. After 10 years as a prosecutor specializing in war crimes, Schiff accepted the posting to Berlin.

"Herr Jung, our evidence suggests these weapons are now Hezbollah's possession. This year, their proxies Islamic Jihad and al-Musawi Corps conducted attacks in Germany, France, and Italy. These weapons may be used to kill my fellow citizens and yours. If your government acts now, Germany can help prevent future attacks."

Jung leaned forward and put his palms down flat on the table. "Herr Schiff, are you demanding the German government open an investigation, raid this facility, and arrest these men?"

Schiff smiled. "No. I am encouraging the German government to take decisive action to prevent potential embarrassment in the future. If Israel seizes the arms, their source will become public, and the German government will be embarrassed since it had a chance to act and didn't."

"Your statement could be taken as a threat."

"I am sorry if you think I am threatening Germany. That is not my intent. I want you to understand that if these weapons leave Germany, we will do our best to prevent them from reaching our enemies. As I am sure you know, seizing them now is much easier than finding and capturing them later. This is Germany's chance to stop the shipment."

Weber put his arm on Jung's forearm as a way of saying be quiet, and he wanted to speak. "Herr Schiff, thank you for coming and for bringing us this important evidence. We will let you know what we decide to do. However, if these photos come from an Israeli undercover operation observing German citizens that is not authorized by my government, I ask that you shut it down. If you inform me in the next 24 hours you have ended your illegal surveillance, I will consider the matter closed. If not, we will pursue diplomatic and, if warranted, criminal actions against those who conducted an illegal surveillance operation on German soil."

"Herr Jung, Israel understands your concerns." Schiff left knowing he didn't commit to when they would stop watching the bunkers. Late tomorrow afternoon, he will call Herr Jung to inform that the surveillance operation has been shut down. By then, Israel will know if the weapons have been moved.

THE SAME DAY 8:03 A.M. LOCAL TIME, RIESA

Ghulam stood by the bunker complex's gate and watched the six trucks hauling 40-foot-long, intermodal shipping containers on trailers trundle down the access road. Each truck was assigned a bunker and a crew to load it. To move the crates faster, Ghulam rented six forklifts which arrived on Thursday. They would be returned either Friday afternoon or Saturday morning. With four men loading each truck with specific weapons in a specific sequence, loading went quickly.

By three o'clock, the trucks were on the road to Trieste, and the forklifts returned to Dresden. His job finished, Ghulam turned his car in at Dresden International Airport and boarded a flight to Frankfurt. Saturday, he would begin a four-day trip that would bring him to Dallas via Toronto and Mexico City.

RESTON, VIRGINIA, THE SAME DAY, 12:07 P.M. LOCAL TIME

August in Reston, Virginia, is spelled hot and humid. By noon, the humidity was close to 70 percent and the temperature in the upper 80s and headed for the low 90s.

Sweat started to run down Rachel Simms's back as she walked from her car to the Italian restaurant and her clothes clung to her body as if she had jumped in a pool. She wasn't sure if her sweat was from anticipation, fear, or the heat and humidity. She was also 10 minutes late and hoped the woman she was meeting for lunch hadn't left.

Rachel told the maître d' she was meeting a friend; the man nodded and said softly, "Your lunch companion is already at a table."

Janis saw Rachel coming and stood up so the two could shake hands. Just before she left for Israel, Janis had her hair styled in a short, pixie cut parted on the right side. It was much easier to take care of in the hot summer temperatures in Israel and Dallas. She wore a comfortable pair of cowboy boots known in Texas as ropers, a faded pair of boot-top jeans, and a loose-fitting pink blouse open at the neck. The only cowboy garment she wasn't wearing was a hat.

As soon as she sat down, Rachel gushed. "Elizabeth, I am so sorry I am late, but I got caught in traffic. How long have you been waiting?"

"Not long." *I began searching the area around the restaurant for surveillance since a little after 10. I found none and if I did, I wouldn't be sitting here.*

They ordered drinks, and for different reasons, both chose something non-alcoholic. After lunch, Janis planned to climb into her TBM 850 and be home in Dallas for dinner.

Rachel wanted a clear head. For the past few days, she'd been trying to script what she was going to say ever since Janis called her back and agreed to meet for lunch.

Yesterday, right after Janis' El Al flight landed at Newark, she flew the TBM to Leesburg Executive Airport, where the ground crew had the rental car waiting on the ramp. Dinner at the Marriott in Reston was via room service. After leaving Aliyah a message saying she was safe and sound back in the U.S., Janis went to bed.

Rachel had tied her graying shoulder-length hair in a ponytail and, for a woman Janis guessed was sixty-ish, her long hair made Rachel look a decade younger.

"Elizabeth, for the record, I am taking the day off. So, we're on my time. However, I do want to give you an update on Bishop."

I knew she couldn't leave the agency at home or in this case, the office. "I'm all ears."

"I believe the agency informed you that Walt Bishop is dead, and I am now your case officer."

Janis didn't react. *I'll bet the agency suspects me.* Her tone of voice was neutral. "Mr. Nasher called to let me know."

"Good. Three things. One, the official Fairfax County coroner's report was backed up by an agency forensic scientist and stated Bishop died from a massive heart attack. He'd had one before. There were signs of cyanide in his blood, but not enough to warrant ruling Bishop's death as a murder."

Rachel's subtle nods as she spoke made Janis think she was telling the truth, and she waited for the next two items.

"Two, Bishop was a traitor and passed Top Secret CIA intel to Hezbollah and the Iranians. I did most of the analysis and am convinced he sanctioned operations without agency approval. And three, I was promoted. They gave me Bishop's job as the Deputy Director for Operations – Middle East and the Arabian Gulf. I'm now one of a handful of female assistant directors and the only one in an operational role. Monday is my official first day in my new position. Hopefully, I won't make the same mistakes Bishop did."

Janis took Rachel's hand. "Congratulations." They held hands awkwardly for a few seconds before Janis pulled hers back.

"So, that takes care of business."

Janis looked at the waiter standing by the table and suggested he give them a few minutes. "Let's figure out what we want to eat, and then you can tell me why you wanted to meet for lunch."

Both looked at the menu. Choices were made and recorded by the waiter who left. Now they could talk.

Rachel looked nervous and looked down at the table, suggesting the subject was very personal and difficult. She looked up. "Elizabeth, this is very hard for me, so please let me stumble my way through what I want to say."

Janis bobbed her head.

Rachel felt vulnerable. "During the debriefing sessions, you said you lived with another woman for many years. From that, I assumed that you are.... are... a lesbian. Am I correct?"

Janis nodded once noticeably as a way of saying yes.

The torrent in Rachel's mind opened, and tears flowed down her cheeks as she told abbreviated versions of her failed marriages. Her confession ended with, "I want to know more about what a relationship with another woman is like."

Janis reached across the table and took Rachel's hands in hers. "Why?"

Their main courses arrived, which gave a natural pause to the conversation. Rachel blushed. "It started when I bought a porno tape of a guy and two women. Most of the tape has the two women making love, which really turned me on. Then I bought several more with women making love and wore them out from watching them so many times. So, I switched to CDs where the images are much better!"

Janis laughed. "What do you want from me?"

"Help."

"In what way?"

"You're the only lesbian I know who can answer my questions! Look, the intelligence analyst in me is hard to put on the back burner, and I need facts."

"Why don't you go to a lesbian club? There will be lots of women who would love to initiate you?"

Rachel looked down at the table and then at Janis. She didn't say anything.

"Let me guess. You are afraid. You don't know what to do or what to talk about, or someone at the agency will find out. Being openly gay at the CIA is not career-enhancing. Worse, you may be disappointed or rejected. Most important, you don't know what to wear."

Rachel laughed at Janis's last reason. "All of the above."

"So, you want a primer?"

"Yes."

"When?"

"Today would be great. Maybe we could go back to my house and talk if you don't have a flight to catch."

Janis thought for a few seconds. "O.K., I'll follow you home, and we can talk as long as you want."

Rachel's three-bedroom, split-level house was in a well-kept neighborhood with large trees. The entranceway opened into a combined family and living room with a fireplace and a huge-projection screen TV. The kitchen was on the opposite side of the TV.

"May I get you a glass of wine? There's a bathroom just up the steps and on the left."

Janis took the opportunity to take a quick look around Rachel's house. Down the hall from the bathroom was the master bathroom and a room she assumed was a guest bedroom. Across from the bathroom was a room Rachel used as an office.

Rachel handed Janis a glass of red wine and motioned to the black leather couch. "If you want, we can sit outside, but I suggest we stay inside and enjoy the air conditioning."

They sat at opposite ends. Janis leaned back against the bolster. "Do you mind if I take off my boots?"

"No, please do. Make yourself comfortable."

Janis's boots clunked as they hit the hardwood floor, and Janis noticed that Rachel used her toes to push off her pumps with one-inch heels. She wasn't wearing pantyhose under her skirt, and her toenails were painted pink. Under the TV, Janis could see rows of CDs.

"Is that your collection?"

"Some of them. The rest are in my bedroom with my toys." *Now, why did I say that?*

Janis pulled up her legs to sit cross-legged. Rachel pulled up her feet and folded them under one side of her butt. "So, what do you want to know?"

The questions came one right after another. Some were about sex; others were about how and when Janis knew. Others were about reactions from others when she is seen holding hands with another woman. Most were about what a lesbian relationship was like.

Janis was careful not to tell Rachel all her experiences or use last names. She wanted to make it very difficult for Rachel to use the information against her if their conversation was being recorded.

Rachel asked what Janis thought about lesbian clubs, and Janis said they were a great way to meet someone and dip her toe in the water, so to speak. Janis' other suggestion was to place a personal ad in a paper and screen the responses.

By now, they had finished the first bottle of wine, and Rachel went to her wine refrigerator. She turned to Janis and asked, "Why don't you pick the next bottle?"

Rachel stood by the sink and Janis could see she had a nervous, strange look on her face. "What's wrong?"

The new Assistant Director of Operations shook her head, and Janis could see her eyes starting to well up. "What if no one finds me attractive?"

Instinctively, Janis wrapped her arms around Rachel as she started to sob. Rachel leaned back and wiped her eyes with the back of her hand.

Janis gently put her hands on both sides of Rachel's head and looked into her eyes. "Rachel, you're very attractive and sexy. Any woman would love to have you as her partner. If not, she'd be crazy."

Rachel started sobbing again. "But I don't know what to do?"

The grandfather clock in the entranceway informed them that it was four. The pause gave Janis a chance to change the subject. "Rachel, what's downstairs?" Janis asked the question because she saw several martial arts trophies in Rachel's office.

"Oh, I have a mini-dojo and some exercise equipment, and I use it to work out and practice.

"What discipline do you practice?

"Karate and jujitsu. I started when I was in operations and practice to maintain my skills and stay in shape."

"Rachel, how about we do some katas and work up a sweat."

"What disciplines do you practice?"

"Tae Kwon Do, kendo, aikido and now, I'm learning krav maga." *It came up in the debrief, but Rachel probably wasn't focused on that.*

"I'm impressed."

"Go change. I've got some workout clothes in my bag in the car."

The two women alternated katas before they enjoyed an intense sparring session. When they were done, Rachel put her hand on Janis's cheek, "You're really good."

"Thanks. You're not so bad yourself. As you know, when you were in the field, being able to defend yourself can be a matter of life and death." Janis laughed. "I'm all hot and sweaty, some women don't like it, but I do."

Rachel kissed Janis on the cheek. "I'll remember that. Thanks for taking the time to talk to me."

Janis pointed to the door. "Let's shower, and then we're going out."

"Where?"

"To dinner in D.C. and then to a lesbian club. You need a social life."

"I'm game."

THE SAME DAY, 8:49 P.M. LOCAL TIME, WASHINGTON, D.C.

Dinner was at a Chinese restaurant in Georgetown. Just before nine, the pair walked into a club called Phase One located on 8th Street, SE in Washington D.C. As they entered, Rachel was very nervous so Janis guided her to a chair at the bar where they could look around.

Janis reminded Rachel that the first person that approached her may or may not be the person she'll leave with that night. They attracted hunters who saw fresh faces and, after a few minutes, found an excuse to move on.

Rachel's nervousness evaporated as she saw women of all ages. Clubbing, she concluded, was not just a young woman's sport. She was sipping a glass of wine when she heard her name. "Hi, Rachel, I would never have imagined seeing you here."

Janis looked at the speaker. The woman was about her age with a trim figure. She had a hairstyle like hers but with longer hair on the left than the right. The woman's hair was a mix of dark and light colors that looked white and black in the light.

"Daffy, my goodness. I'm so glad to see you." Rachel turned to Janis and said, "Daphne Stafford, this is my friend Elizabeth Harris. Daffy and I used to work together."

Daphne Stafford pulled up a free bar stool and looked at Janis who, she assumed by her dress and very butch hairdo, was the male in the relationship. Janis kept her distance and sipped her wine, and she didn't want to do anything that could be interpreted that she and Rachel were a couple. "Rachel, are you still at the same place?"

Rachel nodded. "I am, and I was just promoted to deputy director."

Daffy held out her glass of wine. "Congratulations. I'm impressed, but you were always an outstanding analyst and case officer."

Rachel looked seductively over the rim at Daphne, "So what are you doing these days? I haven't seen or talked to you in a long time."

"Oh, I retired from the Air Force as a light colonel four years ago and got a civil service job with your military counterpart." Translation – I retired as a lieutenant colonel and have a job with the Defense Intelligence Agency.

"You didn't hang around to make full bird?"

All three knew full bird meant full colonel. It received the slang nickname from the eagle insignia worn by full colonels in the Air Force, Army, and Marine Corps.

"No. We may be in a new century, but when it comes to gays and lesbians, the Air Force is a bunch of Neanderthals. So, I retired. Between my pension and civil service pay, I'm making a good buck and like what I do."

Rachel turned to Janis. "Daphne listens in on other people's conversations, translates and analyzes them. The last time we worked together, Daphne spoke German, Russian, Arabic, French, and Spanish. Did I miss any?"

"Yeah, I've learned Pashto since then."

Janis nodded. "I'm impressed."

Daphne looked at Janis. "What do you do?"

"I'm retired."

"What did you do before you retired?"

Daphne's interrogation had begun. "I was in the security business and worked for firms like yours."

The retired Air Force officer's eyebrow rose noticeably at Janis's answer. Rachel put a hand on Janis's and Daphne's forearms. "I've got to go to the little girl's room. Don't either of you leave before I get return."

Both Daphne and Janis said, "We'll be here," at the same time, and then laughed. Janis waited until Rachel was out of sight. "Daphne, we're not a couple. Rachel has been bi-curious for years, and so we came here. I'm in a relationship."

"So, this will be her first time with a woman?"

"Yup."

"Fantastic. I'm single and looking for another partner. Introducing her to our world will be special."

Janis held up her glass and tilted it toward Daphne. "This is all new, different, and exciting to Rachel. You're a perfect tutor since you know all the dos and don'ts in the intelligence world.""

Daphne nodded and took a long sip from her glass of wine. "Perfect."

Rachel walked back up and hung her purse on the chair. "Miss me?"

Daphne said, "Yup" and held out her hand. "Let's go dance and start catching up."

While Janis watched them dance, getting closer and closer, a young woman sat down where Rachel had been sitting. "I see you're the odd woman out. May I buy you a drink? I'm free."

Janis looked at the woman who was young enough to be her daughter. She was very, very pretty with sparkling eyes and long hair that cascaded down over her breasts. "Sorry, but you read me wrong. I just made the introduction."

"So, you're a matchmaker?"

"Not hardly." Janis looked over the young woman's shoulder. "They'll be back soon and may want to sit here." In other words, I am not interested; please leave. The woman took the hint and left with her drink.

While Daphne and Rachel were dancing, two of Daphne's friends introduced themselves to Janis. One was a retired Army intelligence officer, and the other was, like Daphne, retired from the Air Force. Over their shoulders, Janis could see Daphne and Rachel's foreheads touching as they danced.

Rachel and Daphne came back holding hands, sipped on their drinks, and after chatting for a few minutes, went back to the dance floor, leaving Janis alone with Daphne's friends. Janis desperately wanted to leave. She spotted Rachel and Daphne on the dance floor, and instead of moving, they gently swayed to the music with their lips locked together.

When Daphne and Rachel returned the third time, Janis had their wine glasses filled and paid the bill. After listening to the conversation among the four women, Janis waited until the other two women meandered off before she said to Rachel. "My job is done, and I'll exit stage left."

Daphne looked at Rachel. "I'll make sure Rachel gets home safely."

Rachel gave Janis a hug and whispered 'thanks' in her ear.

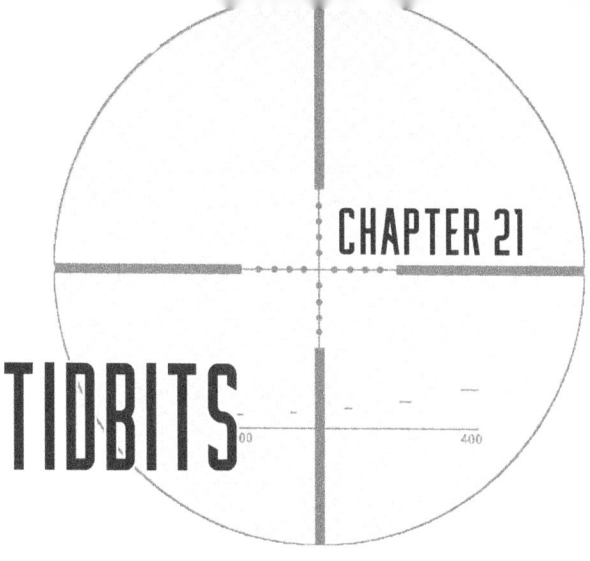

CHAPTER 21

TIDBITS

F ive were in the conversion class, a young couple in their twenties, and a man and two women, and Janis. She had done her required reading and homework. On each trip to Israel, Janis had a list of ruins or religious sites to visit. Sometimes, Aliyah was her tour guide, and other times, Janis went alone. She had not told Aliyah the reason for all the visits, only that she wanted to see the "sights."

Today's lesson was on why the Jewish New Year – Rosh Hashanah – was originally celebrated for two days. Today, only Orthodox and some Conservative Jews celebrate Rosh Hashanah for two days. Long before the common era, Rosh Hashanah was a minor holiday held on the first day of the seventh month in the Hebrew/ Lunar calendar. Back then, it was a precursor to Sukkot, the festival celebrating the harvest that came two days later.

Why two days? In 2002, it was the Jewish Year 5761, 3759 years before the common era (B.C.E.). Back then, communication was slow, and rabbis wanted to ensure the holiday was celebrated on time, so a second day was added.

At the end of the class, the instructor asked Janis and the couple to remain for a few minutes. "You three are ready. We would like to have the ceremony on Friday night, the 6ᵗʰ which is *Erev* Rosh Hashanah. This way, you can start the new year as Jews. Any objections?"

Janis shook her head. *Now I must find a way to get Aliyah here. It will be a huge surprise.*

MONDAY, AUGUST 19ᵀᴴ, 2002, 1:53 P.M. LOCAL TIME, TEL AVIV

In the conference room, Aliyah sat in silence with two Mossad analysts. On the screen were clips from the CDs showing Hezbollah soldiers loading the intermodal container. After the third clip and as the "resident" expert on Abd al-Bari Ghulam, Aliyah was convinced that he and Hezbollah had three options to get the weapons to Lebanon.

Option one – truck them through Austria, Hungary, Serbia, Bulgaria, Turkey, and then into Syria. The trip would take at least two weeks and require documents and bribes at each border crossing. Aliyah assessed this option as being too risky.

Option two – truck them to a port in either Italy or France and bring them to Lebanon or Gaza by ship. No one at Mossad thought Hezbollah would risk putting the weapons on a neutral container ship and wait for the weapons to arrive in either a Lebanese or Syrian port. To Aliyah, a ship Hezbollah or one of their proxies owned made the most sense.

Option three – stash the weapons in caches throughout Europe. This would provide a ready source for teams already in place or smuggled in. This was the choice Aliyah and Mossad feared the most since it would force Mossad to rely on European police organizations to find the weapons.

The debate over the options ended when Aliyah was handed a note stating that a known Hezbollah front company acquired the 3,000-ton *M.V. Star Lynn*. After the purchase, the ship's registry and flag were changed from Panama to Mongolia. The 1998 – 1999 edition of *Jane's Merchant Ships* noted that *Star Lynn* could carry up to nine 40-foot containers on her decks and cargo in her hold.

Venice and Trieste were the closest ports to Riesa. As a free port, Trieste made the most sense. The containers would be considered foreign goods in transit within the EU. They couldn't be searched unless the police were given a valid reason to do so. To do that, the Israelis would need to convince an Italian judge to issue a warrant and lead the police directly to the trucks. To do so, would take time and they would have to show the videos from their surveillance of the former Soviet army base in Germany. An Italian judge might view them as illegally obtained and refuse to act. Then what? In Aliyah's view, one that was shared by Reznik, it was better that they find the weapons and then decide what to do.

A contact at Mano Maritime, an Israeli shipping company, learned from the Port of Trieste that *Star Lynn's* owners had requested a berth to load cargo. *Star Lynn* + six containers + re-registering + Hofer + money transfer from Hezbollah all added up. She gathered her notes and went to talk to Reznik.

LANGLEY, THE SAME DAY, 4:25 P.M. LOCAL TIME

When Rachel walked into what used to be Bishop's office, she was surprised to see her name already on the wall plaque by the door. Betsy Quist put the list of the items she could request to refurnish her office in the center of the clean desk.

Quist, who had been in the agency for almost 20 years, was grinning from ear to ear when Rachel entered. "Good morning, Rachel. Congratulations on your promotion. It is about time we have estrogen at the operations decision-making level. By the way, you look marvelous! If I didn't know better, I'd say you were glowing!"

Rachel, who'd known Betsy for years, laughed. *That's what spending the weekend in the arms of an extraordinary woman like Daphne Stafford will do for you. I have never felt this sexually satisfied in my life.*

The admin she would share with others continued. "Rachel, I cleaned out Bishop's personal stuff. Security will be here later this morning to change the code on the office cipher lock and the cabinets. I inventoried his working files and verified they are all there."

"Thanks. Betsy, one of my first tasks is to get a handle on all, and I mean all the human assets he controlled, and all the operations Bishop was running. To do that, I want to see the file first and then, when I'm ready, set up a private meeting with the players."

"No problem. If you need help deciphering Bishop's hieroglyphics, I can help you." The admin turned serious. "How many of our people did he get killed?"

"Betsy, I don't know the total, but I know of six agents, all in either Lebanon or Syria."

That's how day one started. On day two, Rachel was knee-deep in Bishop's file on a source in Damascus and another in Beirut.

In the CIA's investigation into Bishop, there was no doubt Bishop had deliberately misled the agency for at least 10 years. The agency's official investigation concluded Bishop was a lone wolf, and the postmortem she did on Bishop supported that analysis. She was reading a report summarizing the weapons shipments received by Hamas and Hezbollah when the phone near the edge of her desk rang. "How's your first day and a half at the new job been?"

Rachel recognized Daphne's strong Maine accent. "Fun and exciting. I'm still glowing from the weekend."

"Me too."

"I have to be out at CIA for a meeting on Friday morning, so I'll drive out Thursday afternoon so we can have fun."

"Great. What time do you think you'll be out here?"

"Don't know. I'll call you when I get on the road."

Rachel felt pressure in her loins. It was a new but enjoyable feeling stirred by the anticipation of more sex with Daphne.

TUESDAY, AUGUST 20TH, 2002, 4:25 P.M. LOCAL TIME, ADRIATIC SEA

Star Lynn docked in Trieste on schedule at 5:00 a.m. on the 19th. The port captain and his staff weren't the only ones who noted the ship's arrival. From a roof in the town overlooking the port, two Israelis focused a 1,000mm telephoto lens on *Star Lynn*. They recorded 72 pallets of 55-gallon drums and two pallets wrapped in black plastic being loaded. Next came six pallets stacked with wooden cases that looked as if they contained weapons and ammunition. With the hatches to the hold closed and battened down, six containers matching those in the photographs taken in Riesa were hoisted aboard and chained down.

With its cargo on board, *Star Lynn* took on fuel and provisions before backing away from the pier. It headed into the Adriatic just after three in the afternoon. The Israelis missed the 30 al-Musawi Corps fighters who came on board in ones and twos.

M.V. Star Lynn fastest cruising speed was 10 knots. Abul Zafar, the 3,000-ton freighter's captain, estimated the ship would need just over two days to sail the 460 nautical miles from Trieste to where the Adriatic emptied into the Mediterranean. At only 150 miles at its widest point, the Adriatic doesn't give any ship much room to maneuver, much less hide. There was even less sea room at the heel of Italy's boot where the Adriatic was only 50 nautical miles wide.

Zafar wanted the *Star Lynn* in the Mediterranean as fast as possible, hoping the ship could disappear in the shipping traffic. It was 1,000 nautical miles from the Adriatic to the eastern end of the Mediterranean and what Zafar believed to be the most dangerous part of the voyage– the last 250 nautical miles to the Lebanese coast.

Star Lynn's bow rose and fell about a meter as the 250-foot-long ship plowed through the Adriatic. Zafar's legs gently absorbed the pitching movement as he surveyed the blue water around him from the bridge.

Below him, sparks from welding torches flew as his augmented crew welded half-inch-thick sheets of case-hardened steel to create eight-gun mounts for 12.7mm heavy machine guns. One was installed in the bow, one on the stern, two on each side, and two on the bridge's roof. The steel shields would stop anything up to 12.7mm armor-piercing rounds.

Additional boxes for RPG rockets and ammo cans filled with loaded AK-47 magazines were positioned at each fighting position. The crates containing SA-16s were lashed down on the roof of the bridge and Zafar's standing order was that unless they were in their bunkroom sleeping or bathing, every man wore their ammunition vest and kept their AK-47s within reach. His orders from Hezbollah's Shura Council leader were to not allow *Star Lynn* to be captured.

WEDNESDAY, AUGUST 21ST, 2002, 3:46 A.M. LOCAL TIME, DALLAS

Janis stared at the ceiling. This was the second night she couldn't sleep more than a few hours at a time, and she knew what had caused it. At first, she wrote it off to stress, knowing she was about to turn 55.

Her brain and heart were telling her two different things. Her head told her that she needed to go back into retirement. She knew she could do the work, but she was afraid. Janis wasn't afraid of dying or being killed. She feared missing detail on an operation that would lead to others being killed.

Other reasons were spelled A… L… I… Y… A… H… Their relationship had grown well past just sex, and Janis believed their mutual affection was a complication.

The old feeling and rush from taking a contract in her 20s and 30s was long gone. Once again, she was a hired gun, right out of a Western movie. As radical as she was when she was a student at the University of Wisconsin and a member of the Students for a Democratic Society's Action Wing, she would never have believed she would be called *The Red Star of Death*. But here she was, a professional killer again!

When Janis first agreed to work with the Israelis and the CIA, she believed the decision was mostly about self-preservation. She didn't want to be arrested by the FBI or blackmailed into working for the CIA or the Cuban *Dirección de Inteligencia*. She thought the excitement of being at the top of her game as a hired gun might return.

Now, she had a purpose. *La Estrella Roja de la Muerte* was now an avenging angel for the State of Israel and maybe the CIA. In the back of her mind, she wondered what Rachel would ask her to do?

The hunt for Abd al-Bari Ghulam was Aliyah's focus. Both wanted to take out the entire Shura Council but that was considered an unacceptable escalation, so Ghulam was the target. Janis believed she was going to be ordered to kill him.

Several times while alone in Aliyah's apartment, they talked about, "What do we do after Ghulam?" It was a code phrase for what comes next in their lives. Neither had a good answer nor knew when "after Ghulam" would occur.

Mossad was Aliyah's life, and Janis feared Aliyah might say no to a life together. That fear was just as strong as her fear of failure.

THE SAME DAY, 10:03 A.M. LOCAL TIME, LANGLEY

The CIA analysis of the August 4th attack at the Meron Junction bus stop in Israel reached Rachel's desk earlier this morning. Ten, including the suicide bomber, were killed; another 50 were wounded. Hamas claimed responsibility. The report was clinical, factual, and cold reading. Despite having seen hundreds of these reports, Rachel still became angry when she read them and imagined the suffering endured by those who were attacked.

Eighteen days earlier, on July 17th, an Islamic Jihad suicide bomber killed himself and four others and wounded 40 more. Islamic Jihad meant their parent, Hezbollah sanctioned the attack, and Abd al-Bari Ghulam was involved by association.

The tally inside the folder listed 40 attacks inside Israel in the first eight months of 2002. The body count was 232 dead and 1,505 wounded. Rachel wondered how many more the Israelis would absorb before they reacted militarily.

Rachel was determined to find and capture Abd al-Bari Ghulam outside the U.S. If he was inside, she would push the FBI hard to act, if for nothing else, the attack in Los Angeles.

The call from Grant Hershey inviting her to an impromptu meeting with the FBI interrupted her study of suicide bomber attacks. The topic was Bishop, and more Hershey did not say.

She was surprised by the meeting's location – a conference room off the main lobby and outside the security perimeter of the CIA. These rooms were used by the procurement staff to meet with contractors in an unclassified environment and by HR for job interviews.

Rachel arrived three minutes late, and the second surprise was seeing William Smith III and Gale Reddington, a female Special Agent, sitting in the room. The woman said her first name was spelled G A L E, not the more common G A I L.

Smith III asked why they were not in a secure conference room. Hershey's terse answer was that no classification level was established to warrant using such a room. His answer irritated Smith III.

"Mr. Hershey, Miss Simms, the reason we are here is that the FBI has launched an investigation into the death of Mr. Walter Bishop. At the time of his demise, Mr. Bishop was the CIA's Assistant Director of Operations for the Middle East. The FBI believes that Mr. Bishop had classified material in his home that may have been compromised or stolen. After seeing the list of money transfers to his offshore accounts, we further believe he was a traitor. The FBI suspects that others, either inside or outside CIA, wanted him silenced. Based on our investigation, we have a list of potential suspects and individuals we would like to interview within the agency."

Grant held up his hand. "Mr. Smith, we understand the FBI has a job to do, but the Fairfax County Coroner ruled Mr. Bishop died from a massive heart attack. Independently, the CIA's forensic team came to the same conclusion. I believe the FBI has a copy of the coroner's report. I am sure the CIA would be happy to release our forensic analysis to the FBI to help put this matter to bed."

"Mr. Hershey, the examination of Mr. Bishop's remains was done by the CIA and a county examiner, not an FBI coroner. Our forensic lab is the most advanced in the country. Our medical examiners have seen the report and think the killer used hydrogen cyanide to assassinate Mr. Bishop."

"Do you have any proof?"

"No. Right now, our working hypothesis is that Mr. Bishop was murdered. We have filed paperwork to exhume Mr. Bishop's remains and conduct our autopsy."

Hershey leaned forward and tried to keep the anger out of his voice. "Mr. Smith, Ms. Simms and I think you are chasing a mirage. The leadership of the CIA is convinced that Mr. Bishop was a traitor who worked alone. If you feel he had accomplices, then please go find them. Counter espionage in the U.S. is a mission of the FBI, am I correct?"

Smith bristled at the reminder of his agency's role. "The FBI is well aware of its mission. Central to our investigation is resolving whether Bishop was murdered. In our view, once that is cleared up, we can then investigate the espionage angle."

"Who are your suspects?"

Smith III smiled. "We have reason to believe that Elizabeth Harris whom the CIA has retained as a covert operator murdered Bishop. In the U.S., murder of a federal employee is a crime, and the investigation falls under the jurisdiction of the FBI. I can assure you that the FBI is prepared to go to court to get all legal documents about Ms. Harris's relationship with the CIA. Our filing will include any records, meeting notes, debriefings, conversations, etc., she may have had with the late Mr. Bishop."

Hershey nodded to indicate he understood Bishop's real purpose of the visit. He'd already checked with the agency's legal office, and before he left for the meeting, the CIA's general counsel called the Attorney General of the United States. Based on what Hershey was told, the attorney general was satisfied with the coroner's report, and after a preliminary investigation, none of Bishop's contacts lived in the United States.

Hershey's next statement did not surprise Rachel as she listened to his cold, formal tone. "Special Agent Smith, you do realize that to go to court to acquire the documents you are seeking, you must have the approval of the Attorney General of the United States? He, not you, will determine whether to request them from the CIA through existing inter-agency protocols or the courts. So, have you talked to either the head of the FBI or his boss, the Attorney General about this matter?"

Smith III stared at Hershey. "No, we have not spoken with the director. We have, however, sent him our recommendations and are confident that he will approve our requests. And, if the CIA does not cooperate, the FBI will contact the Attorney General or other powerful friends to force the CIA to comply."

Hershey didn't move. His voice remained calm, but forceful, but it did not hide his annoyance. "Special Agent Smith, you are playing in a sandbox that could be career-threatening to both Special Agent Reddington and you. I strongly suggest you abandon this witch-hunt. You tried once to meet with Ms. Harris and were suspended for 30 days without pay and formally reprimanded. Do you want to risk a more significant punishment? If that is all we have to talk about, Ms. Simms and I have work to do."

THE SAME DAY, 6:21 P.M. LOCAL TIME, TORONTO, CANADA

The U.S. immigration officer at Pearson International Airport looked at Dawud Hafeez's Jordanian passport and then at the clean-shaven man standing on the other side of the glass of his kiosk. The scanner beeped, saying the photos and documents matched what was in the computer.

Through a unique arrangement between the U.S. and Canadian governments, when Hafeez exited immigration and security, he was legally on U.S. soil even though he was still physically in Canada. Hafeez again showed his passport and boarding pass at the gate before walking down the jet bridge. When he got to his row, he put his bag in the overhead bin and took his seat, 24B, on the two-seat side of the aisle of the American Airlines MD-80.

Once seated, he smiled at the man sitting next to him and buckled his seatbelt. Other than saying hello, Hafeez read a book for the entire flight to Dallas. Around midnight, Hafeez, whose real name was Abd al-Bari Ghulam, unlocked the door to the safe house in Dallas's Arab community in Plano, TX.

THURSDAY, AUGUST 22ND, 2002, 8:56 A.M. LOCAL TIME, TEL AVIV

After listening to the data compiled by Mossad, the prime minister ordered the Israeli Defense Forces to find and stop *Star Lynn*. If the ship is carrying weapons, his orders were to bring *Star Lynn* to Haifa.

He also said he didn't want to ask the U.S. for help finding *Star Lynn* unless it was necessary.

One piece of intelligence that gave Aliyah confidence that they could find the *Star Lynn* was when the ship was re-flagged, the 22-year-old freighter was given a new name and radio call sign EX4BMA. Scimitar Shipping did not change the International Maritime Satellite (INMARSAT) phone number when it changed the registration from Panamanian to Mongolian. The IMARSAT directory showed the ship's name, radio code, and phone number.

Aliyah was worried *Star Lynn* could disappear in the Mediterranean and dock in Lebanon before the Israelis could find it. In the IDF command center, two plots were made, one using a 10-knot cruising speed and the second, the freighter's maximum speed of 12 knots. They had six days to find the *Star Lynn* steaming at 10 knots, five if traveling at 12.

Rings on the chart showed *Star Lynn's* potential daily progress toward the Lebanese ports of Beirut or Tripoli. Latakia or Tartus in Syria were also possible destinations but unlikely given that Hezbollah controlled the Lebanese ports. Gaza was controlled by Hamas and was ruled out as a destination since Hamas and Hezbollah were rivals in the Byzantine world of Middle Eastern politics.

On the same chart plotting *Star Lynn's* possible routes, the track of the Israeli Air Force's Boeing 707 converted to electronic intelligence gathering was drawn along with two lines showing the detection range of its sensors. The plane's planned path took it 1,500 kilometers (~810 nautical miles) west of Lebanon before turning north for 300 kilometers (~162 nautical miles) and returning to Israel.

The Israeli Navy's two *Sa'ar 5* class corvettes, each with a team of *Shayetet 13* commandos, the Israeli version of the Eurocopter Dauphin helicopter, and three *Sa'ar 4.5s* missile boats were already in a picket line, 150 kilometers apart. The helicopters from each ship were searching for the *Star Lynn* along the shipping lanes approaching Lebanon.

The most traveled and direct route was east straight across the Mediterranean, allowing *Star Lynn* to blend in with other ships. Once it passed the Greek Island of Crete, the captain could sail around Cyprus, adding a day to the sailing time to Lebanon unless the destination was Latakia in Syria. Or head directly to Beirut or Tripoli. Aliyah believed

Star Lynn would take the most direct route to Lebanon since the risk of capture increased each day *Star Lynn* was at sea.

So far, there had not been an electronic sniff of *Star Lynn*. It had yet to make the regular daily reports via either short-wave radio or satellite phone to its owners, Scimitar Shipping. Looking at the chart and the track of the Boeing 707, an idea formed in Aliyah's mind.

When Aliyah explained what she wanted to do, the watch commander said he would alert the Boeing and Unit 8200, who asked her to try to keep *Star Lynn* online for at least a minute. From a phone in the command center, Aliyah dialed a number, and it rang six times before someone answered. "Motor Vessel *Star Lynn*."

Aliyah spoke in idiomatic Arabic. "Hi, this is Salma from Scimitar Shipping. I noticed in the company log that *Star Lynn* has not made any daily status reports since leaving Trieste. Does the ship have a problem?"

The name Salma appeared in several intercepts. Aliyah had no idea of who Salma was or her role other than she worked at Scimitar. There was no sound for what seemed like ages, but she didn't get a dial tone which added to the time the satellite link was open. Another voice came on the line.

"This is Captain Zafar. Everything is going according to our planned schedule on file at Scimitar."

"So, you are planning to dock after the Sabbath?"

"I am."

The irritation in the man's voice was obvious despite the distance the call traveled. Aliyah's voice went from the command center via landline to where it was transmitted to an INMARSAT satellite 25,000 miles above the earth. The magic of telephony sent a signal to the phone on the *Star Lynn,* and the connection was made.

"Excellent. I shall note in the company log that *Star Lynn* is operating normally, and the ship will arrive as planned. Will you need fuel and re-provisioning when you arrive?"

"Please note in the log that no one is to contact *Star Lynn* until we call just before dark on Saturday. You should have been told that. And yes, we will need food and fuel."

"I will do that. Do you have any other instructions or notes you want me to make?"

"No."

"Thank you, may Allah be with you."

When she heard the dial tone, the watch officer was smiling. *Mitsuyan!*!!

Antennas on the Boeing 707 picked up the signal and located the ship. The vessel was using its S-and X-band search radars intermittently, and the signatures were recorded. Now, the crew on the Boeing could track the ship's progress.

In the command center, *Star Lynn's* location was plotted, and the watch commander ordered IDF's C-130s equipped for search and rescue to take off. They had hemispherical windows on the fuselage that the photographer could use to take pictures. Until the C-130 returned in about three hours with photographs, there was nothing to do but wait.

Based on *Star Lynn's* position, a point 185 kilometers (~100 nautical miles) due west of Beirut was designated as the point where the intercept would take place. The ships on the picket line were ordered to converge on the *Star Lynn* for what was now dubbed Operation Trident. It received its name since everyone in the command center hoped Israel would put a spear into Hezbollah's plans.

THE SAME DAY, 1:07 P.M. LOCAL TIME, WASHINGTON, D.C.

The drawing and notes on the blackboard of the FBI conference room were centered on a photo of Walt Bishop. One line went out to a box labeled Hofer and Associates. Another went out to a box named Hezbollah. A third went to a box listing senior Iranian officers in the Revolutionary Guard Corps and the Quds Force. A fourth went to a list of terrorist organizations. A fifth titled 'Potential Killers' in which there was one name – Elizabeth Harris. Another box had a list of offshore banks where Bishop had accounts.

Smith III was studying a document on Hofer's family when the administrative assistant for the Senior Special Agent in Charge of the FBI's Criminal Investigative Division entered. "Special Agent Smith, Mr. Grimaldi wants to see you right now."

Special Agent Smith III knew an order when he heard one, even though, technically, the woman couldn't give special agents orders. "Right now?"

"Yes, sir. He is waiting for you in his conference room."

Smith III tossed the document on the table. "Special Agent Reddington, I'll be back shortly, hopefully with news on our requests to subpoena Ms. Harris for a deposition."

He followed the woman, wondering why Grimaldi wanted to meet in his conference room unless there were others in the meeting. Smith III ran through several scenarios and concluded that he wanted to discuss his investigation of Elizabeth Harris.

Grimaldi was at the end of the table in his customary chair when Smith III walked into the room. He didn't recognize the mousey-looking woman with large, round, black-framed glasses who said she was from HR. He'd met the other man – Jeffrey Hutchinson – from the FBI's Office of the General Counsel when he was notified of his suspension. Hutchinson's presence caused a sense of foreboding and a knot in Smith III's gut. He immediately forgot the name of the woman from HR.

Grimaldi waited until Smith III sat down. There was no offer of coffee or something to drink and none of the people in the room had a beverage of any kind which signaled this would be a short meeting.

"Special Agent Smith, the purpose of this meeting is to discuss your separation from the FBI. We will allow you to retire, effective today, with a pension if you agree to specific conditions. Or you can allow the bureau to investigate your recent actions and determine your future. If you are cleared, you can continue in the bureau. However, if the bureau discovers you have failed to meet its standards and decides to take judicial action, you may lose your pension or, worse, spend time in jail."

Before Grimaldi could continue, William Smith III said one word, "Why?"

Grimaldi held up his hand and looked at the woman from HR whose head moved slightly up and down and then to Hutchinson, who also nodded more forcibly before Grimaldi continued. "Mr. Bishop, twice you were told to back off Miss Elizabeth Harris. After you refused to follow orders the first time, you were suspended without pay, reprimanded, and reassigned. Second, you were authorized to determine if Mr. Walter Bishop had accomplices, and if so, who were they? You were NOT authorized to investigate his death. What makes matters worse, you were assigned to mentor Special Agent Reddington, who just graduated from the academy. You embroiled her in the obsession you have with Elizabeth Harris. In short, Smith, you can no longer be trusted to be an FBI special agent."

"That's bullshit, sir. There's a connection between Harris and Bishop. I have evidence. All I...."

Grimaldi put up his hand. "Stop. I don't want to hear what you have to say." Grimaldi nodded to the man sitting to his left. "Mr. Hutchinson."

The lawyer slid a folder across the table to Smith III. "This separation agreement grants you full retirement based on twenty years of service. FBI records show that you have eighteen years and seven months of service. The director has graciously given you credit for the remaining months to bring you twenty years. However, to receive this generous offer, you must sign the agreement today. Through it, you agree to three conditions. One, you will not speak or communicate in any way with anyone, even through material released after your death, about Elizabeth Harris. Two, you are not allowed to discuss any investigation in which you were involved. Three, you cannot reveal why you were terminated and retired. If the bureau suspects you have violated this agreement, we will investigate. If violations are found, you will face prosecution that could cost you your pension and its associated benefits."

Smith III waited until he was sure Hutchinson was finished. "And, if I don't agree to these terms, what happens?"

"As Senior Special Agent Grimaldi noted before, you will be suspended and, after the FBI digs into your past, probably terminated for cause and possibly prosecuted. In either case, you lose all your retirement benefits. The FBI wants you out of the bureau now and will pay for you to leave."

"How much time do I have to decide?"

Grimaldi looked at his watch. "About five minutes. We can leave you alone if you would like."

"You don't give me much choice, do you?"

Grimaldi's voice was carefully measured to not betray his annoyance at Smith III. "Smith, we didn't go off half-cocked. You did. This is the price you have to pay."

Smith III opened the document and started reading. When he reached the end, he pulled out a pen and signed both copies. Once he finished, he put his badge, pistol, phone, and access card on the table.

CHAPTER 22

HIGH SEAS TAKETOWN

SATURDAY, AUGUST 24TH, 2002, 1:38 A.M. LOCAL TIME, ON BOARD STAR LYNN

A t one in the morning, the stars above *Star Lynn* shone brightly in the cloudless sky. The sea was a black expanse with a barely discernible horizon. The darkness was familiar to Captain Zafar when he walked onto the bridge just after one in the morning.

Star Lynn was blacked out and not showing any lights, violating international maritime regulations. Zafar didn't care. He wanted the Chinese-built freighter to be as hard to spot as possible on the ship's last night at sea.

Every four hours, the watch noted the ship's course and speed on the chart taped to the aft bulkhead of the bridge. Zafar checked the chart and used his thumb and forefinger to measure the distance from the ship's midnight fix to Beirut. They had about 205 nautical miles to go. He easily did the math in his head – at 12 knots, *Star Lynn* would be entering Beirut's harbor in just over 17 hours.

Satisfied everything was still going as planned, Zafar poured himself a mug of coffee and dropped two lumps of sugar into the steaming hot mixture. A sip told him that he had the mix right, and he set the mug on the small tray next to the captain's chair.

If the Israelis were going to attack, Zafar suspected they would come inside 100 nautical miles from Beirut.

From what he could tell, the ship had not been overflown, or at least no airplane came down low enough to look. They had seen only four merchant ships, none closer than five nautical miles. The scope next to the helmsman indicated no ships within 10 nautical miles. Besides the strange phone call that he will deal with after *Star Lynn* arrives in Beirut, Zafar was beginning to think they would make it safely.

Satisfied everything was in order, Zafar would let the crew sleep until 0200. He put his walkie-talkie next to a silver box with a small antenna, a covered toggle switch, a red button, and a green light. The switch turned the transmitter on. A green light indicated the receiver connected to the detonator in the 100 kilos of SEMTEX in the hold was receiving the radio signal from the box. Pushing the toggle switch under the red cover would set off the plastic explosive and blow *Star Lynn* apart.

Until today, Zafar kept the transmitter in the safe in his cabin. Zafar saw himself as a ship captain, not a suicide bomber, and suspected one or more of the Al-Musawi Corps fighters on board the ship had a similar device.

THE SAME DAY, 2:32 A.M. LOCAL TIME, ON BOARD THE I.N.S. HETZ

Lookouts could see the *Star Lynn* through their long-range, infrared binoculars. The freighter was two kilometers ahead and 20 degrees off the 70-meter-long Israeli Navy's *Sa'ar 4.5* corvette's port bow. Abeam, three kilometers away, *Hetz's* sister ship *Romach*, trailed *Star Lynn* on the merchant ship's port side.

The Israeli assault was supposed to begin at midnight but was delayed after the photographs taken by the C-130's crew showed the *Star Lynn's* new fighting positions. These made a helicopter assault too dangerous.

C-130s dropped 20 more men, and two more Zodiacs by parachute to the task force. Operation Trident now included four ships, *Hetz, Romach,* and two newer, *Sa'ar 5* ships, *Lahav* and *Hanit,* each with two Dauphin helicopters aboard.

While the C-130 with the extra men and equipment was enroute, the helicopters transferred the 20 Shayetet 13 commandos from the two *Sa'ar 5* corvettes – *Lahav* and *Hanit* – to *Hetz* and *Romach.* The newly arrived soldiers brought copies of photographs of the *Star Lynn* and a new plan for the attack. With half the commandos on board *Hetz* and half on *Romach,* the ships sped up to 20 knots and closed on *Star Lynn. Lahav* remained five kilometers from *Star Lynn's* port side and *Hanit* took up a similar station to starboard.

Orbiting 20,000 feet above *Star Lynn,* a highly modified Israeli Air Force Boeing 707 was spoofing the merchant ship's radar. Radar waves bouncing off the Israeli ships were distorted by the 707's jamming equipment. What *Star Lynn's* radar detected was seen as electronic noise and filtered out by the radar's software. Hence, its radarscope was clear. No one on the bridge was checking the radar scope so it didn't matter.

On each *Sa'ar 4.5* corvette, two Kevlar-reinforced Combat Rubber Raiding Craft a.k.a. "Zodiacs" shoved off from the side. Each had 10 men plus a coxswain who steered the boats toward the *Star Lynn* at 25 knots.

The boats from *Hetz* raced toward the freighter's port side, and those from *Romach* went up the starboard side. Once alongside the ship, the most dangerous part of the attack, getting on board, would begin.

THE SAME DAY, 2:49 A.M. LOCAL TIME, ON BOARD STAR LYNN,

Hamid Bagdhadi, the lookout on the port bow, thought he saw something. He swung his heavy night vision binoculars toward a flare of white light. The object was well beyond the night vision binoculars' range, so he went back to his regular binoculars with their wider field of view. Still nothing, but convinced he saw something, Baghdadi keyed his small hand-held radio.

"Bridge, port bow lookout. I saw something abeam of us that is beyond the capabilities of my night vision binoculars. Do you have anything on radar?

Zafar walked over to the radarscope. "Standby." He saw a contact at 13 nautical miles on the port side. Zafar changed the range scale to show only contacts within five miles, and nothing was on the scope. "We see nothing close but keep a sharp lookout."

On the Boeing 707, a linguist listened to the entire conversation and alerted the flagship, the Israeli ships, and the assault teams.

Baha Gazzah, the leader of the Al-Musawi fighters on *Star Lynn,* knocked on the door to the bridge. Zafar waved him in. "Captain, I think we should get everyone up."

"I agree."

Zafar nodded and picked up the mike that connected him to the ship's loudspeaker system. "Crew, wake up, wake up. We are going to action stations. Be alert. If the Israelis attack us, they will come before dawn."

THE SAME DAY, 2:51 A.M. LOCAL TIME, ON BOARD STAR LYNN

What Zafar didn't know was that the Shayetet 13 commandos coming up both sides heard his announcement. The four team names were *Alef, Bet, Gimel,* and *Dalet* – the first four letters in the Hebrew alphabet. *Alef* and *Bet* were assigned to board on the stern and bow of the port side, and *Gimel* and *Dalet* had similar assignments on the starboard side.

On the bow of each of the two lead boats, the snipers spotted the stern sentry. At 75 meters, the raid commander *Seren* (captain) Uri Gluck and leader of Team *Alef* authorized a shot. Gluck, crouched behind the sniper in his Zodiac didn't hear the shot from the Galil Galatz sniper rifle. He did, however, see the man drop.

A padded grappling hook was fired from a specially modified gun and landed with a soft clunk. After a sharp tug to ensure it was secure, Gluck started up the rope ladder on the starboard side. The deck was five meters above the water. Once on board, Gluck crouched behind a stanchion to provide cover for the other nine men on his team coming up the ladder.

Bagdhadi thought he heard a grapnel land from his position on the port bow. Suspecting a boat, he leaned over the side. A round from a suppressed Galil carbine known as a Gillon hit him in the forehead, and Baghdadi's dead body draped over the railing before falling back on the deck.

THE SAME DAY, 2:53 A.M. LOCAL TIME, ON BOARD STAR LYNN

Segen (Israeli equivalent of a first lieutenant) Gabriel Danzig, leader of Team *Bet* was the first man over the port bow railing. The other nine men in his team followed and began to work their way aft.

At the stern of *Star Lynn*, *Seren* Gluck drove his knife into the throat of the first man coming out of the hatch. He peeked into the passageway, and seeing no one between him and the interior stairs, known as a ladder, he started up to Team *Alef's* primary objective – the bridge.

THE SAME DAY, 2:54 A.M. LOCAL TIME, ON BOARD STAR LYNN

On the aft starboard side, Team *Gimel* under *Segen Mishneh* (second lieutenant) Geffen was pinned down. They were spotted coming over the railing. Geffen was seriously wounded by fire from a machine gun on the wing of the bridge. Only five of his 10 men managed to get onto *Star Lynn*. The other five were hanging on the ladder while the five onboard exchanged fire with the *Star Lynn's* defenders.

THE SAME DAY, 2:56 A.M. LOCAL TIME, ON BOARD STAR LYNN

On the starboard bow, *Segen Mishneh* Dov Haretz led all 10 members of Team *Dalet* aft toward the bridge. Just past the forward 12.7 mm gun position, Haretz stepped out from behind a bollard. Four rounds and a long burst from an AK-47 stitched him across the chest from one shoulder to the other. He was dead before his body hit the deck. His men were pressed against the cargo containers and exposed.

Via radio, *Segen* Gabriel Danzig took over Haretz's team and his men began to work toward Geffen's trapped team. Bursts from machine gun positions on both wings of the bridge stopped them and pinned the Israelis down.

THE SAME DAY, 2:58 A.M. LOCAL TIME, ON BOARD STAR LYNN

Inside the bridge structure, Gluck left a fire team of two to cover their backs and led seven men from compartment to compartment killing anyone they found. In a passageway on the deck below the bridge, a grenade was rolled toward the Israelis. Gluck and his men quickly retreated around a corner. The grenade smoked and hissed but did not go off.

Gluck peeked his head around and saw three men coming out of a compartment. The first knelt on the floor and raised his AK-47. He was knocked backward with three 5.56 mm bullets in his upper chest. The other two went down in a spray of blood as short bursts from Team *Alef* stitched their bodies.

On the deck passageway behind the bridge, a man stuck an AK-47 around the corner and emptied the magazine toward Gluck and his men. The bullets went high and ricocheted off the steel, filling the air with lead fragments. Gluck shot the defender as he released the bolt on his reloaded AK-47.

Through a porthole to a door leading to an outside wing of the bridge, Gluck spotted two men firing on Danzig and Team *Bet* with an RPD machine gun behind a steel shield. The Israelis opened the door and shot the two men in the back before they could react.

Two grenades bounding down the passageway sent Gluck and his men retreating down the ladder. The concussion and noise from the blasts hurt their ears, and fragments pinged off the steel walls.

Again, Gluck started up the ladder and again, a hissing grenade bounced down the stairs. In one motion, he scooped up the grenade and tossed the egg-shaped, Soviet-made RGD-5 around the corner. Shrapnel was still ricocheting off the steel bulkheads when they charged around the corner and killed the two Al-Musawi Corps fighters.

THE SAME DAY, 3:04 A.M. LOCAL TIME, ON BOARD STAR LYNN

On the bow and the starboard side, things were not going well for teams *Bet, Gimel,* and *Dalet.* From the port wing of the bridge, the al-Musawi fighter kept up a steady stream of fire from RPD machine guns protected by half-inch thick, case-hardened steel. The 5.56mm bullets from the Israeli Galils rung the steel like a bell each time they disintegrated when they hit the shields. By deploying his men on the main deck and the wings off the bridge, Gazzah kept the Israelis pinned down on the bow and port side.

The Israelis hid behind the ammunition boxes welded to the deck and anything that could protect them from the hail of bullets raining down on them from the superstructure. The longer the fight went on, the worse it became for the Israelis. Each man carried only 300 rounds and by now, most had consumed half of what they carried. Five of the commandos were dead, and four more were wounded.

Gluck sensed the battle was at a critical point. He ordered the men who didn't make it over the railing on the port side to be picked up by a Zodiac and brought around to the port side to reinforce his team.

Believing it was only a matter of time before his men overwhelmed the Israeli commandos, Gazzah urged them to keep shooting. He had more men and more ammunition and ordered his men to push down both sides of the deck to flush out the Israelis. Gazzah believed steady fire from the superstructure would cover his men. Once his men overwhelmed one group, he could do the same to the other.

On the port side *Samal Rishnon* (staff sergeant) David Gutman worked his way down to a pair of large bollards mounted on the deck. Peeking around them, Gutman could see the two machine gunners on the port side. He slid a 40mm grenade into the launcher attached to the bottom of his Gillon and took a bead on the RPD gunners.

The first grenade bounced off the armor plate and exploded in the air below the third deck where the machine gunner was located. The RPD gunner realized the man with the grenade launcher was a greater threat than anyone else, spun around, and sprayed the deck where David Gutman was hiding. Bullets pinged and ricocheted around Gutman sending lead, copper, and steel fragments into his arms and legs.

Gutman calmly popped out the spent grenade's brass case and slipped another into the firing chamber. He stuck his head and shoulders above the bollard and aimed at the overhanging deck above the RPD gunner. The M441 fragmentation grenade banged off the steel a few feet below his point of aim and exploded.

Shredded by the shrapnel, the RPD gunner and his assistant collapsed on the deck. The break in the fire let Gutman fire a third grenade at the RPD gunners above the bridge.

They collapsed from shrapnel wounds and were replaced by two more men. The enterprising gunner thought he could get a better angle on the Israelis by standing on the railing and shooting down. He got off one burst before three streams of red tracers converged on him sending his bloody torso over the side of the ship. The second man cowered behind the steel shield spraying bullets wildly.

Inside the bridge structure, Gluck was about to rush through the hatch onto the bridge when a man wearing a bulky vest and holding a plunger stepped out of the bridge. Before his thumb could move, the two men behind Gluck pumped three round bursts into his head blowing his brains and skull all over the passageway.

On the bridge, Zafar, the only man left alive, was standing at the wheel. The others were dead or helping Gazzah. When Gluck stormed onto the bridge, Zafar reached for the aluminum box that was still on the tray in front of the captain's chair, stopped and raised his hands above his head. "I am Abdul Zafar, captain of *Star Lynn*."

Gluck ordered in Arabic. "Captain, stop the ship. Immediately!"

Zafar pointed at the ship's engine telegraph that sent signals to the engines. Gluck nodded hoping the telegraph was not connected to a bomb. Zafar moved the telegraph arm from its current position to "Stop" once and repeated the movement leaving the arm in the "Stop" position. He then confirmed the order via the internal phone system.

On the second deck, Gazzah felt the ship slow and looked up at the bridge. He could see an Israeli soldier in the porthole and reached into his pocket to pull out a similar box to the one Zafar didn't use. Gazzah extended the antenna and was about to push the toggle switch forward when the first of three 62 grain, green tipped M855 5.56mm bullets hit him in the chest and upper arm. The box flew out his hand as his arm jerked from the impact of a bullet, bounced off the railing, and dropped into the Mediterranean.

With the Israelis in control of the bridge and upper deck and their leader dead, the remaining 16 Al-Musawi Corps soldiers surrendered. Zafar spent five minutes coaxing the two men in the engine room to leave their station, and he promised they would not be shot by either Gazzah or the Israelis.

Star Lynn was now wallowing in the long swells of the Mediterranean. Uri Gluck's watch read 3:33 when he radioed that the ship was taken. Minutes after he made the call, a Dauphin helicopter hovered over the bow to hoist the most seriously wounded Israelis onboard. Of the 40 Shayetet 13 commandos that made the assault, six were dead, and four were seriously wounded and needed immediate evacuation. Another dozen had wounds that were not life-threatening but would need medical attention.

THE SAME DAY, 3:59 A.M. LOCAL TIME, ON BOARD STAR LYNN

Nothing was done to clean up the ship other than to drape the dead Al-Musawi Corps fighters in white sheets. The most seriously wounded were flown to *Lahav* to be treated and the corvette was dispatched to steam at full speed to get within helicopter range of Haifa so they could be flown to a hospital. The others were treated on board *Hetz.*

With the explosives and detonator disarmed, Zafar was allowed to stay on the bridge and guide his ship under the supervision of three Israeli naval officers. On either side of *Star Lynn,* the two Israeli corvettes – *Romach* and *Hetz* maintained station 500 meters away as the freighter trailed *Hanit* by 500 meters.

SUNDAY, AUGUST 25TH, 2002, 12:05 P.M. LOCAL TIME, MOTORSPORT RANCH, CRESSON, TEXAS

There was not a cloud in the Texas sky, letting the sun raise the asphalt track temperature to 120°F. Under her driving suit, Janis wore a "cool suit" through which cold water was pumped. Under it was another layer of fireproof underwear driving suit. Even with the cold water being pumped through the "cool suit," sweat dripped down Janis' back, soaking the undergarment as she worked the steering wheel, gear shift, and pedals.

On her fifth lap of the 3.1-mile-long course during the 30-minute period, Janis' shifted into fifth gear as the 906 tracked wide exiting Turn 1. A slight turn of the wheel angled the Porsche toward the entrance to the difficult right-left-right combination of Turns 2, 3, and 4. The 2-liter flat-six engine behind her back was just passing 7,200 rpm when Janis' pressed on the brake pedal with the ball of her right foot. At the same time, she rocked the outside of the same foot to blip the throttle. This was while depressing the clutch with her left foot and moving the shift lever with her right hand from fifth to fourth, then to third for the decreasing radius Turn 2.

A gentle flick of Janis' wrists and the front tires of the car built in 1965 bit into the abrasive pavement. The car didn't have power steering so there was no boost to help her turn the front wheels and their five-and-a-half-inch wide contact patch.

Janis pushed down on the accelerator and felt the rear end slide. A slight correction with the steering wheel had her lined up perfectly for the entrance to Turn 3 and set the car up on the fastest possible line through Turn 4. Turn 5 was taken at full throttle in fourth. Janis lifted slightly entering Turn 6 and ran the engine up to its 8,500-rpm limit in fourth to use all 220 horsepower on the short straight before lifting off for Turn 7. Braking hard, Janis pointed the car at the apex of Turn 7. As the car drifted toward the edge of the track, Janis shifted up into fifth and passed two cars before downshifting through the gears to second for the 180⁰ left hairpin that was Turn 8.

The car's acceleration pushed her back into the fiberglass bucket seat as she kept the lateral g forces right at the limit of adhesion so the car wouldn't slide or worse, spin as she came out of Turn 8. The gentle esses before the entrance to Turn 9 were taken at almost a straight line. The flat-six was turning nearly 8,000 rpm when she downshifted into third and turned right into Turn 9, a wider radius 180⁰ left turn. With the gas pedal floored, she shifted back into fourth for the short straight into Turn 10 that was, like Turns 2, 3, 4, the make-or-break corners for a good lap time. If Janis exited from Turn 10 on the ideal line, she could maximize her speed down the following straight.

Janis pulled the gearshift lever into fourth as she exited Turn 10. After shifting into fifth, she lifted momentarily to point the nose of the 906 at the exit to the slight left-hander that was Turn 11.

At her braking point to the entrance to Turn 12, the Porsche was going close to 170 miles an hour. She pushed hard on the brake pedal while shifting from fourth and then into third, kept the rpm in the heart of the 906's power band. Her exit from Turn 12 was followed by a quick shift up into fourth with the gas pedal floored before downshifting into third for the entrance to Turn 13, a 90⁰, increasing radius right-hander.

Turn 14 – a 170⁰ left-hand turn in which after turning toward the apex, the driver could keep accelerating. To be fast, Janis had to keep enough power on the car to have the 906 right on the edge of adhesion, but not so much as to create a time-losing slide. Turns 15 and 16, both increasing radius left-handers, let her shift up into fourth entering the start-finish straight to start another lap.

During the session, there were only 10 other cars on the course, six were big-bore sports racing cars with V-8 engines and four were race-prepared Corvettes. For most of the session, they were well spaced out.

The checkered flag waved her car told Janis the session was over. She pulled into the pits and parked where Classic Porsche had set up shop. Once she had unstrapped, unhooked the cool suit, and climbed out of the 906, Lester from Classic Porsches handed her a bottle of water and a clipboard with her times. He maintained her car and was grinning from ear-to-ear. Despite the heat, Janis now held the course lap record for sports racing cars. Way cool!

Inside the air-conditioned clubhouse, she drained another bottle of water, showered, and changed clothes thinking she had a perfect day at the track. On weekends, the TVs in the bar played a motorsport event or showed cars going around the track. Instead, the TV screen showed the Israeli prime minister standing on the deck of a ship.

His tone projected both anger and pride as he spoke. "I am standing on the blood-stained deck of the *Motor Vessel Star Lynn* captured by the Israeli Defense forces after a fierce battle early Saturday morning. The six containers behind me on the *Star Lynn* are filled with weapons and ammunition destined for Hezbollah. The weapons were sold to Hezbollah by Hofer and Associates, a German arms merchant with a history of supplying weapons to terrorist organizations. Earlier this month, the weapons and ammunition were transported by truck from Germany to Trieste and loaded on board *Star Lynn*."

The grim-faced prime minister moved to a spot just forward of the bridge on the port side. The prime minister pointed to the bloodstains on the bulkheads and the cartridge cases still littering the deck. "Normally, diplomatic procedures suggest that I make my next point through a formal protest. We have already done that. However, I want the world to know that this action would not have been necessary if the German government had acted promptly. Israel provided them with the location of the weapons and the organization buying them while they were still stored in Germany. At the time, the German government could have seized the weapons. Instead, the Germans did nothing. Israel was left with no choice but to act in its own defense."

Janis forced herself not to cheer. Instead, she ordered a beer that meant no more driving today and stepped outside to make a call.

THE SAME DAY, 12:06 P.M. LOCAL TIME, DALLAS

Just over 90 miles to the east from where Janis was watching the TV at the racetrack, Ghulam's cell phone buzzed. A voice said, "Turn on your TV and watch CNN." After watching the press conference replay and the talking heads interpretation, of what transpired, Ghulam was mad. Then, as he thought about what he was watching, he smiled. The attack he has planned will be retribution for the Israelis stealing Hezbollah's weapons.

Ghulam did not arrange the transportation, so he was not worried that he might be blamed for the loss of the weapons. They were secure and safe when he left Germany. Allah will decide his fate.

CHAPTER 23

TO CATCH A CUBAN

MONDAY, AUGUST 26TH, 2002, 7:30 A.M. LOCAL TIME, ZURICH

einz Berg watched the news conference with the Israeli prime minister that was carried live on Swiss television. On Monday morning, the political and foreign policy analysts were having a field day with the implications of the prime minister's comments.

Thinking Hezbollah might blame him for the loss, Berg was terrified. Even though he had nothing to do with the shipment, he was afraid Hezbollah would come after him thinking he sold them out when they find out that he shut down Hofer and Associates.

THE SAME DAY, 6:38 A.M. LOCAL TIME, DALLAS

When Janis was in the U.S., she'd call Aliyah when she got up, and Aliyah would call Janis when she returned to her flat after work. At first, Aliyah resisted Janis' offer to pay her phone bill; she gave in when she saw her phone bill showing their 20 to 30-minute calls often cost more than a hundred dollars each.

"Good morning." Janis was expecting Aliyah's call.

"Hi! Did you see the news?"

"I did! Very exciting. Congratulations." Janis knew not to ask for details on an operation for which she had not been cleared.

"Thank you."

There was an awkward 10-second silence before Aliyah spoke. "My mother is unhappy that I want to spend the high holidays with you, but at least she did not explode. Maybe she is coming around."

Janis felt a sense of relief. She was afraid that Aliyah would not come.

"If you can get me tickets to arrive on September 5th and go home on the 17th or 18th, that would be perfect. Reznik has approved my leave and said the chase for Ghulam will go on."

Cool! "Aliyah, I'll arrange for them tomorrow morning."

"*Mitsuyan!!!*"

TUESDAY, AUGUST 27ᵀᴴ, 2002, 3:26 P.M. LOCAL TIME, LANGLEY

Like many things in the CIA, seeing, hearing, and doing unexpected things is often the norm. In her new role as an assistant director, Rachel Simms had things coming at her in ways she never would have expected. From the top, her boss was fond of handing her hot potatoes, expecting she could devise a solution to put the fire out.

The latest came from Nasher in a phone call in the form of three questions:

Nasher question 1 – "How's your Spanish?"

Rachel – "Passable."

Nasher question 2 – "What do you know about Hector Ordonez?"

Rachel – "Wasn't he the Cuban intelligence officer looking for Elizabeth Harris?"

Nasher question 3 – "Yes. Did you know he has been in and out of the U.S. four times since March and has again started asking questions about the Harris woman?"

Rachel – "No."

Nasher – "You're going to meet with Señor Ordonez and put the fear of God in him."

Nasher words were taken as an order. "Where?"

"Miami, where else?"

"Is this my op?"

"Yup. I'll get you access to what we know about Ordonez."

"What am I supposed to do?"

"That's why they pay you the big bucks as Deputy Director. Figure out what to do, but this can't become public. Remember, we're not supposed to operate in the United States."

"Understood. When am I supposed to be there?"

"He's arriving on the 30th, and the meet is supposed to be on the 31st. You've got eight days."

"Eight! I count four."

"No, you have eight. All day on the 27th, all night on the 27th, all day on the 28th, all night on the 28th, all day on the 29th, all ..."

Rachel laughed and cut Nasher off. "Who's he meeting?"

"That we don't know."

"Is the FBI involved? This is their turf."

"They will be when you tell them. I have a CIA-friendly FBI contact named Gene Rostow in Miami. I'll give him a heads-up you're coming and why. I'll also run the traps here in D.C., so Rostow gets what he needs, and the FBI gets credit if there is an arrest. Betsy will give you his phone number."

"Thanks. I'm taking Reeder with me."

"Good idea. Don't fuck it up."

Rachel was left listening to a dial tone. Shit, I'll have to tell Daffy we can't be together this weekend.

THE SAME DAY, 3:26 P.M. LOCAL TIME, DALLAS

The auction catalogs and personal letters from their company presidents were sitting on Janis' desk. The documents were responses to her request asking to let her know if they knew if any 1969, 1970, or 1971 Porsche 908/2s or 908/3s were for sale. Neither had one coming to an auction, but said they knew several owners who might be interested in selling their cars. With her permission, they would arrange a conversation with the owners and help in the transaction if needed.

While Janis was looking at the catalogs, her mobile phone rang. "Hello."

"Elizabeth, it's Rachel. I need to talk to you for a few minutes. If I gave you the address of the local FBI office, would you go there and call me on a secure phone?"

"No need to. I still have the secure mobile phone Bishop gave me. What's a good number, and I'll call you back?"

Janis wrote the number down and opened her gun vault where the Iridium phone was kept charged.

Rachel answered on the first ring. "I didn't know you had a CIA phone."

"Does the agency want it back?"

"No. When you get a chance, send me the serial number so I know you have it, and we can keep the code keys current."

"Will do. What's up?"

"Does the name Hector Ordonez ring a bell?"

"Yup. He's a colonel in the *Dirección de Inteligencia* who was looking for me. Why?"

"The one and only. I'm supposed to meet Ordonez and tell him to stop looking for you."

"Oh." *Earlier in the year, the Cubans were looking for me. Apparently, they're still interested. There's no way I will work for them, ever.*

"Can you be in Miami on Thursday?"

"I can. Why?"

"On Friday, Ordonez is meeting with an unknown source, and we suspect the subject is you. I'd like to have you watch the meeting with me. We'll pay your daily rate that is in the contract."

"I'll be there. Where are you staying?"

Janis copied down the name and said she'd be there by noon Thursday, the 29th. Miami Executive Airport was only about four and a half hours away in her TBM.

CORAL GABLES, FLORIDA, FRIDAY, AUGUST 30TH, 2002, 12:36 P.M. LOCAL TIME

The place in Little Havana where Ordonez was meeting his mystery contact was a café recessed into a row of storefronts. Most of the tables were outside on the wide sidewalk under umbrellas.

FBI agents in a van parked across the street would photograph the meet, and a parabolic mike hidden in the van would record anything said by Ordonez and his contact.

Janis was introduced to Gene Rostow as Elizabeth Harris, and Harvey Reeder arrived first around eleven-thirty. They picked a table on the far-right side that let them see all seven tables. Rachel and Gene Rostow meandered around the street looking for counter surveillance before they sat at a table closest to the café's door. Earpieces attached to their sunglasses connected to mikes clipped under their collars let them communicate.

Harvey put a hand on Janis' thigh even though he knew she was gay. This was, he whispered in her ear, Little Havana, and he was just trying to seduce a beautiful woman. Politely, she moved his hand away and mouthed fuck you.

With her hand over her mouth, Rachel coughed loudly as a signal that Ordonez had arrived. The overweight Cuban sat at a table diagonally across from Janis, facing the sidewalk.

Ordonez opened a copy of the Miami Herald and glanced over the top to study those passing by. He'd waited 16 minutes before another man sat down at the table.

Before they made eye contact, Janis lowered her head, so the wide-brimmed sun hat prevented Ordonez and his guest from seeing her face. "Reeder, look at me and do not turn around. Ordonez's guest is Bill Smith the Third."

Rostow looked at Rachel, his tablemate. "Who's Bill Smith the Third?"

"A fired FBI agent."

"Harvey, look at Elizabeth. Gene, look at me." Rachel was afraid that Smith III would see people he recognized.

They need not have bothered. Smith III focused on Ordonez and put the Manilla envelope he was carried into the café in his lap. "How's the coffee here?"

His words were recorded in the van, and the agents would tell them if any illegal activity was happening. Rostow, the only one Smith III didn't know, occasionally looked at Smith III.

"I heard it was excellent. You need to try the colada."

With the challenge and responses out of the way, Smith III relaxed and rested his hands on the table. A colada, a heavily sweetened espresso usually served in a large cup, was placed in front of him.

The man in the van radioed, "They're making a deal for a transcript of the debrief of a woman named Harris. Today's exchange will be the only one made in person, and the remaining three will be via remote drops. Smith III asked if Ordonez had the first quarter million dollars, and Ordonez said the cash was in his briefcase."

Janis glanced at the table long enough to see Ordonez put a briefcase on the table and pop the latches open. Smith III pulled the briefcase to him, opened the lid far enough so that Janis and Gene could see stacks of bound $100 bills. Satisfied, Smith latched the case and put it on the concrete next to him. He slid the two-inch-thick 9" x 12" manila envelope across the table. Ordonez opened the clasp and pulled out several sheets. Slowly, he examined them.

The discussion was enough for the men in the van to call for backup and were told the supporting agents were 15 minutes away. Rostow replied, "We don't have that kind of time. We're going to arrest both. Janis and Rachel, you detain Ordonez. Reeder and I will go after Smith who we want alive."

The men in the van radioed that the Cubans agreed to pay three-quarters of a million for the remainder of the debrief. When he received the last payment, Smith III would provide the woman's address.

Rachel spoke softly but loud enough for the voice-activated mike to transmit her words, "Elizabeth, please don't kill the son-of-a-bitch."

Janis nodded. "Understood."

As Smith III finished his coffee, he spotted Rachel and bolted down the street. Rostow and Reeder went after him along with the two men from the van.

Ordonez sat quietly, waiting for the hubbub to die down. This allowed Janis to slide into the chair Smith III had occupied. A gentle wave of the hand told Rachel, "I've got this." Rachel stayed at her table and paid the bill while she listened.

Janis held a napkin to her nose to cover the lower part of her face, and her oversized sunglasses hid everything else but her cheekbones. She spoke in Spanish. "*Señor* Ordonez, I understand you are looking for me."

Ordonez made a face. "Who are you?"

"*La Estrella de la Muerte.*"

Ordonez blanched noticeably. "How do I know that is true? Can you prove it?"

Janis assumed that Ordonez read the file the Cubans kept on her. "Sure. I worked for Enrique Payá, and my graduation test was killing a Cuban army colonel who murdered a Cuban general in Angola. I shot him in the head in the Los Maristas. I was trained at a camp in the Escambray Mountains and was friends with a German you know as Monika Arnsdorfer. What else would you like to know?"

Rachel joined them. "Colonel Ordonez, I am Rachel Simms, a Deputy Director of the CIA. Do you speak English?"

Ordonez nodded. "I do."

"Good, then we will continue in English. If you need translation, either my associate here or I will switch to Spanish."

Ordonez again nodded.

"Please give me the envelope that Bill Smith III gave you."

Ordonez complied. Rachel opened the clasp and pulled out the contents far enough to see the Top Secret/Specially Compartmented Information/Code Word Deadly Canary markings on the top of the page. "Colonel, the way I see we go from here is that you have two choices. One, we can arrest you for espionage. We heard enough of your conversation and, along with the classified material in this envelope, to convict you. Or two, you can agree to help us. You are more valuable as a defector than as a spy for us in Cuba. You need to let me know within the next 30 seconds." She pointed to the two men wearing suits crossing the street. "Those FBI agents are coming to arrest you. And, while I know our prisons are nicer than yours, my guess is that you would enjoy freedom more than a six-foot by 10-foot cell."

"If I agree to help you, then what?"

"As long as you do not lie to us, we will give you a new identity and make sure you will live comfortably. If you wish, we can try to sneak your family out of Cuba. If we think you are providing us disinformation, we give you back to the Cuban government."

"My wife won't leave. She writes and believes the propaganda shit she writes. I am worried about my two sons."

"So, what is it going to be?"

Ordonez smiled and looked at *la bandida*. "I'm delighted to meet you and am glad you are not looking at me through a gunsight."

With that, Ordonez opened his arms expansively. "I'm yours. I want to defect. When does the debrief begin?"

Catching Smith III took longer than either Reeder or Rostow expected. The fired FBI agent was not about to let go of the briefcase. Since he spent much of his career in Little Havana, Rostow redirected the backup cars of agents to get in front of Smith III.

They zigged and zagged down several streets before Smith III ran into the arms of two FBI agents who forced him to the ground and read him his rights as he was being handcuffed. By the time Rostow and Reeder arrived, Smith III was bent over the hood of their car being patted down.

Smith III looked at Reeder and then Rostow. "Just like I told these two agents, I want a lawyer."

Reeder got his face close to Smith III. "Buddy, you're going to need lots of them. And, if I find out that you caused the death of any of my friends, you're not going to need a lawyer, you're going to need an undertaker to stitch your body back together, assuming they find enough pieces to put in the casket."

Smith III sneered. "Reeder, you just violated my civil rights by threatening me. Did you guys hear that?"

Rostow spoke for all the FBI agents. "I didn't hear a thing other than you wanted a lawyer. The traffic around here is deafening."

At a CIA office in Miami, Janis waited patiently in a conference room while Rachel arranged for Ordonez to be transported to a safe house for his debriefing. When Rachel came into the room, she held up her hand as if to say, I know what you are going to say. "Only nine people know the debriefing exists. They are Walt Bishop, Harvey Reeder, Jim Green, Greg Nasher, the Director, Betsy Quist, the individual who transcribed the interview, me, and Bill Smith III. Of those, only Green, the transcriber, and I know the file name. Several attorneys at the DOJ knew the debrief would happen but nothing more and don't have any way to gain access to the file."

Janis barely contained her anger. "You left out Gene Rostow. He's FBI and now knows the code name. Now, the FBI will get Smith's computer and a copy of the file which they will use to convince a jury he's guilty."

"Calm down. We can control access to the file due to its classification, the jury will be given an overview of the material, but not any specifics."

"I should never have agreed to be debriefed by the CIA. This was and still is my biggest fear."

Rachel put her hand on Janis's arm. "I know this is hard, but you're going to have to trust me on this. One, I will find the bastard who leaked this to Smith III. Two, I will talk to the Director who will talk to the Attorney General and get Smith's copy of the file back without being copied. Three, William Smith III will spend a long time in jail."

"I don't want him in jail, I want him dead along with the bastard who stole the file from the CIA."

"I can't do that."

Janis looked at Rachel coldly. *But I can. This leak must be plugged, permanently.*

SUNDAY, SEPTEMBER 1ST, 2002, 9:00 A.M. LOCAL TIME, BEIRUT

Grim and subdued would be the best words to describe the atmosphere in the room where the Shura Council met. All had seen the Israeli press conference carried by all the international networks. The loss of *Star Lynn* was the first item on the agenda.

Talal Hamiyah, the man responsible for coordinating all attacks outside of Lebanon and one of the men to whom Ghulam reported, began with a review of how the weapons were procured and the acquisition of *Star Lynn*. When he finished, Imad Mughinyeh, Hezbollah's senior military commander, asked if Ghulam had made any mistakes. The answer was, "No, none that we can tell. We used front companies and special accounts to hide the purchaser, and we used Hofer and Associates many times."

Mughinyeh had a list of questions. "Did anything happen out of the ordinary?"

"Yes and no. Gerd Hofer was not available. We made the deal with his business partner, a man by the name of Heinz Berg. On our prior buys, he handled the money transfers and documents on all our previous purchases. We don't think he was the leak."

"Have you talked to Berg or Hofer since *Star Lynn* was captured?"

"No."

Mughinyeh tapped the table with his forefinger, "I suggest you do. They are infidels, and their loyalties may be elsewhere."

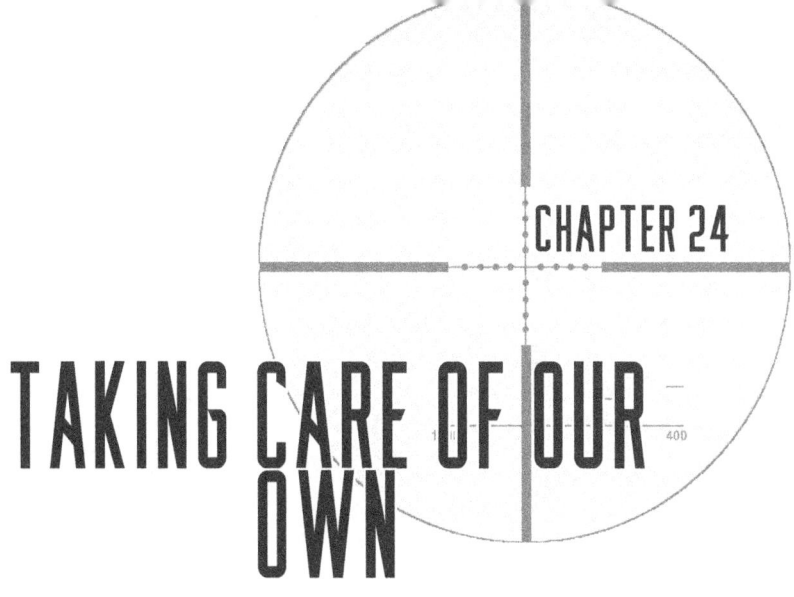

CHAPTER 24

TAKING CARE OF OUR OWN

J im Green was unlocking his car when Rachel Simms shoved him against the car. His keys went flying, Green tried to turn around, but she pressed his cheek against the car while she handcuffed him and patting him down. Then Rachel spun him around so she could look into his eyes.

Green yelled, "What the hell do you ..."

"Think I am doing? This is what!" Rachel slammed the pages from Janis' debrief against his chest that had Green's fingerprints on the pages Smith III handed Ordonez.

Green looked at his boss defiantly. "The bitch should be locked up as a menace to society."

"That is not your call. Who else was involved?"

"I want a lawyer."

"You haven't been arrested, at least not yet. Who else was involved or did you give the file directly to William Smith III? Tell me now or instead of turning you over to the FBI, I will have you taken to a CIA interrogation center where we will get the information from you."

"Go fuck yourself."

Green didn't see the man who jabbed a syringe into his neck. He collapsed and was shoved into a black suburban in the next parking place. Rachel tied his feet, shoved a ball gag into Green's mouth, and buckled the strap behind his head.

Rachel, who was wearing latex gloves, picked up Green's keys and tossed them onto the front seat of the analyst's car. She told Harvey Reeder, "Do what you can to get him talking. We need to get to the bottom of this quickly."

Reeder nodded. "This won't take long. I'll call you later."

THE SAME DAY, 6:19 P.M. LOCAL TIME, NEAR NEW HOPE, VA

Jim Green shook his head to try to clear the cobwebs. He could tell he was blindfolded and didn't like the taste of the rubber ball gag. Green could feel he was tied to a chair with his feet bound to the legs. The cold steel against his skin told him that his pants and shirt had been removed.

Reeder removed the blindfold from behind, and Green blinked in the bright light. A naked 100-watt bulb was directly over his head and bathed him in light while the rest of the room was dark. Green couldn't tell where he was.

"Green, I am glad to see you are awake. I will ask the questions, and you will answer truthfully. If you don't, I have four choices: one, drugs; two, electric shocks; three, beat you; or four, all the above. One way or the other, you will tell me the truth. Shall we begin?"

Harvey Reeder unstrapped the gag. He wore a mask to hide his face and a voice synthesizer to disguise his voice.

"Go fuck yourself."

"Defiant, are we?" Reeder slapped Green's cheek hard enough to leave fingerprints.

"Who helped you?"

"The bitch needs to be in a jail cell or six feet under."

Reeder slapped both of Green's cheeks. "Not an acceptable answer, try again."

Green just glared at the CIA operator. Reeder had done harsh interrogations earlier in his career, and while he didn't like them, they had their time and place. Some dragged on for several days, and others took only a few hours. He was hoping this would only take a few hours but was prepared to wait Green out.

Reeder pulled over a small cart with a stainless-steel tray, several small bottles and a half a dozen syringes. "What I have here are three of my favorite drugs, scopolamine, sodium thiopental, and amobarbital. I have the option of using them in combination or individually. So, which will it be? Drugs or are you going to answer my questions."

The long-term covert CIA operator unwrapped a syringe and was about to jab it into the bottle of sodium thiopental when he looked at Green's face. His eyes were wide open with fear.

"What happened to waterboarding?"

"Takes too long and is way too messy. Plus, I need two or three others to hold you down. So, what's your preference?"

"You're going to kill me, aren't you?"

"That depends on you. The longer this goes, the greater the risk to you."

"This will never hold up in court."

"Who says you are going to be arrested. Your condo has already been searched, and we have lots of incriminating evidence. The real question is whether or not you will live to be tried."

Green set his jaw. "Smith called me about two weeks ago. We agreed that the Harris woman belonged on death row someplace and said he could make that happen. So, I downloaded a copy of the file and gave him roughly 50 pages at a time. I never gave him an electronic copy."

"What else did you give him?"

"Rachel's analysis on Bishop's treason that included all of his Hezbollah and Iranian contacts."

"Did he pay you?"

"Yeah. He gave me twenty-five grand and promised me another twenty-five when he was paid from selling the info."

"So, you committed professional suicide for nothing?"

"Murder in every state in the U.S. and other civilized countries is illegal. That bitch Harris is a murderer. So, I gave him the file."

Reeder jabbed the needle into the bottle of sodium thiopental, filled the syringe, and jabbed it in Green's bicep. "Jim, we're about to see if you are telling the truth."

He looked at Green whose eyes were already starting to get glassy. Reeder went through the same series of questions, and the only additional information he got out of Green was that he had a safe deposit box in a Bank of America branch in Tyson's Corner stuffed with reports on what he believed were illegal activities of the CIA inside and outside the U.S. It took Reeder a few minutes to get Green to tell him where the key to the box was located.

Satisfied Green was telling everything he wanted to know, he filled a syringe with diazepam and jabbed it in Green's arm. He slumped over, unconscious.

A woman, at least by her clothes, stepped out of the shadows. She also wore a mask with a voice synthesizer and latex gloves. "First thing tomorrow morning, tell Rachel so she can tell the IG. They'll get access to the box so the agency can assess the damage."

"Will do. Now, let's get Green back in his car and take care of him."

Later that night, police and firemen responded to the report of an explosion in a deserted parking lot in Chantilly, Virginia. The police report noted that the vehicle's VIN tags had been removed and the body was burned beyond recognition which made determining the cause of death impossible unless they could compare the teeth to dental records.

FRIDAY, SEPTEMBER 6TH, 2002, 8:46 A.M. LOCAL TIME, DALLAS

When Aliyah came out of customs on Thursday, Janis noticed she was favoring her left leg and was drawn and pale. She waited until they hugged and kissed before she offered to bring the Yukon Denali to the curb. Aliyah said it wasn't necessary. She was just stiff from sitting for the past 16 hours – 12 and half from Tel Aviv to Newark and three and a half more from Newark to Dallas.

Janis didn't argue and believed Aliyah's leg bothered her more than she wanted to admit. And, yes, she'd seen a doctor, and they wanted to take more x-rays after the high holidays before they decided what they could do, if anything.

Not seeing Aliyah in the kitchen when she finished her workout and daily run, a sweaty Janis sat on the edge of the bed. Aliyah was face down and sound asleep. It was nearly 10:30 a.m. Sweat dripped down her body as she used her index finger to trace her spine from her shoulders to her butt before she started caressing Aliyah's inner thigh. Aliyah began to stir, and a moan of pleasure came out of her mouth as she rolled on her back and spread her legs, inviting Janis's hand to start working its magic.

Aliyah stretched out her arms and pulled Janis's face toward hers. Just before they kissed, she stopped…. "Ohhhhh, you're all sweaty. I like that." After they kissed, she whispered, "You can wake me this way any time."

"My pleasure."

"Please make love to me. I don't know what I missed more, seeing, or making love to you."

"Before or after I take a shower?"

"How about we take a shower together and start in there?"

THE SAME DAY, 5:17 P.M. LOCAL TIME, RICHARDSON

That evening, as Janis set up the table for dinner, Aliyah looked at the two candlesticks. "What are those for?"

"It is Shabbos, and we are going to light candles."

"Are you doing it just for me?"

"No. We're going to synagogue after dinner."

"Why? We've not gone before."

"I know, but there is always a first time. Tonight, I have two surprises for you."

"Any hints?"

"No, but I am pretty sure you will like them. And, when we get home, we'll make love all night long."

Aliyah's eyebrows went up. "*Mitsuyan!* I know I'll like that."

"What are you taking for pain?"

"Hydrocodone and meloxicam to keep the inflammation down."

"How long have you been taking it?"

"Just a few days. I know why you are concerned, and I am too. I took a hydrocodone tablet while you were gone, and it knocked me out."

"So, when are you going to get your leg fixed?"

"After the high holidays. The doctors aren't sure if there is enough bone or if it is strong enough to allow them to put in an artificial hip. So, they are talking about other options. I will have more exams and tests when I get back."

"So, what are the options?"

"One is they take it apart, put it back together with more wire and screws, and try to graft bone onto it to strengthen it. That will take between three and six months to see if the grafts will take. The danger is that if my hip comes apart, it may rupture my femoral artery, and then I am dead. The only other option is amputation. Before I left, they gave me a forearm crutch to help take the weight off my leg. I left the crutch in Israel, so we ought to buy one."

"Done."

THE SAME DAY, 6:56 P.M. LOCAL TIME, RICHARDSON, TEXAS

Aliyah was surprised when Janis led her to a seat in the second row of the sanctuary and on the center aisle. This was the first time she'd been in an American synagogue. Aliyah was impressed with the stark beauty and simplicity of the sanctuary that contrasted to the ones in Israel, most of which were decades, even centuries old. She was amazed that Janis knew her way through the prayer book and the liturgy of the service.

After the sermon, the rabbi asked Janis and another couple to come to the bema. Standing on the raised platform where the Torah's were kept, the rabbi told the rest of the congregation that these three had finished a conversion course and after he blessed their conversion, they could now call themselves Jews. He then raised his hands and blessed the two women and man.

When she returned to her seat, Aliyah hugged Janis and whispered, "I had no idea. Why didn't you tell me?"

"I wanted it to be a surprise. I'm no longer a *shiksa.*

"Why did you take the Hebrew name of Rachnav Stern?"

"Do you know who Rachnav was?" The shake of Aliyah's head told Janis the answer. "When Joshua arrived a Jericho, he needed intelligence on the Canaanite defenses. Joshua sent two men into the town to reconnoiter. The Bible calls them spies; today we would call them special forces. When the King of Jericho learned they were there, he sent men to find them. Rachnav owned an inn, although there are some who would call her a madame, and she hid them from the Canaanites. Later, these men and others Rachnav knew opposed the King of Jericho, opened the gates to let Joshua's men inside. After the city was taken by the Israelites, Rachnav converted to Judaism and married Yehoshua, one of the leaders of the tribes. Hence, she became one of the first converts."

Aliyah smiled and kissed her lover. "And Stern is star in Hebrew, which I bet comes from *The Red Star of Death.*"

Janis kissed Aliyah. "You are a very smart woman. That's why I love you."

When they arrived at Janis' house, it was almost ten o'clock, and Janis asked Aliyah to sit on the couch, saying she'd be right back. Janis dimmed the lights as she returned to the living room and handed Aliyah a small maroon jewelry box. "I need you to put this on me."

"What's is it?"

"It's Emily Stone's Star of David. She was killed at Cedars Sinai, and her family asked me to wear it in her memory. Her death started me thinking, and I began to read about Judaism. The more I learned, I realized the religion and its rich culture filled a void in my life. After my trips to Israel, the idea of becoming Jewish was a no-brainer."

Aliyah connected the ends of the chain and then gently turned Janis around to admire the silver six-pointed star with half-carat sapphires at the star's tips. "It's beautiful, and welcome to the tribe. I love you so much."

"Thank you and I love you too. Please sit down, Aliyah, I am not done with surprises."

Aliyah sat back down on the couch and took a sip of the glass of wine she had started when they got home. Janis knelt in front of her.

"Aliyah, my love, will you live with me for the rest of our lives?" She held out a flawless round, six-carat, D-clarity diamond. On the band, there were three half-carat flawless diamonds on either side of the main stone.

The Israeli woman put both hands on her mouth as she gasped. "Ohhhhh, my God… It is beautiful!" She slipped the ring on her left ring finger and then remembered the question. "Of course, I will."

Aliyah wrapped her arms around Janis who started to kiss her while her hands pushed up Aliyah's dress. *I cannot turn her down. She loves me unquestionably and I have the same feelings. This was not what Reznik intended to happen. A ring on my finger will be something that will be hard to explain to him. He sees my relationship with Janis as nothing more than an assignment to recruit and manage an expendable asset.*

MONDAY, SEPTEMBER 9ᵀᴴ, 2002, 3:06 P.M. LOCAL TIME, OTTOBEUREN

The mission given to Ayad Okasha by his client was simple. Find Gerd Hofer and Heinz Berg and gather information to help Hezbollah determine if they tipped off the Israelis.

Jalil's father came to Germany from Turkey in the mid-1950s as one of thousands of guest workers. After 15 years of "good behavior," Jalil Okasha became a German citizen. He married a woman who was also in the guest worker program and five years his junior. Ayad, the third of the couple's three children, was born in 1970.

Ayad graduated from the University of Cologne and became a defense attorney. To help look for evidence the police may have missed, he founded a private investigation firm. Most of his clients were Germans of Turkish or Middle Eastern descent. In the past, Ayad had defended men accused of conducting or plotting terrorist attacks and was sure Hezbollah paid his fees through a series of front companies. He didn't have proof, but his clients gave him names of companies to bill, and the money was transferred from a bank in Lebanon called Byblos.

This time the call asked him to find Hofer and conduct the investigation himself. Ayad had seen the news about Hofer, *Star Lynn* and read the editorials in German papers.

His first step was researching public records to see if a death certificate for either Heinz Berg or Gerd Hofer was filed. None were. Next, Ayad checked to see if either man had legally changed his name in Germany. Neither did.

A credit check of Hofer and Associates was clean and noted the firm used Commerzbank. A call to the German Federal Tax Office told Okasha their individual and corporate taxes were current.

Both Hofer's and Berg's passports were renewed within the past year. He found nothing when he checked Branch A of the German Commercial Register, which listed all the companies licensed as partnerships. In Branch B, the list indicated Hofer and Associates had been dissolved. Corporations are created and shut down all the time so that fact was not unusual. The timing – August 31st, 2002 – on which it ceased operations was of note as was no mention of a successor. Neither Berg nor Hofer was listed as officers in any newly formed companies.

When Okasha arrived at Hofer's house, the gate was locked, and a small sign gave a realtor's phone number. He dialed the number and made an appointment to see the home and the estate's 250-hectacres.

On a hunch that Hofer may have had a business jet, he drove to the Bodensee Airport on the shores of Lake Constance. In the general aviation terminal, the young woman volunteered that Herr Hofer used to keep his Falcon 50 in their hangar. His pilots were let go during the summer when the airplane was sold. She wrote down the registration letters of the jet on a company business card.

House for sale, airplane sold, and business shut down are legitimate moves signifying Hofer and Associates was no longer in business. He could have decided to retire, and the transaction with Hezbollah was his last deal. Or that he was in hiding. Okasha decided he would wait until he visited Hofer's house before he reported to his client.

WEDNESDAY, SEPTEMBER 11TH, 2002, 2:58 A.M. LOCAL TIME, FRANKFURT, GERMANY

Three black Mercedes vans stopped in front of the house in a wealthy suburb of Frankfurt. The members of the German Federal Police's *Grenzshutzgruppe* 9 or GSG9 men spilling out of the back were dressed in black, wore Kevlar helmets and vests, and carried suppressed Heckler & Koch MP5SD sub-machine guns.

GSG9 was formed in the aftermath of the 1976 Olympics Massacre as a dedicated counterterrorism and hostage rescue team. The unit's organization is based on the Israeli Sayeret Maktal model and routinely trained with the British, American, and Israeli counterterrorism units.

The house had a small front yard guarded by a fence. Night vision goggles let the men see if any laser beams or infrared sensors were tied to an alarm. There were none, and the men stacked up, three on each side of the door while two scanned the street.

Two more swung the battering ram and the door buckled. The ram was tossed to the side, and the two men who banged open the door became number four on each stack that went into the house and fanned out through the house in pairs.

Doors were shoved open, and flash/bang grenades were tossed into each room. The high-intensity light activates all the photoreceptor cells in the eyes blinding a person for at least five seconds. Someone not prepared for the flash will have spots that impair their vision for several minutes, making it difficult to aim a pistol or rifle. The bang also causes temporary hearing loss and disturbs the inner ear creating balance problems.

One member of the Al-Musawi Corps was trying to get his suicide vest on when he was cut down by a burst of nine-millimeter bullets from a suppressed MP-5SD. The fight inside the house was violent and short. Only two of the eight residents survived, and none of the GSG9 officers were injured.

In the six-story apartment building in Mainz, GSG9 had two apartments to raid – one on the sixth floor and one on the third. With both teams in position, the raid commander on the sixth floor counted down from three, and within a half second, the doors to the two-bedroom apartments were knocked down.

The Al-Musawi Corps fighters spilled out of the cots set up in the living and dining rooms of the sixth-floor apartment. Blinded by the flash-bang grenades, they fired wildly, and their bullets tore chunks out of the concrete walls before they were cut down. When the firing stopped two minutes after it started, all eight men in the apartment were either dead, dying, or being disarmed.

There were only six men in the third-floor apartment. Four were wounded and captured, and two were killed. Again, none of the members of GSG9 were injured.

In both operations, captured mobile phones and computers were taken to the unit's command and control vans for immediate exploitation. By tracing the numbers, four more safe houses were identified, one more in Frankfurt and one each in Hamburg, Cologne, and Berlin. Within an hour of the first raids, doors of the suspected safe houses were being busted down by other detachments of GSG9.

By dawn, GSG9 had killed or captured 70 members of the Al-Musawi Corps. At nine in the morning, the Minister of Justice read a short statement telling the German people about the raids. He noted at the end of his statement that never again will Germany ignore actionable intelligence provided by a friendly nation as it did in the *Star Lynn* incident.

At 9:55 in the morning, the Minister of Justice walked into his office, deliberately ignoring Adolf Weber sitting in a chair, waiting for his 10:00 a.m. appointment. Weber was ushered into the minister's office a minute after the scheduled time not knowing why he was summoned.

"Herr Weber, the purpose of this meeting is to inform you that you are being terminated, effective immediately. You will be paid until this Friday, September 13th."

Weber was surprised and tried to control his anger. "Herr Minister, would you please explain why?"

"Herr Weber, I think you know why but in case you don't, I will give you the short version. Both Herr Jung and you ignored very credible evidence that Hofer and Associates had sold weapons to terrorist organizations and was about to sell more. Those weapons were stored illegally on German soil, and you were told the locations. You were also shown evidence that German and international laws on arms sales were violated. Not only did you ignore the evidence, but your official notes implied the evidence the Israeli government offered was not credible when the exact opposite was true."

The minister tapped his desk with his forefinger as he spoke. "Herr Weber, if you and Herr Jung had done your job, Germany would have avoided the embarrassment that followed the capture of the *Star Lynn*."

"Sir, the evidence was illegally obtained. The Israelis set up a surveillance operation on German soil without our permission. It would have never held up in court."

"Herr Weber, the government acts on tips from concerned citizens all the time. You could have justified a raid on well documented tip."

Weber shook his head. "Sir, the goddam Jews are always crying wolf and see a terrorist or suicide bomber on every corner. If we acted on every tip they provided, our jails would be full of German citizens, some of whom might be innocent."

"Herr Weber, Germany is part of NATO and NATO includes the Americans who were attacked just over a year ago. Many of those attackers lived in Germany. If you watched the news this morning, GSG9 captured or killed 70 terrorists and their weapons, explosives, and suicide vests that could have been used to kill innocent German citizens. The intelligence came from the Americans, Israelis, and German citizens."

The minister stopped and took a deep breath. "Herr Weber, you will be escorted to the personnel department to sign your termination papers. The government will not provide a good reference. And, I might add, I know about both your and Herr Jung's attitude toward Jews, and it is in your official record. My recommendation is that you change them. Now, get out of my office."

THURSDAY, SEPTEMBER 12ᵀᴴ, 2002, 9:56 A.M. LOCAL TIME, OTTOBEUREN

Okasha's appointment was at nine. Before they began a tour of the house, the real estate agent said his firm was retained by a law firm, not the owner. The agent said the owner was anxious to sell the property. To Okasha, this suggested some flexibility in the 15,000,000 Euros price. Neither fact surprised Okasha.

After the tour of the empty house, the realtor showed him the immaculately kept gardens and lawn that told him the owner was being billed for the expense. Out in the meadow, Okasha spotted a rectangular shaped mound where the grass was higher and greener. He wondered if the area was an old flowerbed. The size was much too large for a grave.

In the afternoon, Ayad struggled with what he should tell Hezbollah as he looked at his notes. He could say Hofer and Associates liquidated their assets and shut down their business which he believed was the truth. The Germans could have decided they had enough money and retired.

Or he could imply Hofer and Berg were on the run. He had facts to support his first hypothesis but none for the second.

Investigating the mound of dirt might create more questions than answers. *First, I need permission from Hofer & Associates, which still had title to the estate. What if he says no? Then what? To ask the police to investigate, I need a reason. Probing by myself or asking an investigator to do it entails risks I don't want to accept.*

What if the police find Hofer's body, then what? I would be asked questions for which I don't have answers and are not covered by attorney-client privilege. So, do I want to risk going to jail and losing the business that is making my family wealthy?

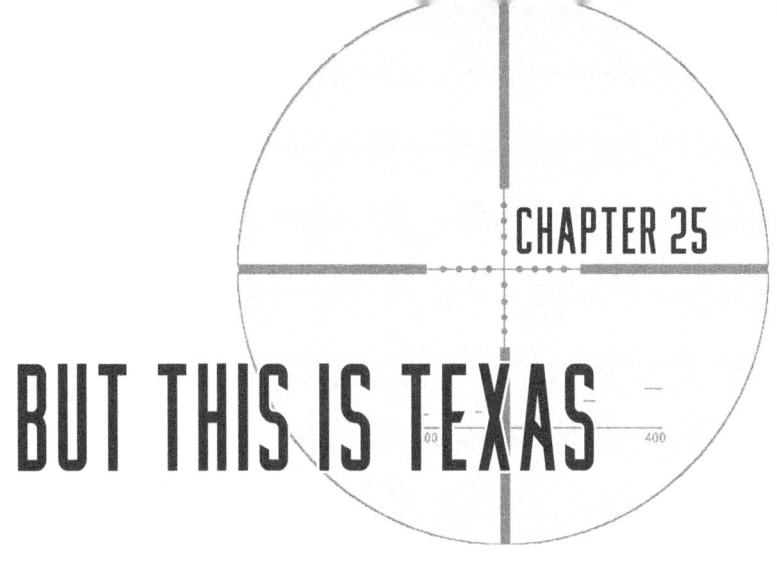

CHAPTER 25

BUT THIS IS TEXAS

SUNDAY, SEPTEMBER 15ᵀᴴ, 2002, 10:42 A.M. LOCAL TIME, DALLAS

Tailgating at Texas Stadium before Cowboy games begins around three hours before kickoff when pick-up trucks, SUVs, and vans arrive, and people start unpacking grills. Neither Aliyah nor Janis had ever been to a professional football game and wanted to enjoy the entire experience. The temperature was in the low 80s when they started walking through the tailgating area. The pleasant aroma from the rubs used on the meat being grilled filled the air and made both women hungry.

Jason Winthrop invited Janis and Aliyah to watch the Cowboys' home opener against the Tennessee Titans from his suite. Besides his family, Winthrop said there will be owners who will want to talk to her about her Porsche collection, which now includes a rare 1973 Porsche 911RS with the Touring package.

The street-legal car had a 2.7-liter, fuel-injected, air-cooled engine, back spoiler, and Koni adjustable shocks. It could easily be converted into a race car. The lights and radio were not working, and Classic Porsche would make the repairs before the car would be put on display for a month.

Based on the noon start, Winthrop suggested they arrive in the parking lot before eleven since getting to his suite might take 30 minutes. And it would also give them time to make their first pass at the buffet before the game started.

The two were holding hands as they walked toward the famous stadium with the hole in the roof when both stopped and listened. At first, Janis wasn't sure. Then she looked at Aliyah and they nodded at the same time. They'd heard the distinctive rattle of AK-47s.

At the entrance to the parking lot where all the tailgating was occurring, Ghulam stopped the white Ford Econoline passenger van long enough to let eight men get out. They all wore black pants and shirts, body armor and Kevlar helmets, ski masks, and carried AK-47s with nine spare magazines in web gear on their chests. In a holster strapped to their thighs, they carried Glock 9mm pistols with one 15-round magazine in the gun and four more in thigh pouch pockets.

The attack plan was simple. Start at one end of the tailgating lot and walk to the other end, killing as many as they can. The survivors would get back in the same van and drive away.

Ghulam had not seen the brief U.S. news reports on the GSG9 raids on the morning news. When he called the numbers last night from his burner phone to alert the teams to attack the Frankfurt and Berlin airports, he did not know that those phones were already in the hands of the GSG9.

The first two men out of the van started shooting on the opposite side of the row. Six fans were wounded as the other fans scrambled for cover or ran. The eight men walked in a ragged row, shooting from the shoulder, and shouting *Allahu Akbar* – God is Great.

What Ghulam didn't anticipate was that this was Texas. Many of the tailgaters had firearms in their SUVs and trucks and many were combat veterans. Most had pistols, but some had shotguns and rifles ranging from M-16s to lever-action hunting rifles and started shooting back.

Ghulam's attackers were less than 20 yards down the row when the first two men dropped dead, their bodies riddled with bullets. Out in the open between the rows of vehicles, they were vulnerable.

The men stopped and looked for those who were firing at them. All around them, they saw heads popping up over hoods, around the fronts and backs of the vehicles as the tailgaters fired back. Bullets were coming from every direction.

Omar Chakroun, the team leader, calmly dropped an empty magazine from his AK and shouted to the other men to keep moving and sweep both sides to suppress the fire. Windows caved in, holes appeared in the sides of cars and trucks as the terrorists kept moving, but their numbers were dwindling.

Three more of Chakroun's men went down. He spotted the white van driven by Ghulam, reloaded, and yelled for the remaining two men to follow him as he started running. If he could survive the gauntlet, he would get to safety.

Janis told Aliyah to go to the gate where she'd meet her as stray bullets whined overhead. Heading toward the fight, Janis dodged one car just in time to see Chakroun stagger and fall face forward on the concrete. Behind him, seven other bodies dressed in black were sprawled on the concrete.

Janis looked at the driver of the white van passing in front of her. Their eyes locked as she recognized Ghulam. A cop blew his whistle and pointed in the direction he wanted the van to go. As Ghulam drove off, Janis memorized the license plate.

A frantic 10 minutes later, Janis found Aliyah by the gate, scanning the crowd. Janis grabbed her by the hand and walked behind a column, where she dialed 911.

Janis had to shout over the ambient noise to tell a skeptical operator that the police needed to look for a white van with Texas plates. She had to give the plate number three times and spell Ghulam's full name twice before the operator understood the name.

Everyone coming into Texas Stadium was being patted down. They walked into the suite at 11:55 a.m. just in time to hear the PA announcement about the attack. None of the people in the suite, most of whom had arrived earlier, had heard the gunfire, or knew what happened just outside the stadium.

The PA announcer kept those in the stands informed. While there was some panic, the cordon of police outside and inside the stadium kept a stampede from happening. Despite the attack, the game and the spectating went on. After all, this was Dallas, and the Cowboys were playing.

Jason's clients kept her from dwelling on the attack by asking about her Porsches and talking about theirs. Janis tried not to be distracted, but what she saw outside played through her mind as she described her hunt for a Porsche 908 or a 910 with a 2.2 six-cylinder engine.

For most of the game, Aliyah talked to the wives about living in Israel. She wanted to ask Janis about what she saw, but this was neither the time nor the place. At TV timeouts during the game, the local CBS affiliate provided updates. Eleven spectators and all eight terrorists were killed, and 31 wounded. One report noted that the terrorists were hit by bullets of many different calibers.

Back in her Yukon Denali after the game, Janis turned to Aliyah. "I need to call Rachel Simms from a secure phone before we go to Kol Nidre services tonight. I know it is Yom Kippur, but I am sure Reznik will take her call and get her current photos of Ghulam to give to the FBI. And, oh-by-the-way, I am going to services armed, something I never thought would be necessary in the U.S."

THE SAME DAY, 5:32 P.M. LOCAL TIME, DALLAS

After the attack, Abd al Bari Ghulam parked the van at the Valley View Mall, walked 100 yards to his rented Chevrolet Impala, and drove back to the safe house. He was sure he'd seen the woman with sandy brown hair who stared at him before but couldn't remember when or where.

The house was empty, and he put the dead fighters' clothing and personal items in plastic bags. He then went to the storage facility where, under a false name, Ghulam stored weapons and ammunition. The bags were tossed into the facility's dumpster.

When he turned on the news at five-thirty, every local channel had detailed coverage of the attack, an artist sketch of him, his name and several aliases, and the license plate of the van. Fox News had a counterterrorism expert whose sources said he was the suspected mastermind behind the attack at Cedars Sinai and recent attacks in Europe.

Ghulam concluded he was now a marked man and, in the short term, will not be able to leave the United States. He had three suicide bombers at another Dallas safe house with AK-47s and ammunition. They needed to attack, and the sooner, the better.

CHAPTER 26

NOT THE FINAL SOLUTION

TUESDAY, SEPTEMBER 17TH, 2002, 11:58 A.M. LOCAL TIME, DALLAS,

When she bought the tickets for Aliyah, the only day Janis could book business class seats on the DFW – Newark and then Newark – Tel Aviv flights were on the 19th. The delay, approved by Reznik, gave the two an extra day together.

Aliyah liked several Chanel make-up products which were very expensive in Israel. She grinned when Janis said they could also stop at the Victoria Secret store at the NorthPark Mall. Janis offered to drop Aliyah off at the main entrance to save wear and tear on her fiancé's leg, but her lover insisted they park and walk-in together. Janis rationalized that Aliyah was trying to put on a brave face.

Janis thought she was lucky to find an end spot in a row for the Porsche 911 Turbo in the covered parking just south of the main Neiman Marcus entrance. It was in the lower 90s and the sun was out as they walked Janis always had her head on a swivel. Suddenly, she stopped. "Aliyah, look over my shoulder to the left and tell me what you see."

"Four men wearing bulky jackets."

"What else do you see?"

"Their right hands look like they are keeping something close to their body, like a.... Oh shit, I can see the end of the barrels. They are carrying AKs and may be wearing suicide vests."

"Bingo."

The men were now about 150 feet from where they stood. Janis pecked Aliyah on her cheek. "Look again. Recognize anyone?"

"Yeah. Ghulam."

"This is another attack. As good as I am with a pistol, there's not much I can do at this range. So, we're going to create a distraction. That female cop over there has no idea of what is about to happen. When I yell, you get under cover and stay there."

"No, I am coming with you."

"No, you are not. First, your leg will make it difficult for you to keep up, and two, you don't have a gun." Janis glared at her lover. "Stay here, and I'll be back in one piece. Trust me, this is something I know how to do."

Janis stepped into the line of traffic, causing an oncoming car to screech to a stop. She ignored the cursing driver and yelled as loud as she could, "Abd al-Bari Ghulam." He turned toward the voice and started to raise his AK-47.

The female police officer by the entrance saw the weapon and yelled 'gun.' People started running for cover as the policewoman keyed her radio to call for backup. Out of the corner of her eyes, Janis saw two more police officers run out of the mall entrance as she drew her S&W MSP 9mm Compact. Her purse was now slung across her shoulder and neck and pushed onto her back and out of the way.

Ghulam hesitated while he looked at the female police officer with the drawn pistol and then at Janis, trying to determine who was the more significant threat. The men made the decision for her when they started firing at the police officers. They were not worried about a crazy 55-year-old woman yelling and running toward them. Janis stopped, aimed, and fired one round before starting to run again. The Al-Musawi fighter crumpled to the ground, his left lung and heart destroyed by the hollow point bullet.

Attacker number two spun around and sprayed the area where Janis had been moments before. He left himself exposed long enough to go down in a hail of bullets from the Dallas Police officers. The third attacker hid behind a car and started shooting well-aimed bursts, alternating between where Janis was hiding behind cars and the policemen. The female police officer didn't have enough cover and AK-47 bullets hammered into her body and Kevlar vest. She rolled on the ground, moaning in pain.

Ghulam fired a short burst and backed away from the fight. The second time he shifted positions, Janis moved to cut him off. She felt a hand gently touch her shoulder and whirled around, ready to kill the person, only to see Aliyah. "What the fuck are you doing here? I told you to stay back there."

"I want to see the life go out of Ghulam's eyes."

Janis made a patting motion and then yelled at the two police officers to cover her. She got a thumbs-up from one, and the pair began firing a series of double taps at the car where the third attacker was hiding. When she popped up followed by Aliyah, the terrorist stood up to get a better shot and took four rounds in his body from the two Dallas policemen.

With Aliyah limping behind her, Janis wove between cars, trying to keep Ghulam in sight. She heard Aliyah groan loudly in pain and stood up to regain her balance. Ghulam turned to the noise and fired. Aliyah spun around in a mist of blood, screaming in pain as she went down.

Janis pumped two rounds in the direction of Ghulam, knowing she only had thirteen in the pistol and two twelve-round magazines in her purse. Her memory said she'd fired three shots which meant she had to reload after she pulled the trigger ten more times.

She crawled back to where Aliyah lay bleeding. A man and a woman crept around the car. The man held up his hand. "I'm a doctor, and she's a nurse. We'll take care of your friend. You go kill the bastard who shot her."

In the distance, Janis heard the police and ambulance sirens. Time was of the essence, and she didn't want to let Ghulam get away. She popped up for a second and saw him darting between cars headed for the north side of Northwest Highway.

Janis weaved through the parked cars, bobbing up every so often to search for Ghulam. She wanted to get within 25 yards before she pulled the trigger. Ghulam had a fully automatic, longer-range AK-47 that fired larger, more powerful bullets, which made closing risky. To get his attention, she yelled his name.

Ghulam stopped, spotted Janis, and let loose a 10-round burst from his AK. The bullets tattooed the side of the car and shattered the front window and door glass but didn't harm Janis who made herself as small as possible behind the engine and front wheel.

Janis raised her head long enough to see Ghulam duck down to reload. Bent over, she went around two cars and was now within about 30 yards. For her, he was now in range.

Ghulam stood up and fired two bursts at the closest police officers chasing them, spun around, and fired at a pair approaching from the east. Janis could see they were still a long way away, and to get to Ghulam, they would have to cross an empty parking lot.

Janis rested her elbow on the hood of a car and took a bead on Ghulam. The shot smacked him in the chest where he had several spare magazines. She was not sure if the shards from the hollow point round hit him and before Janis could get another aimed shot off, Ghulam pointed his AK in her direction. She dove for the ground and crawled to another car, closer than the one she had just used for cover. While she was moving, Janis was showered with shards and chunks of glass as car windows came apart from the hail of AK-47 bullets.

When Janis popped to take a quick peek and Ghulam was 10 yards from her swinging his AK in her direction. Bullets started heading her way before she could get off a shot. The first M43 bullet went through the soft flesh on her left side and started to yaw as it exited her body making a jagged hole. The second 122 grain one hit just below the collarbone and went through her body leaving two round holes. The third went into the car. The fourth 122 grain, 7.62 X 39 round slammed into her Rolex at over 2,300 feet per second. The impact shattered her wrist joint as well as the radius and ulna bones where they joined her left wrist. She heard her M&P 9mm Compact clank when it hit the pavement.

Janis screamed in pain. The impact of the bullets spun her around and forced her to sag to her knees. What was left of her hand hung by a strand of muscle and ligaments. Janis pulled the kerchief she was wearing as a fashion piece, folded it over, and tied it around her arm a few inches up from the bloody end. With her teeth and her right hand, she tied a tourniquet and pulled it tight, wincing in pain. The flow of blood stopped.

The other wounds hurt, and she could see blood oozing out of them, but she was not hemorrhaging blood like she was a few minutes before. She pulled a switchblade out of her purse and cut the remaining strands of tendon and muscle, dropping her hand to the concrete. As Janis did, she bit down on the strap of her purse to keep from screaming.

Janis was madder than hell and determined to kill the son-of-a-bitch who shot her and Aliyah. She picked up the M&P, wiped the bloody grip off on her pants, and suspected she had a few minutes before she passed out.

I will not let myself die until I kill Ghulam, which is why I practice with either hand all the time.

Under the car, Janis could see Ghulam's feet as he moved from car to car. He sprayed the car she was using for cover. The long burst of 7.62 X 39 mm bullets shattered glass, went through the doors, and thudded into the engine block, but did not hit her.

When she heard the assault rifle's bolt clang open saying to Ghulam, "I'm empty, put another magazine in," Janis staggered to her feet and fired a double tap into Ghulam's chest from five yards. He staggered from the impact of the 115-grain hollow point slugs. What she didn't anticipate was that Ghulam had his Glock 19 pistol in his left hand. He got a well-aimed shot off using the body of a car to support his bleeding body.

The round whistled past Janis's head and shoulder. Janis felt herself getting weaker and the M&P 9mm pistol harder to hold up and aim. She saw Ghulam re-aiming his Glock. Hours of practice took over. Up came the muzzle of her M&P and when the front sight was on his bloody chest. The M&P 9mm Compact did what it does best – fire accurately.

With one hand, it was harder to control the recoil. Weak from the loss of blood and her wounds, Janis brought the muzzle back down on her target and squeezed again. Between her shots, Ghulam got a shot off that slammed into the hood just in front of her. Janis's first single-handed shot hit Ghulam in the upper chest, about six inches below his neck. The second one hit the bridge of his nose and shredded Ghulam's brain.

Janis looked down. She was leaking blood from her side, the end of her left arm, and shoulder and felt as if she had been stabbed three times by a hot poker. Slowly, Janis sank to back down to her knees. *This is what bleeding to death from a gunshot wound is like. But at least I killed Abd al-Bari Ghulam.*

THE SAME DAY, 12:48 P.M. LOCAL TIME, DALLAS

Janis felt as if she was in a drugged haze which wasn't too far from reality. She lay on a gurney with an IV in her right arm and a cannula under her nose. The doctors in the emergency room stopped the bleeding, gave her some fresh blood as she was being prepped for surgery.

The nurse came over and checked the monitor.

"Nurse, where am I?"

"Presbyterian Hospital. We'll take good care of you."

"What are they going to do?"

The woman's nametag said her name was Jasmine Magsaysay, and from her looks, Janis guessed she was a Filipino. "Patch you up. Unless they find something horribly wrong, you should be out of the operating room in a couple of hours."

"What happened to my hand?"

"It's being prepped. Dr. Unger is going to try to reattach it."

"Oh…. Where is my friend Aliyah?"

"You mean the woman with long black hair and dark complexion."

"Yeah, that's her."

"She's down the hall, they're waiting for the x-rays. Why?"

"Her name is Aliyah Skylar, and she is my best friend in the world. I want to see her before they take her into the OR."

"I don't think that is possible."

Janis forced herself to bend forward at the waist, grimacing noticeably from the pain that brought stars to her eyes. Her lower left arm was a bloody bandage. "If you don't take me, I will go there myself."

The Filipino, who had come to the U.S. after graduating from Sillman University which was affiliated with the U.S. Presbyterian hospital system, looked at her and saw the fire in Janis' eyes. "Give me a minute."

She went down the hall and Janis could see her talking to a man and another nurse. All three looked in her direction. The nurse came back. "Lie back down. I'll take you there, but you'll only get about two minutes with her."

"Thank you."

Jasmine pushed the gurney into position so she could hold Aliyah's right hand. The engagement ring was still on her finger, and she was barely conscious. "Hi lover. We're going to get through this."

Aliyah nodded weakly. "Do you know what they are going to do to me?"

Janis shook her head.

"I was hit by two bullets, one in just above my vagina and one in the top of my pelvis."

Janis could see Aliyah was heavily sedated. "They think they can save my leg."

Gently, Janis squeezed Aliyah's left hand. "I will love you no matter what they do. I'll be there when you come out of surgery. Trust me. See you in a couple of hours."

"*Mitsuyan.* I love you too."

Jasmine got in front of Janis and pushed the gurney down the hall. "May I talk to the surgeon who will going to operate on Aliyah for a minute."

"He's already in the operating room waiting for her."

"How long will her surgery take?"

"I don't know, probably a couple of hours. I must get you to a different O.R." Jasmine grinned at the patient on the gurney. "Close friends, my ass. That was an engagement ring on her finger."

Janis lay back on the gurney and smiled. "Yes, it is. We call it a live- together-for-life ring."

"One more thing. Can you put us in the same room?"

"I'll see what I can do, but no promises."

"Thanks." Janis closed her eyes.

Janis's surgery took just under three hours, and she'd been in the hospital room when she woke as a nurse was changing one of the IV bags. The nurse gave her some water as the anesthesia still left her groggy. There was still not a second bed in the room.

She asked the nurse about Aliyah who said she would check. Dozing off, she woke at the sound of voices when Aliyah was wheeled into the room. She was propped up on her right side with soft foam blocks. When the orderlies left, Aliyah opened her eyes. "Janis?"

"I'm here, Aliyah."

"We made it this far."

"Aliyah, we're going to get out of here as soon as possible so we can be together."

The Israeli took a deep breath and tried to keep from dozing off. "Deal. The thought turns me on."

THURSDAY, SEPTEMBER 19TH, 2002, 11:00 A.M. LOCAL TIME, DALLAS

Janis woke up dog-tired and ached all over. The end of her left arm throbbed, although she thought today, it throbbed less than yesterday. She remembered the gunfight vividly and thinking that after killing Ghulam, she would die.

After that, it was a blur. Janis vaguely remembered Dr. Unger, the surgeon who operated on her, saying they would not be able to reattach her hand. Until the doctors removed the big bulbous bandage at the end of her left arm, she wouldn't know how much was left.

It was hard to get a decent night's sleep since the nurses woke her up every two hours to take her vital signs. Then, at 6:00 a.m., one came in to ask what she wanted for breakfast.

Breakfast done, she was still groggy, and her left arm ached, much more than the other wounds. Aliyah was dozing when the floor nurse entered, "Ms. Goodrich, The Dallas Police Department would like to send two officers and an attorney to take your formal statement. Do you think you are up to it?"

"Sure. How about after one. I want my attorney present as well. May I have my phone so I can call him?"

"Use the one next to your bed. I'll get your jewelry, what's left of your watch and wallet from the safe."

Janis looked over at Aliyah who was still sleeping on her right side.

A smiling Jasmine came in smiling with a small plastic bag with the remains of Janis' Rolex President, mobile phone, ring, necklace, diamond ring, and her wallet and purse. "I normally don't come up to the wards 'cuz I work in the OR. When they brought you in, we all thought you and your friends were victims of some crazy who shot up a store. I didn't know you were a hero who killed some terrorist mastermind. Everyone's talking about it. I'm impressed."

Janis grimaced as stabs of pain swept through her body as she shifted positions and moved what remained of her left arm. She was trying not to take painkillers, but the nurse advised her to stay ahead of the pain curve.

"Don't be. I got myself shot three times in the process."

"After you call your lawyer, the floor nurse's instructions are to get a urine sample from the bag attached to your catheter. If there's no blood, we'll take it out. And then, later, get you up and walking. The more you walk, the faster you get out of here. The doctors will be here before lunch to replace your bandages."

"I've got to pee so let's see if there is any blood."

By the time Scott Raisbach, a defense attorney from Don Joyce's firm arrived, Janis had the bed propped up to 45^0. She still felt as if someone had beaten her with a hammer.

Shortly after Raisbach walked in, Dr. Hogan, the surgeon who operated on Aliyah, came in to examine his work. He started to pull the curtains closed when Aliyah stopped him and pointed to Janis. "My roommate gets to hear everything since she volunteered to care for me for the rest of my life."

Dr. Hogan looked at Jasmine, who was smiling. Janis raised her right hand. "True statement. I made the offer last week before we both managed to get shot up."

Dr. Hogan laughed. "Aliyah, O.K., do you remember what I told you we did when you were in post-op recovery."

"Yes sir, you rewired my pelvis and leg, put in some new plates, took out the old ones, and grafted in some artificial bones. If the grafts take, I should be able to walk again."

Dr. Hogan nodded. "Not bad. O.K., I am going to take a look at my handiwork." He pulled on a pair of sterile gloves and gently peeled back the bandage that covered most of Aliyah's left hip and midsection. He smeared some more antiseptic cream on the stitches and looked at the drains. When he finished applying a new bandage, he stepped to the front of the bed so Aliyah could see him. "There's no sign of infection, which is good. In a few minutes, a nurse will come in to take some blood so we can make sure your body is not rejecting the grafts. You must stay in this position for a couple of days. Then, we'll get you sitting up and get you on your right foot. No pressure on the left for a few months. I've left a prescription for pain medication. Stay ahead of the pain curve. If the pills are not strong enough, ask for something stronger. Questions?"

Aliyah shook her head, and Dr. Hogan said he would see her tomorrow. And as he left, a woman came into the room. "Janis, hi, I'm Doctor Roberta Unger. Do you remember me?"

Janis nodded. "Barely. I was very groggy."

"I'm not offended. I was the surgeon who operated on you." The pain in her left arm had subsided to a dull throb that was not as bad as earlier in the morning.

Dr. Unger gently slit the bandages with scissors, and very quickly, there was a pile of bloody gauze in the tray. With her index and forefinger, Dr. Unger pressed gently on the end of Janis' arm.

"Do you want to see?"

Janis nodded and bent her left arm so she could see the end which was about six inches below her elbow. It was red around the stitches and much of the skin was black and yellow and swollen. Before she could say anything, Dr. Unger said, "The discoloring is normal and should be gone in about a week along with the swelling. You should be easy to fit with an artificial arm which should be in about a month."

Unger waited until Janis put her arm back down so the nurse could start applying a bandage. "They all look good. We'll put a compression sleeve over the bandage on your arm. The good news is the other bullets didn't hit anything vital in your body. Assuming no infection, your wounds should heal completely in three or four weeks. We'll try to give you solid food today. Once we take the IVs out, we want you up and walking around. Any questions?"

"How big will the scars be?"

Dr. Unger smiled. "At first, they will look ugly, but I'm a plastic surgeon and when they are fully healed, the scars will be barely noticeable. Just so you know, I'm an Army reservist who worked in a field hospital during Desert Shield and Storm, so I know how to fix gunshot wounds."

Janis nodded. "Thank you."

Laughing, Dr. Unger said they spent about 20 minutes plucking bits and pieces of her Rolex out of what remained of her arm before they could close it up.

As soon as Dr. Unger left, Raisbach began coaching them on how to answer the police officer's questions. By the time he finished, Janis was ready for a nap when the three men from the Dallas Police Department came in. Janis told them that Aliyah could hear everything she said since Aliyah was with her during the shootout.

Before the police officers asked any questions, Janis asked how the female police officer was doing. The officer was down the hall in the same wing and would be fine. Five civilians were wounded, and none were killed. The only people who died were the terrorists.

After Janis recorded her statement, the police officer asked how she recognized the terrorists. She said she saw the barrels of the AK-47s and recognized Ghulam from the picture on TV. Janis did not say she was the one who called 911 on Sunday.

Another note was made. The officer asked Janis if she was employed and she said no, not full-time, she was a contractor and only worked a few days a month. That seemed to satisfy the officer.

The officer looked at Aliyah and asked the same question. "I work for the Israeli government."

"Is there someone we can call to verify your identity?"

"I have my passport and identity card in my purse. And, if you need, I can give you my supervisor's name and phone number." Aliyah gave him Reznik's name and phone number.

The last question was, "Would Janis come to Dallas City Hall for a ceremony to receive an award?"

Janis took a deep breath, looked at the police captain, and shook her head. "I am truly honored that the city wants to do this, but I prefer to remain as anonymous as possible. Any publicity will just put a target on my chest for some crazy to shoot at. I'm happy to answer any questions, but that's all."

The captain, whose nametag said his last name was Williamson nodded. "I understand."

Scott Raisbach thought it was time for him to speak. "Captain, my office has already submitted the necessary paperwork to ensure that my client's name will be redacted from the police report and that her contact details will remain confidential."

"Ms. Goodrich, I understand your desire to remain anonymous. However, there will be other agencies who will want the report and to interview you."

"I understand." *I know who they are.*

FRIDAY, SEPTEMBER 20ᵀᴴ, 2002, 10:00 LOCAL TIME, ALEXANDRIA, VIRGINIA

Bill Smith III preferred to appear in court wearing a dark suit, white shirt, and red tie, knowing this was the last day he would wear one for many years. He'd agreed to a deal in exchange for giving back all the information he stole from the FBI and what Bishop and Green had given him from the CIA's files.

The judge for the U.S. District Court for Eastern Virginia, a man in his late 50s, entered. The bailiff called out, "All rise."

After sitting, the judge looked at Smith III and the prosecutor. "The purpose of this session is to formally approve the plea bargain in the matter of the United States versus William F. Smith III. Mr. Smith, please stand."

Smith III stood, and the judge asked him if he had reviewed the agreement with his attorney and understood its implications and requirements. The fired FBI agent said, "Yes, your honor, I do."

The judge nodded. "In that case, as per the agreement, you are hereby sentenced to 20 years in a Federal Penitentiary with no chance for parole and a fine of $250,000. The sentence will begin immediately, and credit will be given for time already served in jail."

The judge banged his gavel, and Bill Smith III was led out of the courtroom to a small anteroom, where he changed into an orange jumpsuit. His attorney would deliver his suit to his wife, who had already filed for divorce. She had agreed to keep his clothing and other personal effects in a storage facility while he was in prison.

SATURDAY, SEPTEMBER 21ˢᵀ, 2002, 9:00 A.M. LOCAL TIME, DALLAS

When Janis walked back into her room after her morning ritual in the hospital of walking up and down the ward for 10 minutes, sitting for five, and then doing the routine twice more, she was surprised to see Rachel Simms waiting. Rachel hesitated to hug Janis. "How are you doing?"

"Despite the extra holes in my body and one less hand, I am doing well, thank you. When did you get in?"

"Last night. After I leave here, I have an appointment with Captain Williamson at the Dallas Police Department. I believe he will understand the sensitivity of the situation."

"I'm sorry you were dragged into this mess."

"Don't be. I can't tell him much about you other than to assure him in writing that you were acting as a private citizen. Under Texas law, you were acting within your rights as a concealed carry holder by trying to prevent a crime. If he pushes back, you and I will be jumping through hoops and spending more time with CIA and Justice Department lawyers. And then, God forbid Congress decides to get involved. By the way, I am the only one in the agency who knows your real name. Where is Aliyah?"

"They're taking a scan of her leg. She'll be back any minute."

"When do you get out of the hospital?"

Janis felt a stab of pain and massaged the end of her arm which was covered by a tan compression sleeve that helped reduce swelling. "Me, early next week. Aliyah has already started using crutches to get around, but I am hoping they'll let me take her home soon."

Rachel looked around the room and seeing no one, she whispered. "The debrief of that Cuban colonel who was looking for you is going well. He's a treasure trove of information."

CHAPTER 27

THE FIGHT GOES ON

BEIRUT, SUNDAY, SEPTEMBER 22ND, 2002, 8:33 A.M. LOCAL TIME

Rather than take their usual seats, Ahmad Busaid, the senior member of the Shura Council, directed the other members to chairs along the long sides of the table. A large TV sat next to a video recorder at the far end of the table. Once the members were seated, Busaid nodded to the man at the far end who pushed the VHS cassette into the recorder.

"Comrades," Busaid intoned, "what you are about to see are recordings of the news from American TV stations after the two shootouts in Dallas. The last of which killed Abd al-Bari Ghulam. Once we watch these, the implications from these attacks are the first item on our agenda."

None of the seven members of the Shura Council spoke as they focused on the 45" TV set. For those who didn't speak English, the man operating the recorder stopped the tape, translated, and pushed play again.

There was some security footage from the North Park Mall, but most of the tape was taken from Texas Stadium where reporters stood next to bullet-riddled trucks and blood-stained concrete. The outrage and desire to bring those who planned these attacks to justice was clear, even those who did not speak English.

When the tape ended, Busaid raised his hand. He had watched the tape at least half a dozen times, parsing each word, each implication. "What I am about to say is not open to discussion. We shall call off any planned attacks on the American homeland. To continue to do so will only result in attacks on Hezbollah by the Americans that may keep us from destroying Israel."

He looked at Talal Malmiyah. "You will issue the recall and ensure our men return to Lebanon safely. Take care to ensure that any weapons left behind are stored where we can retrieve them some day in the future."

Busaid's next instruction was directed at Farhad Madhavi, the man responsible for training the al-Musawi Corps at its base in Iran. "Madhavi, you will study this tape and learn whatever lessons we can from it. Clearly, our fighters could have killed more infidels."

He then clasped his fingers and rested his forearms on the table. Busaid was waiting for comments when the fanatical Malmiyah smacked the table with the palm of his hand. He believed any casualties inflicted on the enemy were good at whatever the cost. Now that he had everyone's attention, he said, "Does it bother anyone besides me that an infidel woman killed Abd al-Bari Ghulam?"

The head of the Shura Council nodded sagely. "Our sources have tried to determine the identity of this woman, but it is a closely guarded secret. This tells me she is CIA. And I suspect CIA is already planning to attack Hezbollah. If we kill or try to kill her, it will only increase the infidel Americans' anger and thirst for revenge against Hezbollah. Therefore, we will let Allah find ways to punish this woman. We will not."

No one challenged Ahmad Busaid's ruling. To do so could be detrimental to one's position, even life. The meeting shifted to other topics, such as who will replace the martyred Abd al-Bari Ghulam.

TUESDAY, SEPTEMBER 24TH, 2002, 9:07 A.M. LOCAL TIME, ZURICH

Every day, the fear in Berg's gut intensified and he was afraid Hezbollah would try to kill him. He wondered if he was paranoid when he decided to stop driving a car. Instead, he took taxis he flagged down on the street. The difference was inconvenient but safer unless the driver was a Hezbollah assassin.

Berg was afraid Hezbollah would blame him for the *Star Lynn* incident, even though all he did was sell them the weapons and shut Hofer and Associates down. Berg rationalized that now that Ghulam and Hofer were dead, they would leave him alone. Best, he thought, live quietly and modestly, and create several layers identities between Hofer and Associates and himself.

Fischer und Sohn sold Hofer's collection of Nazi artifacts to a wealthy German. The weapons went to a licensed gun dealer in the U.S. It took an extra week before the paperwork to legally export them from Germany and legally import them into the United States was approved. Another collector bought the furniture for a million Euros.

All that was left was the house with its grounds. The agent had several interested buyers. Berg spent his time creating a labyrinth of accounts to hide the origin of the money he now controlled. Eberhard Bauer – his first escape name – was about to disappear.

THE SAME DAY, 1:50 P.M. LOCAL TIME, DALLAS

The day Aliyah had been waiting for was finally here. After making his rounds, Doctor Hogan told Aliyah that he would release her later today. She was to call his office to schedule a weekly check-up for the next month. He gave her a prescription for physical therapy and recommended several centers near the hospital.

Not expecting to bring Aliyah back to her house today, Janis drove the '65 Porsche 365SC to the hospital. The sunroof was open, and with the temperature in the low 80s, the weather was a perfect day to drive a car that didn't have air conditioning. Aliyah, when told which car she had, told Janis to go back and get the Yukon.

While she waited for Janis to return, Aliyah walked up and down the ward's halls for more exercise and to keep rebuilding her strength. She could now let her left foot touch the floor and was wearing the short skirt and a blouse Janis had brought earlier when she was allowed to wear something other than the hospital gown.

Just before lunch, a woman from the accounting office came to her room to go over her bill. The clerk confirmed that the hospital contacted Chalit, the healthcare insurance company Aliyah selected as a Mossad employee. Chalit asked for the final bill to be accompanied by a form signed by Aliyah. The woman admitted that the hospital and Chalit were likely to go back and forth several times before they settled the bill. Janis signed the forms saying she, not Aliyah, would be responsible for any fees not covered by Chalit. Satisfied, the woman went to her office, and Aliyah and Janis went to lunch in the hospital's cafeteria.

Mid-afternoon, a nurse came into the room saying Aliyah could leave. She was followed by an aide pushing a wheelchair. Aliyah objected, and the aide said the hospital's insurance policy required that she be taken to a waiting car in a wheelchair. No exceptions were permitted. Aliyah made a face, sat down, and placed the underarm crutches across her lap.

As Janis held the door open, Aliyah slid her crutches into the Yukon, pivoted on the ball of her right foot, and sat on the passenger's seat. Once the door was closed, she said, "I just received a letter from the rabbi at the reform synagogue in Amsterdam. As you know, gay marriage became legal last year in The Netherlands. He will be more than happy to marry us on either Sunday, December 15th or the 22nd. So, my love, we have a wedding to plan. But before we do that, we are going to make love."

MONDAY, SEPTEMBER 30TH, 2002, 8:28 A.M. LOCAL TIME, PHOENIX, ARIZONA

When Ordonez negotiated his asylum agreement, he wanted to live someplace that was warm year-round. As a young intelligence officer, he spent two years assigned to the Cuban U.N. mission in New York and hated the winters. His first choice was Florida, a state the CIA rejected out of hand. The CIA found him a job in Phoenix with a company that made golf equipment that was willing to train him.

A month after he defected, a representative from the Cuban mission to the U.N. delivered an envelope to the U.S.' U.N. mission addressed to Hector Ordonez, c/o The Central Intelligence Agency, Langley, VA.

After being fingerprinted, tested for dangerous chemicals, and x-rayed, the envelope was sent to Langley and delivered, unopened to Ordonez. In the presence of his debriefers, he used a knife to slit open the top. He dumped out the papers stapled together, looked at the top sheet, and laughed. "My wife has divorced me, and Castro got the local Catholic bishop to approve terminating my marriage. The grounds are not enough revolutionary fervor and desertion of my family. I will miss my children, but not my wife. Now I can go meet some single American women."

SUNDAY, NOVEMBER 2ND, 2002, 7:06 LOCAL TIME, BUTNER, NORTH CAROLINA

When prisoner 25771-055 at the Federal Correctional Complex Butner 1 didn't respond, the guard called for the cell door to be opened. As soon as he saw foam on the lips of William Smith III, he called for medical personnel.

The complex has the largest medical facility in the Federal Prison system and within minutes of Smith III arriving in the emergency room, he was pronounced dead. The time of death would be determined later by a forensic team. The preliminary cause of death was cyanide poisoning, and the warden immediately authorized an investigation into how Smith III could have been killed or how cyanide was smuggled into his cell so he could commit suicide.

There was no public announcement of his death other than to his family, the FBI, and the CIA. Rachel Simms was notified later in the day, and she called Janis to let her know that Smith III was dead.

When Janis hung up the phone, she smiled. The second half of the leak about her identity had been plugged without her lifting a finger. She was back to no loose ends other than Rachel. The CIA Deputy Director of Operations was never going to talk since she was involved in silencing Jim Green.

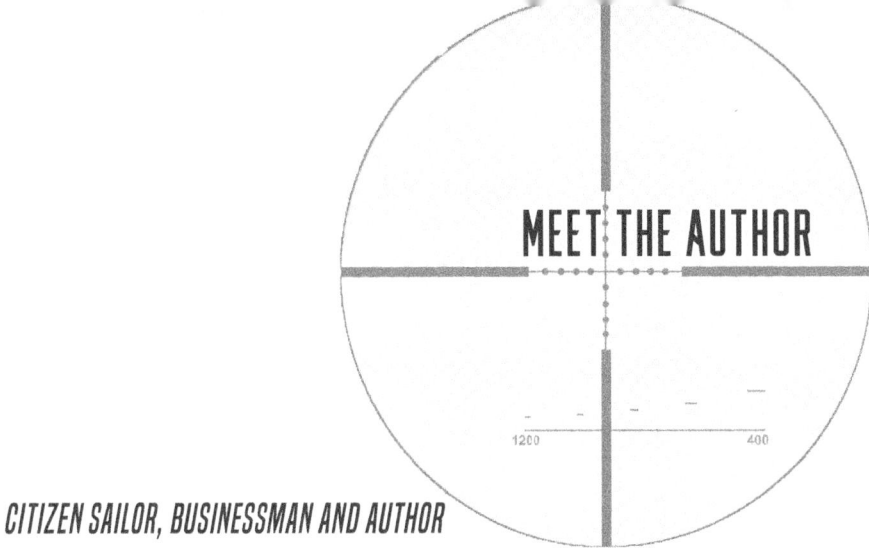

MEET THE AUTHOR

CITIZEN SAILOR, BUSINESSMAN AND AUTHOR

Marc is a combat veteran of Vietnam, the Tanker Wars of the 1980s and Desert Shield/Storm and retired from the Navy as a Captain after 26 years of service. He is a Naval Aviator with just under 6,000 hours of flight time in helicopters and fixed wing aircraft. Captain Liebman has worked with the armed forces of Australia, Canada, Japan, Thailand, Republic of Korea, the Philippines and the U.K.

He has been the CEO of a $50M aerospace and defense contractor and a partner in two different consulting firms advising clients on business and operational strategy and sales and marketing. He speaks on American history, from the American Revolution to the War of 1812, as well as selected topics on aviation, foreign affairs, getting published and leadership.

His latest career is as an award-winning novelist. Five of his 13 novels have become Amazon #1 Best Sellers as well as winning other nationally recognized awards. The Liebmans live near Aubrey, Texas. Marc is married to Betty, his lovely wife of 53+ years.